Keeping Chelsea's Secret

A Historical Romance Novel

By

Gina Rose

Keeping Chelsea's Secret

Copyrighted 2014

Paperback ISBN-13: 978-0-9960940-4-7, ISBN-10:
0996094040
Ebook ISBN-13: 978-0-9960940-5-4, ISBN-10:
0996094059
Paperback ISBN-13: 978-1499603583, ISBN-10:
1499603584

BISAC Codes:
FIC027000   FICTION / Romance / General
FIC027070   FICTION / Romance / Historical / Regency

Prologue

1801
The Sheraton Estate
England

"Celia, we forgot our picnic basket and I'm starving," Chelsea complained, placing her latest catch in the wicker basket, with all the other fish she'd caught since morning.

"You're always starving Chelsea. I swear, one day you'll be as big as old Hattie if you don't learn to tame your appetite."

Chelsea snorted at her sister, "Come now Celia, I'm a growing girl. I need to replenish myself regularly, especially after a day like today where I've been hard at work providing our supper," she said with a puffed up chest, clearly proud of herself.

"A growing girl, indeed! Just look at you dressed in those raggedy breeches and boots, with your hair stuffed under that ugly old cap. No one would ever say you were a girl, dressed like that. You know Papa says it's time for you to put such foolishness behind you and start dressing like a girl. Really, Chelsea, you are quite the little hoyden. How will you ever find a husband unless you start behaving like a lady?" Celia lectured her sister in her most authoritative tone. She was her older sister after all, even if only by three quarters of an hour.

The identical twins, age two and ten glared at each other for a moment until Celia broke, saying "Fine! I'll go back and get the stupid old picnic basket, but this is the last time, Chelsea. You always have me fetch this and that. It is not fair. I'm a lady not a footman."

"Pish tosh! What do you know about being a lady?"

"You are so incorrigible," Celia groaned in exasperation.

"Oh, go on with you and hurry up!" Then, she felt her line tug. She quickly yanked it up out of the water, "Look! I've already caught another one while you've been standing there dallying around. Papa will so be proud," Chelsea beamed as she held up the fish for inspection.

Celia growled. With a huff and a twirl of her skirts, she scurried off through the woods.

Chelsea put the fish in the basket and stood to stretch her legs. She always enjoyed being out of doors. She loves the sound of the running stream trickling by and the birds singing. Yes indeed, nature is a wonderful thing. 'Why should I want to behave like a girl, only to be cooped up inside doing wretchedly boring things all day like practicing stitches and silly old pianoforte lessons', she inwardly grumbled. 'Dressed in those stifling clothes, where one has no freedom of movement.'

'No! I will never give up the outdoors or my boyish ways. If I don't find a husband, so be it. Let Celia do it. She is the heir to the title after all since Papa has no sons. The barony will be safe whether I marry or not.'

'Besides, marriage would not suit me at all. What man would want a wife who can fish better than he fishes and shoot better than him, not to mention out ride him? No, I will never marry,' she assured herself with a soft harrumph.

'It's not that I dislike men, not at all. Indeed, I love and admire and yes, somewhat envy them, if one must be honest with oneself. I love the way they have freedom to be who they are without restriction. If only I could have been born a man as Papa always laments. Alas, I was born with the affliction of being a member of the gentle sex.'

She was startled out of her reverie by the sound of snapping twigs. "Celia?" she cried out, somewhat alarmed. She was answered by silence so eerie that it made her skin crawl. Her eyes darted around looking for the source of the sound but the trees were so thick beyond the small clearing that she couldn't see very far into the wood. She listened quietly; still she heard no other sounds. Even the birds were quiet now. She strained her ears more but still heard nothing.

A sense of self-preservation made her start. She gathered up her basket and tackle, preparing to take her leave of the stream when a deep voice said from behind her, "Are you alone then child?" Instantly, fear gripped her. She froze with her back to the voice.

"Such a lovely child you are," the deep voice murmured. She flinched when she felt a light touch on the back of her neck. The stranger ran his fingers along her skin. Intense fear gripped her now, with icy tendrils, crawling all over her body, causing her to quake. She shivered, unable to speak.

"Turn around. Let me look at you," the voice softly commanded.

When she didn't move, he put his hand on her shoulder forcefully turning her around. She found herself looking into the face of what could only be described, as some kind of demon. His eyes were a strange mixture of brown and yellow and were alight with an unholy shine. His gaze devoured her, making her feel exposed and vulnerable.

A tall man, who was no more than five and thirty, towered over her. The top of her head barely reached his chest. He had long dark brown hair gathered together at the base of his skull with a leather tie. He was dressed in tight fitting buckskin breeches with Hessian boots. His sweat dampened white linen shirt outlined his broad shoulders. The sleeves were rolled up revealing the taut muscles in his forearms.

He looked as though he had been traveling for some time. Dust coated on his boots. Sweat pooled under his armpits and down his chest. It was glistening from his forehead and his throat. His breathing seemed heavy and erratic as if he had just run a foot race. The way he was looking at her made her squirm with fear.

"Ah…eyes made of blue crystal…beautiful boy," he breathed as he began to stroke her cheek.

She was suddenly relieved that he mistook her for a boy and not a girl, alone in the woods. She saw no reason to correct him in his misconception. Indeed, it would be far wiser to play along until she could get safely away.

"Why are you alone out here in the wood lad?" the stranger asked as he continued to stroke her cheek.

Chelsea took a step back, saying, "Please sir, I just finished fishing and am about to return home. My Papa is waiting for me. I'm already late so if you will excuse me, I'll just be on my way."

She tried to turn to move away but he grabbed her hard by the shoulder with his fingers digging into her flesh.

"Hold there, what's the hurry? I'm just getting to know you now, my bonny lad," he said through clenched teeth.

Chelsea dropped her basket and tackle then. She started to struggle to free herself but that only seemed to make him angry.

His grip tightened. He spun her around pressing himself to her back. Then, he started grinding his hips against her. She became aware of a hard ridge in the center of his hips as he undulated against her.

"See what you do to me lad," he breathed harsh, hot into her ear. He started groping her legs and buttocks.

"You're just the right age to appreciate what I can teach you," he said in a husky voice.

Chelsea didn't know what he meant by that but she knew that this was wrong…terribly wrong. She renewed her struggle, to no avail.

He pulled at the back of her shirt to remove it from her breeches. He ran his hand up and down her bare back in several rough pawing strokes.

She continued trying to wriggle free of him but he wrapped his big hand around the back of her neck and squeezed hard to subdue her. Then, suddenly he drove her face down into the ground. With his other hand, he ripped away the back of her breeches and started fondling her exposed buttocks.

"Aye, you like that, don't you?" he panted.

Chelsea couldn't speak. He pushed her face into the moss on the ground, holding her down by the back of her neck. Chelsea whimpered. He chuckled, as though he were amused by her soft cries.

In one swift, savage move, he ripped her trousers away and began to grope her. She understood then, that she was in imminent peril.

Chelsea started to pray now. What else could she do? This monster was clearly intent on harming her and there was nothing she could do to stop him. She grew still and quiet. She realized then, he was undoing his breeches.

"Come lad, spread your legs now, It will be easier on you," he snarled.

Instead, Chelsea clenched her legs closer together with all her might in a feeble attempt to thwart him but he did not notice the action as he commenced with his unholy assault.

Just when she thought she would swoon from the pain, she heard another male voice. She could tell by sound of the other man's voice that he was younger than the monster who was assaulting her.

"Nigel! What in the name of God are you doing to that boy?" the younger man raged.

Nigel stopped long enough to acknowledge the other man. "Go away Damien, this doesn't concern you!" he growled at the interruption.

He let go of her neck, gripping her shoulders with brutal strength, to keep her pressed down. She was able to turn her head to look at the man named Damien now.

He just stood there staring, his emerald green eyes locked on hers. His mouth was agape with a look of shock and utter disbelief on his face.

It seemed like an eternity before he pulled himself together. Finally, he ran toward them. He threw himself at Nigel, knocking him away from her. She lay there a moment too weak and frightened to move, listening to their struggle. She heard Damien shouting.

"It was you that harmed Jacob! I will kill you, you sick bloody bastard!"

She summoned the strength to get up then and started scrambling around trying to find her breeches but realized there was nothing left of them except for torn rags.

She decided to run just as she was but before she did she saw that Nigel had Damien down. He was beating him savagely. She wanted to help but after quickly scanning her surroundings, couldn't see anything to use as a weapon.

The young man, her savior, must have been knocked unconscious because he was no longer moving. Horror surged through Chelsea. She feared he could be dead. That devil, who he'd called Nigel, kicked Damien in the ribs for good measure. Then he made a move toward her. He came to an abrupt halt as his gaze took her in. He just stood there glaring at her with a look of disgust on his face.

She was facing him, naked from the waist down with her plaited hair mostly visible now. Her cap had gone askew during her search for her breeches. Now, he could plainly see that she was not the boy he thought she had been. He made a sound of revulsion then quickly dashed off into the wood.

She stood there for a moment, violently shaking and trembling. She looked over at Damien. He was bleeding from his eyes, nose and mouth.

Afraid that the gallant young man who had saved her was dead and that the monster would return, she turned. The motion caused her to lose her cap altogether. She ran... ran as fast as she could on her sore weakened legs until she arrived at a clearing where she stumbled and fell, hitting her forehead on a rock. She knew no more as darkness grabbed her in its cold embrace.

*****

"Chelsea! Oh sweet Jesu! Chelsea....wake up child! Chelsea can you hear me?"

Celia watched as her father cradled Chelsea in his arms, wailing at the heavens. "Sweet God in heaven who did this to my little girl?" He rose with her limp bleeding body clutched tightly in his arms and started walking toward the manor.

Celia followed behind, tears streaming down her face. Her poor sister! Who could have done such an evil thing? What if Chelsea dies? What has been done to her? Why was she naked and bleeding? She trembled as she tried to imagine what horrors Chelsea must have suffered.

She continued behind her father as they made their way back to their home. How was her sister ever going to be the same? After this...

Chapter One

1810
Mayfair, London

"Aunt Matilda, must we have this conversation again? Damnation! I know what is expected of me but I am only seven and twenty. Can you not allow me to live in peace another year or two before I'm forced to take a wife?"

Damien Alexander Vane, the ninth Marquess of Devonshire stood against the marble fireplace mantle of the Dowager Duchess of Fairhaven's Mayfair mansion, glaring at her in frustration. "I mean really Aunt, every time I turn around you start harping at me about my duty to the title. I know what my duty is, believe me, I know and I loathe it. You know I never wanted this fate so just let me move at my own pace. I'm plenty young enough to marry and produce an heir before I cock up my toes."

"Now now Damien, don't fuss on so. I know that you have not accepted your lot in life but dear, it is past time that you did. Your brother has been dead seven and ten years. If your father, God love him, was capable of telling you himself, he would say how proud he is of you and that you will make a fine duke when he passes on. It is just a matter of time now, you know, that my brother dies. The surgeons say he cannot possibly last more than another month or two in his condition. I dare say, you should straighten up and take charge right this minute, young man because your duty is calling." The middle aged Aunt Matilda said glowering at him.

She was a handsome figure of a woman at the age of nine and forty with lustrous red hair and sharp green eyes.

"Aye… Aye, I suppose I owe it to father," Damien allowed on a deep sigh before walking over to the sofa across from his aunt. He plopped down onto it without ceremony.

He rubbed a hand through the front of his hair. "It's just that I can't abide all the balls, parties and the scheming mama's with their simpering daughters. The whole tradition of the marriage mart makes me ill. It stinks of greed and hypocrisy," he complained. "I just wish Jacob were still here to assume the title so I could live my own life."

"Hear me well Damien, just so you know. I'm serious and will put up with no more of your dallying around. I will cut you out of my will and leave you without so much as a farthing," Matilda bristled. "You know I love you, Damien but heed me, I will cut you off and leave everything to that weasel cousin of yours…oh what's his name…oh yes, Reginald. That's right dear; I will leave all my estates and my entire fortune to Reginald if you don't find a wife this season."

Damien laughed, rolling his eyes. "Is that fool even still alive? Last I heard he was tiptoeing through the jungles of the West Indies trying to make his own fortune. Surely, he's contracted malaria or been eaten by a very large snake by now."

"Behave you devil! He is my youngest brother's only child. I'll not have you say such things about him…even if he is a dandy," she said with an air of indignity though she had a crooked smile and a mischievous glint in her eye.

She knew she had Damien right where she wanted him. He would do whatever he had to do to secure her fortune.

Damien sighed, running his hand through his hair. He shook his head, as if by doing so, he could clear his mind. "Alright you win, but I can tell you now that I refuse to go to Almack's. If you want me to find a wife, you will not interfere. You will allow me to select the balls and parties that I wish to attend. And don't try to choose a bride for me either, I will choose for myself," he said broodingly.

"With your golden looks, title and fortune, you will have your pick of this season's crop. I dare say, all the ladies will swoon at your feet," she said with a smile trying to lighten the mood.

She lost her smile however when she looked at him. She couldn't help but see the aura of darkness in Damien's eyes...that same darkness that had been there for so very long. It worried her.

"Damien what troubles you, dear?" she asked in a more somber tone.

Damien growled. He huffed out a harsh breath and said, "Nigel! He is returned from India."

Nigel took his family to India soon after that fateful day in the woods, the day his whole world changed. That was the day he realized that Nigel was Jacobs tormentor. Nigel was the reason for his brother's shame and suicide. Nigel was responsible for ruining so many lives.

He must make him pay for his crimes, but how? 'Should I publicly denounce him for a pederast? Should I hire some thugs to rough him up and send him off on a transport ship to Australia? Should I challenge him to a duel?' he silently wondered. There had to be a way to make Nigel pay.

Damien would never forget that day nine years ago. He could still see the crystal blue eyes of that beautiful youth filled with tears and terror. His eyes pleading with Damien for help as he lay there on the ground while Nigel violated his poor little body.

The sight of the boy being assaulted had propelled Damien back to another time thirteen years before that day. After the initial shock of what he was seeing registered in his brain, he was dumbstruck with the paralyzing memories for several moments.

He remembered hearing a voice on many a night in the nursery when he was five years old and his poor brother Jacob was nine.

He couldn't see clearly in the darkened nursery but he heard the voice, the voice that he now knew to be Nigel, telling Jacob, 'You like that don't you lad,' as he kept him pressed face down on the mattress while he…Damien shook his head to rid himself of the vision. Nigel deserves to die. By God, he would see to it. The only question is how and when.

His Aunt's voice brought him back to the present, "I never liked Nigel. He always made my skin crawl. But tell me, why do you hate him so, Damien? All these years, you have hated him and have never told me the reason why."

"Some things should never be discussed. It suffices to say that Nigel is an animal, unfit to live in decent society," Damien said with a stern voice that brooked no further discussion.

"I'm sure I don't want to know the specifics. I trust your judgment, but what will you do? What can you do? Nigel is a duke for heaven's sake. You can't just kill him!" Matilda said, not realizing how close to the mark she really was.

"Besides, from what I hear, he is only going to be in London long enough to marry off his daughter then he will return to India and his tea plantation. Perhaps you won't even have to see him, dear," she said in an attempt to look on the bright side.

"I dare say he won't want to leave his plantation unattended for more than a few months. He will marry that mouse of a daughter off to the first bidder or rather the first one he can lure with her fat dowry," she snickered.

They sat in silence for a few moments before Matilda found a new subject.

"Oh Damien dear, I hear that Baron Sheraton… you remember the baron dear, he has brought his daughter Celia to London for a few weeks for a small season. He is eager to see her married since she is one and twenty and will soon be on the shelf. She is an heiress, you know, to not only a fortune but a title as well…though your title is much more impressive darling. I hear she is quite beautiful. You should make yourself known to her as soon as possible before someone else moves in and sweeps her away," she said casually.

Damien growled, "Enough Aunt! I will find my own wife!"

"Yes, yes dear, I'm just making small talk…pay no mind to me, love," she said with a coy smile.

"Well, I'm off to my club, I have a meeting with Jarrett," he said as he got up and went over to kiss her on the cheek. "Don't worry, I know my duty. I am resigned to it." He then quickly took his leave before she could make more mischief.

Behind him, Matilda smiled a knowing smile. She was glad to see Damien cooperate even if she had to trick him with the threat of that ghastly sniveling cousin Reginald inheriting her fortune…as if.

*****

"Ho Damien!" Jarrett Wellstone greeted Damien as he entered Whites on St James Street.

Damien returned the greeting, joined him at his table, and ordered a brandy. Turning to his friend, he asked, "So that bastard has returned, has he?"

Jarrett, the son of his father's late steward has been a lifelong friend of Damien. He is also a highly successful Bow Street runner, commissioned by Damien to monitor his Cousin Nigel's whereabouts and activities.

Until recently, the job was mundane but now that Nigel had returned to London, Jarrett would no doubt, be set the task of following his movements more closely to make sure he did not commit any more atrocities against children.

"Aye. So far all is quiet on the home front as they say. He's spending his days and his fortune escorting his wife and daughter around to the modistes and shoemakers to outfit them both for the season. He is actually going to try to marry his daughter off this season, can you imagine? Good luck I say, have you seen her? God's bones! A more homely lass, I've never seen," he said with a mouth twisted as though he tasted something bad.

Damien can't really remember what his cousin Tess looked like. She was a young girl the last time he had seen her, "around the age of nine," he supposed. "She must be about eight and ten now", he mused. "That's about the right age to find a husband."

What he remembered of her was that she was a shy little chit who preferred to stay out of sight whenever her father was around, hiding bchind her mother's skirt as if hoping to become invisible.

"Perhaps the modiste can help her along with some pretty frocks to enhance her female attributes. Show enough cleavage and one's face becomes inconsequential," he said with an air of disdain.

Jarrett chuckled at that, saying, "Hate the whole family, do you?"

"Am I that obvious?" Damien asked with a rueful smile.

"Just a smidge," Jarrett teased.

The two men sat in silent contemplation for a few moments before Jarrett broke the quiet.

"Seriously Damien, what are you planning to do about Nigel? You cannot just kill him outright. He is a duke for Christ's sake! Though, he does deserve to be killed, you have to be practical."

Damien's right eye twitched. His jaw clenched as he suppressed a flash of memory of why he wanted to kill Nigel. With a dark look at his friend he said, "I could challenge him to a duel."

Jarrett sucked in a breath, saying, "Damien, you know what will happen if you kill him in a duel. You will be forced to leave England. You cannot do that now, not with your father on his deathbed. No my friend, you will have to come up with something else. Perhaps we could set a trap of some kind. Snare him in the act so to speak. Of course we would have to fix it so he can't actually harm a child but maybe we could set it up so we can catch him just before he commits the deed," Jarrett said smiling, clearly liking his plan.

"No! That's not good enough punishment for him, Jarrett. You know he is a monster. He is responsible for my brother's death. Nothing will satisfy me but his own death. I want to personally send the bastard straight to hell," Damien snarled.

Jarrett darted a quick glance around the room to make sure no one heard what he had said then looked at his friend with his most frank and earnest expression, "Look, I'm not going to try to stop you, but I cannot help you kill him. I can look the other way, maybe point the investigation in another direction but that's as far as I can go with it."

Damien loved his friend and would never bring harm or dishonor to him by involving him when it was time to kill Nigel. He just needed to have someone to confide in, someone to listen to his plans. He knew his friend would never reveal to the magistrates that he had killed Nigel. They had a lifelong bond and the only other person besides himself that knew of Nigel's crimes was Jarrett.

Jacob never told anyone else what happened to him or who did it. He was too ashamed and swore Damien to secrecy. Damien was too young at the time, to fully understand, what had happened in the nursery. He was too young to know exactly what it was that he was swearing secrecy to.

From what his brother told him before he killed himself, it was one of many times that he was accosted thusly, but he would never tell Damien who the villain was.

No, instead at the age of four and ten, he got into his father's gun cabinet, took out one of the dueling pistols, went to the pond, and blew his brains out. The note that he left behind did not detail any of the troubled thoughts that would lead him to commit such an act. It simply said that he could not go on living with his shame.

His father never understood the meaning of the note and succumbed to deep depression with the loss of his first-born son. He never really came out of it. He became an introvert rarely leaving the ducal apartments of Evansdale, their ancestral home.

Damien rarely visits his ancestral home because he cannot bear the ghosts of Jacobs suffering. Shaking himself free of his dark contemplations he said, "Of course I would never ask you to do such a thing. I appreciate all you've done so far. No, my friend, this is my problem. I will solve it and take full responsibility when the time comes."

Jarrett wanting to cheer his friend up a bit moved to change the subject. "Are you going to the Simpson's ball tonight?"

"As a matter of fact, it so happens, that I am. Aunt Matilda has been up to her antics again, trying to push me to get leg shackled. Today she actually got me to agree to do it by the end of the season. So it seems, that I have become an eligible bachelor for the taking," he said rolling his eyes. "I guess it's time to settle down and do right by my family and title since my father could die any day now. I just wish I didn't have to go through the dog and pony show."

"Lord, never say that I get to have all the opera singers and actresses to myself now. And what will you do with your mistress the lovely and incomparable luscious Lila?" Jarrett asked in mock horror.

"Lila and I parted ways a few weeks ago. It was time after all, I became bored with her. The relationship ran its course, so I cut it off clean. I left her with the lease on the house paid through the end of the year and five thousand pounds. If she's smart, she'll invest it somewhere and never have to work on her back again," Damien said without emotion.

Jarrett looked at his friend incredulously, "How could you just let her go like that? My God man, are you daft? She has the nicest bosom I have ever seen. Enough to make a man think he's died and gone to heaven."

"Aye, that she does, but the last few months she became lazy and predictable. She just wanted to lay there and let me do all the work. I was paying good coin for that. When a man is paying out thousands of pounds to set a woman up with all her fripperies and jewels and a house to keep her in and all she wants to do is lay on her back and….well it just wasn't worth it anymore," Damien said with the same emotionless tone.

"I see your point. I wonder if she has a new protector yet," Jarrett wondered aloud.

"You can't afford her, Jarrett. You'd better stick with the opera singers and the actresses," Damien said with a rueful smile.

Jarrett laughed and made no further comment but continued to sit there with a thoughtful expression on his face.

Damien smiled inwardly, knowing that he was taking a mental accounting of his finances to see if he could take on the lovely luscious Lila. "Oh well, perhaps Jarrett could work a deal with her through the end of the year. The lease is paid up until then, after all. She has plenty of new baubles and her wardrobe is up to date.

Maybe I should even put in a good word for him, he thought. Aye, I can send a note around to her this afternoon, making the suggestion."

With that decided he smiled, clapping his friend on the back, "Well my friend, if I'm to suffer through the Simpson ball tonight I should go home to rest up. What time will you be there?"

"Oh, I thought I would show up fashionably late, around ten or so. What time will you be there?"

"The same. I can come round to collect you, if you'd like. Perhaps we can make a short time of it and go over to Maude's for some cards, drink and wenches after. I hear she has a new crop of girls to choose from," Damien told him.

"That would be grand old boy!" Jarrett replied smiling.

*****

Damien and Jarrett entered the Simpson's ball at half past ten dressed in their formal black and white attire. Both men were stunning in their appearance. The sea of people parted when Damien lead the way through the ballroom.

He was already bored. He could hear the whispers of women behind their fans, the giggles of the debutantes and the admonishments of their scheming mama's.

"Sit up straight dear!"

"Smile gel, how can you catch his lordships attention, frowning so?"

"He's the heir to the Evansdale dukedom you know!"

"I hear he's a rakehell!"

These were just a few of the comments Damien heard as they braved the gauntlet.

"How can you stand the scrutiny, Damien," Jarrett asked.

"I can't stand it but I'm going to have to suffer it until I find a worthy candidate to be my marchioness," Damien said, rolling his eyes with utter disgust.

Jarrett snickered, asking, "And just what qualifications do you have for this nameless, faceless paragon?"

"Now that's a question I would like an answer to myself. Frankly, I don't care if she's a scullery maid as long as there is a spark between us. Of course, don't let Aunt Matilda hear me say that. She would die if I actually did marry a scullery maid. No my friend, I just want a wife I can be happy with for the rest of my life. A woman I will not mind being faithful to. Because believe it or not, once I take a wife my roguish ways are over. I will be a faithful husband as my father was, as was his father before him. It's how it is with us Vane's. We mate for life so they tell me, so she has to be special. Not one of these silly chits spilling over the rim of the ballroom. Look around! Not a one of them is unique. They all look like they were cut from the same dull cloth!" Damien complained.

Jarrett laughed, saying, "That's a fairly tall order Damien. I wish you the best of....Good God man, would you look at that!"

Damien followed Jarrett's line of sight across the ballroom. He found himself looking into the eyes of a Goddess.

Aye, a living Goddess with hair so black that is cast a blue sheen when the light touched it just so. Her skin was a creamy alabaster that looked as smooth as a babe's bottom.

She was dressed in a pastel blue gown with a bodice low enough to tease a man's senses but high enough to remain modest. Her figure was so lush and voluptuous that it begged a man to grab hold. It left his hands aching to touch and squeeze.

He couldn't quite tell but from where he stood, it looked like she had crystal blue eyes. Huge blue eyes that were staring back at him. "Who is she?" he asked, in awed wonder.

"I don't know but she's looking at you, you lucky bastard," Jarrett grumbled.

"Whoever she is, she will be my marchioness as soon as I can manage it. Where is Aunt Matilda? I need an introduction," he said scanning the room for his wayward aunt.

"Ah look, there she is. How fortuitous for she's conveniently placed not too far from my wife!" Damien said with satisfaction, moving in that direction.

"It's a little early to call her your wife, old boy. What if she already has a husband?" Jarrett asked as he followed closely behind.

That comment brought Damien to an abrupt halt causing Jarrett to bump into him from behind.

"She better not have," he said suddenly struck with a powerful stab of jealously over this phantom husband. He collected his wits and started moving again in the direction of his aunt never taking his eyes off his Goddess.

He finally reached Matilda. "Aunt, how are you this evening?" he said as he took her gloved hand in his own bringing her knuckles up to his lips for a kiss. "You look lovely as ever," he said smoothly.

"Oh, how you do go on, you devil. What are you buttering me up for?" she asked suspiciously.

"You wound me, Aunt. Why would I need to butter you up? I know you love and adore me and will give me whatever I want. All I need do, is ask," he said with a playful grin and a twinkle in his eyes.

She swatted him with her fan on his shoulder, saying, "You forget that I practically raised you."

"Actually aunt, I was wondering…Do you know who that lovely black haired Goddess is? She's over to your left standing beside that gruff looking old man."

"Damien, you know I'm under strict instruction not to interfere, dear." She said with a sniff and a lifting of her chin.

Damien's smile faltered, "Be serious aunt. Do you or do you not, know who she is?"

"Well dear, of course, if you would lift your restriction and allow me, I would love to introduce you to the lovely Lady Celia Sheraton," she said with pointed effect.

Damien's jaw dropped open but he recovered and shut it quickly. His eyes alight with green fire, he said, "Now Aunt! Introduce me… now."

"Of course dear, if you're sure," she winked at Jarrett. "Follow me, gentlemen."

Damien growled in frustration at his facetious aunt. She wasn't alarmed. In fact, she was grinning from ear to ear. "Yes Damien, you should not be so quick to rule out your aunt's advice in the hunt for a wife," she mused as she led the way over to Lady Celia.

*****

Celia was feeling nervous at her first society ball. Never in her life, had she been in a room with so many people. She felt a little plump compared to all the skinny blonde haired china dolls in attendance. She felt like she stuck out like a sore thumb, with all the stares she received, by both men and women.

"Why did Papa insist on coming to London? Three weeks is not enough time to find a husband anyway. Why can I not be allowed to pick a husband from the local gentry near Papa's estate? I'm sure there are plenty of fine eligible bachelors to choose from." Not that she would really know; beyond church and the occasional invitation to tea, she rarely left Sheraton Manor long enough to analyze the field.

At one and twenty she wasn't really eager to take a husband but her father insisted that he was getting old. He needed to be assured his title and his lands will be in good hands once he's gone from this world. So, after much arguing and convincing, here they were in London, staying at her Aunt Gertrude's town house in Grosvenor Square. 'Now, I'm attending balls with stuffy old snobs,' she inwardly grumbled. 'With Papa standing guard beside me looking so fierce, who would want to approach me? Why, I have not even been asked by a single gentleman to dance,' she pouted. 'Oh, they look at me, sure and I can tell they want to approach but you can see the fear in their eyes when they see Papa. I'm going to have to speak with him about this,' she determined.

'He cannot expect me to find a husband when he is standing there ready to tear off the head of anyone who dares to look at me. Of course, he cannot really help himself after what happened to poor Chelsea so many years ago.'

'Such a tragedy. Poor Papa just cannot forgive himself for not being able to protect her. He would move heaven and earth for his family. It is so unfair that he lives in constant fear that he will lose another daughter if he doesn't remain vigilant.'

'Oh, now there's a fine specimen of a man,' she observed as a handsome man came into view. He was tall and broad shouldered with golden brown hair with streaks of blonde running through soft waves. It was unfashionably long, but not too long that he should need to tie it back.

'Oh my, that chiseled jaw, and are those green eyes? Oh, I do so love green eyes. Oh my, he's staring at me, goodness he's so handsome. Should I be staring back like this? What if he gets the wrong idea and thinks me some kind of a wanton?' Celia's face heated up. She became nervous. She tried not to stare anymore but she could feel his eyes on her. 'He's talking to that nice dowager duchess...oh I cannot remember her name. They seem very friendly, perhaps I can slide over there later and ask her who he is and get Papa to approach him later for an introduction.'

'Oh, lord the dowager duchess is leading him over here. Oh my heavens! Calm down Celia, it's all right, he is just a man, not really the Godlike creature he appears to be.'

Chapter Two

"Celia darling, may I make known to you, my nephew, Damien Alexander Vane, Marquess of Devonshire and his companion, Sir Jarrett Wellstone. Damien, Jarrett, meet the lovely Lady Celia Sheraton," the dower duchess introduced them, smoothly.

Damien never imagined a woman could be as beautiful as Lady Celia. "She truly is a living Goddess," he thought in awe. He took her gloved hand in his and slowly brought it to his lips, never taking his eyes off hers.

"Lovely indeed," he breathed softly, placing a kiss on her hand.

"My lord, how nice to meet you," she replied, a little bit breathlessly.

Damien held onto her hand a little longer than propriety allows before releasing it. However his eyes continued to hold hers captive a few seconds longer.

Jarrett cleared his throat, breaking the spell. Celia blinked her eyes, turning to Jarrett. He took her hand in his and placed a kiss on her knuckles as well.

"Enchanted," he said softly.

She blushed prettily, saying, "Nice to meet you Sir Jarrett."

Damien noted the gruff older man beside Lady Celia. On closer inspection, he realized that he did indeed remember him but he seemed to have aged decades beyond the years it had been since he has seen him last. He was still a big burly handsome gent but his hair had silvered and there were deep worry lines around his eyes.

He extended his hand toward him, "Lord Sheraton, nice to meet you again sir."

The baron accepted his hand, in a firm-clasping shake. He replied through tight lips, "My lord, it's nice to meet you again, as well."

Damien realized that Lady Celia's father was a protective man. To pay him his due respect, he said, "Sir, may I have your permission to dance with Lady Celia?"

The baron looked at his daughter as if trying to determine whether she would welcome his attentions. She looked at him, the two communicated silently with their eyes. He finally said, "Aye my lord that would be acceptable, you may dance with my daughter but mind you, no more than once and keep an appropri…"

Lady Celia hurried to interrupt him, "Papa really, I'm sure his lordship knows the rules." The baron blustered, turning red, but said nothing more.

Lady Celia smiled at her father, then turned to Damien, "My lord, I would love to dance," she said with a breathtaking smile.

Damien placed her hand on his arm, leading her out on the dance floor. He bent his head toward hers, murmering, "Your father is quite protective of you Lady Celia. I assure you, that you are quite safe with me."

She threw him a quick blushing glance, "He can't help himself. Everywhere he looks, he sees the big bad wolf. He's afraid that I'll be snatched up and taken away from his protection."

Damien chuckled, asking, "The reason you are here is to find a husband, is it not, Lady Celia? How can you be expected to find one, if your father won't relax his hold?" Damien noticed that she stiffened ever so slightly by his comment.

"Well, as I said my lord, he can't help it," she said in a tone that brooked no further comment on that topic.

Damien persisted, "If I had a daughter as lovely as you, I no doubt would feel the same."

He could see the blush on her cheeks as he swept her into the twirling steps of the waltz that was already in progress. He noticed how well she fit into his arms. He was tempted to draw her nearer but he knew her father was watching closely for any slip of decorum so he held the urge at bay.

"My aunt spoke of you this morning. She said that you were only in London for a few weeks. Do you think you will have found a husband in that amount of time, Lady Celia," he asked a little mischievously.

Her eyes rounded large and she turned a deep crimson, "My lord you are being too forward."

Damien smiled, "Not at all, Lady Celia, I have a feeling that you will indeed find a husband in a few weeks, maybe even less. I dare say, that you could find a husband this very night if your father wasn't hovering so near, scaring away all your prospects," he teased.

"My lord really, you should not speak to me so," she admonished unable to look in his eyes now.

"Lady Celia, I too have a weakness where you're concerned. It seems I cannot help myself either. I confess that you are by far the most beautiful creature I have ever had the privilege to look upon. I am quite overcome."

Damien noted that Celia was trembling slightly, "Forgive me Lady Celia, you are correct, I am being forward, but I have only a few weeks to press my suit. I cannot afford to dally around when someone else may whisk you away if I am not persistent. Sir Jarrett for example, he noticed you first, you know. Without his keen observation I might never have found you."

"Your suit, my lord?" Lady Celia questioned. "Aye, my suit. I'm here for the same reason you are, Lady Celia. I'm in search of a wife before the season is over," he said looking into her eyes. "Do you think we would suit?" he pressed.

"My lord, we have only just met. I couldn't begin to assume such notions," she blustered.

"Ah, of course, you want a proper courtship. Aye, we should take a few more minutes to get to know each other before we go to the parson," he teased.

The dance came to a stop. Damien led Lady Celia back to her father. Not wanting to leave things to chance, he decided to act swiftly and addressed her father. "Sir, may I have your permission to call upon Lady Celia on the morrow?"

The baron looked at his daughter. Once again, they silently communicated, "My lord, we would be honored for you to pay us a call."

Damien was elated. He could already imagine his wedding night with Celia spread out before him with her raven locks loosed and splayed out on the pillow, with her arms open to receive him. He imagined himself kissing every inch of her body starting with her....

"Ahem," he cleared his throat, trying to shake off the images before they became painfully obvious to everyone. "I shall be there around tea time then. Would that be satisfactory, Lady Celia?"

"That would be fine my lord, I shall look forward to it."

Damien took her hand in his and placed a gentle kiss upon it. He made a bow and departed in search of Jarrett, who had disappeared while he and Lady Celia were dancing.

Damien couldn't believe his good fortune. Lady Celia, with her lush body with her full bosom; nicely rounded hips and ample backside was just how he preferred his women. 'Ah…and her exquisite hair and eyes… hmmm…yes, she would make a perfect wife,' he inwardly gloated. 'Of course, she's right, we only just met tonight but there was that spark. I felt it and I am sure she did too.'

*****

'I liked him well enough, I suppose,' Celia mused to herself. 'Of course, he was forward and he is too arrogant but still, he is handsome and has most of the attributes I would want in a husband but then again his title is a bit lofty for my liking. Not quite, what I had in mind.'

'Papa wants to be sure that whomever I marry will care for his estate after he has gone. The marquess probably already has lands and estates that he is responsible for. He might not wish to acquire Sheraton and all that goes with it or worse he might take me away to one of his estates and I could never stand for that.'

'No, whomever I marry, will have to agree to live at Sheraton. I should speak to Papa about this. Well, it is too soon to consider such things.'

'His friend Sir Jarrett was more what I had in mind for a husband. He is just a knight and probably doesn't even own an estate so he most likely wouldn't mind living at Sheraton and he is very handsome with his blonde hair and green… or were they hazel eyes?' She couldn't remember. 'Yes, I must speak with Papa about this.'

"Celia darling, are you ready to leave this wretched place and go home?" the baron asked, forcing her out of her reverie.

"Of course Papa, I would like to speak to you on the way home about the marquess," she said quietly.

"Did he do something untoward?" he demanded.

"No, No Papa, it's nothing like that. I will explain in the carriage. Someone might overhear us here," she said looking around for open ears.

"Well, let's quit this place," he said taking her by the elbow and guiding her through the throngs of people.

Once they were safely ensconced in the carriage her Papa said, "Well now lass, tell me about the marquess."

"It's quite unsettling, actually. He spoke to me of marriage. He said that he was there for the same reason I was and that he wanted to be married before the season was over. He said I was the most beautiful woman he had ever seen. However, I started thinking that he may be a bit too lofty for me, you know. He might take me away from Sheraton. I could never tolerate that. I really had my heart set on someone more along the lines of his friend, Sir Jarrett. He is just a knight and probably does not have any other estates or fortune, for that matter so he would probably be willing to live at Sheraton. Oh, I do not know Papa, I am so confused. What should I do?"

"Child, don't stress yourself just now. The marquess is a very wealthy man. He would make a fine husband. You don't have to live at Sheraton you know. As for Sir Jarrett and his lack of land or fortune, you need not really worry about that considering your own. This is only our second day in London. We still have plenty of time to find eligible bachelors for your consideration," her Papa advised.

"Oh but Papa I must be allowed to stay at Sheraton. Who is going to take care of Chelsea when you're gone?"

"Well, we may have to put her in Bedlam, dear or perhaps a convent. You know she will never be normal again. She will never take a husband. Indeed, who would have her?"

"No Papa, I won't hear of it, we cannot send her to Bedlam or a convent. No, Chelsea will stay with me at Sheraton and that's the end of it," Celia admonished him.

"You can't decide who your future husband should be based on what's best for Chelsea. You have your own life to live, daughter. Chelsea is lost to us dear, you must accept it."

"She is not lost Papa! She is not! I refuse to hear this! How can you give up on her like that? How can you?" she demanded.

"I'm sorry Celia, I know it must sound harsh but if she doesn't come around soon, what are we to do with her? She's violent and could be dangerous to any children you might have. You don't want her to hurt your children, do you lass?"

"Chelsea is not violent. She would never hurt a child, Papa! You know this! It's just your shame of her that makes you say such things. You simply can't forgive her for what happened," Chelsea cried.

"Lass, you are so mistaken. Don't you know child, it is not Chelsea I cannot forgive. It's myself... I cannot forgive myself for not being there to protect her from that animal. It's not her shame, it's mine. But surely, you can see that she will never be like she was before. You can't make decisions about your future based on hers," he said in a pleading tone.

"I'm sorry, I know it was wrong of me to say that you can't forgive her for what happened but you do need to forgive yourself. You have worked so hard since then to protect us, especially me."
She saw an opening to discuss the other topic she wanted to broach. "You know Papa, there aren't monsters everywhere. Perhaps you should ease up a bit while we're in London. The marquess was the only man brave enough to talk to me with you standing beside me like an angry bear," she teased.

"Aye, I'm going to protect my little girl. London is the devil's playground. He has many minions lurking about, looking for an innocent like you. It is my duty to see to it that you do not fall victim to some fortune hunter or worse. But I see your point, from now on I will try not to look so fierce" he said, then kissed her cheek. "You are my little girl Celia, no matter how old you are. I love you, daughter. Never forget that."

Celia hugged her Papa and snuggled up beside him, "I love you too, Papa."

*****

"Have you seen my marchioness?" Damien asked when he finally located Jarrett a half an hour later near the card room. "I lost track of her after our dance when I went in search of you. I wonder if she's still here, I thought I might ask her for the supper dance."

Jarrett laughed at his friends presumptuousness and said, "Alas my friend, I went to drown my sorrows. I never saw her again after you swept her away."

"She is exquisite isn't she? I'm sorry for sweeping her away from you. I know you saw her first, but I was completely captivated. I couldn't control myself," Damien said with genuine sincerity.

"No worries mate. Women of her breeding are not in search of poor lowly knights with no fortune. I guess I will just have to stick with the opera singers. Oh, I say that reminds me, are we still going round to Maude's after this dreary affair?"

"You're not. I forgot to tell you, that I got you a late assignation with the luscious Lila tonight," Damien grinned.

Jarrett sputtered, turning wide-eyed, "The hell you say, old boy. Are you pulling my tail?"

"Indeed I'm not, when I got home this afternoon, I wrote a message to her, asking if she would like to take you on through the end of the year. She wrote back that she would love to. You won't have to put out the expense of putting her up in a house and all that go with it since she is well set for the time being. It's the perfect arrangement," he said clapping him on the back.

"You should probably leave now before it gets much later. Lila doesn't like to be kept waiting."

"I say Damien, that was right nice of you, but how can I repay you?"

"Just keep your eyes on that bastard Nigel and consider us even. Now let me go so I can find my marchioness. You can take the carriage; just have it returned early because I'm to have tea with Lady Celia on the morrow."

"Don't worry Damien, we'll figure out a way to get Nigel. He can't keep escaping justice," Jarrett said solemnly.

"Be off with you now," Damien said as he scanned the room looking for Lady Celia.

Jarrett quickly took his leave with an extra spring in his step as he headed for the ballroom exit. Damien chuckled lightly as he watched him go. "Enjoy Lila, my friend," he mused.

He walked around the ballroom for a few more minutes. Finally, he decided that he should seek out his aunt to see what became of Lady Celia. She must have gone home because he couldn't see her or her father anywhere.

After finding his aunt and her confirmation that Lady Celia did indeed, take her leave, he decided to go on to Maude's. He could use a little female companionship, after all. It's been three weeks since he has lain with a woman. After being around Lady Celia he had a particular itch that needed to be scratched. Outside, he hailed a hack, giving instructions to Maude's.

*****

"Lord Devonshire, it's been a long time since you've visited my establishment. You must've heard about my new crop of lovelies," she preened.

Maude was a tall and beautiful middle-aged woman with an ample bosom and flaming red hair. She went into business for herself when she was too old to attract her own protectors. She was a shrewd businesswoman, reputed to run one of the cleanest brothels in all of London. A man didn't have to worry about contracting the pox at her establishment as she kept a doctor on staff to see to the girls regularly.

"Hello Maude. Indeed, I have heard. I was hoping to find something that might interest me. I say, you wouldn't happen to have any black haired beauties tonight, would you?"

Damien experienced a brief flash of guilt for asking for a black haired woman as if any could compare to Lady Celia but he was feeling a bit maudlin. Since he couldn't have the real thing, perhaps a cheap imitation could tie him over until his wedding night.

"You rogue; you always did prefer the dark haired chits. It just so happens, I do have a lass to fit that description. It is her first night on the floor so she is somewhat shy but I think you will find her satisfactory. Her name is Sara. She comes to me from Scotland so she has a bit of an accent. Let's see, where did she get off to? Oh, there she is, over there beside that palm. Do be kind to her Lord Devonshire. I would hate to lose her as I have had many gentlemen praise her beauty and I think she will be very good for business. I have not agreed to let her take on any clients as of yet because she needs to learn the trade and get her confidence up. I think you would be an excellent tutor for her first time. Let me go speak with her to prepare her. I'll be back momentarily. Do have a drink on the house while you wait."

"Of course, Maude. My thanks."

Damien ordered a brandy. He watched as Maude spoke to Sara. She was quite pretty and young. He could tell she was shy and nervous. She darted a glance his way with trepidation in her eyes but then she gave an affirmative nod to Maude, took her leave, and went up the staircase.

Maude returned to him, "She was delighted to receive you, of course. I sent her upstairs to prepare. Why don't you would finish your drink? She'll be ready in about a quarter of an hour. You'll find her in your favorite suite."

"Is she a virgin, Maude? She seemed a little scared."

"Lud no, she isn't a virgin. She's a poor war widow. Her husband was killed. She lost everything so she made her way to London. She is actually hoping to find a protector but I told the gel that I would let her work here until she could find someone suitable. You wouldn't be interested, would you Lord Devonshire?" she asked with a hopeful eye cast on him.

"I'm to be married soon so I shouldn't take on any arrangements that might embarrass my future wife but I will ask around to some of my friends to see if they might be interested," he said. He was beginning to feel somewhat unsure of his decision to come here tonight.

After all, it wouldn't do for Lady Celia to hear that he was visiting a brothel the very same night he met her and practically proposed.

'Well, declarations haven't made. There aren't yet any real expectations so I might as well indulge myself.' he considered silently.

Shaking off his guilt, he said, "Perhaps if she pleases me I will consider taking her on with your usual finder's fee, of course. But mind you, I make no promises"

"How is dear Lila? I hear that you've cast her off."

"Lila is fine. She will be under the protection of another gentleman through the end of the year. After that, it's my hope that she will leave this business and set herself up with the dress shop she so often spoke of, or better yet, find a husband."

"Lila will never settle for a husband, you know that. Her attentions are not easily held for long," Maude said matter of fact. "She was my most popular girl, you know, until you whisked her away," she said with a sigh.

"True, she really isn't the marrying kind, is she?" Damien mused aloud.

"Well dear, take your time and enjoy Sara. I have to mingle, you know. Stop and see me on your way out. I should know how she performed, in case I need to give her more instructions before she starts seeing other clients… or in case any other arrangements need to be made," she said with a pointed look before taking her leave.

Damien finished his drink and made his way up the stairs in search of Sara. He felt a little nervous and wondered if she had ever been with any other man besides her husband.

"That's almost as bad as having a virgin," he inwardly grumbled. She might not have learned any useful skills as a wife beyond lying on her back. He preferred his women to be active participants. Casting doubts aside, he entered the room. She was awaiting him on the bed, completely nude.

Her body wasn't as lush and full as Celia'ss but she was shapely and firm. He noted that it didn't look as though she had ever born a child, as she still had the firmness of figure that signifies youth.

"Hello Sara," he said, shutting the door.

"Hullo milord," she replied timidly.

"Please call me Damien," he said, trying to put her, as well as himself, at ease.

"Aye, hullo Damien," she said with a shy smile. She cast her eyes down when he started removing his cravat. He watched her closely, as he continued to undress. He removed his evening coat first, then his waist coat. He walked over to the sideboard, poured two glasses of brandy, and walked over went to the bed where she lay. He handed one of the glasses to her, "Here, take this. It will settle your nerves."

She took the brandy and sipped it. He removed his shirt, then sat down on the edge of the bed to remove his shoes and hose. All the while, he never took his eyes from her, so he could gauge her responses to him. She was clearly scared but determined in her course.

He stood up to unbutton the front panel of his breeches but instead of removing them, he moved toward her and asked, "Is it true that you are a widow?"

"Aye, tis true milord. My husband were killt four months past."

"Did you have children with your husband Sara?" he asked softly.

"Nay, we didnae have time to have a babe afore he left… to go to the war," she said clearly uncomfortable with the discussion.

"How long were you married before he left?" Damien asked, now genuinely interested in her story.

"We were together only for a fortnight afore he left," she said almost defensively.

"If I had a wife as bonny as you, I wouldn't have left to go to war," Damien said, feeling a little sorry for her now.

"Weel, he didnae have a choice. He were pressed into service one night after leavin the tavern," she said with her chin up.

"Ah, that explains it," Damien said, as he sat down on the edge of the bed beside her again. He reached over, stroked her hair, and ran his thumb along her jaw. "You are quite lovely, Sara."

He continued a slow methodical caress as he ran his hand down her neck, then moved toward her breasts. He palmed her breast and lightly pinched her nipple, saying, "You have a beautiful body, too."

He could feel slight stiffening in his breeches. "Would you like to touch me, Sara?" he asked softly.

She looked at him with big round eyes, the color of ginger and honey, and tentatively reached toward his chest. She lowered her palm to his stomach and lightly caressed before inching lower to reach inside his breeches. She shyly wrapped her hand around his arousal and started a slow sensual massage.

Damien threw his head back and groaned. It felt nice… but not right. "How old are you Sara?" he asked, while she was administering to him.

She stopped, blinking her eyes at him, but remained mute.

Damien put his hand over hers, removing it from his breeches. "How old, Sara?" he asked again, in a commanding tone.

"I um…um…weel, I'm to be five and ten on my birthday next," she said nervously.

Damien immediately jumped up from the bed as if he had been lying in a bed of hot coals and just now felt the burn. "Bloody hell! Don't tell me you're just a child!" he shouted.

She cowered back against the pillows, warily watching him pacing about the room. He ran his hand through his hair, shaking his head in disgust.

"How can this be? How did a girl of four and ten end up here? What is this nonsense about a husband killed in the war?" he raged.

"Please milord, tis true. I am a widow. My Papa married me off because he has seven daughters and he couldn't afford to keep me. My husband were a no good drunkard but he took me off Papa's hands, then got himself pressed into service. I've nowhere else to go but here," she said, crying now.

"How many men have you been with besides your husband?" he asked.

"Just you milord," she said wiping her eyes.

"Well, you aren't going to be with me. I cannot abide the idea of having sex with a child, widow or no." He rushed to button up his breeches, jerked on his hose and shoes, then his shirt. He threw on his coat and stuffed his cravat in his pocket.

"Get dressed," he barked at her. "I'll be back in a few minutes. When I come back, be ready, because I'm taking you out of here."

He walked out the door, fairly slamming it behind him. What in the world was Maude doing, hiring babies to whore in her brothel? Of all the disgusting things! He stomped down the staircase to find Maude. He was breathing fire by the time he reached her. "How much for the child, Maude?" he said, through clenched teeth.

Maude smiled, "So, she was satisfactory then?"

"No Maude, she was not satisfactory. She's a bloody child, barely out of her leading strings. I do not have sex with children. When did you stoop so low, as to bring children in here to whore for you?

"Now wait just a minute, Lord Devonshire. I will have you know that I care for the poor dear. She has been here for three weeks. I have yet to ask her to service any clients before tonight. The poor child has nowhere else to go, what was I to do? Just throw her out on the streets? No, my Lord, I could never do such a thing. I only asked her to service you because I knew you would be looking for a new mistress, since you cast Lila aside. What better place for a young widow to go than to be placed under your protection?"

"Spare me your humanitarianism, Maude. How much for the child?" he demanded, in an angry tone.

"For you, my lord, five hundred pounds. That's a very good bargain. She will only require a little training. She understands the basics," she said, with a wink and a sultry smile.

"Fine, I will send my man down here on the morrow with your money, but I'm taking the child with me now," he said in a huff. He turned around, heading back toward the staircase.

He stomped back up the stairs, and down the hall, to the suite he had left her in. When he opened the door, she was dressed, waiting primly on the side of the bed.

"Have you gathered your things?"

"Aye milord, I'm ready," she said, clutching a bag on her lap.

"Good, let us quit this place. I'll be taking you to my Aunt Matilda's where you will find employment with her. Under no circumstances are you to speak to anyone of this, do you understand me?"

"Aye milord, thank you milord"

"Good, shall we?" he asked, extending a hand to take her arm.

*****

When they reached Aunt Matilda's, Damien explained to the butler that he was to take the child and give her a place to sleep for the night. He promised he would be come back on the morrow, to speak to his aunt about finding her employment. With that said, he left and went to his townhouse.

God, what a bloody debacle! His only hope was that Lady Celia never heard of it. From this moment forward, he was going to be faithful to Lady Celia. Feeling very frustrated and sexually unfulfilled in his barren wasteland of celibacy, he silently vowed that his condition was even more reason to press his suit to get her to accept his proposal as soon as possible.

He should have just gone home after leaving the ball. What a revolting development! Well, soon it would be different. Soon he would be a married man. He and Lady Celia would have many years of sexual bliss.

All he needed now was a good night sleep to usher in the morrow. Then, he can see could press upon Lady Celia, the need for a speedy wedding. First, he'd have to propose, of course. Surely, she would see the wisdom of the match and accept.

Chapter Three

"Lord Devonshire to see you, Lady Celia," Peterson, her Aunt Gertrude's butler, said with his usual sour expression.

"Thank you, Peterson, please show his lordship to the drawing room. My father and I will receive him there," Celia said. She hurried down the hall to fetch her father from his room. She wanted him to be there when she received Lord Devonshire.

She felt sure, being alone with the marquess was not a good idea, especially since he was so forward in his speaking. It seemed best to have her Papa present to keep him in check.

She knocked on her father's door, calling, "Papa. Lord Devonshire is here. He's awaiting us in the drawing room."

Her father opened the door. He was smiling broadly, "That's fine, lass. Shall we go to him, then?"

"Yes Papa, if we must," she said, with a scrunched up nose.

"Dear child, do try to show a little more enthusiasm for the marquess," he admonished.

"Oh. Alright, Papa!"

They headed to the drawing room. Upon entry, they saw that Damien was standing in front of the window looking out on to the street. His hands clasped together behind his back in what appeared to be a very relaxed pose.

He was wearing tan breeches and Hessian boots. His topcoat was made of dark blue superfine with a tan waist coat. His cravat was impeccably tied. It put emphasis on his fine strong jaw.

He turned toward them when they entered. For a brief moment, he seemed startled to see her father at her heels. She inwardly giggled at the expression on his face. Clearly, he was hoping to have time alone with her.

"Lord Devonshire, it's good to see you looking hale and hearty," the baron said.

"Thank you, sir. Might I say that it's good to be here on such a fine day." After a firm handshake with the baron, he cast his eyes toward Celia. He took her hand bowing to place a soft kiss on it.

"Lady Celia, you are indeed a vision of loveliness," he said softly.

"Please have a seat Lord Devonshire. Celia dear, why don't you ring for tea? Oh, and see if Peterson can drum up some of those little strawberry tarts that Cook makes so well. I'm feeling a bit peckish my dear."

Damien sat on the sofa across from the baron and hoped that when Lady Celia finished with her father's request she would choose to share a sofa with him. He was quite put off by the presence of the baron since his being here would make it impossible to woo her into accepting his proposal.

When Lady Celia returned from requesting the tea and tarts, she sat on the sofa next to her father. Damnation!

She gave Damien a radiant smile, "How is your dear Aunt Matilda, my lord?"

Damien cleared his throat, "As fine as ever," he said somewhat lamely.

He didn't want to think about his aunt after the tongue-lashing she gave him, not even an hour ago, for bringing Sara to her last night. Not that she didn't want to take the child in, no, it was more about where he'd found her.

She decided that Sara was just the right age and disposition to make a fine ladies companion. She said she would see to her training herself. Then, she would find a placement for her with one of her friends.

Damien was quite relieved that she would be so gracious towards Sara but his ears were still stinging from the set down she delivered for his being a shameless "rakehell", as she termed it. Though she did say, he scored some merit by realizing she was just a child and taking her away from Maude's.

"She's a lovely woman," Celia said, breaking into his brooding.

After a few of moments of awkward silence, the teacart finally arrived. Celia poured everyone a cup and passed around the tarts. Damien passed on the tarts but was grateful for the tea.

Celia wasn't interested in the tarts either but the baron was munching away with a certain amount of gusto proving that it might not be a wise thing to let him go too long without sustenance, if the ravishment of the tarts were any indication, that is.

Damien gazed at Celia. He couldn't help but marvel at her beauty. She was wearing a blue and white striped day gown with a delicate lace fichu that hid away her ample bosom. Her hair was pulled back in a loose knot. Curling tendrils about her face and neck made her a sheer vision of perfection.

He wondered how she came to the age of one and twenty without having a husband but then looking over at her father, it all made perfect sense.

"Yes she is a dear, I would be lost without her," Damien replied with as much sincerity as he could muster given his deteriorating mood.

"And Sir Jarrett? How is he?" Celia asked

That threw Damien a bit, "Well uh, Sir Jarrett is fine, actually."

"How did you and he meet?" Celia asked with wide expecting eyes.

"Sir Jarrett's father was my father's steward. We grew up together as a result."

"Ah I see. He seems to be a nice man," Celia said demurely.

Damien didn't want to keep talking about Jarrett but he was floundering for a topic of discussion.

"You would be hard pressed to find a more honorable man," he allowed.

"I say, Lord Devonshire, I hear that your father is in poor health," the baron piped in.

"Aye sir that's true. The surgeons do not expect him to last much longer. Perhaps another month or two," Damien said solemnly.

"Oh! Well, to be sure my lord, you have our deepest condolences. Your father is a fine man. Haven't seen him in years but since our estates were so near one another, we used to have the occasion to share a pint or two, now and again at the old ale house," the baron said with genuine respect for the duke.

"Indeed my lord, please accept our condolences. If there is anything we can do, don't hesitate to let us know," Celia said with sorrowful eyes for the plight of his father.

This visit was taking on a dark, dreary tone. Not good for his purposes.

"Thank you Lady Celia, that's very kind." 'Where do I go from here,' Damien wondered.

"Excuse me, Lord Sheraton, but this just came for you," Peterson entered the drawing room with a small tray carrying a message for the baron. Damien was relieved to have the interruption, given that the course of the conversation was progressing so poorly.

"Excuse me Celia darling, Lord Devonshire. It seems to be rather urgent, I shan't be a moment." The baron got up and went over to the window to better see his missive.

Celia and Damien sat in awkward silence while the baron read his message. Damien couldn't keep his eyes off Celia. However, he could not help but feel frustrated with the presence of her father. "I must find a way to have a moment alone with her to press my suit".

"If only her father would leave the room for just a few minutes. Perhaps there is something in the missive that will require his immediate response." He found himself wondering where the spark was that he felt last night at the Simpson affair. It was clear she felt something for him then, too, but today she seems so calm and indifferent.

'Perhaps she's just nervous with her father looking on.' He completely understood now, why she is still unwed at her age. With a father like that crowding round, what potential suitor would tolerate it?

'Well, I am made of sterner stuff,' Damien assured himself. 'If I can't get a moment alone with Lady Celia today, I can always sweep her away into the garden or balcony after a waltz at the next ball we attend together.'

'On the other hand, if push comes to shove, I can always go straight to her father and ask permission to marry her. Surely, her father expects that to be the conclusion to this course of events. What father would turn me down?' he asked himself.

"Well now, Celia dear, it appears we are going to have to go back to Sheraton Manor for the next day or two to handle a situation with the mill," the baron said after reading his message. Then, an idea seemed to spark. He said, "I say Lord Devonshire, would you like to come along and see Sheraton Manor? It's part of Celia's dowry, of course. We would only be gone two, maybe three days, at most. I hate to interfere with your courtship by taking Celia away just when you are getting to know each other." The baron was smiling, clearly proud of his idea.

He didn't pay attention to his daughter while he was throwing this idea around like so much rubbish or he would have seen the daggers in her eyes. The last thing Celia wanted was to have Lord Devonshire's non-stop presence for three days. "Oh lord Papa, what are you doing to me?" she inwardly cried.

Damien, on the other hand, was quite pleased. He instantly pulled from his despair over not being able to find time alone with her. 'Clearly, her father approves the match or he wouldn't have made the suggestion. Yes indeed, things are looking up,' Damien decided.

"That's an excellent idea, sir. Of course, I would be honored to travel with you and Lady Celia to Sheraton Manor. I have a couple of issues I have to take care of before I can get away, though. When would you want to leave?" he asked.

"I suppose we could leave at dawn if that suits your purposes," the baron said.

"That would be excellent sir. Dawn it is then." Damien was very pleased with this turn of events."

"Are you sure this isn't a matter we should handle alone, Papa?" Celia asked hopefully.

"No, no, my dear, don't worry your pretty head about that. It's not a serious situation after all. I should be able to have everything rectified within a couple hours of our return. No, my dear, this will be an excellent opportunity for you and Lord Devonshire to get to know each other better and for him to view the estate. Yes indeed, an excellent opportunity. Almost tailor made, I dare say," the baron beamed.

Peterson entered the drawing room again, "Sir Jarrett Wellstone to see Lady Celia," he announced with an expression of disdain.

"Sir Jarrett, how lovely to see you today," Celia said as she fairly jumped up from her seat to receive him. She was smiling broadly with real joy by his unexpected visit. Damien on the other hand…was not so happy.

"Lady Celia, you are a vision to heal my poor wretched soul," Jarrett said as he bowed over her hand to place a kiss upon it.

Celia blushed and nervously patted her hair before reclaiming her spot on the sofa.

"Do sit down, Sir Jarrett; we were just having some tea. Would you care to join us?" Celia offered.

"Why that would be excellent my dear, thank you," Jarrett said, before addressing the baron and Damien.

"Lord Sheraton it's good to see you. Damien, always a pleasure," he said with bows to both men before taking a seat next to Damien. "It's a fine day is it not?" he addressed no one in particular.

"Oh, yes it is. I would have loved to have gone for a walk about the park but I knew that I was to have callers today so I postponed until the morrow. Alas, even those plans must be cancelled as we are to return to Sheraton manor for a few days to resolve some kind of issue with our mill," Celia said clearly lamenting this prospect as she poured Jarrett a cup of tea. "How do you take your tea, Sir Jarrett?" Celia asked

"Straight from the tea pot will be fine Lady Celia," Jarrett said.

Celia handed him his cup of tea with a sweet smile and a flush of color upon her cheeks, that made her appear slightly feverish, Damien observed. He didn't remember her blushing for him like that. He was steaming beside Jarrett but everyone seemed to be oblivious to the fact. How dare he show up and try to poach the Lady Celia away from him.

"Is that so? 'Tis a shame indeed, perhaps the weather will remain fine until your return and you'll have an opportunity to go to the park then. It's always lovely this time of year," Jarrett said, with a note of disappointment in his voice.

"Yes it is, isn't it? A shame, that I have to leave, I mean," Celia agreed as she gazed at Jarrett.

Damien noticed how the two of them were eyeing one another. He was struck by a stab of jealousy that felt like a knife to his gut.

So to retaliate and squash the mooning going on between Lady Celia and Jarrett he said, "The baron has been kind enough to invite me along to tour his estate since it's a part of Lady Celia's dowry. He thought it would be an excellent chance for us to get to know one another." "There, take that!" he thought with a sense of smug satisfaction.

"Oh Papa I have a grand idea. We should have Sir Jarrett go along, too. The more the merrier, I always say," Celia said in an excited tone that she hoped would communicate to her father her interests in Sir Jarrett so as to give him an opportunity to get to know her better as well.

Damien sat in stunned silence, breath held awaiting the baron's response to this madness. Something isn't right here; Lady Celia is supposed to be making calf eyes at me, not Jarrett. Perhaps she's a bit more nervous about our marriage than I realized. It's not every day a woman is proposed to by a marquess after all.

"Er...uh, why uh, of course... of course, we would be delighted to have you along, Sir Jarrett, if your schedule permits, that is," sputtered the baron, clearly taken off guard by Celia's suggestion. But what could he do? He could not be rude and deny his daughters request with Sir Jarrett right there. Indeed, it would be most inhospitable to refuse. Then again, perhaps it would be interesting to see who would win his daughters hand, after a jaunt to the country, with everyone in close proximity. 'Nothing wrong with a little competition,' he reasoned.

Smiling he said, "Yes, that's a fine idea daughter, a fine idea indeed. We plan to leave here at dawn and we shouldn't be gone any more than three days, Sir Jarrett, if it's convenient for you."

Jarrett cast a nervous glance at Damien, wincing slightly when he noted the anger in his eyes and his clenched jaw. He looked at him apologetically before answering, "Uh…yes, I think my schedule can accommodate a short trip. Of course, I would be honored to accept your kind invitation Lady Celia."

It would be rude to refuse Lady Celia's offer wouldn't it? Of course, he had no choice but to accept. Certainly, Damien would understand this and forgive him.

"It's not my intention to court Lady Celia after all. "I'm just paying proper homage to the lady after making her acquaintance as any decent fellow would do. I only came here today out of friendly courtesy," he thought in an attempt to soothe his guilty feelings over the matter.

"Good, then it's all settled! We are sure to have a grand time of it," Celia beamed.

"Jarrett, since we will be so close to Evansdale perhaps you could go over to visit your mother. I'm sure she would be glad to see you," Damien said to indicate his displeasure with this development.

Jarrett, understanding Damien's not-so-subtle message retorted with barely perceptible irritation in his voice, "Yes, of course you're right; it's been an age since I've seen her. Perhaps you would like to accompany me to see your father."

He would just have to speak with Damien and assure him that he meant no transgression by his acceptance of Lady Celia's invitation. 'Damien is a logical man and will see the right of it.'

"Good, good. Well Celia, gentlemen, I have some matters to see to. I'm sure Celia needs to see to her packing, so if you don't mind, we'll just meet here on the morrow at say, seven, and then set off. The trip shouldn't take more than three hours by carriage. You gentleman might want to ride your own mounts rather than be cooped up in the carriage with Celia, myself and her maid," the baron said, standing to indicate that the visit was concluded.

Everyone stood up and Damien and Jarrett made their bows, said their goodbyes, and swiftly took their leave.

Once outside, while waiting for the groom to bring their horses, Damien decided it was time to put Jarrett in his place.

"Just what do you think you're doing Jarrett? Isn't Lila enough for you, must you have Lady Celia too?"

"Damien, surely you realize that it's not my intention to undermine you with Lady Celia. I was just paying a friendly social call, nothing more. How was I to know that Celia would invite me along? What could I do but accept?" Jarrett said in a placating voice. "It would have been rather rude for me to refuse and you know this," he added hoping Damien would see reason.

"Aye… it would have been rude to refuse but what I take issue with is that you showed up here at all today when you knew I was to see Lady Celia today for tea," Damien huffed.

"I was only paying a social call as I said but I knew I would find you here. It was my hope that we could go from here to the club so I could tell you how my night with Lila went. I swear, I meant no harm in coming here. Please say that you believe me," Jarrett pleaded.

"Well, just so you understand that I will be proposing to Lady Celia as soon as I can have a few moments alone with her. I believe the Baron approves the match. His invitation today shows that he is in fact, encouraging it," Damien said, somewhat mollified by Jarrett's apparent remorse.

"So, shall we go to the club then?" Jarrett asked hopefully.

"Not today, I need to take care of some matters before I can leave. You can tell me all about you and Lila while we're on the road to Sheraton Manor."

The groom brought around the horses. Both men mounted and headed off in the direction of their own home, each feeling somewhat pensive about the trip, but for entirely different reasons.

*****

"Well missy, you certainly set yourself up for an interesting time," the baron said after Lord Devonshire and Sir Jarrett left. "Both men are now locked, head to head in a direct competition for your favor. You do realize that's what you've done, don't you?" he asked with an arched brow.

"Papa, you know I would do no such thing. It is just that when you invited Lord Devonshire along, I was a bit angry with you. And his lordship seemed so smug when he told Sir Jarrett of your invitation. It seems as though you're pushing me toward him. It's almost as though you two are in cahoots and I'm not sure that the marquess and I would suit at all. I do not dislike him mind you, it's just that I told you I would much prefer someone like Sir Jarrett, so I thought; why not give him the same opportunity as Lord Devonshire, that's all. I certainly do not want them to come to a disagreement over me. Of course, I won't let it come to that. I will simply treat them both the same. That way they don't think I favor one more than the other," she said wringing her hands.

'Clearly, Papa is right and I could be setting the scene for a feud between two lifelong friends. I don't want that at all,' she fretted. 'Oh, what to do? There has to be a way to keep things peaceful between Lord Devonshire and Sir Jarrett.'

'Well, I won't worry about this now. They are lifelong friends after all, I'm sure I'm not first woman they've competed for. I will just treat them both the same as I told Papa and everything will be just fine.'

"Well lass, you are a great beauty and either man would be lucky to have you. I won't interfere with your choice in the matter but I will make it understood to you now, that I prefer Lord Devonshire. He has great wealth and he is to become a duke soon, sooner rather than later, sadly. Can you imagine the life you could lead as a duchess my dear?" he asked, with a wistful look in his eyes.

"Papa, his title matters not to me in the least. As for my being a duchess, I shouldn't like it at all if it takes me away from Chelsea and Sheraton Manor. Please understand that."

'How can Papa think I would be as shallow as that? Why, the very idea, that I would marry the man simply to become a duchess is preposterous.'

'Lord Devonshire is an arrogant man and no doubt, it's because he's lived his whole life, being treated with the deference due his station. It's no wonder he thinks he can waltz right into my life, quite literally, and press his suit upon me and expect me to fall at his feet groveling my acceptance. Indeed, the arrogance of the man; and Papa in alliance with him! Hmfp!'

"The next few days should tell one way or the other. I don't want to rush you into a decision but I would like to have you betrothed before our time in London is over. We have much to do at the manor and time is of the essence. I'm sure, however you decide; you will find happiness. They are both fine gentlemen. I understand that Sir Jarrett is one of Bow Street's most successful runners. They say he always gets his man, maybe this time he'll get you, eh," he chuckled, then added, "I dare say, the next few days should prove very entertaining."

"I'm glad you're enjoying yourself, Papa," Celia grumbled. "Well, I better start packing. See you at supper, Papa." She kissed him on the cheek and quit the room with a swish of her skirts.

'Very entertaining indeed,' the baron mused. 'Sir Jarrett might just come out the winner for Celia's hand. Well it wouldn't be so bad, he seems a fine lad.'

'If only poor Chelsea could find a husband, then I could die a happy man. Why, she cannot even stand to be around me without violent hysterical reactions much less a stranger trying to press his suit. No, poor Chelsea will never marry. 'Tis sad, perhaps it would be better if Celia picked Sir Jarrett, then Chelsea wouldn't be alone in the world when I'm gone.'

'Oh me, that reminds me, I better send a note ahead and warn Dickens that we are to be home tomorrow and let him know that we are bringing the marquess and Sir Jarrett so he can have rooms prepared. And make sure Hattie knows to keep Chelsea out of sight. It wouldn't do to have her come face to face with them and have her go all to pieces. That would be the end of either of their suits.' With that decided he went to the writing desk and dashed off his missive.

*****

Damien lay in bed thinking about Lady Celia. "Did I imagine that spark between us last night at the Simpson ball?" He relived the moment they saw each other from across the room, when their eyes locked together. They had been pulled together by a strong magnetic force. 'Aye, her reaction to me was as strong as mine was to her, I know it.'

'What went wrong between then and now? How could she have had such a powerful response to me one moment and then the next be so cool and aloof? Is she afraid to show her feelings out of some kind of irrational fear that I would think less of her? Perhaps that's it.'

'Surely, she wouldn't prefer Jarrett to me. Jarrett has no fortune and could never give her the life I can. No, she isn't really attracted to Jarrett.'

'Her response to him today was probably just from nerves. The way her father hovers round and she probably isn't used to male attentions other than his. He probably kept her cloistered away at Sheraton Manor her whole life.'

'Hell, if I had a daughter as beautiful as Lady Celia, I would do the same no doubt. It is probably quite a chore keeping all the randy young bucks in the area at bay. Aye, he's a wise man to keep such a close eye on Lady Celia.'

'I just need be clever to find a way to get her alone so I can woo her. Perhaps with a few heated kisses she will succumb and see that we are perfect for one another.'

'Of course, I can't take things too far. She isn't some light skirt to be taken in a hayloft or up against a wall. She's a lady and should be treated as such but there's no harm in a few hot seductive kisses to make her see my way.'

'Though, if I spend too much time with her, I'll be hard pressed, literally, to keep my hands off of her. Her body is so ripe for loving; just the thought of her lying naked beneath me drives me mad. I must get her to accept me and soon. I can't remember the last time a woman affected me so.'

'I've always taken what I wanted and never looked back when my interests died. But Lady Celia, well, I don't think I could ever lose interest in her. I can't wait until our wedding night when I will school her in the art of lovemaking. The look in her eyes last night promised a great passion inside her just begging to be released.'

'I wonder if Jarrett is enjoying Lila tonight. He probably has her legs high in the air right about now. Perhaps I shouldn't have been so quick to give her up. Celibacy is harder than I ever imagined he reflected as he became painfully aware of his raging erection. I suppose I'll have to take matters into my own hands........' and so he did with visions of Lady Celia to spur him on.

Chapter Four

"It's like you said Damien, she just lays there and lets you do all the work. I don't even think she enjoys lovemaking at all. I used all the tricks I know to bring her around but she just wasn't very responsive. Though she does have a sweet body, it hardly matters if she isn't enjoying it. It kind of takes the wind out of a fellows sail if he's giving it all he's got and the wench is stifling a yawn, you know," Jarrett complained on the way to Sheraton Manor.

They were about two and a half hours into the trip and would be there soon. They were making good time and hadn't had to make any stops. "No, I don't think I will be seeing her again. Like you say, it's hardly worth it," he concluded

"She wants to open a dress shop. Perhaps she wants to put this life behind her. She should if she doesn't enjoy it. A non-responsive mistress is hardly a profitable occupation," Damien said. "When she first started acting that way I thought she was bored with me but I can see now after it was the same with you that the problem lies with her. It's a comforting thing to know I haven't lost my knack for pleasing a woman especially since I'm to be married soon."

"Aye, tis true, you would want to please your new lady wife. How long do you think it will be before you marry?" Jarrett asked.

"I have to propose first, after that I would like to do it by special license and have done with it right away but I get the feeling she would prefer to have the banns read instead. Either way, I would like to be married by the end of the season. I don't fancy a long drawn out courtship."

"I can't blame you there, she's a fine…" Jarrett was going to call her a fine piece but cut his words off so as not to offend Damien further than he already had the day before.

Damien looked at him and wondered what he was about to say but thought better of asking him to finish his thought. He shouldn't have reacted the way he did towards Jarrett. He could see that now.

It's just so frustrating not being able to have his moment alone with Lady Celia that it's hard to contain the possessive feelings he has about her. It's silly to be jealous of his best friend. Jarrett would never do anything to dishonor him.

"Isn't that the forest where the incident with Nigel happened?" Jarrett asked as they neared the outer perimeter of the Sheraton estate.

"Aye, about two hundred yards into the wood there's a stream where the child must have been fishing. I never did figure out who he was or where he came from. He must have been a gypsy lad."

Damien had spent about a week asking around in the village about a boy matching his description but no one had any idea who he might be. There had been a band of gypsies in the area so he assumed the child must have belonged with them. The gypsies were closed mouth and refused to help Damien with any information so he reached a dead end.

"Tis a shame you never could find out who he was."

"Aye, that it is," Damien agreed.

"The Sheratons didn't know who the lad was either?" Jarrett asked.

"Truthfully, I never thought to ask the Sheratons. I knew the baron didn't have a son. The child was dressed like a pauper so I never even consider it. I guess in hindsight it could have been a stable lad from there but I was too young and distraught to think of all the possibilities. I'm sure if the child belonged to the Sheratons we'd have heard about it somehow. Our estates are close enough that communication on such an issue would have reached our ears but we never heard a thing."

Damien was a bit ashamed of himself for never once considering the child could have come from the Sheraton estate. He supposed he wouldn't make a very good detective.

"Tell me again how you and Nigel happened to be in that area. I might do a bit of snooping around while we're here so I'm not so much under foot."

"We had just come from the village. We decided to race but my mount came up lame with a stone lodged in his hoof. I removed it but the horse got spooked as I poked around looking for more stones. He reared up and took off running into the wood. Nigel went after him on his mount. I followed behind on foot. By the time I reached the stream Nigel had already attacked the child," Damien explained.

"What a bloody bastard," Jarrett growled, shaking his head in disgust.

"Aye. Then, of course, we fought. I didn't have time to see which way the child ran. When I woke up he and the child were gone with no indication which direction they might have gone. The child's fishing basket and tackle were lying by the stream. The remains of his breeches were strewn about. Ah, here we are, Sheraton Manor up ahead now. I don't know about you but I'm ready to stretch my legs," Damien said. He was relieved to change the topic when the estate came into view.

"It's a grand place isn't it?" Jarrett commented.

"Indeed it is. I think it was built in the late sixteenth century. I would have to check with the baron about that to be sure. It's in excellent condition for its age. I've heard that they modernized it quite a bit; it even has hot water piped in," Damien said in a proud fashion as he gazed ahead at the manor.

A sprawling stone structure rose up around the bend. It was scenically placed on the crest of a hill providing an excellent view of the countryside below. The manor was quite impressive with its fortifications. The landscaping was lush with fountains and statuary. It was almost as nice as Evansdale, Damien observed.

Damien and Jarrett pulled their mounts to a halt on the side of the road to allow the carriage to catch up and pull ahead of them so they could follow them in.

Shortly after they arrived they were met by the butler. "My lord Sheraton, it's good to have you home sir. Lady Celia, how nice to see you well," he said with genuine joviality.

"Thank you Dickens. This is Lord Devonshire and Sir Jarrett. They will be staying with us until we return to London. I trust you have their rooms ready," the baron said.

While the baron was conversing with the butler, Damien stood back looking up at the house. He couldn't quite say why but he had the feeling he was being observed from one of the attic windows. "Perhaps a chambermaid is interested by our arrival," he surmised.

He shook off the feeling and proceeded to follow the others inside. Upon entry to the house, Celia bounded up the grand staircase without so much as a by your leave, disappearing down the eastern hall.

She must have had an urgent need to take care of; understandable after being cooped up in a carriage for three hours.

The foyer was decked with white marble floors. They were overlaid with a huge red Persian carpet that had an elaborate design of blue, green and yellow woven throughout. The walls were painted a pale yellow and were topped with white crown molding. The chandelier was massive with at least a hundred candles inside it. Greek statues adorned the corners of the large space. The focal point of the room was an impressive grand staircase that curved gracefully. It ended with a landing that allowed you to go down halls leading both east and west.

"Gentlemen, Dickens will show you to your rooms where you can freshen up. We'll have luncheon at noon. There'll be a footman at the end of your hall that will show you the way to the dining room when its time. Since neither of you brought a valet, I will lend you mine if you've any needs. His name is Quinn. I think you will find him quite proficient in the art of tying a cravat. Just tug on the bell pull. He will be glad to assist you. Oh, and each of your rooms has a water closet with a copper tub with hot water piped in. That's part of our recent renovations. Quite handy I must say," the baron said proudly.

"This way if you please milord's" Dickens said as he lead them up the staircase.

Jarrett was completely in awe of the palatial estate. He had never been inside Sheraton Manor so he had no idea it was so exquisite. With this as part of Lady Celia's dowry, it's a wonder she wasn't scooped up ages ago. Damien didn't really seem as impressed but then again he had Evansdale and various other lavish estates, so such luxury was commonplace to him.

He supposed you would have to be a poor knight like himself to fully appreciate its grandeur. A fellow could become quite spoiled living in a place like this. Compared to the cozy comfort of his bachelor apartments, this was like being at the Taj Mahal.

*****

"Oh Chelsea darling I'm so glad to be home, I missed you so," Celia said embracing her sister. "London is so dreadful and smelly. I wish I never had to go back."

"I'm glad you're home, too. Who are those men you brought with you?"

"The tallest one is Damien Vane, the Marques of Devonshire. The other is Sir Jarrett Wellstone his companion. He's a Bow Street runner, Papa tells me. Papa invited them along because Lord Devonshire is courting me and well, I would like for Sir Jarrett to be, if you must know. He is far more appealing to me than the lofty marquess. Did you see how handsome they both are?" Celia beamed.

"No I didn't really get a good look at them. You say that Lord Devonshire's name is Damien?" Chelsea wondered aloud, with a bit interest, as the name seemed vaguely familiar.

"Why yes, as a matter of fact, we met at the Simpson's ball. He has been breathing down my neck ever since. Papa is determined that I should marry him and he has practically already asked. But I'm just not that impressed with him. He's so arrogant. If I were to marry him, I would have to leave Sheraton Manor. I could never leave you, darling," Celia said, plainly distressed by the prospect.

"Oh, but Sir Jarrett, my, when he looks at me I go all aflutter in my belly and I start blushing like a wanton. He's so sweet and handsome and so courteous too, he just melts my heart."

"You should marry whomever you want to Celia. Don't let Papa and Lord Devonshire bully you," Chelsea stated firmly.

"I know you won't of course, but I do so wish you would meet him, Sir Jarrett, I mean. You'll admire him dear, I know you will. Even with your aversion to men you won't be able to help yourself. If I could just figure out a way to get Lord Devonshire out of the picture without causing a strain on their friendship I would propose to Sir Jarrett myself," Celia said, then, giggled at the prospect of her proposing marriage.

"What will you do if Lord Devonshire proposes?"

"I'll put him off somehow. I simply can't bear the idea. We'll be having luncheon soon, then afterward I thought I would convince them to take a tour of the gardens with me. I plan to treat them both the same and not show any preference one way or the other. Perhaps Lord Devonshire will realize that we wouldn't suit and step aside, then I will pursue Sir Jarrett," she snickered.

"Be careful Celia, you know how dangerous men can be. You wouldn't want to find yourself in a situation where you could be compromised or…harmed. If Lord Devonshire is determined enough marry you, he might think to have his way with you to better convince you. You remember how it was with Julia Rawlins. The same could happen to you," Chelsea fairly snarled.

"Yes well, I think there was more to that story than Julia told me. I think she wanted to be compromised. But rest assured, I won't make such a mistake," Celia said in an attempt to calm her sister's obvious agitation.

"If Lord Devonshire tries to harm you, I'll kill him," Chelsea said with a curled lip.

"Chelsea, don't say such things. Calm yourself dear, I didn't mean to upset you. I'm sure all will be fine. I'm probably making more out of Lord Devonshire's feelings for me than there is. It's just that Papa seems so determined. I feel as though they are working together for the match. The very idea that Papa would invite two gentlemen here, shows how determined he is to see me married right away. You know how protective he is with us where men are concerned. Well if the truth be known, Papa didn't exactly invite Sir Jarrett. I did. He invited Lord Devonshire. The marquess was so smug about it in front of Sir Jarrett that I felt compelled to suggest we bring him along with us. You should have seen the look on everyone's face. It was priceless. Papa sputtered. Lord Devonshire had steam coming out of his ears. Poor Sir Jarrett turned red as a beet and started stammering," Celia said clearly enjoying herself as she relayed the tale.

"Papa says he won't interfere with my choice but he said that he prefers Lord Devonshire because I would become a duchess someday. His father is ill, you know and not expected to live much longer. So he is soon to become the Duke of Evansdale," she added.

"A duchess? I can just see you now," Chelsea laughed.

"Not me, I shudder to imagine. Well dear, I better go get cleaned up and changed for luncheon. Will you be alright, knowing that there are strange men in the house?"

"I'll be fine dear, I won't go all to pieces, I promise. It's true that I don't trust men, but you know the real reason I act the way I have all these years is because I can't bear to be around Papa. I don't want to hurt his feelings. The hurt I see in his eyes when he looks at me is just too devastating. It's easier to pretend that I fear all men, including him, so I can avoid the pain for both of us," Chelsea lamented, then looked down to hide the sadness in her eyes.

She would never forget that day, about seven years ago, when she ran into Papa was in the library. She had gone down in the middle of the night, to get a book, because she was having trouble sleeping. She didn't know he would be there that late at night.

He had been drinking and started ranting at her when she entered the library. "So, missy you decided to sneak down here for a book, did you? Too good to show your face at a decent hour, eh?" he said with a drunken drawl.

Chelsea had never seen her father like that. She stammered, "P-Please Papa don't be angry with me." she pleaded

"ANGRY?" he shouted, "I'm not angry, I'm disgusted. I can hardly stand to look at you. Every time I see you it's like a festering old wound and it starting to stink," he slurred, then he hid his face in his arm on his desk and started weeping with anguished mumblings. Chelsea was devastated. She couldn't understand his drunken slurs as he cried with his head down like that. It was a sad pitiful mewling sound like a dying animal. That was the first time she had been around her Papa in many months.

Every time she saw him he looked at her with eyes so full of pain that she could barely stand to be around him. But that was the first time he ever told her how he really felt. It was just too much.

She got so angry that she picked up a chair, hurled it across the room and started screaming, "Shut up! Just shut up!" She ran from the library and hadn't been around him since.

Papa tried to see her the day after that but she refused him. She heard him crying outside her door, begging for forgiveness.

That's when she decided to refuse to have anything to do with anyone but Celia, Hattie and Jenny. It was just too painful to be around "Papa. He simply couldn't forgive…well it wasn't long after that when she moved to the attic and began living a life of relative solitude.

Celia reached out, stroking her hair, "I know love, and you are so brave and strong. I'm sure it's not easy to put Papa away from you. I know how much you love him. He loves you too, you know. He blames himself for not being there to protect you. He wishes that someday you could find happiness. I know that you will darling. You just need time to heal and you will. You'll see." She bent down and kissed her sisters cheek, "I'll come see you tonight alright?"

Chelsea looked up with tears welling in her eyes and nodded her head. Then she stood up, embraced her sister tightly, saying, "Please be careful Celia."

*****

Chelsea's breath rushed out of her body as she recognized Damien. Hidden from view of the trio sitting on benches in the garden she could clearly see him. 'It can't be but it is. It has to be,' she told herself. 'He's older yes, but it's him nonetheless.'

She dropped down to the grass and sat huddled behind the shrubbery with her arms wrapped around her knees rocking back and forth as she relived the memory of that awful day. The shock on the young man's face.

His emerald green eyes were wide and washed with horror as he looked on while the monster savagely assaulted her. She started shaking her head to cast off the memory.

Adrenaline started coursing through her body. She found it difficult to breathe as the fear gripped her with its familiar icy tendrils. "I have to get out of here," she realized. She frantically jumped up and started running, blind with panic, through the garden until she reached the wood just beyond.

She stopped cold, realizing she was several yards into the forest. She hadn't been back in the wood since that awful day.

Suddenly she thought of the dangers that lurked in the forest. She started pacing back and forth like a caged animal. Every sound she heard snapped at her nerves like the lashes of a whip all over her body. Unable to decide whether she was safer here or back at the manor, she wildly searched around for a safe place to hide.

She saw a fallen tree, ran over, hunkered down beside it, allowing the fear to have its way with her. She curled herself into a tight ball to hold the shivering at bay.

Lost in the memories she soon went inside herself as she often did for the comfort and protection that the nothingness offered her. When she was found that day, so long ago, she was unconscious. She remained in a catatonic state for many weeks thereafter.

Since then she would sometimes drift into a similar state temporarily when the memories would assault her mind. It never really lasted more than an hour or so but it always had a cleansing effect. She welcomed the peace now and allowed it to happen. She had worked very hard over the years to control these episodes so that she wouldn't become completely lost, fearing that one day she would never return.

Until today, she had not had such an episode in well over a year. Today, she saw Damien and it all came rushing in on her. She felt powerless to stop it from happening.

Once inside herself she was wrapped in a comforting darkness that would eventually revive her spirit. Several hours later, she emerged somewhat disoriented until she remembered where she was.

She jumped up, quickly left the forest, and snuck back to the manor. Once she was safely ensconced in her attic apartments she started contemplating the possible opportunities that having Lord Devonshire here would present.

A half an hour later, Hattie burst into her room with her lace cap askew and sweat beading on her brow, "There you are, love. I've been high and low, searchin' for you for hours, child. Where'd you get off to?" she demanded, hands placed firmly on her robust hips.

Hattie was a round portly woman nearing her fifth decade of life. She had a round cheery face and an extra chin or two. She had been nurse to the twins since their mother died in childbirth, where she first served as wet nurse.

She was much like a mother to them. As any mother would, she loved the girls dearly, especially Chelsea.

"You know you shouldn't be out of your rooms with those two gents here. What if one of them 'ad seen you?" she pressed.

"Oh Hattie, it's so awful. I was curious after Celia came up here to tell me about them. I wanted to get a good look at them so I snuck out into the garden and you'll never guess what I discovered," she cried.

"Tell me child," Hattie prompted as she wiped hair off Chelsea's brow.

Chelsea shook her head trying to keep control. "One of the men…Lord Devonshire…is the young man from the forest…from that day, the one who tried to save me. His name is Damien, I remember the name Damien. Oh, Hattie, it's him. I know it. He's older now, of course but it's him. I'll never forget his eyes so green and bright like emeralds."

Hattie gasped, "You never mentioned any names. How could you keep such a thing to yourself and what're you going to do? Should I tell your Papa?"

"No, Hattie don't! There may be an opportunity here and I would like a chance to see if he might know where to find that monster. Surely, he would know where he is. They knew each other after all. I didn't remember their names until today when I saw Damien in the garden. It all came back to me in a rush of memory. They spoke each other's names, and he called the other man Nigel."

She didn't want to tell Hattie that she had a particularly lengthy episode after seeing him so she left that part out.

"I don't like the sound of this child. What'd you mean you want to find the monster?" Hattie scowled.

Chelsea paced the floor thinking for a moment. 'There has to be a way Lord Devonshire can lead me to Nigel. If only I could speak to him, but how?'

"I'm not sure," she answered Hattie. "Have Celia come to me before she goes to bed, I want to talk to her about this, I'll know what to do after I speak to her."

Hattie huffed and tisked, "Lord above we're in for some mighty big trouble, I can feel it in my bones.

*****

Damien lay in bed with a sense of satisfaction. All in all the day progressed quite nicely. He still hadn't had an opportunity to be alone with Lady Celia but he felt certain tomorrow there would be plenty of opportunity. Jarrett had made plans to go over to Evansdale and the baron would be out at the mill seeing to the crisis there. 'That should leave me plenty of time to woo her.' He grinned at the prospect.

He noticed that she was more attentive to him at luncheon and with the exception of inviting Jarrett along with them for a tour of the gardens she seemed to be genuinely interested in furthering their courtship. She mildly flirted and listened eagerly as he recanted stories of his childhood and his days at Eaton. She did seem to be just as interested in Jarrett's career as a Bow Street runner but he decided she was just being polite as any hostess should be.

At least she no longer treated him with the cool indifference she had yesterday when they were having tea. That lifted his spirits and reassured him in his course. He was beginning to wonder if he had made a mistake in his rash decision to wed her. He had never before been so swept away with a feeling of rightness the way he had with her.

The way things went yesterday shook his confidence more than he wanted to admit. Of course, her father seemed to be firmly in his corner so there was no problem there. Being a dutiful daughter she would naturally be swayed by his opinion.

Aye, her father's invitation alone showed that he approved and even encouraged the match. His over protectiveness of her with regard to men seemed to be non-existent now and the idea that he would leave them alone tomorrow to allow him to further his suit with Lady Celia was indicative of his approval. The rest should be easy.

Chapter Five

"Good Morning Lord Devonshire."
Damien stood up as Lady Celia entered the breakfast room. He'd been drinking his morning tea while he waited for her arrival. Jarrett and the baron had already broken their fast and left the manor. Damien was told that he could expect Lady Celia to be down around nine and here she was, right on time.

She looked radiant this morning, wearing a peach colored day gown with a modest bodice. Her arms were covered in long sleeves of sheer lace that matched her fichu. The material of her skirts lay about her hips in a way that drew the eye and gracefully illustrated her voluptuous figure.

Her hair was artfully pulled away from her face with pearl encrusted combs and her raven hair was draped in loose flowing waves down her back. She was even more striking, wearing her hair in such a simplistic fashion. Such magnificence is truly a sight to behold.

He realized he was gaping at her and tried to recover himself, "Ahem…Good Morning Lady Celia."

He watched as she went over to the sideboard and put some toast and fruit on her plate. The footman pulled out her chair. She sat down and looked up at him charmingly with her big rounded eyes. The moment was electrical as their eyes engaged in an arousing interlude.

He realized that he was still standing, then he clumsily sat down. She was so elegant, that her very presence made him feel like a clod. 'Blast! Get hold of yourself man, he inwardly cursed and cautioned himself.'

"May I say you look resplendent this morning, Lady Celia?" he said in an attempt to appear as normal as possible.

She blushed the most becoming shade as she accepted his compliment with a shy nod of acknowledgement then lowered her eyes down toward her breakfast.

"Thank you my lord, it's very kind of you to say," she said sweetly then cast him another quick glance.

"Please call me Damien," he said

"Thank you Damien and you may call me Celia," she allowed with a smile.

Damien couldn't get over the change in her demeanor now that they were alone, well, not completely alone with the footman standing nearby, but almost as good.

She was warm and...responsive with her sweet smiles and blush. Gone was the cool indifference from before. He was glad of it because he was sure that once they were alone it would be different.

What he didn't count on was his on inability to think of a single topic of conversation. Minutes past as he continued to gaze at her, admiring the way the morning light from the windows shined on her like a halo, giving her a celestial look.

He was hard pressed to look away, much less try to come up with intelligent discourse. That spark is definitely there now, stronger than the first, overwhelmingly so. He realized that he felt shy and nervous like a green lad afraid to speak for fear of opening his mouth and removing all doubt that he was a fool.

He inwardly laughed at himself. 'If Jarrett could see me now, stunned into complete silence by the presence of a woman, he would never let me hear the end of it,' he mused. He cleared his throat and hoped that when he opened his mouth the man would emerge and not the boyish fool.

"Celia, do you like to ride?"

"Oh I did when I was a child but not anymore," she said with a sad look in her eyes. She looked down at her plate again but didn't really seem to see her food. She was no longer touching it.

"Perhaps we could take another walk about the garden after breakfast," he suggested, wondering why she wasn't interested in riding. He wanted to ask if she had suffered an injury that made her have a fear of horses but that might seem rude.

"Oh I would enjoy that, Damien," the light in her eyes returned.

"Good, it's a wonderful day for it with nary a cloud in sight." He realized he was grinning and had been nearly from the moment she entered the room. He tried to will his wayward lips back to order but the effect she was having on him was making it rather difficult to do even the simplest tasks, such as controlling one's own smile. Her answering smile was devastating.

"Perhaps we could arrange for a picnic by one of the fountains," she suggested.

"Now there's an idea; that would be grand," he answered, still smiling.

"I will tell Dickens to arrange it then. We could have it set it up by the big fountain on the side lawn," she said.

Damien observed that she didn't seem interested in her breakfast and hoped that he wasn't the cause of it. He would hate for her to miss too many meals and diminish her curvaceous figure. That would be a tragedy.

Gazing at her made his hands ache to touch her and he yearned to feel her comely body pressed against his. He shook his head to clear away his errant thoughts.

"Tell me about Evansdale, it's been an age since I've seen it," she said.

"Honestly, it's been an age since I have seen it as well, I rarely visit."

"Oh?" she prompted.

"Too many ghosts," he teased.

"Never say you have ghosts at Evansdale, surely you jest."

"Well not actual ghosts, only a few sad memories. That's the way of it sometimes with large ancestral homes. So many generations live and die that the structure itself seems to be alive, particularly where the recently departed are concerned. I'm sure you understand."

Damien didn't want to mention Jacob and his suicide. Society tends to view that as a stigma against a whole family, as if to say that the entire lot would one day succumb to the same affliction, thus making all them ineligible for marriage. The notion is quite ridiculous but irrationality always is.

"Indeed, sometimes I feel Mama here, though I never knew her, the halls are alive with her presence," Celia lamented.

Ah, another stigma to be danced around. Women dying in childbirth had a similar effect for ladies. Another silly notion in Damien's opinion. So many things can go wrong with the process that any woman is susceptible.

"Such a depressing topic, perhaps it's time for our walk in the garden," Damien suggested.

"Excellent advice! I shall go and speak with Dickens about our picnic and meet you in the foyer in an hour."

Damien stood and assisted her with her chair. She gave a graceful curtsy and quickly quit the room. He felt like they made a real connection this morning and was pleased at her suggestion for a picnic, he felt sure the occasion would allow him a chance to deepen it.

Things were looking up so with a spring in his step he followed her out of the room and quickly went upstairs to his chambers to freshen up.

*****

"Celia, I thought you said Lord Devonshire was arrogant. Why, I didn't think that at all when I broke my fast with him. I thought he was rather kind and….sweet."

Chelsea worried that she wouldn't be able to pull off the ruse she and Celia had concocted because Damien would intimidate her with his arrogance. But he was so kind and courteous that she felt totally at ease and even more sure than before that her plan to use him to locate Nigel would be successful.

The sisters were identical twins in every way. No one but Hattie could tell them apart if they were ever determined to try and fool someone. Even their father wouldn't know them unless Chelsea was to have one of her episodes in front of him.

When the girls were young they used to make a game of fooling him and the household staff. It was a great source of amusement for two mischievous little girls. Since the incident, nine years ago, society had all but forgotten the existence of Chelsea. After all, she rarely left her attic apartments.

Those very limited staff members at Sheraton who interacted with her were under strict instruction to never mention her name to anyone but the baron or Celia. They were well compensated for their silence with quarterly bonuses.

The effect of the effort was that as far as the world knew, the baron only had one daughter. The Sheraton's had always been fairly private people, both before and after the incident. So society never asked any questions that might illuminate the existence of another daughter. Chelsea merely disappeared from their consciousness.

This would be the first time in nearly a decade that the twins would be attempting to swap identities and it was important that they succeed. Therefore, they both agreed that it would be prudent to have Chelsea make an appearance today as sort of trial run. She would spend the whole day masquerading as Celia rather than waiting until they were to return to London.

It wouldn't do at all for Chelsea to become overwhelmed by the situation and be discovered while away from home. It would cause quite an upset for all concerned. It would be best to see how she handled herself in her own environment, where she was safe within the protection of Sheraton.

"He is arrogant, just you wait and see," Celia said with her chin up as she defended her opinion of the insufferable man.

"We are to take a tour of the garden in an hour and have a picnic lunch in front of the large fountain on the side lawn afterwards."

"Chelsea, are you sure you want to go through with this?" Celia was concerned about her sister spending time alone with the marquess because he is so forward and domineering. How would she respond if he tried to woo her or worse, tried to seduce her. No, this may not be such a wise plan at all.

"More than sure, I'm convinced that this is the only way. Lord Devonshire can lead me right to Nigel and then I can take my revenge. Besides, you said yourself you don't want to marry him. I can help to turn his interests away from you to clear the field for Sir Jarrett. Isn't that what you want?" she asked.

"Of course that's what I want but I'm concerned that you may be getting in over your head, dear. And tell me exactly what you propose to do to have your revenge on Nigel. Surely you don't think to kill him, do you?"

The idea of Chelsea killing the man was horrific. So many things could go wrong and the whole thing could backfire on her.

"I would like to kill him, yes. I suppose that I will have to play that part by ear as the situation unfolds. If nothing else, I can expose the man for what he is. That would serve my purposes as well as anything but killing him would give me great satisfaction," she said with a look of sheer determination.

"I think you need to get thoughts of killing him out of your head. Exposing him is far better, at least you wouldn't hang. The man's life isn't worth the price of yours. Surely, you understand this; say that you do or I won't continue to go along with this farce," Celia pleaded.

Chelsea dreamed of killing that monster for years. His death seemed like the only way she would ever feel safe and free again. Over the years, she often wondered who he could have been and how many other children he had harmed.

She would spend hours in her attic apartments lost in fantasies of vengeance. She imagined herself wielding a sword and taking his head off as he begged for mercy. Or simply shooting him between the eyes, though that wouldn't be as rewarding as her preferred method, which was to bash his head in with a spiked club. However she imagined killing him, she was always the victor in her visions of retribution.

The frustrated imaginings of a wounded child were one thing, but could she really kill another human being? She wasn't so sure that she could call Nigel a human considering his demonic eyes and his monstrous actions.

Even so, she wasn't sure she could turn dream into reality. So she would just simply have to see where this course would lead her. It was too soon to develop any substantive plans beyond locating him.

For all she knew he could be dead by now. Could Damien have already killed him? She would have to probe him for information somehow. She couldn't be too obvious in her queries, of course, because he might become suspicious and that would never do.

This morning, she felt as though he had some dark memories of his own when he spoke of ghosts at Evansdale. Perhaps Nigel's death was among them. "Chelsea, are you listening to me?" Celia broke into her reverie.

"Oh yes, yes of course I understand. Sorry, I was just considering ways to probe Lord Devonshire for information. I was just thinking that perhaps Nigel is already dead. Maybe Lord Devonshire killed him after what happened that day," she said with a hint of hopefulness in her tone.

"I wouldn't count on it. I can't imagine him making such a sacrifice. Such a thing might dirty his boots," Celia said snidely. "You know it's possible that Sir Jarrett brought him to justice, he is a Bow Street runner after all," she added.

"Well, either way we will never know unless I pretend to be you and do some snooping about. I would recognize him if I were to encounter him at some ball or other. So yes, dear sister, I am sure that I should go through with this and I will be very careful and not do anything rash, I promise," Chelsea said with conviction. "Now, I should go check with Dickens to be sure he has everything ready for the picnic luncheon. Wish me luck, love."

The sisters embraced one another and wished each other well and with that, she headed for her assignation with the marquess.

*****

The walk through the gardens with Celia felt more like a walk in the clouds for Damien. Being in her presence and listening to her voice as she chattered cheerfully about this and that was like hearing a symphony produced by the heavens.

Her voice washed over him in a sweet melody that soothed him at the deepest levels of his being. All the darkness in his heart and mind was replaced with the sweetest warmth of sunshine. It lifted him up and he felt as though he floated on a calm such as he has never before experienced.

She spoke of all the books she'd read and all the places she dreamed of going and as she spoke he imagined taking her there. He would see to it that their honeymoon trip would fulfill all of her dreams and more, he decided.

She listened intently when he spoke of his youth and what it was like to live at Evansdale. She asked questions about his family as if she were trying to imagine each and every one of them so that she would know them when she met them.

He spoke of his brother dying but didn't go into detail about the cause and she was respectful of his apparent hurt and didn't probe on that subject for which he was grateful.

Occasionally, she would drift close to him as they walked along the path and their arms or hands would brush against one another. The first time it happened she seemed embarrassed and quickly moved away.

This would have disturbed him had it not been for the blush and the wide-eyed expression on her face. It was as though she was genuinely surprised by the contact, which indicated to him, that she might have been so carried away by the comfort of his presence that she lost all sense of decorum that dictated a proper distance between them. At least that's how he wished to view it.

He couldn't imagine that she wasn't just as swept away by him as he was by her. He wanted to take her in his arms and see how she would respond to his kiss but her maid, Jenny, followed behind and seemed to be keeping a close eye on the proceedings.

He wished he could come up with a legitimate excuse to be rid of her.

"I want to know how it feels to kiss you," he blurted out without realizing what he was doing.

Chelsea stopped dead in her tracks. What did he just say? Did I hear him correctly? She looked behind them to confirm the presence of her maid Jenny and once assured that she was safe, she started walking again but made no comment to his declaration.

'Be calm Chelsea', she warned herself. 'You should expect a certain amount of amour by the marquess since it's his intention to marry Celia,' she reasoned. 'No need to panic, just stay the course.'

'If you weren't such a ninny you wouldn't mind a kiss from such a handsome man,' she silently grumbled to herself. 'It might not be so bad really,' she reasoned. 'He is very nice and would probably be respectful.'

'He doesn't seem to be the kind of man that would take liberties or force himself upon a woman,' she felt sure of that. 'Perhaps he would be a safe choice to experiment with.'

'Maybe you should allow it while you are still safe here at Sheraton to see what would happen. It might be wise to get it over with now since it's probably bound to occur eventually. What could happen with Jenny right there behind us? You'll be safe,' she assured herself.

"You've grown quiet now, did I upset you?" Damien said breaking into her fret.

"I was just mulling over what you said."

"Would it be so bad, then?" he asked.

"I don't think it would be too bad, but you could hardly kiss me with my maid so near," she said.

Damien was suddenly inspired and suggested, "You could ask her to go check on our picnic preparations."

"I'm not sure that would be wise," she countered.

"I would never do anything to disrespect you. I just long to taste your lips," he said in a husky voice.

Chelsea shivered as he spoke those words but it wasn't an unpleasant feeling like the cold grasping fingers that fear always produced. Instead, she felt warmth in her chest and low in her belly. 'What would the harm be in just one kiss?' She asked herself.

"Just a kiss?" she confirmed.

"Aye, just a kiss," he said with softness in his eyes.

Trust. That's what his eyes asked of her. He wanted her to trust him not to take advantage. Oddly, she knew that she did trust him. She has never trusted any man since that day but he was different.

She didn't like to be touched by anyone except for Celia, Hattie and Jenny but she really didn't think his touch would be too threatening. He was the one who tried to save her all those years ago and was severely injured for his trouble and for that, alone she felt she could trust him.

Aye, she could trust him not to hurt her because he was gentle and kind, not arrogant like Celia said. She just had to be brave and allow the physical contact. You might never have another chance to experience a tender moment with a man, since you'll probably never marry and who better than to try it.

Damien was hopeful that she would yield to the idea. It seemed as though she wanted to but he didn't want to press too hard. The last thing he wanted to do was frighten her off.

She's lived such a sheltered life here at Sheraton and her father had probably never prepared her for what to expect between a man and a woman. If he came on too strong it could be disastrous but since he let the words slip out of his mouth, he decided to forge ahead to see what might develop.

She surprised him when she turned to her maid and said, "Jenny, please go and see if Dickens has our picnic prepared."

Damien smiled and when she returned her attention to him, he was delighted to see that she was smiling, too. He waited until the maid was out of sight before he took her hand in his and lightly caressed her palm and wrist.

He felt her tremble so with his other hand he began to slowly stroke her cheek with his thumb. As both of his hands continued to soothe her, their eyes were speaking to one another's.

His were saying 'you can trust me' and hers were answering 'I do' so he gently tugged her toward him, then he slowly bent his head toward her and lightly pressed his lips against hers.

Chelsea instantly felt of jolt of energy shoot through her blood. She almost panicked and pulled away but he increased the pressure ever so slightly. For reasons she didn't understand, the action comforted her.

Then he placed his thumb on the corner of her mouth and gently inserted the tip, prompting her to open to allow him in. She did and gasped when she felt his tongue move inside and start massaging her own. He swallowed her gasp and continued to kiss her for another moment more until finally with a low groan he brought it to an end.

Her hand flew to her mouth and she started rubbing her lips with her fingers. Their eyes remained on each other's as he raised his hand to stroke her cheek while she continued to rub her mouth. Her lips were tingling and felt a little numb. It was a peculiar feeling that she seemed to feel all the way to her toes.

He gently pulled her hand away from her mouth and murmured, "That wasn't so bad was it?"

She shook her head, took a few steps back, and pulled her hand out of his. He allowed the motion and didn't pursue.

He seemed to sense that she was somewhat distressed so he kept his eyes locked with hers as if he knew that it would assure her that she was safe. How could he know that was what she needed? He seemed to be in tune with her body and her mind. The thought was unsettling.

He allowed her to recover her composure and then once he was sure that she was settled, he extended his hand toward her and said, "Shall we go to the fountain now?"

She didn't resist him when he took her arm into his and started leading her toward their destination. She was so stunned by the kiss that she didn't seem to mind the additional contact. 'I wasn't afraid,' she thought in awed wonder.

He was so gentle and his kiss was so warm and tender that it was like a balm to her wounded soul. 'How could this be? I should have been sent reeling into a state of panic. I should have run away as soon as his lips touched mine.'

On their way to the fountain they were met by a running Jenny. When she saw that all was well with her mistress, she slowed to a walk and said, "Your picnic awaits you my lady."

Jenny and Hattie are the only two servants who knew what happened to her and they both felt a deep devotion to her. Jenny had been afraid that she would find her mistress on the ground being ravished by the marquess but was relieved to see that all appeared to be well. Though her mistress appeared a little flushed about the cheeks, she was otherwise unharmed.

Upon arrival at the fountain Chelsea said, "Thank you Jenny, you may take a break and go and have your own lunch. Just be sure you return in about an hour."

"Are you sure my lady? I don't mind waiting," she said eyeing the marquess.

"Truly Jenny, it will be fine. We will be in view of the manor and there will be a footman nearby so go and have your lunch, dear."

"Thank you my lady," she curtsied toward them both and took her leave.

"Your maid is very protective of you," Damien observed. "I find that admirable," he added.

"She was my governess and grew very attached so she stayed on as my personal maid when I became too old for instruction. She is like a mother hen, constantly watching over me."

"She isn't the same maid you had in London, is she?" he asked casually as they were taking their seats on the blanket spread on the ground.

The footman opened a bottle of wine and poured them both a glass. The blanket had a small short legged table in the center just the right height to accommodate their positions on the ground with their dishware set upon it. The picnic basket was loaded up with sliced ham and cheese as well as a warm loaf of bread. There were apples, grapes, and chocolate cake for desert.

"No, that was Liza, she doesn't usually go with me but Jenny was ill and I didn't want her to travel," she lied. She would have to be careful about these kinds of details. Liza is Celia's maid and naturally, it was she that was in London but when they returned, Jenny would be the one to travel with her.

'I will have to warn Jenny in case the marquess asks about her health at some point. It isn't likely that he would but it's best to cover all eventualities. I will have to come up with a way to explain Jenny's presence to Papa too. Oh, this is getting complicated,' she brooded.

"She seems better now," he said with the same casualness.

She relaxed a little; clearly, he was just trying to make small talk, as there didn't seem to be any implications in his remarks.

"Yes, thank goodness she is much improved and will be able to return to London with us on the morrow," she said.

"Your cook must think we are starved to death to have bestowed us with such a bountiful repast," he said smiling, as he helped himself to a piece of ham and cheese.

Chelsea giggled enjoying herself now as he was putting her at ease.

"Though the food is delicious, it hardly compares to the sweetness of your lips," he said with a wink and another brilliant smile.

'She tastes like peaches and crème,' Damien mused as he looked at her lips. He never enjoyed a kiss as much as the one he shared with Celia. Though it was brief, it was sweet, innocent and full of trepidation but bravery, too.

Looking at her blush from his blatant attempt to flirt with her, he knew that she would accept his proposal when he delivered it. Before the kiss, he thought perhaps he might propose while they were here at Sheraton but then he decided that it might spook her if he pushed too hard.

She's like a skittish little foal over the idea of physical contact but brave enough to experiment. 'That's good,' he mused. He would hate to have to deal with a frigid wife. He would just have to be more patient and move at a pace she would be comfortable with. He could wait a few more days but propose he would.

He was more convinced than ever that she was the woman he wanted to spend the rest of his life with. The woman he wanted to father many children with. She would be the beacon in his life and she would keep him straight and true.

Chapter Six

"Tell me how everything is going so far, love?" Celia asked, as she was running a brush through Chelsea's hair. The twins often comforted each other in this fashion. Whenever Chelsea seemed agitated about something she could be soothed by such ministrations.

Not that Chelsea seemed distressed, per say but Celia knew that after such a day as this one, she would welcome her efforts.

She noticed that her sister seemed to be in a dreamy peaceful state of mind and was curious to know the cause of it. She had managed to get through the picnic with the marquess and dinner with all the men, Papa included with none being the wiser.

At the very least, she would expect her to be stressed or melancholy about being around Papa for the first time in so long, but she made no mention of it. She acted as though it were an everyday occurrence.

Celia found this to be curiously strange and wondered if that moony-eyed look on her face was because she was thinking of Sir Jarrett. She hoped not because she already felt that she, herself had a claim on him.

It would be upsetting for Chelsea to fall in love with him then have to live in misery knowing that Sir Jarrett was to be her husband instead. 'If I can manage it, of course. I still have to let him know of my feelings somehow, when this is all over so we can be married,' she silently vowed.

"He's wonderful, Celia," Chelsea said on a sigh. Celia stiffened, "Who is wonderful dear?"

"Damien," she softly replied.

Shocked by that statement Celia stopped brushing her sister's hair and moved around in front of her, "Damien! Oh, Chelsea, what do you mean by that?" she demanded.

"I mean that he is so kind and gentle. He speaks to me with such reverence in his voice and affection in his eyes. It warms me and makes me feel so strange inside. I never dreamed that a man could make me feel this way." she sighed then added, "Of course, it will never lead anywhere as I will never marry and he thinks that I'm you." Chelsea was somewhat depressed knowing one day he would be out of her life.

"Chelsea you can't allow yourself to get carried away. You have to make sure he loses interest by the time this is all over like we discussed," she admonished.

"I know…I know that I could never have him and that one day he will be gone but still…Oh, Celia don't you see? Maybe I can be normal again. If Damien makes me feel this way perhaps all is not lost and some other man can have the same affect and someday……." she trailed off not really believing her own words.

Celia reached for her sister and hugged her tight, "That is wonderful love; of course you can be normal. It's up to you. You have to be willing to take the chance on life instead of staying cooped up in this depressing attic all the time. Maybe this plan will be good for you after all, dear. Perhaps you will enjoy being out in society and it will inspire you to live again then one day you can find a man that you can love."

"Do you really think so?" she asked with tears in her eyes.

"Yes darling, I really think so. First, you have to get through all this though. I really don't think you should set your sights on the marquess. It could go badly if he finds out that we've tricked him," Celia advised.

"I hadn't thought of that. I suppose, I shouldn't have allowed him to kiss …" her words were cut off by Celia's gasp of alarm, "You what?" she demanded. She whirled around and started pacing furiously.

"I knew something like this would happen. I knew that scoundrel would try to seduce you! Chelsea, we must put an end to this right now before things get out of control. What if he tries to…well…what if he becomes persistent and tries…and tries to take even more liberties?" she finally managed to articulate.

"NO!" Chelsea shouted. "I am not putting an end to this. I will carry on and find Nigel to punish him. You cannot take that away from me, you simply cannot. This is my one chance and I will not allow you to stop me. It's the only way I would ever have a chance at anything remotely similar to a normal existence. I must know that evil blackguard is punished one way or another."

"Shush, dear heart, shhhh… please calm yourself," Celia placated as she began rubbing his sisters back in a slow calming motion. "I understand how you feel. I'm just worried for you, that's all. I don't want anything to happen to you when I won't be there to look after you. I worry that the marquess will do something untoward if you don't make an effort to keep him at arm's length. You simply cannot allow him to get close enough to kiss you again, Chelsea. Promise me this."

Chelsea closed her eyes and allowed her sisters gentle massage to comfort her. She steadied herself and said, "You're right, I have a mission and I can't afford to be distracted. I will keep him at bay, I promise. There is too much at stake to chance discovery before I can complete the task."

"Good dear, stay on course and everything will be fine. Perhaps, when all this is over we can explain to the marquess and you and he can come to care for one another but for now you must put all such notions aside," Celia advised.

"It's silly for me to imagine such possibilities anyway. Who would have me if they knew the truth about me? What man would take a wife who has been sullied in such a fashion? No! I will never marry and I must put such foolishness out of my head and keep the marquess at arm's length and do all I can to discourage any further attentions."

"We have had this discussion before, you have not been sullied. After all, despite what that animal did to you, you are still a virgin. Hattie said that you were still intact. If you did ever marry, your husband need never have to know what you've suffered unless you chose to tell him. You were victimized as a child, not sullied. It's not your shame and no one could hold it against you."

Over recent years Celia had tried her best to convince Chelsea that she was not damaged as she thought she was. She just needs to conquer her fears and put the past behind her.

In a way, it's good that the marquess will be showing her some attention so she can have a taste of what life could offer her if she could just put her fears aside. But whether Lord Devonshire would make a good husband is highly debatable, Celia thought.

Chelsea dropped her head and grew silent. True, she did feel safe with Damien but she hasn't been around any other men to gauge her reaction to him. Once she was in London there might be other gentlemen that would have the same effect on her as he had.

Maybe she was finally healing inside enough to try to live again. It would be wonderful to be able to leave her rooms and join the rest of the world. And to marry…and have children of her own someday.

Until being exposed to Damien, she'd never considered the possibility that it could actually be that way. At least he had done that much for her. For that she would always be grateful even if she could never tell him so.

'Damien is my unwitting savior of sorts. He has no idea the impact he has had on my life,' she silently reflected. She must never let him know who she was because she wouldn't be able to bear seeing the revulsion in his eyes.

Firm now, in her resolve, she said, "All will be well, Celia, have no fear. I will be just fine. I guess I should turn in now since we are to leave for London with the dawn."

"Write to me every day and keep me informed on your progress. I will be sick with worry every minute that you are away. Please don't torture me with silence. Promise me," Celia implored hugging her once again.

"I promise, it's really going to be an adventure and I'm quite looking forward to it. I will write you of every detail," she vowed.

*****

Jarrett lay awake wondering at the difference he noticed in Celia's behavior at dinner. She treated him with such indifference that it was mind-boggling. Gone were the soft blushes and the sweet smiles.

Instead, she was fawning over Damien where before she seemed indifferent to him. Damien must have made some real progress with her today while he was alone with her. Oh well, it was ridiculous to harbor any real hopes with regard to her anyway; he has no fortune to offer a wife. Still, a silly part of him did hope and now there seemed to be no reason to.

If Damien and she ever marry, it would be a difficult lump to swallow seeing them together in marital bliss. Perhaps he should go away somewhere. Take a tour of the continent or go to the West Indies to seek his own fortune.

"First, I have to help Damien with Nigel. I have to stay in England to keep him out of trouble at the very least," he grumbled to the empty room.

'There has to be a way to take care of Nigel without killing him. I must find some kind of evidence or a witness because he should be punished for his crimes.'

'I will just have to try harder to find the boy from nine years ago. If I can find him perhaps, he could be persuaded to come forward to help expose Nigel. If he were exposed, he would be shamed and forever ostracized by society.'

'The resulting scandal would ensure that he would no longer have freedom of movement that would allow him to have contact with any potential victims.'

Today, after Jarrett visited his mother, he made no progress when he was poking around in the village. He had tried to ferret out information about men who would be the about the age of twenty that would fit the description Damien had provided.

The only distinguishing characteristic that Damien could give him was that he had crystal blue eyes set under black eyebrows.

True he could have been a gypsy but not likely with such eyes. He had to have been a local boy and he wouldn't rest until he found him. How hard could it be to find a young man with such unusual eye coloring in the small villages surrounding Evansdale and Sheraton? Damien probably never located him because the family would have been ashamed and kept silent to protect the boy's identity. However, if Jarrett could locate him now, perhaps enough time had passed that he would be strong enough to come forward with his story.

'It would be good for me to stay behind with mother at Evansdale for a while so Damien can court Celia without me being present to witness it anyway. Aye that's what I'll do. I'll write to Bow Street and tell them to set a man in place to watch and report to me on Nigel's movements in London and I'll stay here and find the boy.' With that decided he settled his mind and went to sleep.

*****

The trip back to London was pleasant and rather uneventful. Papa only asked once why Jenny was coming along instead of Liza. Chelsea explained that Liza's mother was ill and that she wanted to stay and take care of her. Thankfully, the explanation wasn't questioned further.

Chelsea smiled inwardly, wondering what Celia would do if she knew that Sir Jarrett had stayed behind at Evansdale with his mother. It would be too tempting to know that he was so close and not try to see him. It's just as well that she doesn't know because that could cause their deception to be discovered.

They only made one stop on the way back. That was to dine on the picnic Cook had sent along with them for their journey since they all had opted to skip breakfast in preference to an early start.

She had a hard time keeping her eyes off of Damien during their meal. He was so handsome with his broad shoulders and his sun-streaked hair. He was a perfect gentleman and only mildly flirted since her father was present but he too had a hard time keeping his eyes from her. Papa seemed oblivious to it all as he heartily ate his meal.

While inside the carriage, Papa told her that he had given a lot of thought to what she said about him not being so obvious in his guard. He said he would ease up a bit so as to allow gentlemen an opportunity to interact with her since Sir Jarrett seemed to be out of the picture and she didn't quite care for the marquess.

However, he still maintained his preference for the marquess and called him a fine fellow that any girl would be lucky to snare.

She didn't know the details of the conversation with him and Celia but played along rather well, she thought. She and Celia didn't discuss things like that to prepare her for such scenarios, a mistake that could be costly.

She had better send her sister a message right away and tell her to try and relate as many things like that as possible so she didn't find herself in a situation that would shine light on the ruse.

When they arrived at Aunt Gertrude's, Damien took his leave, promising to be back this evening to escort her to the theater. She gladly accepted and looked forward to the opportunity to see a play. It was to be a version of Hamlet, which has always been one of her favorite Shakespeare tragedies.

In the meantime, she and Jenny put away all the clothes from her trunks. Then she wrote her missive to Celia.

Afterwards, she lay down to take a nap but had trouble finding a calm center to allow herself to drift off to sleep. She was quite nervous being in London with all its bustling activity and large population.

Celia was right, it has a very unpleasant odor and it seemed to be cloaked in an ever-present haze that was rather oppressive. The noise was nerve shattering when taken into comparison to the peaceful quiet of Sheraton. She didn't think she could ever get used to it all. Fortunately, she wouldn't have to be here long.

*****

"How was your trip to the country, dear?" Matilda asked during tea with her nephew. "I trust you are getting on well with Lady Celia," she prodded.

"The trip was very productive I should say and yes, I am getting on well with Lady Celia. I should like to propose to her soon if things continue on this course. She's an angel and I think I have died and gone to heaven," Damien fairly gloated.

"Very good dear, I knew you would be captivated by her. I knew her mother, Marianna and I'm told she has a strong likeness to her. She was a great beauty in her time. It's a shame she died so young in childbed," Matilda lamented.

"Celia herself is a great beauty but she is so much more than that. She is unlike any woman I have ever known. She has a great depth of character to go with her beauty and that will keep her forever alluring," he said, as if in awe.

Damien has come to realize that he was already in love with Celia. He couldn't tell her that of course, because it might make her wary of him. After all, he had known her less than a week and she might think he was just paying lip service to try to get her to accept him.

"Why Damien, you are quite taken with the gel, aren't you?" Matilda beamed.

"I believe that I am," he admitted.

"Do you think she will accept your proposal?"

"I certainly hope so because if not her, then I'll have no other," Damien declared. "I was going to propose to her at Sheraton but she seems a little inhibited and I believe she will require a bit more courtship. She seems nervous like a wounded doe. It fairly tears my heart in two to think that she could have been harmed before. She needs a strong man to protect her, but from what, I know not."

Damien remembered her reaction to his kiss. She was so full of trepidation before and after, but he sensed in her an adventurous spirit so he was not too concerned. He just had to gain her trust then she would accept him. She had to; otherwise he would be cast adrift in a sea of misery for wanting her.

"I can't imagine what she would have to be nervous about. Her father is a very good man and has raised her well. Perhaps she's just shy dear."

"Perhaps," he allowed.

"She has lived a very sheltered life out there at Sheraton. Her father is a very private man and they rarely entertain guests so she's had little exposure to society."

"Do you think her father could be abusive?" He didn't like to think so but it might explain her skittishness. The way he hovered round guarding her could be indicative of his being a strict disciplinarian.

"Heavens no! The baron is a fine man and he does dote on her so. No dear, she's just shy, I'm sure of it," she soothed.

"Aye, you're probably right. The baron was very hospitable and I can see that he loves her dearly. I did make a fair amount of progress with her yesterday. She allowed some minor intimacies when we walked in the garden and she planned a very romantic picnic by one of the estates grand fountains. At first I thought she would prefer Jarrett but after yesterday I'm certain that she has developed some tender feelings toward me." Damien truly believed that. Yesterday he felt that they had connected on a very deep spiritual level.

"Jarrett has no fortune. How could she prefer him to you?"

"I don't believe she is the type to care for such things as title and fortune; she has her own, you know. No, I think the only thing missing in her life is love. I will have to woo her to get her to accept me. She will settle for nothing less, I'm sure of it."

Damien knew that her character was too pure to view things in such a shallow way as to prefer fortune and title to love and happiness. The only way to Celia's hand was through love and affection. He sensed that she was somewhat afraid of intimacy, yet she seemed to have a craving for it.

"I believe you have the right of it dear," Matilda agreed.

Damien cleared his throat and tugged on his cravat, "Ahem…how is Sara?" he asked blushing.

Matilda scowled at him and shook her head, "Sara is fine, you devil. I should have her placed sometime next week as companion to my very dear friend, Joanna. I should think she is rather happy about the prospect."

"She should be happy, anything is better than...well, I'm glad you took her in and helped her. It was most gracious and I commend you on your kindness," he said sincerely. "I had hoped that she would be in her new position by the time I proposed to Celia…skeletons and all that," he added with shame in his eyes.

"Skeletons indeed…I hope you've learned your lesson and never return to such a den of iniquity. Shame on you, Damien," she said shaking her finger to admonish him.

"I'm a changed man, Aunt! Maude will have to find customers elsewhere from now on," he promised.

"You can't fool me, you rogue," she teased.

Damien threw his hand to his heart "How you wound me Aunt," he said in mock horror.

"Oh, go on with you," she said, shooing a hand at him.

"Aye, it is time for me to be on my way. I'm going to my club to put an ear to the ground to see what I can find out about Nigel's activities. Later, this evening I will be taking Celia to the theater." He stood and kissed her cheek, saying his goodbyes.

Matilda smiled as she watched him go. "A changed man, hmpf!" she said to the empty room.

*****

Damien sat at his club reading the newspaper and listening to conversations around him. Nigel wasn't there but he thought that he would be soon. There were some winnings for him on the betting book from a bare-knuckle fight the day before between Lord Rushmore and Sir Henry Stockholm.

Sir Henry gave the other man a sound thrashing from the sound of it and Nigel was one of few to bet in his favor, so he had a tidy sum awaiting his collection.

He couldn't help but feel a little disturbed by the talk he overheard between two blackguards about Lady Celia. Word of her vast fortune and title has spread throughout the ton. It had attracted the notice of such individuals.

He would have to keep an eye on those two. In fact, he would have to keep close to her to make his intentions toward her clear to keep all such scoundrels and rakehells at bay.

Tonight it would be obvious that he had a claim when he took her to the theatre. That should help, but the fortune hunters would hardly let that stop them from pursuing her.

Her loveliness alone would have caused a riot among all the amorous young bucks without her father's vigilance. He would simply lend his presence to the effort and that should take care of any situations that could develop. Between her father and himself, it would appear to all that Lady Celia was out of reach to any would-be contenders.

Damien finally decided that Nigel wasn't coming and made his way to the door. As he was leaving he knocked shoulders with someone, just outside, "Pardon me," Damien said to the man before realizing who it was.

"Nigel!" he blurted out in surprise.

"Ah, Damien!" Nigel returned coolly.

Damien was momentarily struck mute as he stared into the eyes of his adversary. For so long he had dreamed of this moment and now here he was face to face with his long time nemesis. He took a mental accounting of his surroundings and realized that he could do little more than exchange a few words with him without bringing unwanted attention to them. So with a barely containable hate he said, "I see you've slithered your way back to London."

Nigel Cullen the Duke of Warwick stiffened his back and with a twitch in his eye and a tightening of the jaw, snidely said, "Yes I am recently returned for the season for Tess' debut. Perhaps you would be interested in the chit."

Damien snorted at his gall and said, "I wouldn't sully myself, associating with a product of your loins."

The two men glowered at one another for a suspended moment, each sizing the other up for any weaknesses or strengths.

"I see you've grown…'tis a pity; if you were still a younger 'boy' I would teach you some respect like I did your brother. He was such a disrespectful lad to his betters. I see that you suffer from the same affliction," he taunted.

Damien was appalled by the reference to his brother and lunged at him. He grabbed him by the lapels in a fierce hold and slammed him up against the wall outside the club. He was red faced and breathing harshly, "I'm going to take great pleasure in killing you, Nigel" he said with green blazes in his eyes.

"Unh, unh, unh…don't mess up the coat, dear Damien. I've just come from the tailors," Nigel said as he calmly pried away Damien's grip. "We wouldn't want anyone to think we are not gentlemen, after all. I might be expected to challenge you for such impudence and we wouldn't want that," he continued to taunt as he smoothed down his lapels.

Damien realized that he needed to extradite himself from this situation before it spiraled out of control. Reaching inside himself for strength, he shoved away from Nigel and said, "You disgust me!"

"Such a display of love and affection for your cousin…I'm touched," he mocked.

"We are not done, you and I…you had better watch your arse," Damien advised then he turned and walked away. Behind him he heard Nigel call out, "Until we meet again, dear cousin. Do come round and call upon Tess, she would be delighted to see you," followed by a sinister laugh.

His body was raging to finish what they'd started. After all the years of dreaming and planning for this day, Damien was suddenly struck by a sense of insecurity and wasn't sure what he should do. He knew Nigel was goading him and he didn't like being made sport of.

He needed to be in control of the confrontation and he could clearly see that he hadn't been. He couldn't allow Nigel to have the upper hand by allowing him to make the challenge so he would just have to bide his time and wait for his moment.

Soon! He promised himself. Very soon I will have the bastard where I want him. "Bloody Christ!" he cursed aloud as he stomped his way back to his townhouse.

The way Nigel mocked him made him feel like an impotent fool. He let him get under his skin and he lost his ability to think rationally. He was angry at himself for being such an incompetent. How could he expect to best Nigel if he couldn't even control his emotions?

Well, there was no since in thinking about it. It wouldn't do for him to be in such a foul mood when he was to spend the evening with Celia. He didn't want anything to put a blemish on their time together. At the thought of Celia he could feel his muscles relax and he let the tension flow out of his body. He would just deal with Nigel later.

Chapter Seven

Damien was a perfect gentleman when he arrived to escort Chelsea and her maid Jenny to the theatre. The ride there was a different matter however, as once inside the carriage he stretched his legs out so that they rested against her skirts and stared at her in the most intimate way the entire trip.

She couldn't help but feel a little disconcerted and was relieved for the presence of her maid. Having him so near in such close quarters made her heart rate speed up and she felt a little feverish. It was a real struggle to make small talk with him while he was looking at her as if he wanted to consume her. The look in his eyes promised things she couldn't even begin to understand.

She didn't feel frightened by this but it did make her nervous. She wanted to know what those promises were but knew she would never have the courage to discover them. If his kiss was any indication, a girl could quite lose herself in his embrace.

She must remember that at all cost if she is to succeed with her agenda. My, but he was so handsome dressed in formal black attire that it was hard not to stare right back at him with promises of her own. She tried to shake off her wayward thinking by looking out the window.

She felt Jenny poke her in the thigh as a reminder to behave and she inwardly laughed. 'Oh dear Jenny you have no idea how I struggle to behave,' she thought.

What is it about Damien that made her have such feelings and how was she ever going to control them? Why was Celia so dead set against him? What did he do or say to her to make her have such a low regard? She never thought to ask her sister and she didn't volunteer the information.

It must be that she wanted Sir Jarrett and simply couldn't abide the thought of anyone else. And if Chelsea was honest with herself, after spending so much time with Damien, she would have to admit that she didn't want her sister to marry him either.

Not that she was jealous or anything like that....well alright... a little jealous. 'Damien is mine,' she vowed, then jumped from the shock of the intruding thought. 'Where did that come from?' she wondered. 'He isn't mine and he never can be,' she reminded herself.

She felt Jenny poke her again. She cast her a look of annoyance and then looked at Damien to see if he noticed the exchange between them and he must have because now he had to the most wickedly seductive grin upon his face.

She felt herself blush ten different shades and quickly looked out the window again. She heard his soft laughter of amusement but kept her focus on the city passing by and let the heat from of his laughter course through her veins.

'Blast you Jenny Miller!' She cursed inwardly. 'How I am to ever appear to be normal with my busybody maid poking me in the leg every time she thinks I'm acting peculiar? How many ladies have such brazen maids? Damien is likely to think that I'm some kind of a halfwit goose with such nonsense going on.'

"You are being very quiet, Lady Celia," Damien said in an effort to redirect her attention back to him. He was having a little fun flustering her. Perhaps he shouldn't but he couldn't help himself. She was so beautiful and sweet sitting across from him now with her cheeks rosy and her nerves all atwitter.

She was beautifully adorned in a teal evening gown with its modestly cut bodice that drew the eye to hint at the rich bounty he knew that it contained. Her hair was artfully braided and rolled into a design allowing soft curling tendrils to hang loose about her face and neck. She wore pearl earbobs and a necklace to match.

He couldn't wait to lavish her with gifts of diamonds, rubies and sapphires. The Vane jewels had to have been made for her as she would be devastatingly beautiful in them.

"Forgive me my lord; I was just admiring the city. It's so very different from the country," Chelsea said in an attempt to sound composed.

"Quite true," he agreed. "I'm sure it's rather shocking to the system for one who has lived in a rural setting all their life," he said conversationally.

"Yes, it's very unsettling, actually."

Chelsea was very unsettled by the city, indeed. She hoped that he wasn't able to see her stress. She wouldn't want him to think she was a fragile flower that needed to be coddled.

"You should make the most of it however since you are only to be in town another couple of weeks. There are many sites to see while you're here. How would you like to go to the museum?" he ventured.

"Oh, I would dearly love that Damien," she beamed. Chelsea loved history and she knew that the museums here were full of wonderful things from Egypt and Rome. She would be in absolute heaven to see all those wonderful artifacts.

"Well I shall take you on the morrow then," he said with a warm smile.

"Oh that would be lovely, thank you," she blushed. Jenny poked her again but she ignored it this time as the carriage came to a stop at their destination.

The footman opened the door and assisted her and her maid. They were followed by Damien as he exited, offering her his arm. She took it and he led her to the entrance. Jenny followed behind at a discreet distance.

There were throngs of people gathered outside the theatre. They parted like the sea, when Moses raised his staff, as Damien led them through. She noticed the envious looks that she received by the many females in attendance and wondered at it. Why did they look so hostile?

Damien must be considered the catch of the season and she was the target of their frustrations by being here with him. She stiffened her spine and clung a little tighter to his arm and tried not to look at them further as they made their way to Damien's private box.

Once inside, they sat down and Jenny took her place behind them. Chelsea was impressed by the luxurious setting of the theatre. It was so lush and lavish.

All the patrons were decked out in their finest evening attire and all the ladies were spying on other patrons with opera glasses. She noticed many trained on her and tried not to let it bother her. Damien asked if she would like some champagne or lemon-aid and she agreed that champagne would be nice.

He left to go and get their refreshments and Jenny who apparently was unable to contain herself any longer said, "What do you think you are doing making cow eyes at the marquess?"

Chelsea sucked wind and whipped around in her seat, "I was doing no such thing, what do you mean by such an accusation?" she hissed.

"You know very well what I mean; you were batting your eyes and blushing like a trollop. Why you were practically in his lap rubbing legs together the way you were."

"Jenny, you go too far. There was hardly enough room in the carriage for our legs and we were not rubbing them together," Chelsea said indignantly.

"Celia will have my head if I allow the marquess to get too close to you. She warned me that he was a scoundrel. I should write her and tell her how you've behaved. This was a ridiculous idea, coming down here pretending to be her anyway," Jenny said on an angry huff.

"You'll do nothing of the kind, do you hear me?" she demanded.

"Child, what am I to do with you?" Jenny pleaded.

Jenny was a thin, older matronly woman around the age of seven and forty with gray streaked hair kept tightly in a knot at the base of her skull. Spectacles were perched upon her nose. She was formerly the twins governess and she was so moved by what happened to Chelsea that she stayed on. She helped Hattie with her, serving as her personal maid ever since and was very protective of her.

Chelsea loved Jenny like a dear old aunt but she refused to allow her to overstep her bounds. She was a servant after all, not a warden, though she is acting like one now.

She tried a different tone with her and said, "I know you love me and are trying to see to my well being Jenny, but really dear, you shouldn't carry on so. The marquess thinks he's courting Celia, so I must allow certain intimacies to keep the ruse alive. Now please relax and just stay in the background like a maid is supposed to."

"Well, just you mind that I will be watching and if I see anything untoward, I will tell your Papa and put a stop to this farce right away," she said trying to reassert authority over her.

"Oh do hush now, the marquess will be back any minute and we don't want him to hear us talking about this," Chelsea said in a counter move for dominance.

Jenny stiffened her spine, not willing to admit defeat but knowing she wouldn't make good on any of her threats, she sat back and said not another word.

Damien returned moments later with refreshments for everyone and took his seat beside Chelsea. The lights dimmed in the theatre. The patrons quieted when the curtain opened revealing a platform that was to be the castle. The first scene opened with Bernardo saying; Who's there? Francisco answered Nay, answer me: stand and unfold yourself;

Chelsea felt a thrill go up her spine. She has always dreamed of seeing a real performance. She was immediately captivated, immersed in the complicated dialog of Shakespeare.

With so much time on her hands, Chelsea has memorized all of his works and many times imagined herself there in that place and time. She would get Celia, Hattie and Jenny to act out the scenes with her and they seemed to take great pleasure in doing so.

Later in the play King Claudius said, Take thy fair hour, Laertes; time be thine and thy best graces spend it at thy will! But now, my cousin Hamlet, and my son…Hamlet said in aside, a little more than kin, a little less than kind.

It was then that Chelsea felt Damien's hand upon hers. She looked up at him and saw that he was gazing at her with a wanting so deep in his eyes that it made her shiver. He gave a gentle squeeze of her hand to acknowledge the effect.

She moved her eyes back toward the stage and he started a slow sensuous massage of her palm with his thumb. She knew she should pull away but she couldn't bring herself to do it. She closed her eyes and lost herself in the comfort that it brought her.

Her mind drifted and she felt as though she were in the safest place in the world. She drifted back to a time when she was just a small child. She remembered her Papa holding her and caressing her back while she drifted off to sleep. She felt so warm and secure and…..she shook her head in an attempt to gain perspective.

She looked at him again and saw that his eyes were still upon her. He had moved ever so closer. Their shoulders were lightly touching. His head was tilted toward her as he continued his ministrations. She looked away again and tried to focus on the play.

His thumb began a slow trend toward her wrist and he began to rub her pulse. She nearly threw her head back in ecstasy but remembered that Jenny was behind her and would become alarmed.

She became aware of warmth spreading throughout her body that seemed to radiate from her private center. She started tingling on her breasts as the tips hardened in response to the stimulation.

Startled by that, she pulled her hand away. He allowed it but only for a moment when her reached for her again and twined his fingers with hers and gave a gentle reassuring squeeze.

They sat like that through the rest of the play. It was nice, Chelsea decided, nothing to at all to be afraid of.

Damien was quite moved by her response to him. His soul reached out to hers and she answered and embraced it. He wished that he could kiss her again but with the hardnosed Jenny looking on it would be impossible.

Perhaps tomorrow at the museum he could figure out a way to give Jenny the slip and sample her sweetness again. Being so near to her now was driving him mad. To be so close but yet so far away from the object of his desire was very frustrating.

Of course, there was the Hathaway ball tomorrow night, the idea occurred to him. 'I could always take her out on the terrace or walk her about the gardens there.'

That might be a better plan he reasoned. 'I need to make sure I have plenty of time to woo her before the kiss, so she doesn't refuse me,' he reflected. After her response to him tonight, he didn't think she would shy away from another kiss.

In the meantime he would have to content himself to simply hold her hand and bask in the warmth of this simple intimacy.

*****

The next morning Damien arrived to escort Chelsea and Jenny to The British Museum. The museum was a thrilling experience for her and she particularly liked the displays from Egypt, though there was really very little of it beyond artist renderings of the pyramids and the sphinx and a few sparse artifacts. They did have a fairly extensive showing from Pompeii, complete with statues, busts and pottery, however.

Damien was quite attentive and seemed to thoroughly enjoy squiring her through the exhibits. He seemed to be very well read on the histories of ancient cultures and Chelsea was pleased that they had this common interest.

"I wish we could escape your maid so I can sample the nectar of your lips," Damien murmured in her ear while they were viewing a display from Rome.

His voice warmed her and she blushed but made no response to his comment. He was undeterred however as he said, "We could send her to the carriage with some excuse or other, perhaps to retrieve your shawl."

Chelsea stretched her neck around his shoulder to see where Jenny was located. She wasn't in hearing distance as she was still back at the Pompeii exhibit.

"That might not be wise," Chelsea admitted.

"Oh it's very wise," Damien whispered. "In fact, I dare say that it will be life saving," he added as he swept a strand of hair away from her brow and stared into her eyes with a deep intensity.

Chelsea couldn't help herself, she giggled. Damien reached for her hand and brought it to his lips for a sensual kiss on her palm. "Save me, sweet Celia," he breathed.

"Why look, Tess darling, it's your cousin Damien," intruded a screeching female voice. Damien whipped his head around and found himself looking at the clownish Penelope Cullen, Duchess of Warwick and her daughter, not entirely mousey, Tess. Taken unawares by this interruption he was speechless and quite discomfited.

The two ladies made their way closer in a swish of skirts and fluttering lashes. The duchess who would be in the latter part of her thirties was unpleasantly plump, decked in a red and white striped day gown with a lavender pelisse that clashed with her orange-red hair. Her ridiculous bonnet was adorned with various fruits and birds.

The picture she made with her excessive cosmetics, combined with the harsh clash of her ensembles color scheme with her hair was utterly ghastly.

Tess on the other hand wasn't beautiful by common standards but she was put together well in a white day gown and pastel green pelisse with her dull brown hair partially visible under a simple white straw bonnet tied with a matching green ribbon, making her not too difficult to look upon.

Sadly, he feared, she would have the look of her mother some day. She the same beak nose and the same dull brown eyes, with heavy brows that were in much need of a plucking.

"Your Grace," Damien said as he reluctantly accepted the proffered hand of the duchess and placed a mock kiss an inch just above her gloved knuckles. The act made him inwardly cringe. He turned and did the same for Tess as she too was extending her hand, "Cousin Tess, you have grown up well, I see."

Tess blushed and batted her eyes lashes at Damien.

"I've been expecting you to come around Damien, father said that he spoke with you and that you had expressed an interest in paying me court," Tess said brazenly while she cast a jealous eye toward Celia.

Damien was struck silent by the audacity of the little she-devil and returned her comment with a false smile. He felt Celia stiffen beside him and it was altogether an uncomfortable moment.

It appears that Nigel has decided to make another show of duplicity toward Damien at the expense of his daughter and she seems quite game to be his unwitting accomplice. If Nigel were present now he would wring his neck.

Damien looked around him to see if he were there but saw no sign of him then realized that he had been remiss in not introducing Celia. He cleared his throat and said, "Your Grace, Tess, may I make known to you, Lady Celia Sheraton."

The two irksome women eyed her in a hostile manner and looked back at Damien expectantly waiting for further explanation. When Damien didn't provide it after an uncomfortable silent moment, the duchess decided to ignore the introduction and asked, "When can we expect you for tea Damien?"

He cleared his throat again and searched his mind for a way to discourage further comments about his paying court to Tess and said, "My schedule is quite full actually. I'm not sure when I'll have any openings in the foreseeable future. I'll have my man check my appointments to see what I have might have available and send you round a note."

The two women realized that they weren't going to get a commitment from him in front of Celia and decided to let the matter rest and said their farewells. As they were walking away the duchess could clearly be heard saying, "The very idea of parading his doxy around in broad daylight, can you imagine such a thing dear?"

Damien stood there in stunned disbelief. He was floundering in his mind for a way to smooth this over with Celia. He looked at her and saw her hurt expression and groaned aloud.

He took her by the hand sayinb, "Please believe me when I say that I have no interest in courting my cousin. I don't know why her father would have told her such a thing. Please say that you believe me?"

Chelsea pulled her hand out of his and said, "I hardly know what to think about you and those two awful women. They were very insulting Damien and you did nothing to reproach them."

Damien reached for her hand again. This time she didn't pull it away, "Celia, you must know my feelings for you. I wish to marry you and I have known it from the first moment that I saw you across the room at the Simpson ball. I know this isn't the time or the place. I would have preferred to wait a while longer to give you time but please say that you will be my wife," he pleaded.

Damien felt desperate. He was afraid that if he didn't assure her now of his intentions he would lose her after this debacle. His gut was wrenching as she remained silent after his proposal. God knows this wasn't the right time to ask but he didn't have any other choice. It was now or never.

Finally she spoke, "Yes, you're right Damien, I need more time. I can't possibly decide such a thing on such short notice and after such a scene as this. It was humiliating and I just can't think beyond it at present."

Celia pulled her hand away and this time Damien accepted the withdrawal. His heart was in his stomach and he was devastated. He sighed deeply and shook his head, then he put the full force of his eyes upon hers, "Celia please, give me a chance," he said with his soul in his eyes as he beseeched her.

Chelsea was devastated, too. She couldn't believe that Damien stood by and let those two women treat her in such a way. It really was beyond her comprehension.

She wouldn't have been so upset, had he told them that he was courting her but he didn't. He acted as though she were insignificant.

Why that should matter she couldn't say as they weren't really courting and she wasn't really Celia but still, it's the principle of the matter.

Of course Damien and she hadn't made any formal declarations of love or commitment of any kind, prior to that, but he still had an obligation to protect her from slight while he was escorting her.

True enough, they were ladies, if you can call them that, and high ranking ones too; it would have been socially unacceptable for Damien to give them a set down as he is a gentleman and that just isn't done. Perhaps she is being a bit too harsh on him, she allowed. And she does need him to find Nigel.

"I'm not declining your proposal, Damien. I just would like to have more time. We are only just getting to know one another after all," she said hoping to mollify him.

Damien let out the breath he hadn't realized he'd been holding, "Thank you for not throwing me out with the rubbish. I'm sorry I didn't speak up for you but I was so taken aback by their behavior that I was struck quite speechless. I have never liked them and have very little to do with them, I assure you. And as for her father saying such things to her I cannot account," he said in a rush of relief.

"He and I don't get on well but I did see him yesterday outside of my club. We exchanged a few words and he did mention her to me but I can't imagine why he would encourage her in such a way. It's despicable and I will set him straight on the matter next time I see him, I can promise you that" he explained.

Chelsea sniffed and raised her chin, "Well let's not them ruin our day," she said wanting to put the entire ordeal behind them.

Grateful for her graciousness Damien took her hand in his again, softly kissed the back of it. "Excellent advice," he said with a tender smile.

Chelsea couldn't help herself. She melted. How could she combat that smile? Or those eyes? She realized at that moment that she was in over her head where Damien was concerned.

If she were honest with herself she would admit that a part of her wanted to accept his proposal but she couldn't. Not as Celia and he would never want her. Not if he knew.......

*****

The Hathaway ball was a grand affair and was immediately reputed to be the crush of the season. The ballroom was packed and it was stifling hot. Chelsea was surrounded by gentlemen vying for her attention and her dance card was full.

She was becoming agitated by all the gentlemen's attentions. She was starting to feel a little suffocated. She would love to go home but she had her mission and needed to see it through. She would just have to straighten her spine and endure.

Her Papa and Damien both had brooding looks on their faces as they stood sentinel at her side. She was taking a much needed break now as her feet were aching from all the dancing. She hated to slight anyone but she had to decline the next set.

"Can I get you some punch, Lady Celia?" some eager young gentleman asked.

"Do you need a foot stool to rest your feet, Lady Celia?" some other eager gentleman asked, with a hopeful expression as if her acceptance of his ridiculous suggestion would mean the difference between his living and dying.

"Lady Celia, might I say how lovely you are tonight?" another gentleman asked…Lord Davenport or some such. She didn't like the looks of him at all. He seemed slimy and conniving like a snake and she was really dreading the set assigned to him.

Chelsea gracefully fielded all of their questions with as much poise and decorum as she could muster, she was really quite sick of this. All these men crowding around her was more than she could take.

Taken singularly, dancing with each one wasn't too bad but she was glad the only three waltzes were split between Damien and her Papa as she couldn't abide the thought of strangers getting that close to her.

Some of these men had hungry wolf looks and that bothered her immensely but she couldn't let it show. If she did, she could be found out, so to distract herself, she kept replaying last night in her mind when she was at the theatre with Damien and how peaceful she felt with him then. It helped to block out the stress of this unGodly situation.

"Papa, I think I'd like to go to the retiring room for a bit," she murmured in his ear.

"Of course darling, let me escort you there," Papa said as he held out his arm. "Lord Devonshire, gentlemen, please excuse us, we shall return momentarily," he said to the bewildered looking men as they turned to walk away. Damien looked relieved, however.

"Thank you Papa, I just had to get away from them for awhile. It's a bit like being circled by vultures having all those men standing around," Chelsea complained.

"Someone must have spread the word that you're an heiress. The last time we were at a ball, only Lord Devonshire and Sir Jarrett approached you, curious that," he said as he escorted her through the throngs.

They made their way up the staircase to the retiring room and Papa released her and took his place outside the door while she went inside.

There was a very inviting sofa that was unoccupied and she immediately claimed it. It felt good to be off her feet. She sat back and closed her eyes and basked in the cool comforting quiet of solitude.

It didn't last however as it was rudely interrupted by a familiar hateful voice, "Well if it isn't Damien's paramour," the hateful voice said. Chelsea opened her eyes and looked up at to see Tess sneering at her. Wonderful! She sat up to prepare for the obvious confrontation that was to come.

"You know he wants me, don't you?" Tess continued in her hatefulness.

"I'm sure I know nothing of the kind," Chelsea responded.

"Oh yes, he has wanted me for years but I was too young of course," she said trying to convince Chelsea of this absurd fiction.

"If only that were true I might pity him," Chelsea quipped sarcastically. This woman is a real piece of baggage, she thought in complete wonder. The very idea that Damien would want her was too ludicrous by half. He was too good and kind to want such a woman and his cousin too, besides.

"How dare you speak as if you would know his feelings," Tess said, in a near rage. Her face turned red, her mouth pursed tightly and her heavy brow was drawn together; that combined with her beak nose crinkled up gave her face a very unflattering appearance.

"Careful dear, if you suffer a fright with your face all twisted up like that, you will become frozen like that for eternity," chimed in another familiar voice "And it's really quite ugly. It wouldn't do at all for everyone to see who you really are." Aunt Matilda, who had been behind the privacy screen, came out when she heard the exchange and decided to intervene.

Tess rubbed her face and looked at the mirror to confirm that she wasn't really afflicted as Matilda said she would be.

"Really dear, you should show more respect to Damien's fiancé, they are to be married soon and she will be his marchioness," Matilda taunted, clearly having a bit of fun.

"Fiancé?" Tess asked looking at Chelsea incredulously.

Chelsea was shocked by Matilda's statement but decided to play along. "He has proposed… just this morning actually, right after you left us… at the museum," she allowed. That was true at least so it wasn't an outright lie. It serves the blasted cow right at any rate.

The look on her face now was worth the effort. It was another variation of the one before only slightly more comical. She huffed and puffed indignantly, opening and closing her mouth a few times as if to speak but no words came out. Finally, she puffed up her chest, stomped her foot and stormed out of the retiring room.

Chelsea and Matilda looked after her as she made her dramatic exit then looked back at each other and shared a good hearty laugh.

Then suddenly the repercussions of the incident occurred to Chelsea and she said, "Do you think she will tell anyone that Damien and I are betrothed?"

"I'm sure she will dear," Matilda said smiling as she was quite pleased with the situation.

"Oh this is bad, I told him that I needed more time," Chelsea said in a fret. 'Celia is going to kill me, I was supposed to make him lose interest not accept his proposal. Oh no what I have I done?' Chelsea stood up and started pacing. 'This is bad…Oh I must undo this somehow.'

'Maybe Tess won't say anything and no one will know. Oh who am I kidding; of course that spiteful wretch will blab it all over the ballroom.'

Matilda noticed her agitation and said, "Do relax dear; I'm sure Damien won't mind a bit. He is quite taken with you, you know. Why, he has as much admitted that he loves you, you shouldn't……"

Her words were cut off by Chelsea when she gasped, "Loves me?" she asked in disbelief. 'He doesn't love me, he loves Celia. Oh this just keeps getting worse.'

"That can't be....this is bad," she murmured. All her plans are about to blow up in her face. 'When Celia gets word of this she will tell Papa about our ruse and I will be done for,' she thought in despair.

"Dear I don't understand. I thought you were inclined to accept him," Matilda ventured.

Chelsea could feel herself panicking and her breathing was becoming erratic. She sat down on the sofa and put her head in her hands. She started to cry in great heaving sobs.

Matilda was perplexed by this reaction and felt at a loss as to what she should say or do. She started rubbing Chelsea's back in a soothing manner and said, "There, there dear, tell me what the matter is. I'm sure it's not as bad as all this. You and Damien make a fine match and I couldn't be happier for you both. There's no reason to cry. I will explain what happened to Damien and he won't be upset with you, dear. As I said, he is quite taken with you so you've no need to carry on so."

Chelsea pondered this for a moment. Perhaps all is not lost, I could always cry off later. The only drawback, really, is that Papa may want to go back to Sheraton since the only reason we are here is to find Celia a husband.

I could always tell Papa that I would like a couple more weeks in London to court Damien to be sure. I could explain to him what happened and that it isn't really a formal betrothal. That should work, yes that's what I'll do.

"I suppose you're right. It's not so bad but it is a bit embarrassing. Are you sure Damien won't mind?" she asked.

"Oh dear girl, he will be delighted," Matilda assured her.

Chelsea sniffed and blotted away her tears with the handkerchief that seemed to have magically appeared in her hand. Must be Matilda's she reflected as she frowned at it.

"Go wash your face dear and I will go warn Damien what happened. When you've collected yourself just go back to the ballroom with your head held high and all will be well, you'll see," Matilda urged.

Chelsea nodded her head in the affirmative and Matilda took her leave.

What a terrible development! I better prepare Papa, too and I will have to write a very long letter to Celia to tell her of this situation. She will be upset but I will explain to her and assure her that I will cry off as soon as I locate Nigel. What better way to have a man lose interest in you than to jilt him.

Chapter Eight

Twenty minutes later after explaining things to a very happy Papa and getting his agreement that they stay in London, Chelsea made her way back to a widely smiling Damien and Aunt Matilda. 'Oh brother! Everyone is ecstatic about this but me…and Celia of course when she learns of it,' she inwardly groaned. 'Well there's nothing for it except to forge ahead, adapt with the changing elements. I can do this, it won't be so bad.' Her mind settled now she vowed to get through the remainder of the ball.

The night was a total disaster; she came here hoping to spot Nigel but found herself engaged. 'This could only happen to you Chelsea!'

"You've returned just in time for the next waltz, mine I believe," Damien softly spoke in her ear. Chelsea felt herself blush and put her head down.

Damien was overjoyed by the turn of events. When Aunt Matilda told him what happened he couldn't believe his luck. Of course he wanted to twist Tess' head off for upsetting Celia like that but in a way she did him a favor so he would let her keep her head. So much for his 'strict instructions' to Aunt Matilda about meddling. If he would have known that this is what would happen, he would have had her meddle days ago.

It's not quite the way he had wanted it but her hand was as good as secured now. He would give her another week or two to accustom herself to it then he would insist they move ahead with a small ceremony as soon as possible.

She couldn't back out now unless she wanted to be known as a jilt. Such a thing would make it nearly impossible to attract another offer this season. Society tends to be a bit unkind to ladies who jilt…and gentlemen, for that matter. No, once the word is out, which it surely will be before the ball is concluded they will be as good as officially betrothed.

'Well, no matter, I will just continue to woo her and make her see how good it will be between us. I might even consider a lengthier engagement and have the banns read.' Though that idea stuck in his side like thorn, he would do it for her. After all you only get married once, if she wants to have formal wedding so be it.

Of course after tonight he would have to send his notice to the Times announcing their betrothal but that was standard practice. Negative rumors would surely circulate if he didn't. Yes indeed things were looking up.

The only troubling thing for Damien was that Aunt Matilda said that Celia started crying at the prospect of him loving her. Perhaps she doesn't really believe it. He would just have to show her.

She was such a complicated girl that he still couldn't shake the feeling that she might have been abused. Though Matilda assured him that she couldn't have been, he couldn't escape the feeling that she suffered deep wounds inflicted by something. Her reaction just seemed a strange one to have after learning that he loved her.

Perhaps they were tears of joy but he didn't think so, not from what Matilda said. It sounded as though the thought of it terrified her.

"Shall we?" Damien said, offering his arm to Chelsea and leading her onto the dance floor. He held her a little too closely as he swept her into the waltz, clearly demonstrating his pleasure with tonight's turn of events.

Chelsea felt weak and listless but she allowed herself to be spun around and around as Damien led her through the dance.

"So we are betrothed now?" he asked trying to get her to express her feelings on the matter.

"I'm sorry Damien I didn't mean for it to happen. I hope you aren't upset," Chelsea said avoiding his eyes.

"Sorry? Please don't be sorry. I'm perfectly happy and it's my wish that you be as well. I know it's not how you wanted it, especially after this morning but we will make an excellent match, you'll see," he assured her.

Chelsea didn't know how to respond. She wasn't happy about this at all but she didn't want to hurt Damien's feelings by telling him how upset she really was. He would be hurt and confused by that and he didn't deserve that.

As they were dancing Chelsea became cognizant of the whispers of the other dancers as they swept beside them. The rumor had spread and everyone seemed to know. How did it happen so fast, she wondered? Everywhere she looked, people were staring at them and ladies were whispering to one another behind their fans.

Tess must have gone straight to her mother and shouted the story to the rafters in her fit of temper and was overheard; now the whole room seems to be hashing it over. Chelsea shivered and Damien's hold on her tightened in support.

"Perhaps we should take a walk in the garden so you can better collect yourself. You seem a bit overwhelmed," he said, as he twirled her in the direction of the exit.

Once they were out of the ballroom and into the night air, Chelsea felt a little more relaxed. They slowly promenaded down a garden path lit up with Chinese styled lanterns. It was rather pretty, she silently observed.

"Better?" he asked, after a few precious moments of silence.

"Oh yes, much better, thank you," she said softly with her eyes averted.

Chelsea slowly began to realize the vulnerability of the situation. With Papa here tonight they allowed Jenny the evening off and she had no chaperone.

"Perhaps we should stay closer to the ball," she said as she nervously looked back to gauge how far they had gone.

Damien led her to a bench and he urged her to sit. He hunkered down in front of her so he was facing her at eye level. She looked around, somewhat relieved to see that they were still in view of the ballroom, just in case……..

"Is there anything I can say or do to put you more at ease about our betrothal?" Damien asked, breaking into her fearful thinking. He took her hand in his and started his signature massage of her palm. She began to relax further and could feel the tension leaving her body.

She sat in quiet contemplation before saying, "No it's alright, really. It was just a bit of a shock and now everyone seems to know of it. Everyone was staring and whispering and it made me feel terribly exposed."

Chelsea wondered if her confession would mollify him or make him feel angry.

He gently squeezed her hand and laughed softly, "My sweet Celia, this must all be so overwhelming, for a country lass, such as you. London alone can be intimidating without all the balls and the ton to have to deal with," he said, leaning in to gently kiss her temple.

"You are doing admirably well, all things considered. Try not to let it all get you down. If it would make you happy, we don't have to attend any more balls. I never liked them anyway," he added.

Chelsea's head shot up…not attend anymore balls? But I have to, how else can I find Nigel. "Oh no it's not as bad as all that. It's just that tonight seemed particularly… unusual and it was a bit taxing but I'm fine now, really," she said in a rush. "I enjoy the dancing," she added to further convince him.

Damien searched her eyes for the truth. She felt like he could read her so very well. She averted her face away but he wasn't dissuaded as he gently tugged her chin back so he could see her eyes.

They stared into each other for what seemed an eternity. Ever so slowly Damien moved his head toward her and his eyes focused on her lips. He halted briefly and looked back into her eyes as if to ask for permission. Whatever he saw there must have convinced him. He slowly placed his lips upon hers. His tongue gently pushed its way into her mouth and began a slow sensuous mingling with hers.

Chelsea was swept away by the essence of the man. His breath was sweet and tasted of mint and he smelled lightly of bay rum shaving soap. His lips were tender and warm as he deepened the kiss.

She felt herself go limp but he supported her with one hand behind her back and the other was cradling the side of her head. It was a wonderful feeling but then his hand started traversing from her head down the side of her neck as her brought their embrace closer.

She tensed slightly but he began to gently massage her lower back to try to soothe her while he continued his sensual assault. Chelsea shouldn't be allowing this but he was so very persuasive and tender that she found it difficult to deny him. She never dreamed a kiss could be so wonderful or that it would feel so right…but it wasn't right! 'He thinks he's kissing Celia.'

Chelsea pulled out of the kiss and away from him "We mustn't do this now," she admonished.

Damien groaned at the loss of her lips and stood up to recover himself. He ran a hand through his hair and said,

"Of course, you're right. Forgive me, I was quite overcome." "We should go back to the ballroom before we are missed," he added a bit disgruntled. Soon, he reminded himself, soon she would be his wife and he would be free to kiss her whenever he wished but until then he must be mindful of her reputation.

It was remiss of him to forget even for a moment that they were in view of the ballroom where anyone could have seen them. He offered her his hand and assisted her to her feet, then placed her hand upon his forearm and led her back inside.

*****

Chelsea asked Damien to take her for a turn about the perimeter of the ballroom. She wanted to scan the crowd to allow her a view of all the men in attendance. Her hopes was to see the familiar face of her enemy. The night was such a disaster. She hoped to salvage it by somehow locating Nigel.

She ignored the whispers and the envious stares of the hostile females, the gawking males. She managed to get through the greetings of the occasional well-wisher offering felicitations on their upcoming nuptials. Through it all, Chelsea searched her mind for ways to probe Damien about his male relatives, friends and other acquaintances without drawing suspicion onto herself.

She couldn't just come right out and ask for a list of all his known associates, so she settled for what she hoped would be a subtle opener. "Do you have any other friends or relatives besides your Aunt Matilda…and the duchess and her lovely daughter Tess in attendance tonight," she asked with a smile.

"Since we are engaged, I suppose I should know who your friends and relatives are," she added. That shouldn't be too suspicious she assured herself.

"Oh, there are a couple of cousins and fellows here and there that I associate with from time to time and that I see mostly at the club and of course the duke is probably here somewhere," he said looking around the room to see if he could see Nigel.

"But I don't see him. He must be in the card room or some such. I don't think he spends a lot of time doting on his wife and daughter," he added with a snort.

"The duke is your uncle?" she asked, trying to sound nonchalant.

"No, a cousin, on my mother's side of the family. I don't associate with him. He is not a very kind man and I find him rather…distasteful," he allowed. "He owns a tea plantation in India with many slaves. I find that deplorable," he added.

Chelsea felt like she could probably strike him off the list of suspects since he lived in India, although….

"Has he lived in India long?" she probed.

"Quite a while yes, it's actually been in his family for about fifty years so he has lived there since he became the duke," he explained

"When did he become a duke?" she asked to confirm that it couldn't be him. Of course, if she asked too many more questions about him Damien might become irritated.

"About twenty years ago," he said with no apparent notice of her persistence.

Well, she could strike the duke off her list of suspects at least. "Is your family small?" she prompted to allow the discussion to continue.

"Not too small. My father has many brothers and of course there is his sister, Matilda. I have several cousins from that side but poor Matilda never had any children," he told her.

Damien was pleased that she seemed to be accepting their betrothal to the degree that she would want to know his family. He would have to have a dinner party and invite his friends and relatives over to meet her, he decided.

"I would love to meet them," she said.

"I was just thinking that I should have a dinner party and invite family and friends to meet my future marchioness," he beamed his suggestion.

"That would be grand, Damien. When do you think you would like to do this?" she asked, a little too excited about it, she realized.

"Oh, I'm sure something could be arranged early next week. We should have it at Aunt Matilda's however because she has a bigger home and its better for entertaining than mine. Mine is just a bachelor town house and isn't set up to accommodate more than ten or so guests at a time," he suggested. "I will speak to her about it before we leave," he added.

Chelsea was pleased by this development. It would be a good chance to survey his friends and family in one close setting. It's much too hard to find anyone in this madhouse.

Resigned to not finding Nigel tonight she said, "We should get back to Papa now because I still have three dances left to fill before this cursed event is over."

Damien chuckled at that and led her back to her father. 'The poor girl hates balls more than I do. We are perfectly suited. After we are married we can retire to one of my country estates and we will be able to live our lives in absolute bliss,' he decided.

*****

'The last dance and it's with Lord Davenport,' Chelsea inwardly groaned. He eagerly took her arm and fairly pulled her onto the dance floor. He was a tall slim man with black hair, slicked back with what looked like grease. He had long burly mutton chops.

His hands were cold and his eyes were small black, lifeless orbs. He quite reminded her of a snake. His eyes roved over her as if she were a meal he wanted to consume whole.

She didn't like this man at all. She should have never agreed to dance with him, next time, she wouldn't. Thank God, it was the last dance and she could be quit of this ghastly affair. 'What a night,' she reflected as she followed the steps of the dance.

Chelsea was lost in thought and didn't realize that he lead her toward the terrace rather than back to her Papa and Damien until it was too late. She found herself outside being groped and pawed at by a very amorous Lord Davenport.

He pulled her tight against him and tried to put his lips with his sour foul breath on hers. She moved her face just in time to avoid him and started trying to wriggle away from him.

His grip tightened and panic started to set in as unwanted memories began to flood her mind. The futility of her efforts to free herself caused her to become dazed and weak and she felt herself detaching.

Suddenly Lord Davenport was gone and through her hazy vision she saw that Papa and Damien were on the terrace, too. Damien was beating Lord Davenport senseless.

She sank to the floor in stunned silence while the scene played itself out in a bizarre sort of slow motion. It felt as though she were looking through a foggy, darkened glass.

Finally after administering a sound thrashing Damien picked up Lord Davenport by the lapels, hurling him over the terrace railing, into the pond below. Chelsea heard the splash and the subsequent curses of a very angry Lord Davenport. His words sounded as though they were being shouted, with an accompanying echo.

The next thing she knew she was laid over on her side and she felt herself moving toward her quite place. She was barely aware now as Papa and Damien were talking about her. Then the darkness claimed her and all was quiet…..

The baron watched in horror as he saw his daughter's reaction to the assault by Lord Davenport. It couldn't be…no…not Chelsea. 'Oh my God, but it is her. How could I have not seen it before? What's to be done now? I can't let the marquess suspect anything, it could be disastrous.'

He cleared his throat "Ahem…Lord Devonshire, would you please leave us and make sure no one comes out here" he asked his eyes still riveted on his daughter.

Damien was upset seeing Celia on the ground, ghostly white with her eyes wide open, staring blankly in apparent shock. He didn't know what to do. He didn't want to abandon her now, so he asked, "What's wrong with her Sir? Should I go get Aunt Matilda?"

"No.. there's no need to go get your aunt, she'll be alright, I believe she has only swooned. Please, just stand outside the doors and make sure no one comes out here. She wouldn't want anyone to see her like this," the baron implored.

Damien wasn't so sure she had only fainted but decided that the baron was right. He was willing to do whatever he could to protect her even if it meant to leave her in her father's care and simply guard the doors leading to the terrace.

When the baron was alone with Chelsea he sat down beside her and gathered her in his arms and spoke softly to her, "My sweet Chelsea lass, what are you doing child?"

He slowly began to rock her back and forth and continued to coo sweet fatherly words in her ear in hopes of reaching her shattered mind. He didn't know how long this would last but he feared it would be a good hour or so.

'What in the world is she doing here and to what possible end? How could Celia have gone along with such a preposterous idea? And Hattie and Jenny too, they must be in on it as well. Something is afoot here, but what?'

He searched his mind while he held his daughter trying to determine when the switch was made. Of course it happened while they were still at Sheraton. It must have been fairly soon after they arrived.

Aye, he remembered something amiss at dinner the second night. Celia was fawning at Lord Devonshire and ignoring Sir Jarrett. He thought that had been strange but didn't think much of it at the time. He had just assumed that they were getting on well. But he also remembered the way Sir Jarrett was looking at her as if he were trying to understand the change in her, too.

'Clever girls….but why? Why would they risk such a thing and how has Chelsea been able to pull this off thus far.'

He was suddenly proud of his daughter now that he thought of it. He would never have dreamed that she could be in situations such as those that she has been through since their arrival here in London.

Tears welled in his eyes at the thought of her bravery. Oh how he has missed his special lass. So many years since she'd been taken away from him and now she was back. He would never let her go again.

He must protect her secret even if he didn't understand the why of it. He had to give her a chance to live again, he just had to. Celia must have put her up to this so she could have Sir Jarrett. Aye and he stayed behind at Evansdale; the bastard is probably in on it, too. It suddenly occurred to him that they might be planning to elope. 'Oh, what a mess! Lord Devonshire will be insulted when he learns of this. On the other hand, he seems quite taken with Chelsea and her with him and they are engaged after all.'

'Hmmm…there are possibilities here yet to be determined. I shall simply have to play my cards close to the vest,' he decided.

"Aye Chelsea love, your Papa will keep your secret," he vowed with a kiss to her cheek. 'I will just have to keep a close eye on her and make sure she doesn't get herself in a situation like this again. It's a good thing she and Lord Devonshire are engaged as he too will be there to protect her.'

He was quite proud of the way he thrashed that Davenport fellow. Yes' indeed the marquess has very strong feelings for Chelsea. He would have to bank on that for the future outcome after his lordship learned of the ruse.

Chelsea started to stir, then. Relieved that the episode was over fairly quickly the baron said, "Celia dear, wake up, you've swooned lass." Her eyes blinked and she focused on him and smiled fondly at her Papa.......

*****

Damien was pleased to see Celia finally recovered as she and her father came in from the terrace. Most of the balls occupants had gone and they were able to leave in relative obscurity.

Celia tried to put on a brave face as she was lead to the carriage but Damien saw through it. He could see that she was still terrified and off kilter.

When he tried to offer his arm she shied away from him in preference of her father and once inside the carriage she sat quietly by her father side. Neither she nor the baron spoke a word all the way home.

Perhaps she was a bit embarrassed by what happened. He wished her father wasn't there so he could assure her that she had nothing to be embarrassed about.

It was strange the way she fainted with her eyes wide open. It was more like a state of shock than a faint. Damien worried that perhaps Davenport did more than just grope before he could rescue her but he didn't know how to delicately ask.

She was having trouble looking at him now and seemed terribly uncomfortable with his presence. That didn't bode well for their betrothal, Damien feared. After seeing her that way tonight he was more convinced than ever that someone or something from her past had hurt her. It was a mystery that needed to be solved.

Not that anything he found out would sway him one way or the other from marrying her. He just needed to know so he could help her put whatever it is behind her. They didn't need skeletons between them.

But how to broach the subject without aggravating what is clearly a stressful issue for her. Perhaps he could ask her father or Jenny. No, they probably wouldn't talk about it.

Whatever it is, it is more than likely a closely guarded secret that they wish to keep. I will just have to peel the layers away a little at a time until I learn who or what has hurt her and then move heaven and earth to protect her from it, he decided.

Chapter Nine

After exhaustive searching of the villages around the areas of Evansdale, Jarrett found himself back at Sheraton Manor. He decided to speak with the old stable master there to see if he might have any information.

He had to come back and retrieve his journal that was left behind when he departed last, so he thought while there it would be prudent to poke around a bit.

Jonas McBride's family, as it turned out, had been stable masters at Sheraton for the last one hundred and twenty years. So if anyone would have any information about the lads that have served at Sheraton, it would be old Jonas.

"Nay, can't say we ever 'ad no young lads to fit them looks," Jonas said after careful contemplation. "Strange blue eyes, ye say?"

"Yes, a crystal blue sort of color and he would have had black hair more than likely. Would be about twenty years old by now."

"Wat ye want wiv 'im?" Old Jonas asked with a shrewd eye.

"I believe he witnessed a terrible crime about ten years ago and I was hoping to speak with him about it. I've been asked to investigate and to be quite honest I'm coming up empty everywhere I go. It's as though he fell off the face of the earth," Jarrett said with frustration.

"Strange for ye to mention them crystal blue eyes. Only be one round these parts wiv 'em kind of eyes an that'd be the baron's lass. She be about the right age but she's a lass and ye be lookin' for a lad. Of course her mum had the same eyes but she's been gone long past."

Jarrett wondered if perhaps the boy could be related to the Sheratons somehow and asked, "Did the Sheratons ever have any visiting relatives that might fit that description? A cousin perhaps?"

"Nay, the Sheratons be private folk, t'aint many of em neither , they don't 'ave no one comin round to see em. Never 'ave," Old Jonas said assuredly.

Frustrated, Jarrett took his leave of the stable and went to the manor. He knocked on the door and was met by a sunny, smiling Dickens, "Ah Sir Jarrett, nice to see you sir, do come in," he said as he bowed and waved his arm for Jarrett to pass, "How can I help you sir?" he asked once inside the foyer.

"I left my journal behind when I left the other day and I was hoping to retrieve it."

"Very good sir, I'll be happy to go and retrieve it for you," he said

"If you don't mind, Dickens I would like to have a look about the room myself, in case I left anything else," Jarrett said realizing that he packed his bag in a sleep deprived state and could have left other things behind.

"Very good sir, please be my guest and if I can be of further service, don't hesitate to ask."

Jarrett gave him an informal salute and made his way up the grand stair case. He found the room he stayed in and looked around. He spotted his journal and scooped it up then he looked under the bed and all around to be sure he left nothing else. He checked in the wardrobe and found nothing there.

Content that he had everything; he left the room and headed down the long hall with his head down as he was thumbing through his journal. Just as he was near the landing, he looked up and was stunned to see an equally stunned Celia standing in the far end of the opposite hall.

"Lady Celia! I thought you were in London," he called out in surprised confusion as he moved past the landing to go down the other hall to greet her.

Celia was shocked! She had left the attic apartments to go to her room to retrieve her embroidery hoop so she could finish her project. She had no idea she would meet anyone in the hall, let alone Jarrett. She was so shocked she couldn't come up with a single explanation for her presence there.

Jarrett finally reached her and she was stunned anew by how handsome he was. He looked wonderful, ruggedly dressed as he was, with his doe skin breeches and his Hessians; half dressed with his white lawn shirt without a waist coat.

"When did you return from London, Lady Celia?" Jarrett prompted.

"I uh…um…that is to say…" At a loss for explanation she tried to distract him by asking, "How are you Sir Jarrett?"

Jarrett, not one to be distracted, ignored that and said, "Lady Celia, this is strange. I just received a missive this morning from Damien and he didn't mention your return from London. In fact he spoke of your attendance at the Hathaway ball last night and made mention of future plans."

Celia dropped her head and floundered for an explanation. Realizing she was caught out right and not wanting the servants to overhear what she had to say she took him by the hand, tugged it and said, "Come with me."

She led him back down the hall, took him to her room and quickly closed and locked the door. She started pacing and wringing her hands trying to find the words to explain.

"Perhaps you should just come right out with it Lady Celia," he prompted.

She stopped her pacing and faced him, "Yes of course, I should just come right to it," but still she seemed scared to proceed. "I uh…ahem…Sir Jarrett I have an identical twin and it is she, that is in London." There, that wasn't so hard.

Jarrett looked at her as if she were mad and incredulously said, "A twin." Not a question, just a statement.

"Yes, my sister's name is Chelsea. She and I switched identities the day after we arrived here from London so she could take my place with Lord Devonshire."

Celia wasn't sure how much she should tell him so she opted for partial truth. "You see Sir Jarrett, I am disinclined to marry the marquess and it was the plan…well Chelsea and I planned for her to put him off so he would lose interest in me."

"That makes no sense, Lady Celia," Jarrett said.

Celia plopped down on her bed and sighed deeply, "I realize that it doesn't but you have to trust me. I can't tell you the whole story only that it is not my wish to marry Lord Devonshire. Chelsea rather liked him you see and I well…I rather like you," she admitted shyly.

"You rather like me?" Jarrett honed in on that one sentence and the words of it coursed through his veins like lightening. He couldn't believe what he had just heard.

"Yes, are you disappointed?" Celia asked with trepidation. His possibly rejecting her offer of affection was not a thing she wished to consider.

"No, how could I be, but I'm still confused. I didn't even know you had a sister let alone a twin," he said in an effort to get back on topic.

"Yes, well you see, the thing about Chelsea… she is very shy, you know, so she doesn't socialize but she saw Lord Devonshire, when we were all in the garden, and she was intrigued by him. When she and I were talking later that night about it and I explained to her my feelings, we decided to switch so she could get to know him better. She was going to try and have him lose interest in me so he would go away, clearing the field for you," she explained blushing.

She knew her story didn't entirely make sense but it was the best she could do without revealing Chelsea's real motives. She hoped it would suffice.

"Do you switch identities often?" he asked still perplexed.

"Oh yes all the time," she lied.

Jarrett shook his head hoping that he could send her scrambled words into some kind of order. He said, "So let me see if I have the right of it. Chelsea saw Lord Devonshire in the garden and became intrigued and you are… intrigued with me so you two switched places in an effort to send Lord Devonshire's attentions away from you to clear the field for me?"

Celia emphatically shook her head in the affirmative and said, "Yes, that's it exactly." Jarrett whistled a sound reminiscent of an incoming cannon ball then let out a loud breath as if the projectile found its mark. He started his own pacing.

After a moment he sat in the chair beside her bed and said, "This is incredible! You do realize that Damien will regard this as a severe insult, do you not?"

"Well, I had hoped that it wouldn't be discovered, actually. But if it is, perhaps he will consider himself lucky to be rid of me," she said with her chin lifted in defiance.

"Are you suggesting that I not tell him, Lady Celia?" Jarrett asked, marveling at the female mind.

"I can't stop you of course, but I would hope that your regard for me would prevent you from exposing us," Celia was suddenly unsure what would happen now. 'Chelsea is going to kill me,' she thought. 'I have totally ruined her plans.'

"I get the feeling there is more to this than you have explained. But for the moment, I am willing to consider keeping your confidence."

Jarrett wasn't sure how to handle this development. On the one hand, he was elated that Lady Celia preferred him to Damien, which was a first. On the other, he and Damien have been lifelong friends and he owed him the courtesy of telling him of this deception.

Jarrett owed Damien and his family for many things. Without their funding his education, he would never have become the man he is today.

At university he studied criminal law and when he was fresh out of school he was hired by Bow Street with a very fine word of recommendation from the Duke of Evansdale. From there, he performed various services for the crow. In so doing, became knighted, gaining a yearly pension. He owed everything to Damien and his family. To try and hide this…to not tell him will be huge betrayal, but Celia…what to do?

"There are certain things about Chelsea that are not mine to tell. Please don't ask me to elaborate. I know that's asking a lot, but you must understand that her…well, she is very special and it's vital that she be allowed to take my place in London," Celia implored.

Jarrett sensed that there was something on the peripheral of this story that he wasn't seeing. What is it?

"Has Chelsea always been so shy and unsociable?" he asked fishing for more details.

"No, she wasn't always like that. It's only been that way for the last ten years," she allowed.

Jarrett was suddenly chilled. It couldn't be? Could it? Could Chelsea have been the boy….no surely not, that just doesn't make sense, he reasoned.

"What was she like as a child?" he ventured further.

Celia didn't realize what he was angling for and said,

"Oh, she was quite the ragamuffin; always riding horses, fishing and romping about out of doors."

"How did she go from being so adventurous to being so socially withdrawn?" he asked fearing that every answer she provided brought him closer to the obvious conclusion.

At that, Celia clammed up. She realized she had said too much and that Jarrett knew…she looked at him imploringly. He got the message because he didn't ask any more questions.

But she knew that he knew and she was suddenly worried for Chelsea. After a few awkward silent moments with Jarrett staring off into space, she finally asked, "What will you do, Sir Jarrett?"

It all made sense to Jarrett now. Chelsea was the boy that they have been searching for and when she spotted Damien and recognized him, she became convinced that he could lead her to Nigel.

There was no other explanation. "I'm not sure Lady Celia, this is very serious," he said, as he continued to brooding contemplations.

Celia was squirming from the tension of his prolonged silence. She felt as though she were sitting on the edge of a knife. He looked so intense and fierce sitting there silent as a stone.

"Please don't betray Chelsea to Lord Devonshire!" she begged, more to break the silence than anything else.

"Tell me this…is Damien in any danger from Chelsea?" he asked sharply after another moment of silence.

"No, oh no, Chelsea is quite smitten with him, that part is true, I swear it."

"And the part where you are smitten with me?" he couldn't help but wonder aloud.

Celia got up from the bed and dropped to her knees at his feet and said, "I would never lie about a thing like that, Jarrett."

Jarrett was comforted by that and he believed her. If Chelsea isn't dangerous, what harm could there be in allowing her a few more days or even a week or so in London. She would be safe with her father and Damien to protect her if she did encounter Nigel, he reasoned.

"Are you in communication with Chelsea while she is in London?" he probed.

"Yes, she writes to me every day," Celia still on her knees before him said.

"I'll tell you what we'll do... I will be staying with my mother at Evansdale for the foreseeable future. If you hear anything at all from Chelsea that could signify danger, you will tell me immediately. Is that understood?" he asked sternly.

"Yes, of course, that's what I'll do. Oh, thank you, Jarrett," she said grasping his hand, fondly kissing it.

"There's something you should know...Damien wrote to me this morning and told me that you and he are officially betrothed."

Celia fainted dead away.

*****

Jarrett picked Celia up and took her to her bed and gently laid her out. He should have been more delicate in his delivery when he told her that she was now officially engaged to Damien.

He went to her water closet and wet a hand towel with some cool water. He brought it back to the bed and sat down beside her and placed it on her brow. He started patting her hand and calling to her to wake up.

Her eyes fluttered open. She looked at him bewilderedly for a moment then remembered where she was and made a move to sit up.

Jarrett gently pushed her back to the bed by her shoulder and said, "Stay there. I don't believe you are quite steady yet."

"Oh Jarrett, this is awful. What am I going to do? I can't marry Lord Devonshire, it's impossible. What could have made Chelsea do such a stupid thing as to accept?" she complained.

"Actually from what I understand from Damien said it was quite accidental."

"Accidental? What do you mean?"

"There seemed to have been some kind of incident in the ladies retiring room. Aunt Matilda came to the rescue and said that she was Damien's betrothed."

He chuckled thinking of Aunt Matilda and her meddling. She wanted to get Damien leg shackled by the end of the season and by God she's probably done it.

"Chelsea must be beside herself," Celia said, worry in her eyes for her sister. "Well this changes everything. We will have to tell Papa and have him bring her home. We'll explain to Lord Devonshire and hope that he is gentleman enough not to make too big an issue of it," she added.

"I don't think you should do that just yet. It could work to our advantage that he is betrothed to your sister. Sooner or later the truth will be revealed and I have a feeling that when all is said and done, Damien won't care who she is, he will still want to marry her. I say that we should wait it out for a couple of days, maybe a week to see what develops," Jarrett said clearly liking the plan.

Celia mulled that over in her mind and smiled, "Do you think so?" she asked with hope in her eyes. The idea that Chelsea might find happiness, too, made Celia very happy even if it was with the marquess.

"It's possible and quite likely, I should say," Jarrett said smiling in return.

He only felt mildly guilty about it now that he had time to think on it. If things were to go as he hoped, everyone could be happy. Damien could have Chelsea and he could have Celia.

The only real potential problem was what Chelsea would do when she encountered Nigel. He didn't ask Celia what her plans were for Nigel because it was clearly an uncomfortable subject to broach but he needed to know.

"Celia, I have to ask you an uncomfortable question. Please forgive me but I need to know. What does Chelsea plan to do when she finds Nigel?" he asked.

'So, he does know…of course he knows. He's a Bow Street runner with a highly successful reputation. Well the cats out of the bag now so what's the harm in answering?' "She wants to locate him so she can expose him," she said in a matter of fact tone.

"Yes, that was mine and Damien's plan as well. That's why he hired me to find the 'boy', whoever he may have been. We had hoped that maybe enough time had passed that he would be brave enough to come forward. Of course Damien wants to kill Nigel because of what happened but I have told him he has to see reason because Nigel is a duke and you can't just kill a duke."

Celia sucked in a gasping breath, "Nigel is a duke?" she asked.

"Oh yes, he's a duke and he is also Damien's cousin on his mother's side," Jarrett explained.

Celia made an 'O' shape with her mouth but no sound came out. She shook her head and said, "That certainly explains how they knew each other. Chelsea puzzled over it. She couldn't imagine what a nice man like Damien was doing with a monster like Nigel," she finished on a shiver.

"Believe me, Damien hates Nigel and I have a feeling that things could get really ugly when Damien finds out who Chelsea is. All the more reason I feel we should wait this thing out. If I were to send Damien a note telling him what I have discovered, Nigel is a dead man and Damien will have to leave the country."

Jarrett knew the words he spoke were true. There would be no safe place on earth for Nigel when Damien learned of Chelsea's identity. The situation is very precarious.

"Oh Jarrett I'm so worried. What should we do?" Celia asked chewing on her lower lip.

Jarrett looked down at her to gauge whether or not she were steady enough to get up yet. Looking at her lying on the bed like that was too distracting.

"How do you feel now Celia?" he asked.

He moved to sit up and this time he allowed it. He got up and moved back to the chair. She swung her legs over the side of the bed to face him, "Much better now thank you. This is all so worrisome but I don't think I shall swoon again," she said.

"Yes and I fear things will get worse before they get better, but all we can do is wait and watch and keep up regular correspondences with both Damien and Chelsea. If we hear anything from either of them to indicate impending violence, I will return to London right away. I can be there within an hour on horse, if we hear any bad news."

Jarrett didn't want to tell Celia what he had been thinking while she was sleeping. He didn't think either Chelsea or Damien would be willing to simply expose Nigel. He was sure that they both wanted to kill him.

Before, Damien could have been reasoned with, as far as exposing Nigel once the boy was found, but now that they had found the "boy" and he was a she and potentially his future bride…well, that would put a whole new light on things.

Perhaps he should come up with a way to get Nigel out of the country. He could have him kidnapped and sent away on a prison transport or sell him to some Barbary Corsairs.

It happened all the time in this dangerous climate with both France and the American colonies having gone through revolutions. The English aristocracy was particularly nervous and made every effort to cover up anything that could be embarrassing to the crown.

Aristocrats like Nigel, were known to disappear, finding themselves on plantations in countries like Australia or on islands like Jamaica as indentured servants for life or as a slave in Algiers.

Once placed on a transport, if you had no way to identify yourself, you were sold into service along with all the other criminals. And of course the corsairs didn't care who you were, a slave was a slave.

The plan had possibilities but there were many things to consider before he could actually put it into place. It might be better to entrap Nigel somehow and have him publicly exposed but to do that he would have to place a child in danger. So many things consider; so many things could go wrong...

Celia broke into his thoughts, "Shall I ring for tea?" she asked.

"No, I should probably be going before Dickens realizes I haven't left yet," he said reluctant to leave her now. He still couldn't fathom that Celia preferred him to Damien. He looked at her and was awed by her beauty.

What a fortunate man he would be if he could indeed have her for a wife. But before he could seriously consider it, he had to let the relationship between Chelsea and Damien play itself out for awhile, didn't he? But would there be any real harm in kissing her?

Whether Damien and Chelsea actually marry or not, Celia clearly doesn't want him. Would he be betraying Damien, if he were to pursue Celia? He didn't like to think so. He knew that Damien was head over heels in love with Chelsea now and he felt reasonably certain that despite what happened they would end up together, if he knew anything at all about Damien, and he did.

"I hate to see you go," Celia murmured with pouting lips and big doe eyes.

Jarrett was lost... he stood up and pulled her into his arms and kissed her for all he was worth and she kissed him back for all she was worth, too. Before they knew what they were doing they were rolling around on her bed desperately removing each other's clothes.

It was such a heady passionate experience that they were both lost to the ecstasy of the momentary madness. Once he had Celia naked and splayed out before him, he realized what they were about to do,

"Are you sure Celia?" he asked.

"Oh do shut up and kiss me!" was her reply, so he did.

Chapter Ten

Damien was sitting at his club brooding about the night before with Celia. No matter how hard he tried, he just couldn't convince himself that she merely swooned.

He had seen a person in shock before and he knew what it looked like and she was definitely in shock. Sure, it was a terrible thing that happened to her but it shouldn't have caused that kind of reaction.

A simple swoon he could understand but she should have quickly recovered. She and her father were on the terrace a good three quarters of an hour, maybe more. That wasn't simply a swoon.

It was almost as though she were reliving some trauma from a past experience. Her father seemed familiar enough with her condition to keep calm and cool to attend her. It was as though they had both been down that road before.

The only logical conclusion he could reach is that someone had hurt her, but who? He was reasonably sure it wasn't her father; the man clearly loved his daughter.

He had tossed and turned last night unable to get the picture of her laying there like that out of his mind. He wanted to thrash Davenport all over again…and again.

His protective instincts were ratcheted up from the experience and he wanted to find out who hurt her. He wanted to hurt them but how could he broach the topic with her without upsetting her?

He had sent around a note this morning asking her to accompany him for a walk in the park this afternoon. Her reply was that she would love to. Perhaps while they were out, he could speak to her and get her to provide some kind of clue to help him understand what happened and who might have harmed her.

She and her father were content to act as though she had simply fainted as it was nothing out of the ordinary for a lady to do so after such a fright. He supposed he could allow them to keep their dignity and not come right out and demand answers but he could ask a few subtle questions in such a way that she might not realize she was giving him what he was after.

He knew that whatever happened to her, it would have absolutely no bearing on his feelings for her but he had to know. He loved the girl and every moment he spent with her compounded and solidified it.

If only he could show her that she could trust him. He realized that trust wasn't something you could rush, especially with a wounded soul. It had to be earned through patience and constancy.

Well, today he would start by showing her that he was still just as interested in her as ever, more so now that they are officially betrothed. The first thing he did this morning was send his notice to the Times. He also went to see his solicitor about the marriage contract.

This afternoon he would go over the details of that with her father and then he would give her the Vane betrothal ring. That should say plainly that the relationship between them was solid.

Perhaps any embarrassment she suffered from last night would ease away once she had the proof of his affection upon her finger. With that, she might be inclined to open up; at least he hoped that she would.

*****

Chelsea was relieved that Papa didn't seem to realize who she was after her episode last night at the Hathaway ball. When she came back and was wrapped in her Papa's arms, she was sure that all was lost and that she would have a lot of explaining to do.

Apparently it was a very mild episode only lasting a few minutes. Papa said she simply swooned, which under the circumstances was a perfectly normal reaction to such an upsetting ordeal. 'Any woman would have done as much,' she consoled herself.

She only hoped that Damien didn't realize her aversion to him afterward. The idea of him touching her had been too much for her to deal with after such an event. She would try very hard to show him that she was over it and not shy away from his touch again.

 He was to call on her this afternoon to take her for a walk about the park. That would be the perfect opportunity to re-establish their connection, so to speak. She can't afford to do anything further that would cast a suspicious eye in her direction.

Everything about this whole plan seemed to be falling out of her control. First she found herself betrothed...oh and she still hadn't found the courage to write Celia and tell her about that.

She can't hold off much longer considering that Damien mentioned in his request to call upon her today, that he'd sent a notice to the Times making the announcement and that it would print in tomorrow's edition. Oh, why did he have to do that? Drat the man!

Well, there was nothing for it except to go along as planned and gird her loins against all the bumps and grinds along the way. Tonight, before she went to bed she would have to write Celia a message and be sure that it went out with the morning post.

It wouldn't do at all for Celia to read the announcement and come storming back to London before she had a chance to tell her of it herself.

The idea of being betrothed to Damien, even if it was pretend, wasn't so bad really. He was so gentle and kind and he really would make a wonderful husband. If only there was some way they could be together…but when he finally found out what she had done he would surely be insulted and humiliated and want nothing more to do with her.

She would do anything to avoid that now that she actually knew him. He didn't deserve to be used in such a fashion but it was too late now. It was hard not to feel guilty and just throw the whole plan aside and avoid the ultimate conclusion. But she was really in too deep now. Though she hadn't seen Nigel yet, she sensed that he is close.

It was a weird feeling, really. It was like a shadow was lurking but she couldn't quite make it out. She could only catch a glimpse here and there. Chelsea shivered and wrapped her shawl tighter around herself. Yes, Nigel was close, of that she was sure. She just wished Damien didn't have to be a casualty of this private war of hers.

It was hard not to love him. Yes, she had to admit that she must. Why else would he have such an effect on her? That kiss last night was so breathtaking. No other man on this earth could make her feel that way.

Try as she might, she couldn't imagine herself locked in an embrace with any of those young gentlemen that she danced with last night, most of whom made her feel very uncomfortable. No, only Damien had the power to move her so. Only he could wrap her in a feeling of total security and make her lose all her inhibitions.

If she were to ever learn the ways of love between a man and a woman, it would be Damien who would have to show her the way. No other man would do. It saddened her to realize that when this was all over she would be consigned to a life without him.

Less than a week ago, she didn't even know he existed and now his presence in her world seemed vital to her existence. It was too despairing to know that the only experience she had ever had with a man was a horrible nightmare instead of the beauteous wonder she knew she would have with Damien and she would never be able to experience it.

Would it be so bad to allow him to make love to her, just so she could have one pleasant memory to offset the other? Who would blame her if she did? Could she really do it though, she wasn't sure.

Coward! That's what you are Chelsea Sheraton!
Only a coward would let a monster like Nigel dictate
her happiness. Why should she banish herself to a
life of loneliness when the one person in the world
that she could ever love was so near to her?

*****

"Damien dear, how is poor Celia bearing up after
the incident in the retiring room and uh….your
subsequent betrothal? Aunt Matilda asked sheepishly,
before sipping her tea.

"It's really hard to be mad at you, you know, Aunt.
I expressly forbid your interference but your
interference gave me exactly what I want so I have
decided not to give you the dressing down that you
probably deserve," Damien said with a crooked smile
and a wink.

"Yes dear, it was rather brilliant of me, I should
say. Why, what else was I to do when that horrid
creature was terrorizing her so?" Matilda asked with
feigned offence. "It seemed the only way to give her
the comeuppance that was due. I only wish you could
have been there to witness my genius, dear," she
smirked.

"Genius, was it? Well no matter, she and I are
more or less officially engaged and today she will be
wearing the Vane betrothal ring to seal the deal."

Damien was enjoying his Aunts moment of self
congratulation. He hoped that he never got on her bad
side as she was quite the harridan when opposed.

"I should think she will be lovely in the Vane
betrothal jewels," she mused aloud.

"There was another incident involving Celia last night. Have you heard anything about it?" Damien was curious to know if Lord Davenport might have tried to besmirch Celia's character since he was thwarted from his obvious plan to compromise her into marriage. The blackguard wasn't apt to take it laying down when her fortune was at stake.

"I assume you mean that ghastly business with Lord Davenport. I heard that you threw him over the terrace and into the pond but there was no mention of Celia. You should take care to be sure there is no one below when you send debris flying over the rail, dear," Matilda admonished.

"When I saw what he was doing to her, I lost all sense of reason. The bloody sod had his hands all over her," Damien said through clenched teeth.

"Her fortune is bound to appeal to scoundrels like him. You will have to be more attentive of her safety in those kinds of settings," she advised.

"Aye, well the sooner we can be married the better."

"I hope she wasn't too terribly upset by what happened," Matilda probed.

Damien wasn't sure he should tell her the rest of the story but he needed someone to talk to about it.

"Actually, she swooned, or rather her father said it was a swoon," he allowed. "I haven't yet spoken with her to see how she fares today but I'm due to call upon her within the hour," he added.
Matilda, not one to miss a beat said, "What do you mean, 'rather her father said'?"

"I mean if it was a swoon, it was the strangest one I ever witnessed. It was more like a state of shock," Damien admitted exasperatedly.

He felt like he was betraying Celia by telling Matilda but he knew she would never divulge anything he said to anyone else. Matilda had always closely guarded his confidences so he wasn't worried about that, but if Celia knew that he told anyone, she might not forgive him.

"I'm sure it was rather shocking for the poor dear but I'm sure it's nothing to worry about."

"Maybe you're right. It's just that the more time I spend with her the more layers there seem to be that need to be peeled away so I can see who the real Celia is. She seems to be such a wounded soul and I have a desperate need to heal her. I can't explain it exactly, except that something isn't right with her. It's a constant nagging feeling that I can't shake," he confessed.

"Perhaps you should slow things down a bit, get to know her better. Maybe you are having doubts and need time to sort them out. It's perfectly normal to have doubts before one marries. I believe you are suffering from what's called cold feet, dear," she said, with a sardonic smile.

"No! I will have her," Damien fairly shouted. He roughly dragged his hands down his cheeks and sighed deeply. "Perhaps it's just cold feet like you say, but I will have her," he added more calmly.

"I think you have yourself a little too worked up. Relax a bit and just enjoy the courtship. Quit trying to find problems where there are none. Really dear, the girl seems perfectly normal to me" she said, in an attempt to settle his agitation.

"Aye, good advice" he agreed.

They sat in companionable silence a moment then Damien said "Can you host a dinner party with some of the relatives and a few of my friends so we can introduce her around?"

"That would be perfect, dear. When would you like to have it?"

"As soon as you could manage it."

"I should think I can manage a fine affair in two or three days" she beamed.

Damien wasn't prepared for it to happen so soon and it occurred to him that Sara may become an issue and the last thing he wanted was another debacle like there was at the museum.

He cleared his throat and ventured "What about Sara?"

"She won't be invited dear…oh you mean will she be a problem? No, dear I will just make sure she stays in her room," Matilda couldn't help teasing him a little. The rogue!

Damien turned red but said nothing to this, "Well then the sooner the better I should say."

"Very good, today is Tuesday, how does Thursday sound dear?"

"Thursday, it is!"

"Consider it done!"

"Thank you Aunt, you're a real peach. I don't know where I would be without you. I'll send you a list of friends to invite and of course you know the Cullen's are off limits. I should be off now. I want a chance to speak with the baron about the marriage contract before I take Celia to the park," Damien said feeling better already.

"Yes, well see that you never forget it!" she quipped with a wink and a smile.

*****

"This preliminary contract is very generous of you Lord Devonshire but perhaps we are rushing it a bit, considering the way the betrothal came about, it would hardly serve to have you forced into taking Celia just because of a fiasco in the ladies retiring room," the baron said groping for reasons to stall the signing of contracts.

The contract had Celia's name and her dowry included Sheraton Manor whereas Chelsea merely had a fortune with no property. He had to handle this delicately so as not to offend Lord Devonshire but encourage the match at the same time if Chelsea was to have a real future.

"I don't feel forced to take Celia at all sir. I am quite pleased with the outcome regardless of how it came about. I proposed to your daughter yesterday at the museum. She asked for more time to consider, of course but believe me sir, this is what I want. I in no way feel forced into anything," Damien explained.

"Aye your obvious regard for my daughter is admirable my lord and I'm not trying to discourage you. You may continue to consider yourselves betrothed with my blessing, by all means, but I would feel more comfortable waiting to sign the contracts until everyone is sure where they stand. Celia felt like she was pushed into it, you see, and she did ask you for more time. So it stands to reason that the contracts can be postponed until she has a chance to accept what has transpired," the baron insisted.

"It was my hope to be married in the next week or two by special license. I would like to avoid a large wedding and have a more private affair with close friends and family. So, I don't see the need for a lengthy engagement. I don't mean to rush but I'm quite anxious to start my life with Celia, I'm quite taken with her," Damien pressed.

The baron could see that Damien wasn't going to be put off for long with regard to the marriage and felt like his back was against the wall but he had to buy time.

"Perhaps we should leave it up to Celia to decide when the wedding should be. I can't say that I know her mind on the issue," he hedged.

"Of course she will have the final say. I don't want to force her into anything she doesn't want. I will speak to her this afternoon at the park about it. I plan to present her with the Vane betrothal ring, so we can discuss it then," Damien allowed.

"Very good, my lord. I think that is the best course of action to take. I can't see anything at all amiss with the contract. It's very generous of you to leave her marriage portion to any second son and daughters of your union and of course five thousand pounds a year for pin money is more than plenty," the baron said relieved that he didn't have to deny Lord Devonshire his daughters hand in the end.

He would have, if the marquess had persisted, however. He felt sure that Chelsea would stall as well and Damien would have to accept her wishes on the matter.

"She will need a large amount of pin money as she will eventually be a duchess and will need to have funds to accommodate her station. As for our heir, he will have Evansdale and all my other estates so it's only right that her property and fortune should go to the others," Damien said a bit defensively.

"Then, let us not continue further until you have spoken with Celia. I will have Peterson send for her, if we are concluded with our discussion," the baron said as he stood up to indicate the meeting was over.

But Damien wasn't quite finished, "Before I go, there is one thing I would like to ask you. Is there anything I should know about Celia's health?"

The baron was taken aback by the question and sputtered, "Why…uh…that is to say…my lord, Celia is in excellent health."

Damien decided to let it go at that but he was sure the baron was hiding something.

*****

"I hope you don't mind that I brought some bread crumbs to feed the pigeons at the park" Chelsea said as they made their way down the path.

"I think it's a fine idea. I'm sure they will worship at your feet in gratitude," he teased gently. Damien was pleased to see her sunny disposition was back in place.

"There's a fine bench over there under a shade tree that looks like a nice spot to set up the buffet. Of course, we might have been wise to bring along a security detail to control the mob, I hear some of these pigeons are pretty tough characters when a free lunch is in the offing," he added leading her now in that direction.

Chelsea giggled; she loved his sense of humor. "Yes, well, I'm sure I'll be quite safe with you along. I have seen your pugilistic skills," she couldn't believe she just flirted but she did. Her efforts were rewarded with a soft chuckle. "My dear Celia, I would take on great Zeus himself to protect you," he said with conviction.

"I hear his he a pretty powerful lightning bolt but I believe you can take him with your left hook," she teased with a blush and a brilliant smile.

"I will have to increase my daily exercise routine so I don't disappoint."

"You could never disappoint me Damien, never," Chelsea knew she really meant that. Damien was forever coming to her rescue like a knight in shining armor.

Damien assisted her to sit on the bench and sat down beside her. They sat in comfortable silence for several moments while she threw out her bread crumbs.

The birds started gathering around and Damien was touched by the sheer joy it seemed to bring her. She looked like Mother Nature in all her glory. The birds and all the animals of the forest were her children. Damien imagined her being a mother of a different kind…the mother of his children. After the talk with the baron, the thought was firmly fixed in his mind. He waited until she had emptied her bag of crumbs and said, "I have something for you."

He fished in his pocket and removed a small box. He opened it up and presented it to her. Inside was a ring with a large square sapphire stone surrounded by diamonds. "The Vane betrothal ring," he said with his heart in his eyes.

He took her hand in his. "It is my wish that you should wear it." He cleared his throat and added, "I know that you feel that our betrothal was brought about falsely but to me it is very real and it would please me greatly for you to accept this as a token of my promise of marriage. I will make you a fine husband, Celia. I will be true and never stray, this I swear. I will love you until the day I die and beyond. I would die the happiest of men to have had you in my life. Please say you'll wear it."

Chelsea couldn't see the ring for the tears that were welled in her eyes. She blinked and they spilled over and flowed down her cheeks. She didn't know what to say or do.

This was getting too far out of control and it was on the tip of her tongue to tell him the truth when Damien took the matter into his own hands, slowly slipping her glove off and the ring on her finger. He then placed a kiss in the center of her bare palm and it was like a bolt of lightning.

The warmth from that kiss spread from her hand into her whole body and she allowed herself to dream. She saw herself as his wife and the future that they could have. She saw their children and their grandchildren. More tears flowed down her cheeks.

"I've upset you," Damien said, in a low voice roughened with emotion.

"No, no you haven't, I'm just quite overcome," she said in a desperate attempt to soothe his hurt. "This is the sweetest thing that has ever happened to me and I'm deeply touched," she added.

She was afraid to tell him that she loved him too because she didn't feel like she had a right to, but she did, deeply. There had to be a way that they could....

Her thoughts were interrupted when Damien asked, "So you'll wear it, then?"

She threw her arms around his neck and hugged him fiercely. "I don't deserve you, but yes I'll wear it," she cried.

"You have it all backwards, you know. It is I who doesn't deserve you," he said returning her embrace. He moved his head back and gently pushed her from him so he could look into her eyes.

He put the full force of his eyes on hers and said, "Never let me hear you say that again." Then he kissed her with all his heart and soul.

He wanted to show her how much he loved her and needed her through that simple act. He nearly cried out when she started kissing him back.

She was so passionate and warm. He knew that beneath the skittish foal dwelled a woman with a grand passion for life. They were lost in the blissful moment for what seemed like an eternity when Damien slowly drifted back to reality and realized where they were.

He gently pulled away from the kiss and said, "I love you Celia."

Damien sensed that she still needed more time so he decided not to press the issue of when to be married. He was content to let things rest for another day or two. Her reaction to his giving her the ring was disturbing. Why would she cry and say she doesn't deserve him?

When she remained silent after his declaration of love he sighed deeply and said, "I should probably get you home."

*****

Dear Celia

There's something I should tell you......

Chelsea struggled to compose her letter but compose it she must. Oh, how she wished Celia was with her now. She was overwhelmed with guilt and grief. She shouldn't have allowed things to go so far with Damien.

That selfish part of her that is willing to sacrifice him was detestable. She should just come clean and tell him now but she was scared. Scared of losing him forever. She didn't even care about Nigel anymore, all she cared about was that she was hurting Damien.

She would wait to hear from Celia before she acted but she was sure that telling Damien was the only way to salvage her soul. She couldn't go on like this, she just couldn't.

Chapter Eleven

"The poor dear," Celia lamented as she read Chelsea's letter. Celia could tell by reading her letter that she was completely heartbroken.

"What's wrong sweet," Jarrett asked as he nuzzled the back of her neck. They lay naked together like a pair of spoons.

He was surprised that he could generate the strength to be aroused again after their long night of love-making and after the several times that they had already indulged this morning. Why they hadn't even left her room since the first time they made love yesterday afternoon and neither of them had any real sleep to speak of. Just a few cat naps here and there, to replenish their strength.

He marveled at her insatiable appetite and was pleased by her adventurous spirit. It allowed him to teach her many ways to make love and he looked forward to teaching her many more. It seemed like every time they touched each other, even in sleep, their bodies were drawn together in a passionate frenzy. Jarrett cupped her full breast in his hand and gently kneaded and then began to tweak the tip until he got the response he wanted.

He ran his hand down her stomach then slowly moved on to the moist hot center between her legs to test her readiness while he demonstrated what he needed with gentle prodding from behind with the evidence of his arousal.

Celia put the letter aside and allowed Jarrett to work his magic on her yet again. He entered her for a slow rhythmic joining that ended with a mutual explosive release heralded in by both of their shouts and moans of ecstasy.

"You are well and truly ruined now, Celia. I think we need to rest for awhile, you have fairly worn me out," he said as he kissed her in appreciation of their loving.

"You keep saying that then you ravish me again and again," she teased as they still lay in their spooned position.

She remembered the letter and worried that it might have become crinkled or torn and felt around the bed for it. Once she found it she picked it up and started reading it again.

"What does she say love?" Jarrett asked as his thumb lightly traced circles around her belly button while she read.

"She says to tell Jarrett to keep his hands to himself," she laughed.

"Never!" he said then sucked on her neck where it joined with her shoulder in teasing demonstration of his resolve, careful not to leave anymore marks, visible ones anyway. Her breasts were well branded by his claiming.

"Behave you rogue!" she admonished playfully. "This is serious now. Chelsea is deeply distressed and I'm worried for her. Damien gave her the Vane betrothal ring yesterday and she accepted it. It's tearing her apart that she is deceiving him. I don't know how much longer she can pull this off or even if she should," she added emotionally.

"Well now, it sounds as though things are going as I knew they would. Damien has secured her betrothal by giving her the ring. Next he will send his announcement to the Times and they will have to marry to avoid scandal. Now you and I can elope to Gretna Green. We have to, at the rate we're going, you will be with child very soon, if not already," Jarrett with enthusiasm.

"Chelsea said that Damien already sent his notice to the Times and that it would be out in today's edition. I already told you that we can't elope while Chelsea is in London. Just in case there's trouble, we need to be close by. I thought we agreed on this," Celia said a little annoyed.

Jarrett sighed deeply and said, "Of course, you're right. I just don't want you to have a seven month pregnancy after our wedding, so it needs to be soon, people will talk and I won't have you gossiped about."

"We will be living here at Sheraton, who cares what people will say, but we are off point. Chelsea is distressed and wants to end the ruse now. She is overwhelmed by guilt and despair for what she is doing to Damien. She doesn't believe he deserves to be deceived like this and she is even quite willing to give up her pursuit of Nigel to avoid hurting him further. She told me she was going to refuse to see him until she heard from me," Celia explained.

"I need some time to come up with a plan to be rid of Nigel. I have a few ideas but I need to run them by Damien and then I need time to set it up. At least three days or so, maybe a week," he mused aloud then added, "Tell Chelsea about us and that you would like to have more time with me before Damien finds out. Tell her to give up on her search for Nigel and just enjoy her time with Damien in London. Encourage her to continue the betrothal and not reveal anything until you tell her to. Tell her all will be well somehow and she and Damien can be together. Say whatever you must to stall her from telling Damien who she is."

Jarrett's mind was already hard at work coming up with a solution. Perhaps the impact of learning that Chelsea is not Celia won't be so bad if Damien never finds out that she was the child from the wood that day. He will already be so in love with Chelsea that he won't care that he was tricked by the twins and he also wouldn't care about Celia anymore, at least he hoped.

"Yes that's a good idea, we need more time, but how can you be rid of Nigel. You won't be in danger will you?" she asked.

"No, nothing like that. Just leave the details to me. It's best if you don't know anything in case there's trouble with the magistrate," he assured her.

"Trouble with the magistrate? Oh Jarrett, I don't like the sound of that at all, surely you don't plan to kill him, do you?" Celia nearly shouted her distress.

"No, I won't kill him, I promise you. There's more than one way to be rid of him and I can assure you that killing him is the last among them. Don't worry now, promise me," he urged with a hug and a kiss.

Celia forgot all her distress as they began to make passionate love again.

*****

Chelsea was completely miserable today. She stayed locked away in her room curled up on her bed hugging her pillow. She was up most of the night thinking about what she was doing to Damien and began to loathe herself. She was lost to the despair of knowing that she would lose him soon. By the time morning came she had worked herself into real heartache and depression.

She kept alternating between hating herself and wishing she could hold him in her arms. Then, she would remember that he would soon hate her and she would sob inconsolably at the loss. When Damien sent a note this morning asking if she would accompany him to the lending library this afternoon, she replied that she wasn't well. She said that she had a terrible ache of the head and would be indisposed until the morrow at the very earliest. She knew it was cowardly, but what else could she do?

She had written Celia telling her of her predicament and asked her advice. So she really must avoid Damien until she heard back from her sister. She felt sure Celia would have some sound advice and hoped that she would be able to help her with her troubled soul. She didn't even care about finding Nigel anymore.

As a matter of fact she decided to give it up entirely. She simply couldn't run the risk of Damien finding that out on top of learning that she had tricked him into believing that she was Celia. She knew that the hurt he would suffer from the switch alone would be devastating to him and she really wanted to spare him as much as possible.

What could she have done to Nigel anyway, she's not a murderer. She couldn't bear the idea of that kind of exposure so really; all that was left was to try to forget the past and try to live her life as normally as possible when she returned to Sheraton. No, the only thing that concerned her now was knowing that she was deceiving Damien and he didn't deserve it. She had to lessen the damage somehow.

She only hoped that when he did learn of the ruse he would see how much she loved him and that he would take pity on her and love her back. Of course, that was a dream that would probably never be but when one felt as low as she did, dreams are all that was left.

*****

The baron was worried about his daughter. He knew what the problem was but he couldn't say anything to her to help ease her suffering. He knew that since the betrothal, she was depressed about the deception because she never intended to fall in love with the marquess as she had.

He held the letter that just arrived, addressed to Lady Celia Sheraton written in her own hand and debated whether or not he should read it. He needed to know what the girls were up to and to what end. It wouldn't hurt to read it, he reasoned. He could always seal it back up. Chelsea would never know that he'd read it. Curiosity won out. He carefully opened the letter so as not to break the seal.

Dear Chelsea

I am sad to hear that you are suffering so and wish that I were there to comfort you. Please know that it is not all in vain as Sir Jarrett and I have come to an understanding and as soon as he can finish his current business for Bow Street, we plan to elope. Darling, I know that this is difficult for you but I need a few more days maybe even a week before Lord Devonshire is made aware of our ruse. I want to be safely wed to Sir Jarrett before he learns of it. Do not despair, dear sister as I am quite sure that Lord Devonshire's feelings for you are genuine and once he knows the truth he will still wish to go forth with the marriage. I have a good feeling about this dear, and I do believe that we will both find happiness in our efforts. Please refrain from confessing to Lord Devonshire until you hear from me. Just enjoy your time in London and put your guilty feelings aside and enjoy Lord Devonshire's attentions. I agree with you that it would be wise for you to forget about Nigel and move toward the future with the marquess. Don't worry dear; all will be well, you'll see.

Your devoted Celia

'So the girl is going to elope eh'…the baron thought with a smile. 'I knew that sly Sir Jarrett was going to win out,' he chuckled. He knew Celia must have put Chelsea up to this ridiculous farce and now he knew why.

Though he was proud of Chelsea for her bravery and her ability to overcome so many challenges he couldn't help but be angry at Celia for putting her in this situation. Chelsea was clearly distressed with feelings of guilt and he could tell that she had truly formed a deep attachment to Lord Devonshire.

When this is all over he was going to give Celia quite a dressing down, he vowed. He would have to allow this thing to run its course and hope that what Celia said was true, that the marquess would want to go forward with the wedding. What a mess!

"And who the bloody hell is Nigel?" the baron wondered aloud. Surely, she isn't referring to Lord Davenport. I thought his Christian name was Rupert, though I could be wrong.

*****

"Open the door, my lady…I have two missives for you," Jenny said exasperatedly as she continued to pound on Chelsea's door. After a long moment she could hear shuffling around in the room and then the door opened. Lord, she looked awful!

"Two missives?" Chelsea asked bleary eyed. She had made no effort to change out of her night clothes from the night before and her hair was wild and unruly. Her eyes and nose were puffy and red and she had tear- stained cheeks.

"Aye, one is from your sister, and the other from his lordship," Jenny replied, hustling through the door.

"Just look at you, you're a mess dear. What am I going to do with you?" she grumbled "Didn't the tonic I brought you help your headache at all?" Jenny ventured cautiously.

Jenny didn't believe for a single moment that Chelsea was only suffering from a headache. Heartache, more like it. Just what did that scoundrel do to her anyway? She wondered.

Chelsea took the letters out of Jenny's hand, ignoring her inquiries to her health. She immediately opened the letter from Celia and started reading. When she was through reading it, she plopped down on her bed and sighed woefully.

How was she to get through another day of this, much less another week? Well there was nothing for it accept to trudge through it. Celia and Sir Jarrett are to elope but they need more time. Well at least something good will come from this disaster. She only hoped that Celia was right and they both could find happiness somehow. Chelsea sighed again then opened the other message.

Ah… the dinner party at Aunt Matilda's is set up for tomorrow night. It's a good thing it's not going to be tonight. She would have to decline the way she looked right now.

Jenny worked wonders with hair but she couldn't perform miracles and bring the dead back to life. She smiled at that thought, imagining Jenny with a magic wand and waving it frantically at her trying desperately to revive her. Poor Jenny had a mess on her hands, alright. Chelsea read over Celia's message again and despite her better reasoning, she was mildly cheered by the prospect of another week with Damien. Now that she had given up her plan of vengeance she could devote all her time to him.

"Jenny, I think I would like to have a hot bath and I need to decide what to wear to a dinner party tomorrow night where I am to be introduced to Lord Devonshire's friends and family at his Aunt Matilda's," she said after deciding that it was time to pull herself out of her stupor.

Jenny was relieved to see her mistress improved and said cheerfully, "I'll have it taken care of right away, my lady," then turned and left the room so she could put the order in place. Chelsea missed her copper tub with hot water piped in.

It was such a chore for the servants to haul buckets and buckets of hot water up the stairs to fill a tub. It almost made her feel guilty for her penchant for cleanliness. Oh well, such is the life of a servant…sad really.

Chelsea went over to her desk and wrote her return messages and decided that tomorrow would be a new day.

*****

Damien sat at his desk in his library and tried to drink away his depression. Celia didn't want anything to do with him today and he couldn't help but feel slighted. Of course she said she was suffering from a headache but he didn't believe that.

Her reply to his invitation to the lending library today was so evasive as to make him suspect that she was lying. She had plainly said that she would really love to go when he told her of it.

She loved to read and he thought that would make a perfect outing. He didn't want to think that she was lying but he just couldn't help it. Her refusal to attend him today coupled with her actions yesterday at the park when he gave her the betrothal ring, lent to the theory that she was lying.

He tried not to be hurt when she didn't return his declaration of love. He sensed then that something was amiss. Though she accepted the ring and hugged him tenderly her refusal to return his love verbally really stung. He knew that she must feel something for him. He could feel it.

And then, there was the journey back to her home from the park. She had been very quiet and seemed in despair when she should have been elated. She tried not to show it but he noticed that she was fighting back tears.

What is it that causes her to suffer so, and it was a suffering, he could see that now. What kind of hurt had she been through that made her afraid to grab hold of the love he offered her with both hands and bask in the glory of it with him.

It was almost as if she was ashamed of herself, or that she didn't feel she deserved it. Indeed, she said she didn't deserve him, but why did she feel that way? His brooding was interrupted by a knock on the library door. "Enter!" he called out a bit too loudly.

Thompson his butler-valet entered the room carrying a missive on a silver tray. "This just came for you, my lord," he said handing the message to Damien. "Thank you, Thompson. You may be excused," he intoned trying not to sound as though he were too much in his cups, which he was.

Thompson, the consummate professional didn't give any indication that he knew his master was drunk. He left the room and closed the door with his usual style and grace.

Damien opened his note from Celia and read it two or three times. She said she was much improved as Jenny's tonic put her to back to rights and she would love to attend the dinner party tomorrow. Damien was pleased though still perplexed.

Just when he thought he is on the verge of figuring her out, she came back with her sunny disposition and confused him anew. If this going back and forth with her continued, he feared that she may turn him into a pathetic sot. He looked at his empty glass, got up and staggered to bed to sleep it off.

*****

"Excuse me my lord, I don't mean to question your good judgment but should you really allow Lady Celia to go to the dinner party without a chaperone? There is her reputation to consider!" Jenny admonished with her most stern expression.

She didn't like this situation at all. The very idea that the baron would allow his daughter to parade around London with only Lord Devonshire in attendance was shocking. Of course, he didn't know that she was really Chelsea. He probably didn't see any real harm since they were just going to a dinner party at Lord Devonshire's aunts, where the duchess herself would serve as chaperone.

Still there was the carriage ride with a scoundrel to consider. Clearly, the baron was determined in the match between the marquess and his daughter and saw nothing wrong with allowing them to be alone together now that they were 'officially' betrothed.

True, a betrothal was considered as good as a marriage. Courtship restrictions could be eased up without causing scandal…oh, how she wished she could tell him what was really going on but she knew she couldn't betray her mistress like that. No, she could only voice her concerns and hope the baron would take heed.

"I understand your concerns, Jenny but I see nothing wrong with allowing Lord Devonshire to accompany her alone. It's only a short distance to Mayfair. There would hardly be enough time for the marquess to do anything untoward and they are betrothed after all. Put your mind at ease and enjoy your night off, my dear," the baron said with finality.

Jenny realizing that she was being dismissed, stiffened her back and took her leave of the baron and marched up to Chelsea's room in a huff.

The baron watched her go and smiled ruefully. What Jenny doesn't know won't hurt her. He needed to give the marquess every opportunity to fall madly in love with Chelsea so that he would go through with the marriage when the truth came to light.

Sure, it was unscrupulous of him to allow the marquess the opportunity to seduce Chelsea but desperate times call for desperate measures. He didn't believe that Lord Devonshire would force himself on Chelsea but if he were to bed her before they wed then he would surely feel compelled to go through with it regardless of learning the truth.

Yes, he simply must allow every opportunity for the couple to solidify their relationship…at all cost. If the marquess were to bed Chelsea, then he as her father would be in position to demand satisfaction for his daughter's honor, namely marriage.

The only logical thing for Damien to do in such a situation would be to marry Chelsea. It would be unconscionable for a gentleman such as him to refuse to honor a lady of Chelsea's breeding, if he had taken her innocence. Considering what Celia was planning to do, if the marquess didn't fall in love with Chelsea beforehand, he would be outraged and humiliated by the twin's duplicity.

The baron made a big frustrated heaving sigh. It doesn't make a man proud to know that he is putting his daughter in such a position but it must be done to secure Chelsea's future.

*****

"Oh Jenny, really, you mustn't carry on so. I am just going as far as Mayfair where there will be dozens of other people in attendance. There is no harm in going without a chaperone to such an event. I'm sure other unmarried ladies will be there unattended, as well. If Papa doesn't see a problem with it, why must you be so distressed?" Chelsea asked, putting on her earbobs.

"Your Papa doesn't know what I know or he would see a problem with it," Jenny grumbled.

Chelsea finished putting on her earbobs and looked herself over in her cheval glass mirror. Satisfied that she was presentable, she turned to her maid and gave her a hug and said, "Please don't worry, dear. I will be fine in Lord Devonshire's capable hands. He is quite the gentleman and has never done anything inappropriate with me," she assured her.

Jenny wasn't convinced "It's his capable hands I'm worried about," she quipped. "You better see to it that he keeps them to himself," she added.

Chelsea giggled. Poor Jenny was beside herself.

"Lord Devonshire will be here any moment now, how do I look?" she asked striking a pose.

"You look beautiful Chelsea love. There is hardly any sign of yesterdays…uh…headache,"came Jenny's halted reply.

"Good, then I shall go downstairs to the drawing room to await the marquess," Chelsea said, with one last look at her image.

Chapter Twelve

Damien couldn't take his eyes off Celia in the carriage. Tonight she wore a lavender gown with a flirtatious but not too naughty bodice that inflamed his senses.

She wore her hair artfully braided and twisted to form an artful knot on top that was woven with pearls. An intentional stray strand of ringlets hung loose at her forehead lightly kissing the left side of her face and neck when she moved. It was designed to draw the eye to her lovely face and seemed to invite him to twist it about his finger. She was perfection!

When Damien assisted her in the carriage, he gave the covert command to his driver to meander on the way to his aunts so he could spend some time alone with Celia before they arrived. They had plenty of time to dally a bit so he wasn't worried. An extra ten minute extension of the journey would hardly be observed by anyone and it was just the right amount of time to steal a kiss, or two.

He was surprised that the baron declined the invitation due to a stomach ailment and that the hardnosed Jenny was left behind but he wasn't one to look a gift horse in the mouth. He moved from his bench and joined her on hers. "I have to kiss you," he stated before taking her by the shoulders and draping her across his lap.

She gasped, but didn't resist when he joined their mouths in a searing kiss. She smelled lightly of oranges and spice and he was aroused by her essence as he plundered her mouth with his own. She must have been eager for the contact too because she started running her hand through his hair and massaging his head and moaning in ecstasy as he ravished her lips.

Damien was so elated by her passion that he started a slow sensual caress at her shoulder then moved ever so slowly toward her breast. Once there he rested his hand and when she didn't protest he allowed himself the pleasure of kneading and squeezing it gently.

After a moment he was unable to stand the material that separated her soft skin from his hand any longer so he slipped his hand beneath her bodice and nearly cried out at the warmth and fullness it contained.

She was all woman and it pleased him immensely that she wasn't wearing stays to encumber his exploration. The tip of her breast was erect begging for his attention so he tugged and pinched it as he deepened the kiss and still she didn't protest.

Her hand began an exploration of its own as she caressed his jaw and neck. Emboldened now, she moved her hand down his chest, then down his torso and came to rest on to his thigh, just inches from his manhood.

He froze as he realized what could happen if he allowed her to go further so he reluctantly pulled out of the kiss. With a groan he gently set her back in place beside him on the carriage bench.

He cleared his throat and ran his hand through his hair, "Forgive me, that was not well done of me" he managed to choke out as he became aware of his uncomfortable predicament.

His arousal was painful now as it strained against his breeches and it seemed to have a mind of its own as it ignored his inward admonishments to stand down.

"There is nothing to forgive. I enjoyed your kiss Damien," she said sweetly as she made sure her hair was still in place.

"You don't understand; I shouldn't have taken such liberties. Another minute longer and I would have taken you here in the carriage like you were a....forgive me," he said ashamed.

Chelsea realized the implication and she too was ashamed. She would have let him take her here in the carriage like some light skirt. She had been so immersed in the wonder of his embrace that it never occurred to her that she was in danger of being compromised.

But it didn't feel like danger, it was heaven. She composed herself as best she could and hoped that he didn't think poorly of her now.

She was relieved moments later when he said, "I love you, Celia and I don't want to do anything to dishonor you."

She didn't feel dishonored at all and didn't understand why she should. She loved him too and it felt natural to be able to express it. That in itself was a complete marvel to her.

His next words chilled her though, "If I can't make love to you soon, I think I shall go mad. That's why we need to marry as soon as possible."

Damien noticed her withdrawal when he pushed for a quick marriage. Blast and damnation, when will she relax about the idea?

"I'm sorry I'm rushing you, but it's the only way. I must have you, Celia, and soon," he said allowing his tension to show. His words hung in the air and he felt as though she would demand to be taken home because she looked so terribly distressed.

After a few moments of silence she said in a barely audible tone, "I must have you too, Damien."

Stunned by her admission and not sure he heard her correctly he took her hand in his and brought them both to his heart, "Do you mean it?" he couldn't help but ask.

"Yes, it's true, I know now that I'm in love with you but I'm scared Damien. You must give me more time to adjust to the idea of being married. It's not something I can rush into. I know that the reason I'm here in London is to find a husband but it's more Papa's idea than mine. Please be patient with me, I beg you," she implored.

Chelsea hadn't meant to say what she said before but since the words were out she felt she had to explain. She did want him…in the most desperate way but she couldn't commit to marriage until everything was settled with Jarrett and Celia and the truth was finally known.

Damien's heart was soaring; he couldn't believe that she loved him, too. Now the only barrier is this cursed irrational fear of hers. Well, there was nothing for it, he would have to let her set the pace, he decided.

"I have a special license so we can be married any time you're ready. I just hope you will have mercy on me and not make me wait too long but have no fear I will wait for you Celia," he promised and sealed it with a kiss.

He tapped on the roof of the carriage and within minutes they arrived at Aunt Matilda's mansion.

Chelsea was depressed again but what could she do. If only she could come clean and tell him before any more time passed. She hoped that Celia and Jarrett eloped quickly because she was ready for this farce to be over so she could confess to Damien.

He deserved to know who he was in love with and who was in love with him.

*****

There were twenty seven people in attendance for the dinner party. Chelsea clung to Damien's arm as he led her around the large drawing room and introduced her to his family and friends. She was relieved that there was no sign of the dreaded Nigel as she wanted nothing to mar the evening.

She and Damien were in love with each other and she wanted to relish the feeling as long as possible. Sure she was allowing herself to dream but she didn't care right now.

Damien's family were all fine looking people with happy dispositions and several of the men suffered from a naughty wit. She liked them though and laughed at their antics as they teased her about taking on a rogue like Damien.

Some of the unattached gentlemen teased Damien about taking her away from him and she noticed that he didn't seem to think that was so funny. One person stuck out in particular as a very good friend of Damien's, Henry Firth, the Earl of Granville.

He was a young man who had been wounded in the conflict with Napoleon. He suffered a severe limp from the injury but he didn't let his deficiency get him down. In fact, he was one of the most boisterous fellows in attendance and a shameless flirt. But it was all in good fun and it was easy to see the camaraderie between them.

Damien explained that he too was a second son and never thought to inherit his title so he bought a commission in the war. His brother was killed in a riding accident while Henry was recuperating from his injuries so instead of returning to the campaign he was forced to return home and assume his family duty.

"I say Lady Celia, why don't you forget about Damien and run away with me to the continent?" Lord Granville teased with a wink.

"Find your own fiancé' Henry," Damien smiled. "This one's mine and I plan on keeping her," he added.

"Tis a pity, I do believe she adores me already, she just has to be made to see that I'm the better man," Lord Granville said, wagging his eyebrows in a comical manner.

"Gentlemen please, you are going to frighten the poor dear," Matilda playfully admonished.

Chelsea felt herself blush but smiled and said, "It's alright Your Grace, Lord Granville and I are dear friends already," she said with a smile.

"Damien dear, you better keep an eye on this shameless rake," Matilda said swatting Lord Granville on the stomach with her fan. And so the playful banter continued for another moment or so before Damien moved her on to the next group of people.

There were several lovely female relatives in attendance as well as wives of friends and they all seemed pleased by Damien's betrothal to her. Aunt Matilda must have sung her praises because they seemed to like her before she even entered the room. What a nice family, she mused.

Whenever anyone asked when the wedding was to be held Damien said soon, or that they were still trying to decide. She tried not to feel guilty knowing that they might not actually wed.

What will all these fine people think of her when the truth is known? She simply couldn't think about that now. One day at a time, she counseled herself.

Shortly after all the introductions were made, dinner was announced. The meal was wonderful with roast duck in an orange sauce, potatoes with butter and parsley, glazed carrots and asparagus with a crème sauce, with chocolate tart for dessert. Red wine was served with the meal, or cool lemonade if that were your preference. Matilda was quite pleased with her French chef and vowed vengeance on anyone who tried to lure him away from her.

Later when it came time for the drawing room entertainments, several of the ladies played the pianoforte but Chelsea declined explaining that she never learned to play. That was alright with Damien, as he had other plans.

*****

He escorted her out into the garden that was well lit with Chinese lanterns. They walked arm in arm down a path that led to a gazebo. Damien assisted her in and once inside he immediately started ravishing her lips as if he were a starving man and only she could feed his hunger.

She didn't resist. How could she as he was far more amorous now than he was in the carriage. He seemed to forget his earlier behavior and subsequent need for apology as his hands began to rove over her body.

He walked her backwards as he continued his ravishment and gently urged her to lay down on a cushioned bench. He covered her with his body as he deepened his kiss.

No words seemed necessary as they devoured one another. He tugged her bodice and chemise down to expose her breasts to his view and after gazing at her generous bounty he said with awe, "Beautiful," and then he began to suckle her, first one breast then the other and back and forth as if he couldn't decide which one he preferred best.

He ran his tongue between her breasts then began to lavish kisses on the mounds of flesh offered to him. She moaned her appreciation and gave herself over to the moment and began caressing the back of his head. She held his head in place at her breast when he gently pulled at her nipple with his teeth and then licked it in apology.

She became aware of a cool draft on her legs as Damien lifted her skirts and began to stroke her thigh as he continued to worship at her breasts. She whimpered in distress but he deepened the kiss and she responded in kind forgetting that his hand was perilously close to her private center that was aching for his touch but afraid of it too.

She shouldn't be allowing this. It was too much too soon and her heart was racing as the familiar fear started to make its presence felt. She pushed his hand away and pulled out of the kiss. "We mustn't do this," she panted.

Damien looked into her eyes for a suspended moment as if trying to soothe her with the warmth of his gaze.

"We are to be married Celia and I only want to show you how good it will be between us. You are safe with me, I swear," he said as he cupped her woman's mound.

She squirmed and shoved at his hand, "Please, this is wrong," she implored.

She knew he wouldn't hurt her but her mind wasn't ready to accept this. She felt exposed, vulnerable and…conflicted. Part of her wanted to retreat and hide from the moment and the other part of her wanted to reach out and grab hold and take what she wanted. She did want Damien, she loved him and wanted to spend the rest of her life with him but she was so afraid.

What Damien was doing was pleasurable and terrifying at the same time and it conjured up memories that she wanted to forget. The last time a man had touched her body was in an act of violence and it left her damaged inside. She didn't know for sure if she could ever accept a man to have the kind of control over her that the act would bring.

"How can it be wrong when we love one another?" Damien said. He didn't wait for her answer and he moved in and took possession of her lips again. He kiss was so warm and tender with the ability to make her forget reason. She briefly succumbed to the pleasure and didn't realize that he had started to caress her again there on her woman's mound.

probe into her she jerked and cried out in distress. Damien must have confused her outburst for a sign of pleasure because he continued with his sensual assault. She pulled away from his kiss, "Please, Dami…" her thought was lost when he reclaimed her lips in a mind-numbing kiss and she found herself being swept away on a tide of arousal.

As if he sensed her need he slowly continued to move his hand to the warm moist entrance and began a slow rotating massage on the sensitive spot there. It wasn't so bad at first but then she was nearly undone when she felt an almost painful jolt of sensation when he pressed it just so. She bucked her hips in protest.

"Let me bring you pleasure, Celia" Damien breathed as he continued his ministrations.

She relaxed at the sound of his voice and the promise that it made. He slipped a finger into her passage again and began a slow rhythmic motion and simulated the motion with his tongue in her mouth. Chelsea's hips began to squirm and thrust up as he continued his gentle assault.

She could feel herself on the verge of something but she knew not what. It was an almost irritating feeling that she continued to reach toward for some kind of conclusion. She felt that there must be something at the end of this irritation but she didn't have any idea what it was or how she was supposed to get there.

Damien knew the way and he continued with determination to take her there until she was on the verge of a sensation that felt as though she were about to fracture in a million pieces when they heard a voice.

"Damien!" the intruder called out. "Are you out there, old boy?" the voice persisted. Damien froze at first then jumped back from her and started righting her clothing.

He softly kissed her lips as he tugged her bodice back up and promised "We will finish this later" then he kissed her again.

They stood up and hurriedly smoothed their clothing and hair and looked each other over to see if they were presentable and they couldn't help it they laughed quietly. He drew her close in an embrace, "I won't apologize this time Celia because I know it will happen again and it will give you great pleasure when it does. Trust me, you were so close to release that it nearly killed me to have to stop," he whispered in her ear.

The promise made her shiver but it wasn't a bad shiver that always comes when…..Chelsea stood there a moment as she thought that over. There was no real reason to be afraid, she realized. He hadn't hurt her or even tried, he only wanted to bring her pleasure.

They heard other voices now moving closer so reluctantly they left the gazebo and started back toward the mansion. Matilda must have observed their prolonged absence and sent someone to retrieve them in an effort to guard her virtue.

She was glad that the gentleman had the good sense to call out from a distance rather than sneak up quietly. It could have been an embarrassing situation.

*****

When they returned to the party everyone was preparing to play cards. Tables were set up and partners were formed to play whist. Chelsea didn't know how to play so Matilda volunteered to sit out with her so she wouldn't feel out of place.

Chelsea couldn't take her mind off the scene in the gazebo and her reaction to Damien's seduction. It gave her great hope that she had finally conquered her fear of men but she suspected that it had to be him.

She simply couldn't imagine doing that with anyone else. She decided that it wouldn't be so bad to make love with Damien and felt herself blush at the prospect.

"Dear, you were a smashing success this evening," Matilda said breaking into her wayward thoughts.

"You have a lovely family, your grace and I do thank you for allowing the use of your home for the occasion," Chelsea said.

"Dear, please call me Matilda. We are to be family you now, and Damien is like the son I never had. So we shall see much of each other in the future and I do so hate formalities"

"Thank you Matilda. Damien speaks highly of you. I can tell that you are very close." Chelsea liked Matilda even if this betrothal debacle was her doing. She couldn't help but admire the woman and her feisty personality.

"I do hope that you are adjusting to your impromptu betrothal. I realize that you weren't inclined for an immediate engagement but that wretched tart provoked me so and I simply couldn't let it stand. I had to put her in her place and it was the first thing that came to mind," Matilda explained.

"I enjoyed it as much as you did. The look on her face will stay with me forever and I can draw upon the memory whenever I find myself in need of a good tickling of the funny bone," Chelsea assured her, hoping that she didn't notice that she didn't comment on the betrothal itself.

"It was rather comical wasn't it? I dare say, she'll never attract a man with those kind of expressions pasted on her face. She isn't very pretty to begin with and she has a loathsome personality," Matilda said. "But tell me dear, are you terribly upset about the outcome?" she persisted.

"No, not terribly, only a little apprehensive. I hardly know Damien after all and I would have preferred more time for a proper courtship," she allowed.

"It doesn't always take a proper courtship to know when one is in love and I do believe that the two of you are. Am I mistaken?" Matilda continued to probe.

Chelsea grew quiet and reflected on her feelings. Matilda must have noticed her discomfort because she placed her hand over Chelsea's to stop her from wringing them, "Forgive my meddling dear, everything will work out fine between you and Damien. I have a good feeling about it. I have never seen him so content."

Chelsea looked at Matilda with hopeful eyes and said, "Do you really think he is content?"

"Of course dear, just look at him. He can hardly pay attention to his cards because he can't stop looking at you with wanting in his eyes," Matilda said indicating with a flick of her head in Damien's direction. "He will make a good husband and I dare say a wonderful lover," she added.

Chelsea's head snapped back toward Matilda as she was shocked by what she had said. "Please, someone could hear you," she pleaded.

Matilda chuckled at Chelsea's response but made no further comment for which Chelsea was grateful. She looked back over at Damien and he was looking at her with a wanting in his eyes and it made her feel warm all over her body.

It never ceased to amaze her, the effect he had with the power of his gaze. His eyes were so soulful and expressive and he seemed to be trying to see into her heart and mind. She shivered and turned away so she could compose herself.

He made her wish for things she had no right to. She wished she could run away somewhere with him. Somewhere safe from the rest of the world, where no one could touch them. Where they would be free to be lovers and live the rest of their lives in each other's embrace.

If only, she were free to have him…she would have him, she promised herself. Someway, somehow when Jarrett and Celia have married, she would have Damien.

It was strange how much her life has changed in the last week. She never imagined herself here, now with the man of her dreams. A week ago she was alone in her attic reading her books in the quiet safety of Sheraton with no plans for a future. Now she was in love and betrothed sitting at a dinner party with strangers and allowing herself to behave wantonly. It boggles the mind.

Damien didn't think it would be wise to make another attempt at seduction on the ride home so he tried to keep his mind off of her sweet responses to him in the gazebo. She had been primed and on the verge of release just when his cousin Jason came out to the garden, no doubt sent by Aunt Matilda.

The meddlesome woman probably knew he had her splayed out on her back and thought to protect her from ruin. Well, he should be grateful really as he would have been hard pressed not to take it further than he had. He needed to avoid amorous encounters where there was likelihood that they would be caught.

It would be disastrous if she were to be compromised in such a way, even when his intentions were to marry her. He better stick to harmless settings and keep his hands to himself or she would not come to the marriage bed a virgin. Not that that was essential but it was customary to wait to consummate the union until the wedding night.

"How would you like to go shopping tomorrow? We could go to a book store or we could even go to the lending library as we had discussed before. I'm sure you are in need of some good reading material while you are here in London," he suggested.

"I should think that would be lovely Damien," Celia said with a blush. Clearly she had been thinking along the same lines as he. He adored the way her skin turned rosy when she was flustered. It was all he could do to stay on his side of the carriage.

He cleared his throat to clear away his naughty thoughts and said, "Very good then. I will come round in the morning at ten and we shall make a day of it. Perhaps we can have lunch and an ice while we're out."

"I shall be waiting with bells on until the hour," she said.

Good, maybe that hardnosed Jenny would accompany her to keep her safe from his lecherous yearnings. With that settled he relaxed as they were nearing her home and leaned forward to take her hand in his and brought it to his lips.

"Every moment that we are apart is torture to my soul, fair Celia," he said as he kissed her gloved hand then held it awhile longer and rubbed her palm with his thumb as he so often did.

He knew that the action put her at ease and he enjoyed seeing her so. He would like to be able to massage other places on her as well but alas, that would have to wait as they had arrived. He assisted her out of the carriage and placed a respectful kiss upon her cheek and bid her adieu.

Chapter Thirteen

It was a lovely Friday morning in London. The city was bustling with activity and the streets were full of Londoners on their way to various appointments and destinations. The shopkeepers were advertising their wares and food vendors were hawking their meat pies and sausages. The streets were alive and the aromas from the eateries and bakeries were mouth watering as they casually made their way along.

Chelsea was delighted by the selection of books she found at the lending library and couldn't wait to get home and delve into them. She checked out three gothic novels by Ann Radcliffe, The Castles of Athlin and Dunbayne, The Romance of the Forest and The Mysteries of Udolpho. She just adored reading gothic romance.

She also got A Vindication of the Rights of Woman by Mary Wollstonecraft in which the authoress holds a feminist opinion and argues that women are not naturally inferior to men but only appear so because they are kept uneducated, a very heady issue even now nearly twenty years after its publication.

Society preferred to keep women ignorant and justified it by implying that education makes them unattractive and labeled them with derogatory terms such as bluestocking as if to imply that being labeled so means that they were frumpy and undesirable, spinsterish even. It always irritated Chelsea, even when she was a young girl that men had all the advantages in society and women had nothing but what men allowed them.

"I see you are an enlightened woman," Damien murmured as he looked over her choices. After a moment of perusal he said, "Women are their own worst enemy when it comes to the perpetuation of societies dictates with regard to their education," he added conversationally.

"How do you mean?"

"I'm sure you noticed how silly they all behaved at the various balls you've attended. They're all cookie cut-outs of the same ignorant creature. No originality and none of them, with the exception of you of course, appear to have their own brain. It's almost as though they function off of one central unit. There must be a queen dimwit somewhere keeping them all enslaved," he finished with a chuckle.

"I see your point and agree. I felt as though I were from another planet by comparison. But what else can women do if they want to find a husband? They have to follow the rules of society or else be ostracized and forced into spinsterhood," she argued.

"Believe it or not, there are many more men like me out there that prefer individuality, that's why so many men prefer to remain bachelors. There's nothing exciting about the marriage mart and when I saw you I knew I had to act quickly or someone else would scoop you up. Not to put too fine a point on the matter but most men maintain mistresses and I can assure you that those women look nothing like the simpering misses you see at Almack's," he said before he realized that was not a very good point to make. But he was so relaxed in her presence that he lost all reason and the words just flowed out, naturally without effort.

"D-Do you keep a mistress?" she shyly asked.

Now it was time to pay for his stupidity…he sighed then said, "Most men of my station do and I have always kept one but my most recent mistress and I parted ways about a month ago and since I met you I haven't thought of her once. You are all I will ever need in a woman, Celia."

She was quiet for a moment reflecting on his words. She was glad for his honesty and she was pleased to know that there wasn't a mistress waiting in a love nest somewhere. It would be disappointing to know that when he left her, he went to another woman for carnal relations.

"I'm glad that you feel that way and I appreciate your honesty," she said meaningfully.

He was relieved that she didn't ask him for details. The last thing he wanted to do was discuss Lila with her.

"I suppose having a mistress is safer than going to brothels where disease runs rampant," she continued the uncomfortable topic.

"It impresses me that you know of such things and feel free to discuss them. It's true that brothels are cesspools and it would be a wonderful world if there weren't a need for them. If more men could find happiness with their chosen wives perhaps there wouldn't be a need. But because society tells women that they can't enjoy sex lest they be somehow lacking in moral character, they become cold and frigid and a man such as myself prefers an active, willing even adventurous partner in his bed. Another fine illustration of what I meant when I said women are their own worst enemy," he said marveling at the ease in which they were discussing such a delicate issue.

Chelsea considered his words and couldn't help but be reminded of last night in the gazebo. She shivered and felt warm and tingly all over.

"Perhaps we should have lunch, I'm starved," she said indicating an end to the subject. She agreed with his assessment and wished more people were as open minded as he for it would benefit society greatly.

Damien was truly impressed with her intelligence and decided that it was good that they had this discussion because he wanted to make sure she understood what would be expected of her once they were married.

Women were rarely told what was expected of them other than that they should simply lay there and assume their duty with as little enjoyment in the act as possible. He wanted much more from his mate than that and conversations such as the one they just had were a good way to pave the road to his desires.

"Would you care for a meat pie? We could eat that as we walk along or we could go and have a sit down meal at one of the eateries"

"Oh I much prefer to walk, it's been quite enjoyable and it's much easier to converse without open ears listening in," Chelsea frankly stated.

"True, we wouldn't want to set London on its ear with such scandalous discussion. There could be mass panic and people could be crushed to death in the resulting pandemonium," he teased with an expression of mock horror on his face.

Chelsea giggled as he led the way over to a vendor selling meat pies and other pastries. He got them both a pie and they continued their walk in easy companionship as they ate.

Then, without warning, she saw him on the opposite side of the street walking past at a brisk pace. Nigel! She froze for a suspended moment, heart pounding in her chest as she realized what she was seeing. He rounded a corner and disappeared. After an indecisive minute she dropped her pie and gave chase.

Damien wasn't aware of her sudden departure as he had heartily popped the last bite of his meat pie into his mouth and eagerly started thumbing through "A Vindication". He had become distracted by a particularly interesting turn of phrase.

By the time he looked up and realized that Celia was no longer standing beside him she had already dashed away and was now across the street a couple of blocks up and was about to round a corner, obviously in pursuit of someone or something that he couldn't see. He called out to her to stop but she couldn't hear him or ignored him, he wasn't sure which, so he quickly bundled up the books and went after her.

Chelsea watched breathless as Nigel entered a carriage further up the road and was whisked away. She was stunned to find him now after deciding to give up hope of locating him. She was sure it was him; he hadn't changed a bit in all these years.

He still looked just as menacing as he did when she was a helpless child. Her body was pumping with adrenaline now and her hearing was drowned out by the sound of her pumping heart as it rushed the blood through her veins.

She looked around frantically for a hack to rent but saw none. She started pacing back and forth trying to figure out what to do next and didn't hear Damien when he approached and laid his hand on her shoulder.

She shrieked, then jerked and twirled away from him as if he were the very devil. "Don't touch me!" she shouted and continued her pacing.

Damien watched helpless as she paced back and forth like a trapped animal and tried to understand her low mutterings but couldn't make them out. She had a wild look in her eyes as if she weren't in touch with reality and her movements were jerky and shaky as she moved about.

He had no idea what she had seen to cause such a response but whatever it was, disturbed her immensely. He looked around the street trying to get an indication of her distress but saw nothing out of the ordinary. He wasn't sure how to proceed so he just watched her, afraid that she wasn't aware of her surroundings and it was almost as if she hadn't recognized him.

He walked back to the corner and signaled for his driver to come over and pick them up. He needed to get her off the street and try to calm her down.

"Celia…Celia…Celia!" she didn't seem to hear him calling her name. He cautiously walked toward her and placed himself in her path so she was forced to stop. "Celia! What's happening to you? How can I help?" he ventured when she stopped.

She didn't see him as she looked right through him with her eyes wild and bright and unfocused. He gently took hold of her arms just below her shoulders and gave her a light shake.

"Celia, it's me, Damien," he told her speaking gently so as not to disturb her further. She started blinking her eyes and they seemed to focus then. She looked at him bewilderedly and pulled out of his hold.

"Celia what just happened, tell me!" he asked in desperate concern. Though she didn't answer him he sensed that she was finally with him in the here and now.

"Come, let us get you off the street and into the carriage," he said as he reached for her again.

This time she didn't pull away and allowed herself to be lead to the carriage and placed inside. Damien quietly gave instructions to his driver to go to his townhouse but to go to the back alley entrance.

He wanted to capitalize on this opportunity to find out who the real Celia was. He thought if he could get her to his home and give her a brandy, she might relax and open up.

He had to be mindful of her reputation so he thought it would be prudent to go in through the back door so as not to be observed by his neighbors. With the instructions given he climbed inside the carriage and gave the command on the roof to proceed.

*****

The short carriage ride to Damien's townhouse in Grosvenor Square was made in silence. He couldn't fathom what had occurred to cause Celia to behave in such a manner. He was truly concerned now, that she might be mad. He hoped not as that could bode ill for their future together and the idea that their future was being threatened was more than he could abide.

He hoped that once he got her inside his town house he could begin to peel away the layers that make up her being. What would he do if she were mad? He asked himself. That, he honestly didn't know. He supposed it depended on the nature and severity of it.

If she was stark raving mad, then there was no way that they could have a future. But if she only suffered from temporary episodes such as those that he witnessed today and the one from the night on the terrace, then he felt fairly certain that it could be dealt with.

He was heartsick by what he saw and knew that he must proceed cautiously with her or he could lose her forever. He looked at her as she sat quietly in the carriage and wondered what she must be thinking. She seemed subdued now but he sensed her fear.

The carriage arrived at his townhouse and he escorted her inside. He took her up the stairs and into his private chambers and sat her down in one of the chairs at a table there. He walked over to the door and closed and locked it and tucked the key away in his pocket.

He then walked over to the sideboard and poured her a brandy. He brought the remainder of the bottle with him to the table. He placed the glass down in front of her and took the chair opposite her at the table. "Drink!" he mildly commanded her.

Her hand shakily picked up the brandy and she sipped it. When she made a face of distaste he said, "Drink it down quickly so it will relax you."

She did as she was told and coughed and sputtered but remained otherwise silent. He poured her another and said, "You can sip this one."

She made a face at it but then sipped it. She cleared her throat and he could see the tension releasing in her shoulders.

"Now, tell me what happened out there Celia," he said as calmly as he could. He noticed that she hadn't once made eye contact with him and that worried him.

"I'm not sure what you mean," came her soft reply as she stared at her glass.

"Please, don't try to be evasive. We both know what I witnessed," he said firmly

She hesitated a moment then sighed before saying, "I thought I saw someone I knew and gave chase but I lost them. I was probably mistaken anyway as I don't know anyone in London."

Damien took her words into consideration and realized that she carefully avoided saying whether this 'someone' was a man or a woman.

"Was it a man?" he asked cautiously.

Her head snapped up and she looked at him with eyes wide with trepidation and a look on her face that begged him to drop the matter, but he couldn't do that now.

"It was a man, wasn't it?" he ventured.

She nodded her head that it was but said nothing and once again studied her glass of brandy.

Damien wasn't sure that he should ask but he knew it was now or never to get the information he needed, "Was he the man who hurt you, Celia?" he asked with a quiet tenderness.

Startled by the question, her body jerked upwards and she knocked over her brandy. In her clumsy flight from the table, she bumped into her chair, causing it to fall over before she sputtered her denial, "I-I d-don't know w-what you could mean by that," she managed to articulate.

Damien knew that she did. "Celia I can't help but feel that something terrible has happened to you in your past to make you so afraid. I want to help you but I can't if you don't tell me about it," he pleaded.

"I'm fine!" came her emphatic reply. She stood, with as much composure as she could produce.

"Celia if something has happened to you that was beyond your control, I won't hold it against you, how could I when I love you?" he asked trying to assure her.

"I'm fine!" came the same reply, only this time, with anger.

Damien took a deep breath and released it slowly. 'How to proceed?' he wondered. She was agitated and clearly wanted an end to the discussion without being forced to reveal her secrets.

He got up from the table and walked toward her where she still stood. He tried to embrace her but she backed away from him and said, "Don't!"

"Please, I need to hold you," he implored her. He made a move toward her again and she went rigid but didn't pull away.

He wrapped his arms around her and held her close but she was like holding a block of ice. She was cold and hard and wouldn't yield to the embrace. He held on anyway, trying to warm her.

He started caressing her back in slow soothing strokes and he could feel her body ripple with distress. She finally had all she could stand of the contact and shoved away from him. He didn't follow.

"I'm fine!" she said again. "Where are we?" she asked looking around the room for the first time.

"My town house."

"Why have you brought me here?" she asked with a tone of annoyance.

This was not the Celia he knew. This Celia was cold and hard and angry toward him. His heart was aching and he longed to hold her and kiss away her demons.

He knew in his heart now that she was most likely raped at some point in her life but he didn't care about that except that he knew that she suffered from it still.

It had no bearing on his feelings for her. He wasn't so shallow as to expect a virgin as his due. In fact, he found the idea of initiating them intimidating.

He had never been with one but from what he has been told it was an uncomfortable business deflowering them. He just needed to make her feel more comfortable so she would tell him what happened so he can help her deal with it. It now stood in the way of their happiness and he couldn't allow that.

He was convinced that if she were mad from the experience, only extreme stress or confrontations in setting similar to her trauma would set her off. So, how to proceed?

"I brought you here so we could have privacy and you needed the brandy to soothe your nerves."

She drew her shoulders back and tilted her chin up and said, "My nerves are fine, thank you. I shall like to go home now, if you please."

"Celia, please don't shut me out. I can help you but only if you tell me about it," he said as he started moving toward her again. He tried again to embrace her but she took a step back and shook her head.

"I tell you, I'm fine! Why do you persist?" she shouted.

"If you are fine, then allow me to hold you and kiss you," he hedged as he reached for her again.

She didn't move away but stood stone still as he took her in his arms. He moved his head toward her so he could kiss her and she closed her eyes tight just before he would have placed his lips upon hers.

He paused a moment to consider whether or not it was worth it if was going to cause her further distress but he had to re-establish their bond. He felt that it was vital to do so.

He forged ahead with a gentle kiss and she responded with a tight lipped mouth. He persisted until she opened for him and he moved his tongue inside her mouth and deepened his kiss.

After a moment she made a whimpering sound and pulled out of the kiss. She turned her head away but didn't remove herself from his embrace. She was shaking and trembling so that he began to massage her back again. It seemed to help as the tension started to drain away by his ministrations.

Encouraged, he took her by her chin and brought her face back to face him so he could look into her eyes. They were full of tears and her bottom lip was quivering. He was devastated to see her this way and couldn't help himself, he kissed her again. She kissed him back this time with a trembling body and fevered lips.

They began to caress each other frantically and he eventually moved his hand inside her bodice and gently kneaded her right breast. That was a mistake.

She jerked away from him again and said, "You must stop this. Take me home this instant!"

Frustrated, Damien cursed, "Damnation woman! Don't do this...don't shut me out!"

"Take me home now, I say," she demanded.

"You are the most insufferable creature I have....I didn't mean that," he pleaded as she twirled away and was stomping her way to the door.

"Unlock this door!" she demanded after seeing that she was locked in.

"Please don't leave yet Celia! I didn't mean what I said," he cried.

"Yes you did and I would not have you suffer my presence a moment longer, now unlock this door," she shouted.

Damien wouldn't let things stand as they were so he put himself between her and the door and faced her. He grabbed her by the shoulders and kissed her roughly. She struggled and kicked him in the shin causing him to release her, limping and cursing.

He rubbed his shin for a moment and knew that he would have an ugly bruise so angrily he sighed and said, "Fine, if you want to go, then go, damn you. I'll have my driver take you home," then he took the key out of his pocket, unlocked and opened the door.

"Good! I can't abide another moment with such an arse as you," she said as she stomped her way down the hall. He followed behind her running his hands through his hair and shaking his head in frustration. He shouted the order to have the carriage brought around back.

He made one last attempt to reach her, "I don't know what has happened to cause this scene to be played out between us. How can I make sense of it when you won't tell me anything?"

She ignored him and he said, "Celia please, I know that I said things that I shouldn't have but you must know that I love you and I'm only trying to help," he said in an agitated tone.

She continued to ignore him. They stood there inside the back entrance of his townhouse in painful silence waiting for the carriage.

When it was clear to Damien that she wouldn't speak to him further he decided not to say anything else that would further damage their relationship. The carriage arrived and he escorted her out and helped her in. He took her hand and was surprised that she allowed it then placed a tender kiss upon it.

"I'm sorry!" he said then he closed the door and watched the carriage as it carried her away from him. As he did so he suddenly remembered the wild fear in her eyes while she paced and muttered incoherently on the street when he found her and shivered at the vision. He had seen eyes like that once before and has never been able to put them out of his mind. Now he had a new image to haunt him, her eyes…

*****

Chelsea cried her eyes out in the carriage on the way home then she got angry. She has lost him and it felt like her whole world would end. Damn Nigel! Damn me! Damn Damien for not leaving it alone. Why did he have to persist?

Now all is lost and she would never see him again and she will never know the wonders that could have been between them. She should have never allowed herself to dream of a life with him anyway.

It was impossible from the beginning, doomed to miserable failure. It was just as well that he was out of her life so he won't be hurt when he found out who she really was.

Now she would just have to focus on her original objective and locate Nigel so she could make the bastard pay. Now that she knew he was in London, it shouldn't be too difficult to seek him out. How hard could it really be?

She hadn't been in London long and already she spotted him. Surely, she would come across him again. Perhaps balls aren't the way to find him after all, she decided. She would have to plan more shopping trips and other outings that would put him in her path.

Then what? Kill him…She would kill him for ruining her life and causing her to lose Damien. Aye, he deserved to die for that alone. Damien had come to mean so much to her and she loved him with all her heart. She would never have him now. She had no reason to live except to exact her vengeance on that loathsome animal.

Oh, she would take great pleasure in snuffing the lights out of his evil eyes. But how to do it? It would take careful planning and execution. She didn't care if she were caught and hanged. Her life was worthless anyway, but she would hate to harm Papa and Celia with the scandal and the shame it would bring upon them. Careful planning was needed.

First, she had to find out exactly who he is. If she could spot him again she could follow him to see where he resided and then work out a way to kill him. She could follow him down an alley and slit his throat or shoot him.

She smiled a bitter smile….the day of reckoning is upon you, Nigel she silently vowed. He had no idea what was coming and that would give her the advantage. She would make sure that he knew who would deliver him to hell before she gave the killing blow.

The carriage arrived. She was assisted out by a footman. She marched inside with purpose and walked right past her father without saying a word of greeting on her way up the stairs to her room.

The baron watched his daughter proceed up the stairs with a terrible sense of foreboding. He had never seen her so cold and hard with the look of murder in her eyes. Something terrible must have happened while she was out with the marquess. Did he do something untoward; try to force himself on her somehow?

He decided that he would have to probe Jenny later to see what Chelsea might say to her on the matter. If the marquess hurt Chelsea, there would surely be a reckoning.

Chapter Fourteen

He was walking through the forest trying to find his horse and the wood was so thick with fog that he couldn't see where he was going. He heard Nigel talking and moved toward to sound of his voice. When he reached a small clearing he saw Nigel with a little boy. He was holding him down on the ground, hurting him.

He wanted to save the child but he couldn't move because the trees had suddenly came alive and their roots bursts through the ground and wrapped and twined themselves around his legs and his torso keeping him in place to force him to watch the horror unfolding.

He saw the child's face and recognized that it was Jacob. Jacob was crying and looking at him with pleading in his...... strange blue eyes......my brother doesn't have blue eyes, he noted, it can't really be him......

Just then a mighty wind came and he was released from the hold that the trees had upon him and he was hurled through the air and sailed away on the wind until he landed at Sheraton nearby where he saw Jacob again only this time he was walking and holding hands with a little girl with blue black hair and strange blue eyes...

He ran after them as they began to move away from him but couldn't reach them because he slammed into an invisible barrier. He wanted desperately to see who she was because he thought that she must be the prettiest girl he had ever seen.

The girl turned to him and smiled and beckoned him to come but he couldn't get past the barrier to reach them. He beat on the invisible wall and shouted for Jacob to come help him but Jacob and the girl with strange blue eyes...............

Damien sat straight up in bed and his lungs were heaving and he couldn't catch his breath. His heart was pounding in his chest as he struggled to breathe. With great gasping effort he finally sucked down the air he needed and tried to regulate his heart beat.

What the bloody hell was that? He shivered as he remembered the dream, it must have been a nightmare....about Jacob.......and a girl with strange blue eyes, he thought.

He rubbed his face and eyes in an attempt to make sense of the dream but he couldn't. He drank quite a bit last night but not enough to make him dream such insanity. He had dreams of Nigel and Jacob and the unknown child from the wood before but never had there been a girl there.

Clearly, his fight with Celia had affected him more than he realized. There was something about her eyes yesterday that haunted him and reminded him of the boy from the forest. Strange. His conscience must have been telling him that he was wrong in his treatment of Celia yesterday.

He should have handled things more delicately but he was desperate for answers and lost control of the whole situation. He sent a note of apology over to her last evening but he received no reply.

He sat in his library and drank himself into a stupor of self pity at the rejection. The woman was driving him to drink and if he didn't have answers soon he would be driven into permanent drunkenness or worse…madness.

He knew that he was perilously close to the truth when he asked her if the man she saw was the one who had hurt her. As soon as the words left his mouth, her whole demeanor changed and she became hostile.

He needed to find out who the bastard was so he could punish him but he had no idea where to start his search. He needed to see Celia to be sure she was alright. The thought of her suffering because of him was too much to bear.

He got up and washed his face and called for his valet. After a bath and a shave he felt more human and decided to send a note to Celia requesting afternoon tea with her.

An hour after he sent his missive he received her reply. It was a refusal to allow him to attend her, no explanations, just a refusal. Well to hell with her then…If that's the way she wants it, so be it.

*****

Damien found himself standing on the doorstep of his ex-mistress Lila late that night. He was in his cups again and he was slightly swaying as he knocked on the door.

He had been at his club brooding the day away over Scotch whisky and he was in a foul temper. He decided what he needed was sexual release to clear the cobwebs from his brain. Celia had him tied up in knots and he couldn't think straight.

All day long he vacillated between wanting to crawl on his hands and knees to her home and beg her forgiveness to being convinced that he was well rid of her. Right now he was convinced that he was well rid of her and as a free man he could take his pleasure anywhere and with anyone he wanted.

Lila's butler gave him entrance and he staggered his way up the stairs to her room. He burst through her bedroom door and found her lying right where he wanted her. In bed!

"Damien what are you doing here?" Lila asked as she quickly sat up in complete surprise.

Lila was a full figured woman with dark hair and eyes and most importantly very large breasts, just the way he liked his women to be. She was wearing a sexy night rail and looked most inviting to a poor wretch like him.

He walked over to the side of the bed and ran his hand through her loose hair "I've missed you Lila," he slurred.

That was a lie but she didn't need to know it. He had given her very little thought at all since their departing. But she was here and would serve his purpose; she lived off his coin after all.

"You should have sent round a note Damien, you know I don't like surprises," she had the nerve to admonish him.

Damien wasn't chastised a bit as he sat down on the bed and started removing his disheveled clothes. He had a little trouble with his boots and after several frustrated tries he managed to get them off and flung them about the room along with his hose. He unceremoniously jerked off his offending breeches and stood up arse naked on unsteady legs and slurred, "Where's the whiskey?"

"Over there on the sideboard where it always is but it seems like you've probably had enough already," she pointed out.

He grunted his reply and swaggered over to the side board to pour himself a glass. He tossed it back, "Take off that ridiculous night rail," he ordered as he refilled his glass.

"You can't just come in here and order me about Damien," she bristled.

"If you wanna play rough Lila, it's alright with me. It's been awhile since you actually inspired me but one way or another, you'll lose the gown," he promised then tossed down the second glass of whisky.

Lila puffed up her ample bosom and said, "I'm not in the mood to entertain you Damien so why don't you get dressed and leave?"

He walked over to the bed and shoved her back in a laying position so he could fondle her breast then said, "Oh, I think not."

Then he grabbed a handful of the delicate material of her night rail and ripped it right off of her and threw himself on top of her.

He ground his hips against hers and said, "Is this any way to treat your protector?" then he started kissing her roughly.

She didn't put up any resistance as he moved down to her breast and started laving her nipples with his tongue. He squeezed and kneaded the fleshy mounds…..and froze. He stared at her for a long moment then shook his head as if by doing so he could bring her image into focus.

He rolled off of her then and wiped the taste of her off his mouth with the back of his hand and cursed, "God's teeth, I'm a bloody arse."

*****

Damien went home to nurse his shame. He couldn't believe he behaved like such an animal. Thank God he stopped himself before he raped her. He had never behaved so badly before in all of his life. Even a whore like Lila deserved to be treated with a degree of respect by virtue of being a woman and as being weaker than a man.

He went to his private chambers and instructed Thompson to bring him a bottle of Scotch whisky and a glass. Then he holed himself up in his rooms then proceeded to get himself stinking drunk.

Before the night was through he had destroyed his private chambers in a fit of drunken anger, self loathing and continued sexual frustration. Disgusted with himself he had lain down in the floor and wallowed around in the mess like the pig he knew that he was before passing out completely.

Morning came harshly. He found himself still on the floor amidst all the rubble, with a splitting head. Thompson had apparently been in his room and opened the curtains to allow the morning sunlight to abuse him. Probably to punish him for the mess he'd made, he would have to take pity on him and clean much of it up himself, he decided.

But first thing, first. He staggered to his feet and went to wash his face. His cleaned his teeth and poured cold water on his head. He shook his mane like a dog does after a swim and wrapped himself in his robe.

He went over to the sofa, plopped down and thought about what he'd done. How could he ever face Celia now? A tear rolled down his cheek and he reached a finger up to trace the source of the moisture and realized that it came from his eyes and that he was crying. He gave himself over to it and cried inconsolably like a child.

Oddly, when he composed himself, he felt better, renewed somehow. He got up and started picking up his mess then called for his valet to attend him.

He decided that today was a new day and he would go over there and demand to see Celia and not leave until he did. He was determined to could put the blasted quarrel behind them and move forward with their betrothal.

When he got there his new found hopes were dashed to bits when he was told that the lady was not at home. He demanded to see the baron and the baron agreed to receive him.

"My lord, Celia is not home to receive you but I will tell her that you came to call on her," the baron promised.

"Where did she go?" Damien persisted.

"My lord, she and her maid Jenny went shopping and they have been gone most of the morning. Is something wrong my lord?" the baron ventured.

He was curious to know what was going on and Jenny didn't have any information to shed any light on the matter so perhaps he could learn the details from the marquess himself.

"Celia won't speak to me," he said pathetically.

"So I gathered my lord, but why?" he persisted.

Damien debated the wisdom of confiding the story to the baron but his need to reconcile with Celia was paramount so he forged ahead.

"The other day we were walking down the street after leaving the lending library. We were having a meat pie. The next thing I know Celia ran down the street and disappeared around a corner. I gave chase but when I found her she was pacing in the street like a caged animal and had a wild look in her eyes. I finally got her to calm down. When I pressed her for details she became cold and hard and refused to talk. I got frustrated and called her an insufferable woman which was a mistake I now know because at that point she refused to be in my presence a moment longer. I had my driver carry her home and haven't been able to see or speak to her since. It's very distressing."

Damien intentionally left out the part about taking her to his townhouse and locking her in his private chambers with himself. That was a detail the baron didn't need.

After a contemplative moment, the baron cleared his throat and asked, "Did she say what it was that she was after?"

"I managed to get her to admit that she had seen a man that she thought she knew," he explained.

The baron became very quiet with a look of deep concern on his face.

"What do you know about this mystery man?" Damien probed.

The baron looked away from Damien with a haunted expression in his eyes. If Damien needed further confirmation of a tragedy in Celia's past, he had it now by the look on the baron's guilt written upon his face when he turned back to him with the same haunted look in his eyes.

The baron obviously wasn't going to tell Damien what he wanted to know because he looked away again.

"I know that something…terrible has happened to Celia and I also know that this man was likely responsible. I have been able to piece that much together on my own," Damien ventured.

"My lord, forgive me but I have a pressing matter to attend to, you will have to excuse me….."

Damien cut the baron off, "Whatever happened to her makes no difference in how I feel about her. But I can't help her if I don't have the details. Please help me to help her as I can't abide this thing to come between us," he implored.

"My lord, it's not my story to tell. Please don't ask it of me," the baron pleaded in reply.

"Has she spoken to you of our betrothal?" Damien wondered aloud after a moment of silence while he observed the baron and considered his words.

"No, but she did send the ring to me through Jenny and said that I should return it to you personally as she didn't want to take a chance sending it by a messenger since the ring was a valuable heirloom," the baron replied with real regret in his voice.

Damien's heart twisted and wrenched, He felt as though it had become detached as it plunged into his stomach.

"I refuse to accept this!" he blurted out, "Tell her I refused it and I refuse to allow her out of the commitment," he added angrily. With that he removed himself from the presence of the baron and stormed his way out of the house and went to his club to get drunk again.

The baron was stunned by what he'd learned.

*****

"Jenny, we may as well go home. We've been walking out here for hours with no sign of Nigel. We'll just have to try again tomorrow," Chelsea said, with a tired sigh.

She and Jenny had been walking up and down the street for hours near the place where she had spotted Nigel, in hopes of crossing paths with him again. This was the second day in a row with no luck and her feet were tired and blistered.

"Aye, let's go then, my feet are aching something awful," came Jenny's agreement.

Chelsea has been clinging to her mission to find Nigel because to do otherwise was to fall in complete despair over losing Damien. She missed him terribly and wished that she could go to him and fall into his arms and ask for forgiveness but she couldn't, he didn't belong to her anymore.

She hated herself for the hurt she had caused him by refusing to tell him what he wanted to know and already suspected. He was so close to the truth and that scared her.

What she saw in his eyes the last time they were together had been devastating and she knew that he was tormented by her pain and like it was with her father, she simply couldn't bear to be around him and witness the pain that her shame was causing him.

They arrived at Aunt Gertrude's and were met by Papa in the foyer, "Celia, I would like to see you in the library right away, if you please," came his formal stern command.

Chelsea was concerned by his tone and wondered what could be amiss. She followed him to the library and once inside he closed the door for privacy.

"What is it Papa?" She asked nervously.

"Lord Devonshire called today and he was quite agitated about your refusal to speak with him. He said that the two of you had a falling out and that he wanted to reconcile. In fact, he refused to accept the return of the betrothal ring or to allow you out of the commitment and I quite agree with him. You need the protection of a husband and he clearly has a deep attachment to you and you to him as well. I must insist that you allow the marquess to call on you tomorrow and set everything back to rights. This has gone on long enough!"

Chelsea felt chilled by her father's command. Celia was right, they are working together to force the match. Well she was old enough to make her own decisions and wasn't about to allow them to bully her.

"Father, it is none of your concern and I refuse to allow you and Lord Devonshire to push me into a marriage that I do not want," she told him.

"Now you see here, daughter, I am your father and it is my will that you should marry Lord Devonshire. He is a fine young man and will make you an excellent husband. Now, I want you to stop this foolishness and send him an invitation to tea tomorrow. You will reconcile with him. I will accept no refusal," the baron insisted.

Fine, she would do as her father bade her and invite him for tea and then she would tell him face to face that it was over.

"Yes, father, I will invite him to tea" she said sarcastically. "Is that all?" she asked.

"No, you will take his ring and replace it on your finger," he said as he thrust the object at her. She took it and jammed it on her finger painfully and glared at him.

"Also, you will tell me what this disagreement is about," he instructed.

She wasn't about to tell him what it was about but she had to tell him something. She wondered what Damien might have said and decided she should stick as close to the truth as possible without giving herself away.

"He became jealous when I thought I saw a man I knew… from one of the balls. He started questioning me about the man and it made me angry. When I refused to give him any details he called me names and cursed at me. I was offended and decided that I should not have to put up with such abuse," she explained.

"His story was similar," he said with his index fingers pressed together under his chin forming a steeple as he leaned back in the chair considering her story.

When she didn't say more after a moment he said, "It's not uncommon for young couples to quarrel and it's silly to end such a promising match over such a trivial matter. As your husband, he will expect your obedience and you must give it to him. He is not your husband yet but as your betrothed he has certain rights in the same manner. He is not an unkind man and I don't believe he will abuse you physically or I wouldn't insist that you take him on as a husband. I know how your temper is and I'm sure you must have provoked him with your insolence. You should apologize to him right away and not leave the matter to risk."

Chelsea couldn't believe her ears. Why was Papa so set on her marrying Damien? Was he that eager to be rid of her? No, she didn't think that was the case. He thought she was Celia after all. Puzzling.

She put her head down from the chastisement and clamped her lips tight to avoid expressing her anger and making matters worse. If she wasn't careful her father would have her dragged to the parson this very minute to marry Damien and she couldn't have that.

"Yes Papa," was her meek reply. "May I be excused now?"

"Yes you may, but I expect you to have your invitation to the marquess out by messenger within the hour," was his final command.

With an inward growl she rose and swept from the room and as soon as she was out of his line of sight she jerked the betrothal ring off her finger and stuffed it in pocket.

The baron watched his daughter go with sadness. He didn't like to be so harsh and demanding but it was in her best interest to marry the marquess. This was her one chance at happiness and if she was too stubborn to seize it then he would seize it for her.

Once she was safely wed and with child, perhaps she would give up this foolishness of locating this Nigel person that was mentioned in Celia's letter. Apparently he is the man who attacked her years ago and she has somehow learned his identity and is now on the hunt for him.

Aye the lass needs the protection of a husband. One who will keep her fat with child and help her put her troubled past behind her.

He must try to find out what's going on with Celia and Sir Jarrett. There have been no letters between the girls in the last two days that he was aware of and he suspected that was because Celia was on her way to Gretna Green.

He hoped this ridiculous mess was cleared up soon before Chelsea did locate this Nigel person and finds herself harmed or worse. In the meantime he will have to await word from the Bow Street runner that he hired to locate the blackguard. The man has a penance to pay and I will see to it that he does, he vowed.

*****

Damien sat in his room the following morning, pondering Celia's invitation to tea this afternoon. It didn't sound friendly at all; perhaps her father put her up to it. Well, no matter, at least he would have an opportunity to reconcile with her.

He felt sure that once he was alone with her he could soothe the hurt and she would forgive him. At least he hoped so because he had another missive that needed his attentions as well.

His father had awakened and was asking for him. He had to go to Evansdale as soon as possible. He didn't want to leave things as they were between him and Celia without making every effort to reconcile with her before he left.

The message said that his father was doing well and seemed to be on the road to recovery. That was good at least. He didn't have to go rushing over there this instant. He was glad his father was getting better and felt guilty for not being there with him when he regained consciousness.

Reconciling with Celia was foremost on his mind now, so in his return message to his father he explained that he was recently betrothed and needed to take care of a related issue before he could return to Evansdale. He thought he should be there within the next two days. That bought his conscience some time.

When he arrived at Celia's later, he would beg, borrow or steal whatever he must to get back in her good graces. He simply must……..

*****

Chelsea was cold and rigid when Damien entered the drawing room. She was standing by the window facing into the room. Her shoulders squared in preparation for battle. Not good! The butler closed the door and they were alone. They stared at onc another in uncomfortable silence.

Damien broke the quiet, "Thank you for seeing me," he said humbly, moving slowly toward her.

He felt as though, he were a panther stalking his nervous prey…trying to lull her into a sense of security long enough to allow him to get close enough for the kill. He shook his head at the awful thought proceeding toward her. He noticed that her spine straightened even more, if that were possible. Clearly she wouldn't be easily lulled.

He stopped in front of her, dropping to his knees. He wrapped him arms around her backside, pulling her close, so he could breathe her in. He couldn't help it. He needed the contact. She stayed rigid for a moment, then reluctantly cradled the back of his head, as if to hold him in place.

With the side of his face so intimately placed upon her person, he said, "Forgive me."

Chelsea was breathless. She knew she had already lost the battle. She couldn't forgive him, though, because there was nothing to forgive. She held him close and tears flowed from her eyes.

Damien started to kiss her about her hips. She saw that his eyes were filled with tears, too. She whispered, "I do."

"I've been a miserable wretch without you. I can't take it anymore. God help me, Celia. I need you," he said as he continued to worship her hips with kisses.

Chelsea stood immobilized by his admission. She knew that she could never leave him. Just once, she wished to hear her own name from his beautiful lips. She determined then and there to find a way to be with him no matter what. She continued to caress his head and ran her fingers through his hair.

"I'm the miserable wretch, Damien. I don't deserve your devotion," she told him. "I can't fathom what I have ever done to be given such a gift as you," she added on a soft sob.

"Please, say that you'll marry me. I don't care when. Just say that you will have me," he begged.

Chelsea was quiet and she stiffened slightly in his arms again. Damien wasn't about to be put off. He continued, "I don't care what happened in your past. It has no bearing on my love for you…no don't…just listen," he commanded.

When she tried to pull away, he held firm to her hips, "It doesn't matter! The only thing that matters is us. You and me and the future that we can share…and the family that we will have together. That's all I care about. Please don't deny us this," he pleaded.

When she remained quiet, he thought all was lost. He was sure she was going to send him away, out of her life. He just couldn't take the idea of it, so he stood up and took her by the chin gently. He laid his lips on hers, urging her to accept him in the only way he could.

He put every ounce of love he could find within himself behind the kiss, thrusting his tongue into her mouth and mingling with hers. He deepened the kiss. His hands began a slow exploration of her back and her rounded hips.

He could tell that she was loosening up for him now so he continued with his sensual assault of her mouth. She whimpered and started returning his kiss. She too, started an exploration of her own, caressing his back.

He felt a tightening in his loins and pressed himself against her hips, lightly rotating to demonstrate the power she had over him. When she didn't resist, he allowed his hands to traverse down to her luscious bottom where he kneaded and massaged her there, too.

She didn't shy away in the beginning, but as he continued the pressure of his hard ridge against her pelvic, she stiffened and pulled out of the embrace. She was panting hard and had a wild look in her eyes. He thought for a moment she would have one of her spells but then she surprised him by lunging back at him. She started kissing him with a savage hunger. She groaned and moaned, trying to pull him closer, as though she were trying to pull him inside her.

He knew that if he allowed this to continue much longer, he would take her here and now on the floor. He refused to be such a barbarian. He found himself pulling away from her out of desperation to preserve her virtue and his sanity.

With gasping breath, he said, "Celia, please say you'll have me. I think I'll die without you"

"You know I'll have you, Damien," she rasped out. Her chest continued a violent heaving as she tried to compose herself.

Damien was caught between total elation of her words and an amazing sense of awe over the sexual hunger she had displayed. It had been the most devastating kiss he had ever shared with a woman in his life.

If this was what he could expect from her, he would be in sheer ecstasy until his dying day. It was all he could do to will his arousal into submission as he stood there staring at her.

When they were both semi-composed, he asked, "Did I hear you right?"

She nodded her head that it was true. She gazed at him with big round eyes. Clearly, she had surprised herself, as well as him, with her own prowess.

They went back into each other's arms for a suspended moment, willing their heartbeats into a slow mutual rhythm. When they were settled down, he kissed her cheek and pulled back so he could look at her.

"I have to go to Evansdale. I must leave soon. My father has awakened and is asking for my attendance. Please come away with me as I can't bear the thought of our being apart. It will only be for a couple of days. I'm sure your father wont object."

Chelsea wanted to go with him. Of course she did. How could she not? "Yes that would be lovely Damien, when shall we leave?"

"On the morrow with the dawn. Is that too soon?" He asked.

"I shall be ready," she promised, leaning forward to kiss him tenderly. It promised a future.

"And Celia? Put your ring back on," was his soft command as he laid another searing kiss upon her.

*****

Damien was so lost in pleasant thoughts as he waited for his horse to be brought around in front of Celia's town house, that he didn't notice the two women approaching on the sidewalk.

His elation was rudely interrupted by a familiar screeching voice, "Damien dear, what a surprise to see you," the duchess said.

Damien rolled his eyes heavenward before giving his acknowledgement, "Your Grace. Tess." He said nothing more nor made any attempt to sound friendly.

Not to be deterred by his obvious displeasure at seeing them, Tess asked, "Whatever brings you here cousin?"

Damien saw his opportunity to get a dig in and said, "Why, I was paying a call to my fiancé. Thanks to your kind efforts dear cousin, I am now betrothed to Lady Celia and am soon to be a married man. I really can't thank you enough for your intervention on my behalf."

Tess fumed. The clownish duchess sucked wind. And Damien, well, he smiled.

"We'll just see about that! You are to be mine! When father gets through with you, you'll be singing a different tune cousin, of this I swear," Tess threatened.

"I'm all a quiver," Damien taunted with an expression of mock fear.

The two ladies huffed and puffed and swept passed him…good riddance.

Damien felt a little sorry for Tess. It was sad her father had put the ridiculous notion of marrying him into her head and she couldn't seem to let go of the idea. He didn't remember her being such a spoiled bitch. Well, what could you expect from having parents like Nigel and Penelope Cullen. It stood to reason she would turn out to be such a harridan.

Chapter Fifteen

Celia and Jenny napped as they made their way to Evansdale. It was raining, gloomy and rather cold so they stayed under blankets in the carriage to keep warm. Subsequently, they drifted off to sleep.

Celia looked so pretty in slumber. Yes even her snoring pleased him. He couldn't wait until the day when he could wake up in the morning with her in his arms and make sweet passionate love to her.

Damien wasn't thrilled to have Jenny along but he was glad in a way because he knew he couldn't guarantee Celia's virtue after their interlude yesterday in the drawing room. He was resigned to wait until their wedding before bedding her, which with any luck would be soon.

While he no longer thought she was a virgin, he wanted to make their wedding night and their first joining as special for her as possible. Given her past and the obvious pain that it harbored, he would just have to cling to the moments that they had shared thus far.

Though, she would never know it, what they had done yesterday washed clean the stain of the distasteful scene with Lila. He was glad he didn't go through with the insulting notion of bedding her, to get back at Celia for refusing to see him. Had he gone through with it he could have never faced her again, knowing that he had betrayed her in such a way simply because they had quarreled.

He hoped that by bringing her to Evansdale with him, he could accustom her to the idea of marrying right away. He thought that his home would provide the perfect romantic setting for her to realize what they could have together and truly embrace it.

As they neared Evansdale, his spirits seemed to drop ever so slightly. He hadn't been home in so long; he wasn't really relishing the prospect.

He was glad he would have Celia along as a distraction from the memories of Jacob and all the years since that his father had suffered the loss of his oldest son. He was happy that his father was doing well, so really he had a lot to be content with, but still…he missed his brother.

The big sprawling mansion came into view and he lightly shook Celia awake. "We're here darling, wake up," he said softly, as he fondly stroked her cheek.

Her eyes opened and they were smiling at him. She was genuinely happy and it pleased his heart to see it. Beside her, Jenny came awake. They both composed themselves as the carriage traveled up the long winding drive of the estate.

Chelsea gasped at the sight of Evansdale. She had forgotten how massive it was. She hadn't seen it since she was a child. It was like something out of a fairy tale that quite reminded her of Camelot.

It was a huge sprawling palatial structure, built in the Tudor style. There were many spires and multi-levels adorned with huge arched windows. The structure itself was built from limestone, that gave it an eternal feeling, as though it could defy time and its ravishments, and remain forever defiant in its grandeur.

It was scenically placed upon twenty five hundred acres, with large oak trees lining the drive. The feeling was that you were entering a private world. Once inside that private world, you were presented with great regal landscaping features, complete with grand parks and a lake.

The front courtyard was decorated by huge lavish fountains and sculptures honoring characters of ancient mythology. It was overwhelming and left one quite breathlessly in awe.

*****

Once they arrived at the front entrance they were greeted by the Butler Prescott and Mrs. Wellstone, Jarrett's mother. She had served as Evansdale's Chatelaine in absence of Damien's mother, who had died many years ago. She was the head housekeeper. Since the duke never re-married, she ascended to the position mistress of Evansdale.

Of course, Jarrett himself was present as well to receive them as he had chosen to stay behind at Evansdale for a few weeks. Damien was glad to see his old friend. He had missed him dearly. They were all happy to see Damien's return with his betrothed and talk of celebration was bantered about.

After the greetings, Mrs. Wellstone said, "My lord, you will find all is ready to receive Lady Celia and her maid in the Blue Room suite of the west wing. I took the liberty of placing her on your wing. I hope that is acceptable."

"That will be fine, Mrs. Wellstone," Damien replied.

"Very good my lord, we shall have luncheon in an hour. If I may be so bold my lord, His Grace is very eager to see you. He is aware of your arrival, if you would like to take the opportunity to visit with him before he tires," she said smiling.

When Damien nodded his head in the affirmative, she looked at Chelsea saying, "Lady Celia, if you will follow me, I will show you and your maid to your rooms."

Damien watched as the ladies made their procession up the grand staircase. Turning to Jarrett, he said, "My God it's good to see you, man! Let's go have a drink, shall we?"

They headed to the library. Once inside and drinks were poured, Damien said, "Have you any news?"

Jarrett had a hard time looking his friend in the eye initially, but recovered and said, "Aye, after giving it much thought, I have formed a plan to deal with Nigel," he ventured.

Jarrett wasn't sure that Damien would go for his idea but he felt sure that he could persuade him that it was the best option.

"And what is this plan?" Damien asked cautiously.

"I have spoken to Captain Fellows of the Dirty Devil about selling him to the Barbary Corsairs. I didn't give him any names of course but he has done work like this for Bow Street in the past. He is very reliable and has familial connections to Captain Hassan of the Black Viper, who as you know, is a Barbary pirate. He said, with a heavy enough bribe, we could ensure that they would not ransom him later. Once he was taken to Algiers, there would be no way he could ever escape as he would most likely become a slave assigned to work in their rock quarries or the like. It's a brutal existence and the lifespan of such slaves is usually very short," Jarrett told him.

Damien was shocked by the words flowing out of Jarrett's mouth. He would have never expected this of him. However, he did liked the idea of Nigel suffering before he died. He had planned to cause the suffering himself, so he gave it some serious thought before he asked, "How much for the bribe?"

Jarrett released the breath he had been holding while Damien contemplated and said, "Twenty thousand pounds, which is to be given to Captain Fellows in advance."

A king's ransom! Damien was a very wealthy man who could absorb such a loss quite easily, so that wasn't an issue.

"What guarantees do we have that he can successfully sell him to Hassan? Nigel won't go easily and might try to bribe Fellows in his favor," Damien asked.

"I told Fellows what kind of monster the man is and that he is a lofty aristocrat. He hates both, pederasts and aristocrats and would gladly do it for free but he has to keep five thousand to pay for his expenses. The rest will go to the Corsairs to ensure that there will be no need for the usual ransom. And as I said before they have both been involved with Bow Street operations of this fashion before and never double crossed us. Believe it or not, there seems to be an honor of sorts among them once their word is given," Jarrett explained.

"How are we to arrange for Nigel to be captured?" he asked, warming to the plan. To be rid of Nigel and have him become a slave was becoming more and more palatable.

"I know some cut throats that will do it. Again, they have done similar work for Bow Street." Jarrett felt reasonably certain that Damien was going to go for it and was feeling the excitement that always goes with such missions.

Damien sat for a long while contemplating the plan and all the things that could go wrong with it.

"There seems to be a lot left to chance; too many people involved. I need to give this some more thought before I commit," Damien said.

"Captain Fellows will be setting sail in four days, so time is of the essence. I have to have a decision by tomorrow so I can go to London and take care of the particulars," Jarrett advised.

"When were you going to tell me of this plan?" Damien asked, wondering why Jarrett put him in such a pinch.

"I was planning to ride to London tonight but I learned that you were returning and I didn't want to put such a thing down on paper, so I waited for you to arrive. I felt reasonably sure that you would like the idea and we would have plenty of time to work it out," Jarrett said, a little defensively.

Damien sighed deeply and ran a hand through his hair, "Alright, make the arrangements. I will send a note to my man to have the funds ready for you when you get to London," he instructed.

He wasn't sure it was such a good idea but now that he had Celia to think of, he really couldn't afford to openly kill Nigel in a duel. His back was really against the wall. With that decided, he said, "What news of the boy?"

Jarrett knew this was coming and braced himself for it, "I haven't made any headway," he lied smoothly.

"I have another matter I need for you to handle," Damien said. "Once we have Nigel safely away, I need you to dig around in Celia's past to see if you can find out anything about a man who might have harmed her. I believe she may have been... mishandled. There have been several things come to light while I was in London and after putting two and two together I have deduced that this was the case. When I questioned her about it, she didn't deny it and neither did she admit it. When I confronted her father about it, he simply told me it wasn't his story to tell. So, my friend we may have another need of your pirate and cut throat friends in the near future," Damien thought that with Nigel out of the way he could focus his attention on finding the bastard that hurt Celia.

Jarrett was speechless. He had no idea that Damien was so close to uncovering the truth. He wondered what had happened to cause him to be suspicious, "What things came to light," he asked.

"She has episodes...spells...I'm not sure what to call them. She goes into another world almost, whenever something causes her stress. That bastard Davenport tried to compromise her and when her father and I got to her she having one of them. Then, a few days ago, there was an incident out on the street when she thought she saw a man that she knew. She went running after him before I knew what was going on. When I chased her down, I found her in a wild eyed state and she didn't know who I was. She became hostile and cold and refused to tell me anything. She nearly broke our engagement and didn't speak to me for two days. It was very disconcerting," Damien said broodingly.

"It's good you got her out of London, then. So, do you think this man she saw was the man who might have hurt her?" he ventured carefully.

"I do, only the bastard got away before I got there"

"I'll see what I can dig up," Jarrett promised.

*****

Damien's father was lying in bed looking more thin and frail than he had ever seen him. His body had been ravaged by his illness and he looked decades older than what he actually was.

"My son, you have come home," the duke said in a garbled, raspy voice He held his trembling hand out to him.

Damien grabbed hold of his father's hand and squeezed it, saying, "Father, I'm sorry I wasn't hear sooner, but I have recently been betrothed and I had to stay in London to work out the details with her father. I brought her home to meet you if you are up to it later. I think you will love her father, as I do. Her name is Lady Celia Sheraton of Sheraton Manor"

"Ah…one of the barons daughter's. You have done well," the duke said.

Damien wasn't sure if his father's mental faculties were up to snuff because Celia didn't have any siblings but he didn't want to quibble with a dying man so he made no attempt to correct him, other than, "Aye, the baron's daughter."

"Two," the duke rasped out.

"Two, sir?" Damien asked, confused by his father's outburst. But he wouldn't get an answer because his father had fallen asleep. Clearly, the duke was in worse shape than he thought. He had hoped that when he came home, he would see his father sitting up and giving out commands and…..he sighed deeply. He sat there another moment, hoping he would awaken once again. He didn't so after a half an hour, he decided that he should go get changed for luncheon and reluctantly left his side.

Damien's spirits fell after seeing his father and he wanted to see Celia. He needed the comfort of her presence to offset such an unsettling sight as his father's dying visage.

Too bad, the weather was so gloomy. He would love to take her for a tour about the gardens. What he really wanted to do though, was steal Celia away and hide her in his chambers and just hold her for hours but he knew he could never do that…or could he?

*****

"What are you doing Damien? You shouldn't be in here. It's indecent," Chelsea gasped when she opened her eyes and found Damien lying next to her in bed, beneath the covers.

He had been tickling her face with a quill until she was awakened. He smiled at her and dove forward for a tender kiss. She wrapped her arms around him and kissed him back.

He didn't really want to take things further so he pulled back saying, "I wanted to hold you for a few hours, and talk about things," he whispered.

"Things?" she asked nervously

"Just everyday things and maybe what our life will be like together, once we're married," he assured her.

He sensed that she was worried that he might probe her for information again but that wasn't his intention. He just wanted to hold her to ward away the sadness that always enveloped him when he was at Evansdale.

He had waited all day for this moment. He wasn't about to spoil it by talking about things that he knew would upset her. No, he just wanted time to bond with her and if in so doing, she decided to confide in him, then he wouldn't discourage her.

"That sounds nice. You first," she said, snuggling against him with her head on his chest.

He wrapped her in his arms and started a slow stroking of her shoulder with his thumb, "I'm thankful that you agreed to take me back and I hope that you are happy about it as well. I can't wait until we are married so I can hold you like this every night and wake up with you every morning…you snore, you know," he teased with a slight squeeze on her shoulder.

She playfully slapped him on the chest and said, "I do no such thing, you beast." Then she buried her face in his chest, red with embarrassment.

"Only a little and it's adorable, really," he assured her.

She kept her head buried in his chest. For a moment he thought she might be crying because her body was shuddering. He lifted up her face by her chin and saw that she was laughing instead and he laughed too.

"Shhhh…..you will wake up Jenny and get me in trouble," she quietly admonished him but she was smiling widely.

"Perhaps we should lock the door'" he suggested.

She hopped up and skipped over to the door and turned the key. Then she ran and jumped back in the bed, quickly snuggling back up to him under the covers so he could wrap her in his arms again. Once she settled herself, he kissed her on the top of the head.

"You reminded me of a little girl just then, when you were skipping to the door," he remarked with a smile.

"So cute," he said tweaking her nose.
She giggled, rubbed her nose on his chest and shimmied closer.

Damien was in heaven. This is what it was all about, he mused. Having the woman you love in your arms and simply enjoying being together, behaving silly.

The thought caused him a twinge of sadness as he thought of Jacob and the life he was missing out on. Jacob would never know the pure joy of a moment like this.

"I get a little depressed when I come to Evansdale," he said, without really meaning to.

She looked up at him with sad eyes, "Why?" she asked.

"I miss my brother, Jacob. It's not fair that I get to have moments like this while he's….it's just not fair," he finished with a faraway look in his eyes.

"Tell me about him," she urged him.

"He was my hero…he could do anything. He was four years older than I and I followed him around wherever he went. I aped his every move. It used to frustrate him sometimes but mostly he tolerated it with brotherly love. He taught me how to fish and find toads and turtles near the lake. We used to build paper sail boats and send them to their doom in battles with rocks for canon fire," he said, smiling now.

"How did he die?" she asked innocently, not realizing that was such a sore spot for him.

But this was the woman he would spend the rest of his life with and she deserved to know. He couldn't tell her everything of course; it was much too sensitive an issue.

"H-He killed himself," he said softly.

She gasped softly and said, "Oh Damien, I'm so sorry." She kissed his neck and chin tenderly.

"He was only four and ten when it happened," he explained.

"You don't have to talk about it, if you don't want to," she offered.

"It's alright. You have the right to know. He was a sad child. As he got older it became full blown depression. One day he took one of father's pistols, went to the lake and…shot himself," he said, squeezing her closer up against him.

"Is that what you meant before when you mentioned ghosts?" she ventured.

"There aren't any ghosts at Evansdale, but his presence is all around and when I'm here, I feel his suffering and the suffering my father still goes through at his loss."

"I know what you mean. I felt a sense of sorrow when I was exploring the east wing" she told him. Earlier, after luncheon she had explored the palace and felt as though she were connected somehow to a kindred spirit whose presence she could feel all around her. She couldn't quite define it, but she knew someone had suffered here.

"The east wing is where the nursery was," he said noting the coincidence.

"I guess it's like you said before, that these old estates are alive with the past. So many generations come and go and they leave something of themselves behind. The house becomes the steward of their souls."

"Yes, I'm sure that's what it is," he agreed.

He didn't like to think of Jacobs soul trapped here for eternity. But sometimes, it was as though he was still here, watching over the place, he mused with a slight shiver.

"It doesn't scare you, does it?" he thought to ask. Considering that they would have to make their home here someday, it would be a good idea to find out how she really feels about it.

"Oh, not at all. I feel quite at peace here actually. It made me feel wrapped up, secure in a sort of embrace. I can't explain it but it didn't scare me. It was a comforting experience."

He squeezed her shoulder and kissed her temple, "Good, because one day it will be our home and we will fill it with the laughter of at least two dozen children," he teased.

"You have great confidence in my abilities," she teased back.

"Alright, only a dozen, then," he said, smiling at the prospect of their children. Perhaps that would change the feel of Evansdale for him and he would be happy here once again.

*****

Damien woke up just before dawn and realized he still held Celia in his arms. He hadn't meant to fall asleep. They had talked for hours last night and they must have fallen asleep when there was a lull in the conversation.

He smiled as she snored. It wasn't an obnoxious sound; more a light fluttering sound. She looked so peaceful that he wished he could see into her dreams and join her there.

He dreamed of her last night, only it was kind of strange because she was just a little girl and she was holding hands with Jacob. He knew now that she was the girl from the other dream he had but this time it wasn't a nightmare, just a sweet pleasant dream. He wasn't in the dream, only an observer as she and Jacob walked hand in hand through the gardens of Sheraton.

Strange things; dreams. Many people put great stock in their meanings but he never had. He always felt that dreams were just random pictures from your subconscious and memories. If he were to put stock in this dream's meaning, he would be hard pressed to figure out why he kept seeing her holding hands with Jacob.

Maybe Jacob's spirit was still here and he was watching over her somehow...but that couldn't be. The first time he dreamed them together was in London.

Maybe he kept placing them together in his dreams because they were both so special to him. They were the only two people he had ever truly loved in his entire life. He suspected that was more the case, than any ghostly explanations.

He looked at her again, wishing that he could wake her up by making sweet love to her. His body was aching to immerse itself within her. Would it be so bad to do so now?

Many betrothed couples did anticipate their vows, consummating their union before the ceremony but that just didn't seem right to him. He didn't think it would be right for her either, considering her past, whatever it held.

No, the wisest thing for him to do was to remove himself from the bed. He needed to go back to his own chamber and sit in cold water to cool his ardor. With that decided he slowly slipped out from under the covers and quietly left the room.

He went to his room; did just that, then climbed in his bed and willed himself back to sleep.

******

"I'm sorry, love, but you knew this was coming. It can't be helped. I must go to London today and take care of the details of the plan for Nigel," Jarrett said, as he held Celia in his arms, trying to console her.

She was worried and didn't want any harm to come to him. She pleaded for him to stay with her, where he was safe. "There's more that I need to tell you," he added.

"What more?" she asked in alarm.

"Damien is very close to figuring out what happened to Chelsea. Things happened while they were in London and he has come to the conclusion that she must have been…harmed her in the past," he explained.

"What sort of things?"

"Damien witnessed a couple of her episodes. Apparently, there was a situation on the street where she may have spotted Nigel."

"You saw her at Evansdale. How did she seem?"

"Blissfully happy, honestly. It seems that she and Damien have definitely decided to marry, and soon. So you see, I must go to London and take care of all the particulars. Then, you and I can marry as soon as it can be arranged. I could try to get a special license through Damien's solicitor while I'm in town. We can be married at a moment's notice after," he said smiling.

"That sounds wonderful darling, but are you sure that Chelsea was really happy?" she asked. Without giving him time to answer, she added, "Oh, I do wish I could speak to her."

"You know it's not possible. Too risky! Things are good for her now so let's not do anything to upset the boat," he advised.

"I know you're right but she is so close by and I haven't heard a word from her in days," she pouted. Jarrett planted a big wet kiss on her mouth saying, "How about giving me some of your special loving before I have to leave? I will be gone at least two days and it will be torture without you."

She embraced him. Soon their clothes started flying and they were deep in the passionate throws of their union.

Chapter Sixteen

"That be the bloke there, Smithy. Ye distract 'im and I'll cosh 'im on the nob like we planned" Gibbons instructed. Smithy and Gibbons watched their prey, as he exited the rear entrance of the brothel.

It was said that this particular brothel secretly catered to unsavory sexual appetites. Almost anything could be had for a price, including children. It was a loathsome place that operated in relative security from the local authorities.

It was said that Jester, the innkeeper, paid handsomely for the privilege of operating, unmolested by the corrupt magistrate, as he was a 'special patron' of the Randy Knave Inn himself. It was conveniently located about twenty minutes outside London proper and was disguised as a regular Inn.

True, you could get a meal and some ale. And you could even rent a room but with the activity that went on there, you would be far better off sleeping in the mud than to bed down there. Everyone knew what the place really was and it only attracted the most despicable sorts of humanity. Fall asleep there and you might never wake up. Instead, you would likely be found with your throat slit and your cods stuffed in your mouth with your purse turned out empty. No, only the worst of the worst would dare to spend the night at the inn.

Smithy swaggered forward, dressed as a pauper. He placed himself in front of his victim and said, "ello guvna, can ye spare a coin for a poor ole soul?"

His victim never had time to answer, as he was dropped to his knees in a dead sleep, thanks to the efficiency of Gibbons and his handy cudgel.

They quickly tied up their prize and toted him to their waiting hack where they unceremoniously tossed him inside, not caring whether he landed on his head or his arse. They considered him to be human rubbish and figured it was his due. Even two cut throats like Smithy and Gibbons wouldn't grace the doors of the Randy Knave Inn.

A fellow had his self respect, after all. They were a decent sort of criminal, indeed. They had lent their expertise to Bow Street and the tax man too, on many occasions and were quite proud of that fact, and of the heavy purse they always gained from their efforts.

It was easy coin and a fellow shouldn't have to work too hard for his living. All they had to do was rough a bloke up here and there and chase him out of London with the threat of worse if he returned. Or hunt down and collect coin and of course, the occasional nabbing of some filthy bugger like tonight's fine prize. Yes indeed, easy coin.

This particular slob was to be sent off on a ship and would never be heard from again, though they didn't have all the details, they suspected he was to be sold to the Corsairs, which so often was the case. Must be a fancy aristocrat and his family wants to be rid of him, probably his heir. Wasn't their business where he ended up as long as they got paid?

"Another easy one, eh?" Gibbons asked his mate. "Bloke didn't even 'ave time to blink 'is eyes, just dropped down like a stone," he laughed.

"Aye Gibby, ye nailed 'im good, ye did," Smithy said, making a motion with his arm in demonstration of the scene that had just played out.

"Popped 'im right on top of 'is crown ye did," he grinned.

The two sat in companionable silence as they made their way to Gibbon's. It was the designated meeting place where they were to hand their prisoner over to some sea captain's crew members in a few hours.

A few minutes later they arrived at the seaside location where they unloaded their cargo and toted him into the shack. They sat him up in a chair and retied his bindings with his arms behind the back of the chair to make sure he was good and secure. They wanted to enjoy some ale and cards while they waited.

"So, you think 'im to be sold to the Corsair's?" Smithy asked his friend and leader.

"Aint they all?" Gibbons replied with a belch while digging in his breeches to scratch a bothersome itch.

"Aye fer sure, and them that are never come back, I hear tell" Smithy said, then hiked the left side of his arse up and broke wind.

"Jesu Smithy, did ye shite yer breeches?" Gibbons said, with a twisted up face of disgust at his friends deplorable manners.

Smithy snickered "Ah Gibby, ye know Ada's blood puddin' twist me innards," he defended and let another one rip.

Gibbons grunted his response and the two sat there and drank their ale and continued to scratch their itches, break their wind and belch their boredom away while they waited and contemplated how they would spend their coin.

Unbeknownst to the windy duo, Nigel was awake. He was busy trying to press the trigger to release the blade on his custom made spring loaded knife. It was attached to a leather wrist band and was cleverly hidden under the cuff of his coat sleeve. As he calmly worked to angle his wrists just so, he feigned unconsciousness and he plotted. It was a tricky business but not impossible. The leather wrist band was created for just such a purpose and now it would pay for itself.

He realized, from their conversation, it was most likely the one called Gibby was the one with the information. The other man Smithy seemed too dim witted to retain intricate details. Not that Gibby was a genius by any stretch of the imagination but he was clearly the sharper of the two.

When he first came to, he thought it was a kidnapping for ransom, but as he listened to them he knew otherwise. The only thing to do was try to escape but not before he got the information that he wanted. Afterwards, he would send them to their maker with his fine regards.

Clearly, he had an enemy, but who? Only a couple of people came to mind right away. On the top of the list was his cousin Damien. It would be just like that spineless weasel to come up with a plan like this rather than face him man to man on the field of honor.

But still he couldn't be certain, because he was a very wealthy man. As such, he had acquired a few enemies on the road to his ill gotten fortune. He felt reasonably certain that, with the right amount of applied pressure, he could loosen up Gibby's tongue. First he would get Smithy out of the picture then....ah, success!

The blade was released. He quickly sliced through his bindings, rubbing his wrists, careful not to let on that he was freed. After a few moments he groaned and moaned for effect and said in as raspy a voice as he could, "Water... I need water."

Gibbons said "Well whadya know, the ole bum bugger's awake. 'E wants water 'e says. Well we aint got no water, but we aint savages neither, so get the bastard some ale, Smithy."

Smithy grudgingly got up, fetched a mug and sloshed some ale into it. He walked back over to the prisoner and went to hold it to his mouth to help him drink.

In a lightning fast move, Nigel thrust his arm out and sliced the blade across his jugular. He shoved him out of the way, barely hearing the gurgling of the dying man. He jumped up and leaped the few feet it took to get to the other man. He grabbed him by the collar and held the blade to his throat.

"Thanks for the ale," he said, and then added, "But before I imbibe, I think you and I should get to know one another, Gibby."

He jerked him up from the table, dragging the shocked and speechless Gibbons over to the chair that he had occupied mere seconds before. He pushed him down in it. Keeping the blade to the man's throat, he started searching his person for weapons and found a pistol tucked inside his coat pocket.

"Ah…a man after my own black heart," he said, as he examined the weapon. "And it's loaded too. How convenient," he added. Then in another lightening move, he bashed Gibbons on the side of the head with the butt of the pistol and knocked him out.

He set to work removing Gibbons clothes. Then, he carried him over to the rickety small bed located in the far corner of the room, another convenience he noted. He spread his legs and arms out, tying each limb to the bed posts with some rope he was able to scrounge up in the shack.

Nigel was starting to enjoy himself. A little torture, to cap off a delectable evening spent at the Randy Knave, would suit his mood just fine.

He went back to the table and drank some of the swill they called ale. He was thirsty so it would serve. He hunted around the shack for implements to use in the games he had planned for Gibby.

He found some candles and some flint sticks, and plenty of lantern oil. Ah the things he could do with oil and fire to a naked man tied to a bed. The possibilities were endless. "Let's see, knife…check, candles… check… oil…check, what else? Yes, here we are…bowls for the body parts. Very good."

He sat down at the table and took off his boots and hose. He removed his cravat and started unbuttoning his shirt. He stood then and removed his coat and shirt and breeches too. "Could get messy," he mused.

Wouldn't do to go home to that screeching cow Penelope and her prodigy covered in blood. The questions would be tedious. The woman never ceased her nagging. Always pestering him about where he's been and who he was with. Well, he would be rid of her soon enough.

Once he married off his pathetic daughter, he would enjoy killing the bitch so he could remarry and get his heir. He had been giving a lot of thought to his future bride. He wanted to be sure she was young and thin and not some grotesque pig with huge sagging breasts like Penelope.

He hadn't been able to stomach bedding her since his wedding night, which resulted in Tess. No, his future wife would be thin and have very little to nauseate him on her chest. It would be easier to sustain an erection if he wasn't casting up his accounts from rolling around on top of protruding lumps of lard, while he pumped his seed.

Why, if he could find a woman thin enough with no breasts at all it wouldn't be a great effort to perform his duty to his title. He could just flip her over in the dark and do what he had to.

Breasts disgusted Nigel. Everything about women disgusted Nigel but they were a necessary evil, if one were to perpetuate his blood line.

He stretched out his arms, laced his fingers together and turned his hands over backwards, so he could crack his knuckles. He rotated his head about, to loosen his muscles in his neck and shoulders. That done he decided it was time to go play.

He strolled through the room, whistling a cheerful tune and wadding up his cravat, as he made his way to the bed. He ran his hand down Gibbons face a few affectionate times, giving thanks for such a fine specimen to play with.

Then… he slapped him, "Wakey, wakey, Gibby," he called out in a playful tone.

Gibbons eyes fluttered open and he groaned. He tried to move his hand, presumably to rub his bleeding head. Nigel was sure it smarted some.

When Gibbons realized he was tied down, Nigel was nearly unmanned by the orgasmic pleasure from the expression on his face. The terror he saw there was simply delightful. Gibbons opened his mouth to scream.

Nigel immediately stuffed his cravat into his mouth to silence him. He patted him on the cheek, "That's what I like about you, Gibby…always so accommodating."

*****

Nigel felt a little disappointed as he left the burning shack behind. Despite all the games he played with Gibby, he was no further ahead than he was when he started. Gibby must not have been trusted by the man who hired him because he knew absolutely nothing.

He was positive that he knew nothing. No one could have withstood all the things that Nigel did to him without spouting out the truth in sheer desperation. Why, losing the first finger alone should have had him singing like a soprano in an Italian opera, but no, he endured while Nigel carefully removed all his digits and his manly parts too.

Well, it had been entertaining at least, so not all was lost. Nigel lovingly caressed the ear he had nestled in his pocket. He would miss ole Gibby, he had been a really good sport.

Nigel whistled his happy tune as he made his way through town. He really hoped he found a hack soon, his boots were pinching his toes a might.

The more he thought about it, the more certain he was that Damien was behind this. Well, not to worry, he had plans for Damien. First, he had to get him alone with his daughter so he could force a compromising situation and force him into marrying the silly twit.

Once that was done he would have documents worked up, false ones of course, willing Damien's entire fortune to Tess. Then, he would kill him. Since his daughter was still under her majority, he could claim the fortune for himself as her father and manager of the funds.

Yes, that would fix things nicely, of course he would probably have to kill Tess too. And really, who would miss her? He certainly wouldn't. She's just an ugly reminder of what he endured on his wedding night. The only reason he married Penelope in the first place was for her rich dowry.

Now that his daughter was old enough he could gain a new fortune through her marriage. Too bad the old duke hasn't cocked up his toes yet. Perhaps he would wait until the old bastard croaked, to kill Damien. Then, he could have his fortune, too.

Maybe he should pay his respects to the old sod and help him along to the hereafter. Nah, he could wait. No sense dirtying one's hands, if one didn't have to. He was due to expire before the year was out, anyway.

Patience is a virtue after all and good things come to those who wait. He had been waiting for Tess and Damien's union for nearly a decade now. It really was the perfect plan to be rid of Damien once and for all. How to get Damien alone with his precious, though? That was the tricky part.

Perhaps he could work out something. Maybe a house party or some such where couples were wont to partake in a bit of licentious romping up and down the halls after bedtime. Of course, he had better do it soon because he was betrothed to that Sheraton chit.

He would probably have to marry her soon. She probably already had a bun in the oven, the way they quickly announced their impending nuptials. Well, no matter, he could always knock her off, too. So many people to kill, so little time. Alas, there was no rest for the wicked.

*****

Damien and Jarrett celebrated their success over a bottle of brandy in the library of Damien's town house. Damien was glad to have this sordid mess behind him now, so he could look to the future. Things had been going really well between him and Celia over the last few days. They had really bonded while they were at Evansdale, as he'd hoped they would.

He hated to go back to London but she wanted to. He couldn't keep her there any longer unless they were man and wife. Being alone with her in that setting was too tempting and it had been a real struggle to keep his hands to himself. They slept with each other both nights they were there and stayed up late into the nights talking.

They shared so many interests in common and he marveled at her intelligence. It made him proud to know that he had chosen such a woman. He couldn't have done better if he tried. He felt sure they would be perfectly suited in all areas, most importantly, in lovemaking.

They had a few close calls the second night he slept in her room. He felt sure she would have allowed him to go further had he tried. Mostly they just massaged and caressed one another and enjoyed passionate kisses. He was careful not to do anything to bring her to climax, as he was saving that for their wedding night.

A couple of times, he had to push himself away from her and go to the water closet to cool off. She had such a powerful effect on him that he was sure when they finally came together, it would be explosive, such as he has never known.

He found a certain pleasure in depriving his desires in preference to relishing the day when they married and they would come together in the first joining as man and wife. It really put a fine point on his need and it was pleasantly painful.

He was glad when they left though, as he didn't think he could bare it another night. It had been worth every ounce of discomfort to hold her and simply learn about her. She was a complicated woman and he felt that she would never bore him.

He proved that he didn't have to make love to her to enjoy her and that was his intent. To show her that he wanted more from her than carnal relations. He wanted her, the whole being. The real person, that she was.

Damien held up his glass and Jarrett did the same, "May Nigel rot in hell," Damien said. They clinked their glasses together and tossed back their drinks.

******

Jarrett, on the other hand missed his Celia terribly. He was at a complete loss without her. He had been able to obtain a special license through Damien's man and hoped to take her to the parson when he returned to Evansdale. The sooner the better as far as he was concerned. They couldn't afford to wait, the way they had been going at it.

She was such a passionate, adventurous lover, that he could quite lose himself. He had, really. They had made love so many times now that he lost count. He was sure she would be with child by now and the thought made him happy.

Imagining her fat with his child warmed through him as he sat there with Damien, drinking in companionable silence. He didn't feel guilty anymore about Celia but it did bother him that he was keeping secrets about Chelsea from him.

He really felt that it was for the best. It would help Chelsea to not have to tell him such a horrible thing about herself. It's like Celia said, in point of fact, she was a virgin. She would never have to tell Damien what she had suffered unless she wanted to.

It was best all the way around that Damien should never know. That thought helped to salve his conscience. Like finding the boy…he never would find this alleged man that Damien requested he find. He would simply just never find him and eventually Damien would give up on both. He was to be a married man himself, soon and once he had his wife fat with child, all the pain from the past would wither away and die. Good riddance.

The past is for the dead. Damien and Chelsea deserved to live, in happiness. And he would make sure they did by never telling Damien what he knew. He would forever keep Chelsea's secret.

"Well ole chum, I should head home, so I can get an early start to Evansdale on the morrow. I told mum I would be there before luncheon. She really liked Celia and looks forward to handing over the keys she says," he said, standing and stretching his legs.

What Damien didn't know, was that he was leaving London tonight and going back to Sheraton with breakneck speed. They had a wedding to plan and he hoped to have it done in the next day or two.

"My thanks to you, Jarrett. You really went above and beyond our friendship with this one. I can't thank you enough," Damien said as he stood up and embraced his friend.

They said their goodbyes and Damien went to his lonely bed and let his dreams travel where they would. He hoped that they took him to Celia and her loving arms.

*****

Celia hated that it was done without her father's blessing but it was done now and they would just have to accept the consequences when they came. For now, she was going to enjoy her wedding night.

She and Jarrett were having a romantic dinner in her room and soon would be enjoying each other's bodies until they were pleasantly weak and sated. Two days after Jarrett returned from London, they joined as man and wife and they would get to enjoy each other for many years to come.

Celia's cheeks warmed, as she remembered the last time they made love. Well, this morning before they went to the parson actually, such a naughty thing but so much fun.

"When do you think we should tell everyone that we have married? We can't keep up the ruse much longer and now that Nigel is out of the picture, there is really no reason to continue," she said.

She wanted to shout to the world that she was the wife of Sir Jarrett Wellstone and didn't want to be denied that privilege much longer.

"Let's give it another week, to see what develops. I hate to put a snag in their courtship. They were so happy at Evansdale. I just want to be sure that their bond is firmly cemented before we make the announcement. By this time next week, if Chelsea hasn't told him who she really is, then we will do it. I just want to give her as much time as we can," he explained.

"I'm sure you know best, but I want the world to know we are married. I don't want to have to hide like I'm ashamed," she pouted.

Jarrett got up to assist her from her chair. It was time to consummate their marriage and it wasn't food he was hungry for. She gracefully stood and he ushered her to the bed. He started removing her night gown so he could see all her wonderful charms.

Once she was disrobed, he stood back and admired the vision before him. Then, he started a slow disrobing of his own dressing gown, letting it slide to the floor. Then he too, stood in all his naked glory.

They started with a hot passionate kiss, soon landing on the bed, where he demonstrated his love for her with all the passion and skill he possessed. He taught her new things this night and she reveled in the learning.

They brought in the dawn with their loving and stayed hidden away the rest of the day exploring and cherishing one another. The future was bright, Jarrett decided, just before they fell into a deep contented sleep in the late afternoon the day after their wedding from pure exhaustion.

Chapter Seventeen

Chelsea didn't really want to be at the Osgood ball. But with only two days left in London, before they were to return to Sheraton, she thought that she should use the opportunity for one last sweep in the hunt for Nigel. She avoided filling her dance card this time, vowing to only dance with Damien, and only the waltzes, so she could scan the crowds for the familiar hated face, unencumbered.

She really wanted to remove that particular dark cloud from her horizon of happiness. She had decided that before they returned to Sheraton, that she would tell Damien of the ruse and hope that he could forgive her so they could be married soon after. She didn't want Nigel to haunt their happiness.

True, she could just forget about him now that she and Damien were back on course but she knew somehow, that he would always be an issue with her ability to find peace. She simply couldn't stand the idea that he could show up in her life someday, in passing on a street or at a ball and cause a scene that would perhaps reveal her secret to Damien.

She had decided that she would never tell him of her tragedy. Though, he already suspected there was such, he had no idea of the real nature of it and she would make sure he never did. No, she needed to locate him to find out his identity at the very least. Then she would decide what to do about him.

She was exceedingly pleased that Celia and Jarrett had married, taking the real Celia out of the equation in marriage to Damien. Everything was just about perfect now.

She was very apprehensive about telling Damien, however and hadn't quite worked out all the particulars. She didn't want to cause permanent damage between him and his lifelong friend, Sir Jarrett. That was the really tricky part in all of this. How to explain the switch; without hurting his feelings or insulting him; and have him lash out at his friend, too.

She had confidence that hers and Damien's bond was now one of everlasting duration but she knew that he would be angry, at the very least. She had worked hard to show him how strongly she loved him, in preparation for that day and hoped that her efforts would prove effective.

Celia and she, along with a word of advice from Sir Jarrett on the matter, had decided that the safest way to approach it would be to simply say what they had originally said they would. That when Chelsea saw Damien, she wanted him for herself. And Celia preferred Sir Jarrett, for the sake of Sheraton. Still a lot was left out that begged many questions and she hadn't yet been able to anticipate what all of them might be.

Perhaps she should tell Papa about it first and get his opinion. Surely, he would be able to come up with some logical ways to avoid a nasty scene that could result in her losing Damien forever. 'It would all work out somehow,' she told herself, 'it simply must.'

She was pulled out of her reverie when Matilda and Damien both moved closer to her in what almost seemed like an attempt to close ranks. It took her minute to see why, but when she did, it was a mind boggling sight.

There he was, approaching with two very familiar unpleasant women, one on each arm. Nigel, the duchess and Tess walked toward her small group with purpose. They were heading right for them. What in the world is he doing with those two, she wondered. She could feel her heart rate increasing and she looked at Damien and noted that he seemed equally distressed. She cast her eyes toward Matilda and she too, was tensed. What madness is this? She was about to get the most shocking of answers.

"Hello cousin, if I didn't know better I would almost think you were surprised to see me," Nigel said, looking menacingly upon Damien.

*****

Damien was surprised, indeed. Shocked, was more accurate a description for what he was. Nigel was supposed to be in route to Algiers but here he was in the flesh and very angry…at him. Something must have gone wrong…terribly wrong.

He must have bribed Hassan like he figured he might. He must suspect that he was involved with the kidnapping. Well, there was nothing for it but to brace up to it and play this scene out, he determined.

"Why would I be surprised to see you Nigel? You have been back in London for weeks. It stands to reason, that we should cross paths a time or two. You remember our meeting outside the club that day," Damien said, feigning boredom that he did not, could not feel.

Beside him, he felt Celia start to tremble and he moved ever so closer to comfort her with the warmth of his presence. Clearly, she picked up a bad vibration about Nigel and her senses were on high alert.

He needed to get her away from him and soon. No telling what the bastard would say in an attempt to upset her. Devil take it! Nigel focused his attention on her. His eyes traveled over every inch of her body. Then they rested on her eyes, where they stayed locked in a curious gaze, "Shouldn't you introduce me to this creature, Damien? Really, cousin where are your manners," he asked, never taking his eyes off Celia.

Damien debated whether or not he should make the introduction, as clearly Nigel already knew who she was and was using the opportunity to intimidate.

Damien leaned close to Nigel, so only he could hear what he had to say, and whispered, "Really, Nigel we both know that she's hardly your… cup of tea, why bother? I'm sure if you troll around you could find something here more to your…unusual tastes?"

Nigel glared at him for what seemed an eternity. He must have thought better of taking the conversation further. He surely knew he couldn't entirely trust Damien not to let his secrets loose in the crowded ballroom, where many high ranking members of the ton were now gathered, just slavering like hungry wolves for the next juicy piece of gossip.

He shifted his focus back on Damien, then said, "I see that you still suffer from your insolence, cousin. Very well then, have it your way. No worries, we shall meet again…and soon, you may count upon it. Oh and cousin, you really should quit neglecting your responsibility toward your dear cousin Tess. Why, you and she are practically betrothed. It's quite rude of you to shirk your obligations in such a way."

He followed that absurdity up with a disdainful look at Celia ,then he smirked back at him.

Damien laughed out loud at that ridiculous remark but otherwise remained silent, choosing instead to stare Nigel down with his most intimidating stare.

It was Nigel's turn to feign boredom now as he dusted off his coat sleeves and said, "Come ladies, let us quit these undesirables and seek out more suitable company for our exalted stations," and with a sniff and a wave of dismissal toward the group, he ushered his women away, seemingly satisfied with his stinging cut direct.

When they were several yards away, it was as if Matilda, Celia and Damien all drew a breath of relief at once.

Matilda was first to break the tension, "Did he just imply that you are betrothed to that ghastly monstrosity that he calls daughter?" she asked in abject disbelief.

Damien shook his head in wonder of the absurdity of it and said, "If you can imagine that yes, I think that was the implication."

Matilda looked at Celia and said, "Dear, you mustn't believe a word of it. Nigel and Damien detest one another, in case you couldn't tell. Nigel was only trying to make mischief dear, to cause problems for you and Damien."

Celia was still standing there silent with a strange look in her eyes. It wasn't the wild look that Damien had seen in her eyes before on the street the other day but an uncanny look. This was something altogether different. It was more along the lines of hostile intent, almost murderous.

She looked as though she wanted to harm Nigel and her breathing was somewhat erratic. Damien reached for her hand and she flinched but didn't pull away. She immediately tried to compose herself, he observed. He could tell that it was difficult for her but she finally managed to smile at him.

He was relieved that she wasn't evading his touch as she had done before when she was stressed. He said, "Once again I assure you that I have no idea what that is about. The idea that I would want to marry that woman is insane. I don't know what Nigel's game is but he seems intent to play it with or without me. I hope you don't let it upset you further."

She squeezed his hand in assurance but said nothing. It was something at least so he drew strength in knowing that she was still with him even if she was clearly upset.

"Yes dear, pay absolutely no mind to the monster and his madness. He has always been an evil blackguard," Matilda put in.

She looked at Damien then and said, "Perhaps we should take our leave."

That brought Celia out of her silence, "No, we shall not let him drive us away!" she said with conviction. Damien thought that was an admirable response and didn't challenge it. Just then, the first strings of the next waltz sounded and he offered his elbow to her asking, "Shall we, my lady?"

She accepted his arm. He whisked her away into the steps, held her closer than propriety allowed and thanked God that she was alright. He had an uncomfortable feeling that things were about to get really rocky with regard to Nigel. He would have to write Jarrett right away and tell him of this so he could find out what went wrong.

*****

Chelsea wasn't really alright but better than she should be. She was astounded to learn that she had been so close to finding Nigel all this time, as he had been right there under her nose. She had a feeling before that he was close, only she had no idea how right she really was. Damien's cousin?

Amazing, that those two very different people, could have the same blood coursing through their veins. Damien was so kind and good and Nigel was the exact polar opposite.

The way he looked her over tonight made her skin crawl with ugly sensations. She felt like she could use a good hot scrubbing. His gaze was probing and curious. For a moment, she was afraid he might have recognized her but she hadn't been afraid.

One thing that struck her was the fact that being confronted with the demon hadn't sent her into one of her episodes but instead it seemed to make her feel strong. She had a strange sense of invincibility. Her body was rippling with adrenaline, to be sure but not the kind that usually accompanied one of her episodes. This was more of a rush of energy, than the cold icy tendrils that she usually felt. It had been all she could do, to contain the urge to pounce on him then and there in the ballroom and gouge his eyes out with her finger nails. It was really most disconcerting.

So, the monster had a name and she knew him, now. Nigel Cullen, the Duke of Warwick. That was the most unfathomable part…a duke of all things.

Killing him wouldn't be easy. If she were to be caught, she would surely hang but she wouldn't let that intimidate her. She would just use all the cunning and intelligence she had at her disposal to defeat him.

She wasn't that little defenseless girl anymore. She would be able to outsmart him now and she would lure him to his doom, totally unsuspecting of who she was. She was sure she could do it. She had waited nearly a decade for the day of reckoning.

Now, all she had to do was plan it out and execute. It saddened her that Damien had to carry the shame of such an evil relation on his conscience. She knew why he hated Nigel and she loved him for it.

She wouldn't hold this against him, but instead, would find a way to protect him from the bastard by removing him from the family tree. He had obviously threatened Damien tonight. You would have had to have been deaf, dumb and blind not to see it. She wondered at the reason for it.

Nigel must hate Damien for knowing such a dark secret about him. But to provoke him like he had was madness. Damien could have done him in then and there by telling half the ton what a despicable person he was. That would have sent him slinking back under whatever rock he'd crawled out from under, in utter shame and forever ostracized by his peers.

Even his daughter would be ruined from such a monumental scandal. There would be no safe place in the civilized world for him to hide from it. That had possibilities, Chelsea realized.

Perhaps, she didn't have to kill him to destroy him. She would tuck the thought away as a last resort if she couldn't go through with actually killing him, but one way or another; Duke Nigel was going to be destroyed.

She brought herself out of her contemplations and focused on Damien as he led her through the waltz. He was the love of her life. She would do anything to protect him. Whatever Nigel had planned for Damien, he would have to go through her to get to him, she vowed.

*****

Nigel couldn't believe the resemblance of the Sheraton chit to her dead sister. Well, she should, considering they had been twins. 'I wonder if she misses her dear sister,' he mused with a grin.

Nigel remembered the moment of realization when he became aware of the fact that not only was the child a girl but most likely one of the barons daughters... with her signature eyes and her long black hair spilling out from under her cap.

It was well known locally, that one of the baron's daughters had been a hoyden and that she ran amok through the forest like some kind of banshee. Had he known she was the baron's daughter, he would have walked away and never thought twice about her.

She shouldn't have tricked him in such a way; no, she had lured him with her disguise. She must have been looking for it, he concluded. Well, she certainly got what she had coming to her, more than she bargained for, he wagered.

At first, he had been repulsed by the fact that he had taken a girl but he was consoled by the delicious memory of nearly beating Damien to death. It gave him pleasure to know that Damien knew his secret and couldn't do anything about it, lest he bring shame on his family's name. He so enjoyed taunting him with it.

He remembered how much fun he always had playing with Jacob, knowing that Damien was looking on. It always increased his pleasure to be observed, in effect making him a silent partner to the games.

But Jacob had refused to be cooperative in front of his brother anymore, so Nigel had to play the games with him elsewhere. From then on, they met mostly at the folly or the old game keeper's cottage, not nearly as fun without Damien, or the risk of being caught by one of the nurses or maids, but it served his basic needs.

He regretted that he had never taken the time to initiate Damien as well. It just hadn't felt right somehow, with one so young. Just when he was tiring of Jacob, Damien was the perfect age for it, then that fool brother of his had to go and kill himself. Afterwards, Nigel lost interest in Damien altogether.

Until that day in the wood when Damien saw him with the Sheraton brat and the old excitement was rekindled. Then, Damien had to go and ruin it by making him stop and forcing Nigel to thrash him. If he could have kept calm and tried to reason with him, he could have convinced Damien to join him and they could have become partners in the games again, a pity really.

Months later, he had heard about the mysterious disappearance of the chit, through an acquaintance near Evansdale that he often used to keep abreast of useful information while he was in Jamaica. He liked to keep up with Damien and what was going on at the estate while he was away. A man could never be too careful, after all and it was wise to stay well informed of one's adversaries.

When he heard about the missing Sheraton daughter, he knew then that she must have been so overcome by what had happened that she must have killed herself or perhaps her father did it. One never really knows about these things. Maybe she threw herself in the stream from her shame and was taken downstream to her watery doom.

Her body was never found and her father discouraged talk about it by saying the child had gone away but Nigel knew that he was trying to keep it quiet for the shame that his daughter had wrought. He was sure after the talk died down that he would never be connected to her disappearance as no one cared about her anymore. She was just a girl after all. No matter, she was gone now and could never tell a soul what he'd done to her.

Then Nigel decided he needed a new wife, he thought about that day and remembered the pleasure he'd had. He knew that if he found a wife without any womanly features, he would be able to get an heir, so he really owed her a lot. If her sister were any indication, the child he knew in the wood that day would have grown up to be quite grotesque.

He would have to be sure whoever he chose to take to wife was fully matured. He didn't want any surprise developments later on, that would encumber him in his duty.

"Tess dear, why don't you go speak with the Countess of Ravenswood and secure an invitation for Damien and Lady Sheraton for the house party. It would be a good opportunity for you all to get to know one another better," Nigel said, the plan to get them together suddenly coming to mind.

Tess, understanding what her father was about, beamed at the suggestion and said, "I'll go speak with her now and have it all arranged by the end of the ball. I'll personally deliver the good news to Lady Celia."

Nigel smiled at his stupid daughter. She doesn't have to know that he was going to kill her precious Damien after they marry. If she did she might not be so eager to help him with his plans.

The silly chit had had a crush on him since she was seven years old and always said she would marry him someday. Of course, he would help her realize her dreams, what are fathers for?

*****

Later in the evening, Chelsea was feeling weary and needed to get off her feet for a while. She thought a rest in the retiring room was just what she needed.

"Matilda would you mind going with me to the ladies retiring room?" Chelsea asked.

She didn't relish the idea of going alone as there were so many people here and she didn't know most of them. It was comforting to have a companion along.

"Absolutely dear, I could use a bit of a rest myself. These affairs are always so hard on one's feet, you know," came Matilda's reply.

"We shall only be a little while Damien, you'll be alright wont you? I believe Papa has been in the card room since shortly after our arrival, perhaps you could join him for a spell and encourage him to cut the play short before he loses Sheraton," Chelsea suggested with a giggle.

"We should let the baron have his fun while he can, after all he only has a couple of days left in London, and as far as losing Sheraton, the stakes are small at these affairs, so I wouldn't worry about that," Damien said, taking her hand and kissing it tenderly on her gloved palm.

Damien watched the ladies go and decided he would go to the card room, after all to see how the baron was faring. Not that he was worried about him losing his shirt, the man had very deep pockets, but 'a little while' in the retiring room could turn out to be upwards of an hour.

He was moving that way when he spied Nigel and his harpies on the other side of the ball room observing Celia as she exited. He waited to see what they would do.

Nigel whispered something into Tess' ear and she took her leave of him following the route Celia and Matilda took. What is he up to, Damien wondered. 'Perhaps, I should stay right where I am and continue observing.'

Damien was glad that Matilda accompanied Celia to the retiring room. Matilda will make mince meat out of Tess if she tried anything underhanded.

Damien couldn't help but feel that Nigel was up to something, but what? He was bound to retaliate for the kidnapping debacle, so he had better be on alert to circumvent any of his schemes.

Damien was glad that Celia was leaving London in a couple of days. He had decided that he, too, would leave London and go to Evansdale where he could be near her and hopefully persuade her to marry soon after their arrival at their country homes. He felt like Celia was becoming more amenable everyday and it was just a matter putting London behind them.

*****

Chelsea and Matilda arrived at the retiring room and claimed two available comfortable looking chairs with foot rests. It felt good to be off her feet, Chelsea mused. There were only three other ladies present. They were all busily relaying the latest juicy tidbits to one another and didn't seem to really notice their arrival.

Chelsea was just about to tell Matilda that she was looking forward to going home, when Tess came into the room. Matilda made a groan of disgust and squared her shoulders for battle.

Chelsea was surprised when Tess turned a sweet, though quite false, smile in her direction and said, "Dear Lady Celia, I just feel dreadful about fathers behavior earlier, and he does, too, of course. I thought it would be a nice way to make amends if I were to get you an invitation to the Ravenswood house party this weekend. It's going to be a smashing sensation as anyone that matters will be there. Of course, you should bring Damien and," she cast her eyes at Matilda and continued, "Your uh, friend. Oh, do say you'll come, I went to great effort to acquire your invitation and it would mean so much to me if you would attend," she finished in a rush.

Interesting, Chelsea mused, what was she about?

Matilda must have suspected something afoot too because she said, "You mean that your father put you up to it, don't you Tess?"

Tess glared at Matilda but otherwise gave no response to the jab.

That got Chelsea's attention, however. If Nigel was going to be in attendance perhaps she should be as well. Plenty of opportunity to plan her revenge could be had at a house party.

"Are the duke and duchess going to be in attendance as well," Chelsea probed.

"Oh yes, of course, I wouldn't dare go without proper chaperones," Tess said emphatically.

"You say that it's going to be held this weekend, but how long will it last?" Chelsea continued her questioning.

"We are all to start arriving on the morrow and it will last four days," Tess explained.

Chelsea would have four days in which she could come up with any number of ways to dispatch him. The only drawback was that Damien would be there. That would curb her ability to move about undetected. But she felt sure she could manage something.

Perhaps after everyone went to bed she could sneak into his room and what? Hmmm...perhaps she should see about some poison, arsenic perhaps.

Her thoughts were interrupted when Matilda said, "Surely you don't plan to actually attend dear, you are to return to Sheraton and I know your father is quite looking forward to going home."

Matilda was right, her Papa would be another obstacle to overcome. She thought sure he would be amenable if Damien were attending. He seemed to agree to anything if Damien were involved. Yes, she could manage Papa, she decided.

"I'm sure he won't object, a quick jaunt to Ravenswood wouldn't be a hardship and it would mean we could leave London a day earlier," she told her.

Matilda was incredulous, Tess was smirking and Chelsea, well, she was plotting.

Chapter Eighteen

"You can't be serious," Damien said, glaring at Chelsea. How could she have returned from the retiring room to inform him of this insanity?

She must have gone completely mad, agreeing to such a suggestion. Surely, she wasn't taken in by Tess and her machinations.

"Of course, I'm serious. I would love to finish off my time in London with a grand house party out in the country. It's not far from Sheraton, after all. I would really love to go," she said, with her hands on her hips, clearly digging in to defend her decision.

Damien sighed, running his hand through his hair, as he so often did when he was trying to think clearly. Of course, if she was determined to go, he couldn't very well allow her to go without him.

Nigel is clearly up to something. He only wished he knew what it was. He had a bad feeling about this.

He looked over at Matilda and said, "And you couldn't talk her out of it either, I assume."

Matilda looked just as disturbed by the notion as Damien was and merely shook her head that she had not been able to.

He sighed again, "I don't like this, but if there is no way to talk you out of it, I suppose we all shall go then," he said, with great reluctance.

What could Nigel do, after all? He was a member of the aristocracy and had to publicly behave with a certain decorum. Celia really seemed to have her mind set on it. She had no idea how evil Nigel was, so she wouldn't see the danger that he did.

Although, Damien suspected that he, himself might be the one in danger from Tess…he inwardly laughed at that. No, surely, there could be no real harm in this.

He would just stick close to Celia. When he wasn't able to, he would have Matilda or her father look after her to keep any nefarious schemes of Tess and Nigel's at bay. Perhaps, he could lessen the chances Nigel would have if he offered a compromise and agreed to only attend for two days instead of the entire duration.

"However, I would prefer we didn't stay the entire time. Maybe just two days instead of four," he added, after a quiet moment.

"Why don't we play it by ear? If it seems that your cousin is up to no good then we shall leave," Chelsea allowed.

Damien knew that was as good as he would get and dropped the matter. Perhaps her father would object and be more successful than he had been, he thought hopefully.

"We should go find your father and be quit of this place. I have a headache now," he said, giving her a chastising look to let her know that she was the cause of his discomfort.

Celia smiled at him clearly oblivious of her crimes and despite his agitation, it warmed him.

*****

The baron had been no help at all, much to Damien's chagrin, making him wonder if he spoiled her rotten by giving in to her every whim. That's how it seemed, anyway.

Well, Damien would just put a stop to that when they were married. He wouldn't let his wife walk all over him, no matter how much he loved her. A man has to be king in his own castle, after all, Damien inwardly grumbled. He sat in his bed chambers with a bottle of scotch whiskey to nurse his anger.

The woman really was driving him to drink. He was not happy about this at all. His head was splitting, even after three shots.

When he got home he sent a missive by special runner to Jarrett explaining that he had seen Nigel. He asked him to find out what had gone wrong and to see about getting his twenty thousand pounds back. Twenty thousand pounds was no great loss for him but he couldn't see paying for nothing.

Perhaps those two clowns had botched it up somehow. Damien hadn't had a very confident feeling about them as he and Jarrett sat in a hack, watching as they did their work.

Once they had him secured and tucked inside their hack, they had left the scene and assumed all would be well from there. They never thought to watch the transfer between the two cut throats and Captain Fellow's crew.

An error in judgment, that shouldn't have happened, not with something so important as that was. Perhaps Nigel escaped and Captain Fellows never saw him. The ship would have sailed yesterday along with Nigel and Damien's money.

Damien sighed and poured another drink. He should have just taken matters into his own hands and not involved so many others. Aye, he should have killed Nigel himself and now he knew that the only way to be rid of him once and for all, was to do just that.

Perhaps he could plan some kind of accident while they were at the house party. There were usually fox hunts at these affairs. He could always make it look like a hunting accident. He wished Jarrett were here to discuss it.

No, he'd have to handle it himself. It was too dangerous to involve others. He could see that now. Well, he would have four days to come up with something, he supposed.

One thing he knew for certain, if Nigel laid one hand on Celia, he wouldn't care if it looked like an accident or not. He would kill him on the spot, wherever that may be.

Damien tossed back one more drink and summoned Thompson to assist him with a bath and the packing of his bags. He was not looking forward to the dawn.

*****

"Celia, that was a footman from Evansdale with an urgent missive from Damien. I have to leave for London right away; something went wrong with the plan for Nigel. Damien and Chelsea saw him tonight at the Osgood ball and actually talked to him. He was supposed to be…well, gone," Jarrett explained what had disturbed their love play earlier.

"No, you can't go tonight. Why, it's already three in the morning. Wait until you've slept," she pleaded.

"I'm sorry love but it can't be helped. Just try to relax. All I'm going to do is ride out there and talk to my contacts to find out what might have gone wrong. I will be back long before you even wake up, I promise," he assured her.

She lunged for him, with tears in her eyes. He held her tight for a long moment, then pushing away; he escorted her to the bed. He tucked her in, kissing her on the forehead. With great reluctance, he took his leave.

It was a fairly quick ride to the docks. Jarrett arrived at about five in the morning. He was confronted with the shocking sight of Gibbons shack, burned to the ground. He stood in the street, scratching his head in confusion trying to imagine what might have happened.

A few minutes into his contemplations, he heard someone approaching from behind. He turned around quickly and saw a familiar face. It was Elijah Jones of the Dirty Devil crew.

"Knew'd ye be round sooner or later so Cap'n said I should stay 'ere until you showed. Looks like yer cut throats got themselves kill't. There be two bodies found inside after the fire were put out," he said holding out an envelope to Jarrett. "Cap'n said to give ye this," he added.

Jarrett was stunned as he accepted the envelope. He recognized it as the same envelop he had given Fellows. It contained the bank note for twenty thousand pounds. He opened it to confirm his conclusion and he was correct.

"Thank you, Elijah…did any of you happen to see who did this?" he asked, knowing who it was, but asking anyway.

"It were the bloke ye wanted took, I seen 'im leavin' and 'e were whistling' a 'appy tune when 'e came out, 'e were. Give me the willies, it did," Elijah told him with a shiver. "I 'eard evil things goin on in there just afore the place went up in flames. Some kind of demon were in there, laughin' like 'e were bringin' forth the devil 'imself. Me and Paps just arrived to pick the bloke up but we were too late," he said, holding his head down in shame.

Jarrett didn't like the sound of that. Nigel must have tortured them to death to find out who had arranged for him to be kidnapped. He was glad he had made the arrangements with Gibbons anonymously.

Nigel wasn't stupid. He could easily figure out that Damien was behind it. Not good. With a heavy heart he thanked Elijah for the information and gave him two crowns. He knew that he wouldn't be working for awhile since the ship had sailed without him.

He decided to snoop around the remains of the shack to see if anything could be detected other than the obvious. Two men died in a fire. With the bodies being gone, he probably couldn't find anything but it was good to be prudent.

Jarrett arrived at Damien's town house just after dawn and learned that he had already left for the house party at Ravenswood. He borrowed paper and a quill to write a missive explaining all he had learned, then asked the butler to have it posted.

With that done, all there was to do now was return home and wait for further instructions from Damien. With a sick heart and a worried mind he turned his horse toward Sheraton.

*****

Chelsea was rather tired on the morning journey to Ravenswood. She had barely managed an hour's worth of sleep due to her excitement about the whole affair. She had managed to pilfer some arsenic and a small sized mallet that would make a good cudgel, from the kitchen. She felt that she was now well provisioned.

She tucked the poison away inside her reticule and packed the cudgel in her portmanteau along with her knife. She would unpack that herself while Jenny unpacked the trunk. She was a little disappointed that she hadn't able to obtain a pistol. However, she felt that between the poison, mallet and the knife she had brought from home, she should be able to figure out some way to dispatch Nigel.

She had had the knife since she was a child. It was a gift from her Papa so she kept it but hadn't really needed it since she no longer hunted or fished. It had a fairly large blade, but was light weight and small enough to be concealed under her skirts by a strap.

She decided that she would try the poison first as she wouldn't have to get too close to him to actually perform the deed. She went over scenarios in her mind rehearsing possible dialogs for various situations. She was reasonably certain it could work.

She even rehearsed her reaction to the news that he was dead and was quite proud of her dramatic acting skills. Why, if she concentrated really hard, she could actually produce tears.

She had decided that one of the best ways to ensure he partook of the concoction would be to find out what his preference for alcoholic beverages were. She planned to try to obtain a full bottle to pour the poison into. Then, she would slip it in his room, with a handy serving glass. She didn't want anyone to see her doing it, of course, so she had rehearsed reasons why she would need a private bottle of brandy or port for her room.

She thought perhaps she wouldn't even have to request the beverage as Papa always kept a well stocked bar in his room at Sheraton. The Ravenswood's would probably provide such luxuries for the more distinguished persons among their guests. Since Nigel was a duke he would fit that criteria.

So, the first thing she would have to do when she got there would be to locate his room to make sure that it was well stocked. Then, she would have to find out what his favorite drink was and make sure she put the poison in that one.

She sighed; so many things could go wrong with poison, of course. There was no guarantee that he would even consume it. She wished she could come up with a more definitive way to administer it but that might prove impossible.

She could always stay her hand for a day or two and see what his drinking routine was, then formulate a better plan. But since time was of the essence she might have to have a backup plan for the poison.

Her last resort for killing him was to go in to his room the last night of the party and slice his throat or bash his skull in with the mallet…she winced…she didn't like either of those ideas at all. In fact she was fairly certain she would have to be desperate to attempt them.

No, she would have to place all her eggs in the arsenic basket and hope that it would work. She wished she knew with certainty, how much she should give him. She knew that it didn't take a lot to kill a rat but a grown man was something altogether different. She was reasonably sure she brought enough, though, so she wasn't too concerned.

The only thing about poisoning Nigel that disappointed her, was that she wouldn't be able to let him know who his killer had been. She had fantasized so many times about telling him who she was just before she struck the killing blow. Oh well, dreams are one thing. Reality is another, so she must stick with the realistic options and get the deed done.

She had formulated a backup plan to all her other back up plans, to cover the possible eventuality that she wouldn't be able to kill him at all. She decided that, even though it would hurt Damien and Papa, she would expose Nigel for what he was. She would use herself as proof. It was a desperate plan that she hoped she wouldn't have to use. But the option was there, if worse came to worst. It gave her some small comfort.

She thought about the wisdom of bringing Jenny in on any of her plans and decided that she would wait a day or two before she did. This was a dangerous business. She didn't want to drag an innocent bystander into it, especially if she were to be caught.

Even if she wasn't successful in her attempts to kill Nigel; when she was caught, her maid would surely hang for assisting her. While in her own case, it was possible that because of whom her father was, she might be spared the death sentence in favor of transportation. Either would be awful. Truthfully she would prefer death but she didn't want Jenny to be put in the position of fearing either sentence.

She looked at her Papa, Jenny and Matilda as they slept and wished she could clear her mind enough to sleep with them. Damien was riding his horse instead of accompanying them in the carriage, as it was full. She was glad of it because he seemed particularly agitated this morning. She thought that she smelled whisky on his breath but she never really got close enough to confirm it. He was red eyed and had an angry look about him.

She felt bad that he was coming along. She wished there had been some way to avoid it, but he wouldn't have allowed her to go without him. If he hadn't agreed to go, Papa would have never allowed her to.

She sighed heavily again and closed her eyes. She really needed to get some sleep, if she were to stay sharp enough to do what must be done.

*****

Damien was still in a foul mood as they made their way to Ravenswood. He would rather be stripped naked and tied to a tree near a beehive covered in strawberry jam than have to endure the next four days. He had decided that Celia would compensate him for this madness by marrying him as soon as they returned to their homes. Enough was enough and he was not going to be pulled around like some lovesick fool while she toyed with his emotions any longer.

That was the whiskey talking, of course. He had been sipping from his flask through much of the trip as he was still nursing his headache. He didn't get a wink of sleep last night and knew that sleep would be a precious commodity while residing under the same roof as the conniving Cullen's.

His mind had been busy trying to anticipate their agenda. He was sure he had it pretty well figured out. Nigel, in his deluded way of thinking, must have devised a way for his daughter to try to compromise herself with him to try to force him to marry her. Why would Nigel wish for such a match?

Well, whatever his reasoning he was going to be sorely disappointed. Damien wouldn't marry Tess in any circumstance, whether he be tortured or forced at gunpoint, gentlemen's code be damned. It was insanity to even imagine such a thing.

Knowing Nigel the way he did, he felt that there had to be an underlying motive for trying to force such a debacle. It didn't take a great deal of calculation to come up with a sum that equaled fortune. Nigel had always coveted Evansdale and its rich lands and rents. Not to mention the private fortune Damien had accumulated on his own through his investments in shipping ventures. Yes, money must be at the root of it, as was often the case with scheming devils such as Nigel.

He must be aware that Damien was involved in the kidnapping and was willing to stay his hand in retaliation until he could force Damien to marry Tess. In fact, he might try to use that as a means of blackmail.

First, he would have to prove that Damien was involved and he couldn't because Jarrett had hired the cut throats anonymously. Captain Fellows would never divulge the information. He wasn't sure about the pirate Hassan, though. Damien was fairly certain that Nigel never even made it to the ship. He thought he must have escaped the two used for the kidnapping somehow. It was the only logical explanation.

He would have never escaped from the ship with an entire armed crew watching him. 'Great, it's raining now to add to my misery,' Damien grumbled, pulling his greatcoat collar up. He tipped down the front of his hat in a futile attempt to avoid the pelts of the icy rains on his face.

Aye, Celia owed him big for this and he planned to collect. The symbol of his misery came into view, after another half an hour, when rounding a bend the seaside castle came into view.

It sat high atop the cliffs and had a sprawling lawn with very few decorative elements. It was a medieval structure that looked rather depressing in Damien's opinion. He supposed it was the perfect setting to play the impending drama out.

Damien eyed the castle noting the battlements. He tried to calculate how high they were. It was actually an impressive sight. In its day, it was probably virtually impregnable and would have been the safest place to be when an invading army came through.

Damien was sure he remembered hearing about secret passage ways that lead from the castle. They connected to natural caves carved out in the rock cliff that open up to the sea and were most recently used to bring French aristocrats to safety during the revolution. Perhaps he would find time to explore them while he was here.

As a child he enjoyed exploration with Jacob but they never had anything as grand as caves to delve into. Damien pulled his Bay over and allowed the carriage to catch up with him. He took one last fortifying swig from his flask and silently vowed…'let come what may. It's time to get this misadventure over with.'

*****

"Welcome to Ravenswood, how nice of you all to come," Alexandra, the Countess of Ravenswood said cheerfully, as she greeted her latest guests. "With this cursed rain, we were afraid people would decline or be delayed at the very least but we have had an excellent turn out, so far."

The countess was a statuesque middle aged woman with blonde hair and brown eyes. Hers was a genuine smile of delight, welcoming them into her home.

"Thank you for inviting us, my lady, we are delighted to be here," Chelsea said, beaming at the woman.

She was truly captivated by the castle. It was the first time in her life she had seen such an amazing sight and she couldn't wait to explore.

"You're very welcome dear, we are delighted to have both you and your father of course. We have much planned to entertain you, if this rain will let up of course," she said casting an angry eye heavenward.

"Matilda, it's so nice to see you dear." Matilda gave a pleasant return, then the countess turned to Damien, "Lord Devonshire, your presence here will ensure our success. So many people have tried to get you to attend their house parties and here you are at mine. But I hear you are already taken off the market and that congratulations are in order," she said, with a wink.

"Yes, my lady that is true. The lovely Celia has consented to be my wife and we hope to have our nuptials very soon," Damien said, trying to show enthusiasm that he didn't feel.

It wasn't the countess's fault that he was dragged here against his will, so he couldn't very well take it out on her. He cast the object of his temporary scorn a look of genuine love and affection. He might be mad at her but he loved her until it hurt.

"How very fortunate for you both, you make a lovely couple, and I wish you both all the best. Now if you are ready, Alfred will direct you to your rooms. I have placed you all on the same hall for convenience and I do hope your stay here will be enjoyable," the countess said. With that, Alfred took the lead ushering them to their respective rooms.

Chelsea couldn't help but feel Damien and Matilda's discontent but Papa and Jenny seemed as in awe of the castle as she was. Once they were directed to their rooms she was pleased to see that Damien and Papa's rooms were across the hall from hers and Matilda was next door.

Jenny had a small side room on the other side of the dressing room. She felt secure knowing all of her loved ones were so near at hand. She had a mission and was determined to see it through but she was still very much afraid. She wished she could just forget it and enjoy the party but she had to do what must be done.

Chapter Nineteen

Chelsea was exhausted on the first evening of the house party. She hadn't been able to rest and she was out of sorts. She knew that she should get some sleep soon if she were going to be able to stay sharp to affect her plans.

She found out which room Nigel slept in and as she had assumed, the room was indeed, well provisioned with various bottles of liquor. She had yet to see Nigel consume any alcoholic beverages and feared perhaps that he didn't imbibe at all.

She decided that she would observe his habits through tomorrow evening. If he didn't indicate what his preference was by then she would come up with an alternative to alcohol.

All the guests were gathered in the drawing room while the young ladies demonstrated their singing and pianoforte talents. Some were very good and others, like the poor wretch playing now, were pitiful and it was a very difficult thing to sit through when one was as tired and irritated as she was.

The poor dear was miserably unskilled and her voice was atrocious and grating on ones nerves. Many of the other guests were as uncomfortable as she herself was so she would just have to suffer through it right along with them and hope that the next brave soul to entertain them would be more tolerable than her predecessor.

Chelsea was flanked by Damien and Matilda and her father was around somewhere. She hadn't seen him much since they arrived. Papa really loved the castle and was behaving like a young lad on an expedition in a magical world.

It was just as well, she didn't need him clinging about while she tried to dispatch Nigel. She wasn't as confident in her plans now as she was before but she thought that was probably due to fatigue.

In fact, she rather wished she weren't here at all. Poor Damien was as out of sorts as she. Matilda wasn't much better off. All in all, they made a miserable little group.

She wondered if it was too early to retire as that would be one way to spare her poor splitting head from the ivory butchers. She had plans she wanted to put into place to better monitor Nigel. She had been trying to keep her eyes on Nigel as much as she could without being noticed but it was difficult to do because he didn't often stay in one spot overly long. She supposed that he, like everyone else was miserable with the entertainment.

Right now, however, he was staring at her and Damien. Every time she turned around he was casting his evil eyes in their direction. It was quite disconcerting. She wasn't sure that he didn't recognize her. That thought made her stomach hurt and she had quite lost her appetite during supper, as he glowered at her all through the meal.

Damien was aware of it, too. In return he would stare right back with a most hostile glare, but so far his efforts had no effect. She feared that if these two had to remain in close proximity much longer, something was going to happen.

Perhaps, she should suggest to Damien that they leave the house party and go home. He wouldn't try to talk her out of it, she was sure of that, given that he didn't even want to come in the first place. No, I must give it more time, she admonished herself.

She was pulled out of her depressing thoughts, when Matilda whispered, "Prepare yourself, here comes trouble."

Chelsea noticed then that Tess and the outlandishly clad duchess were making a path in their direction. She stiffened her shoulders to prepare herself for battle. In response to that action, Damien looked at her, then followed the path of her eyes. He quietly groaned when he saw them. He too, stiffened his shoulders and took hold of her hand and held it. It was good to show a unified front against these two transgressors, she supposed.

*****

Damien would rather be flogged than to be at this cursed house party. He always hated these things to begin with but this one was particularly bad as Nigel and his harpies were in attendance.

He didn't like the way Celia and he kept watching one another and was on the verge of suggesting that they call it a night, just to put one aggravating day of this madness behind him. To add to his bad disposition was the constant rain that had forced everyone to stay indoors so he hadn't been able to steal away with Celia to have any private time with her.

Now, to put a cap on a perfectly wretched day, here came the two women he most hoped to avoid. Trapped. He braced himself as the duchess heaved her bosom, inhaling to gather the wind she needed, before launching her usually unpleasant discourse.

"Damien you look simply bored dear, perhaps you should take a turn about the room with Tess and I. It's good to stretch ones legs when forced to endure such monotonous entertainments," she said, elbowing Tess to signal it was her move, in the obvious attempt to corral Damien.

Before Tess could affect her move, Damien quickly said, "I was just telling Celia that it was time we all turn in, actually," Damien said, hoping that Celia wouldn't contradict him. She didn't, much to his relief.

"Oh, that's too bad cousin, as I was hoping that you and I could spend a few moments in private converse," Tess said, casting a jealous eye toward his fiancé.

"I hardly think that's appropriate," Matilda piped in, "What could the two of you possibly have to converse privately about?" she asked, with a sardonic smile and a challenging gleam in her eyes.

Clearly Tess and her handler didn't appreciate being thwarted because if looks could kill, Matilda just got a double dose of murder. Matilda wasn't worried though, for she murdered them right back with her own eyes. After a moment of silent combat the other two women retreated from the field but not without a parting shot at Damien.

It was Tess who spoke, "Cousin do not despair, I shall make myself available whenever you can escape your keepers," she said, before joining arms with her mother and taking leave.

Damien couldn't resist calling after them, "Your bones will turn to dust long before I seek you out, cousin."

The two women acted as though they hadn't heard what he said but there was a slight misstep in Tess' gait that gave her anger away. There would be retaliation, Damien was sure of it.

"Damien, you had better sleep with your door locked and barred against that conniving Jezebel. I think she and her mother are looking to have her compromised at your expense" Matilda warned.

"Don't worry, I have already considered this and have taken the appropriate measures. Might I suggest that you two do the same as well. I don't trust anyone by the name of Cullen. Shall we go upstairs?" he replied.

The ladies complied and they all went to their respective rooms. Once inside his own room, Damien turned the key in the lock, removed it and wedged a chair under the door handle.

That should keep her out, he decided. He breathed a sigh of relief. He had made it through the day relatively unscathed.

*****

Several hours later, a sound woke Damien from his troubled slumber. He sat and listened. To his chagrin, it sounded as though someone were trying to turn his doorknob. He jumped up and put his robe on and walked over to the door and positioned himself to accost his intruder.

A minute, maybe two went by when he heard frustrated whisperings, very clearly female voices, right outside his door. It didn't take a genius to deduce who they belonged to. He stood there silently, shaking his head incredulously and debated whether he should open his door.

The decision was taken away from him when he heard a third voice and this one wasn't whispering. Matilda to the rescue again, he realized.

"How dare you try to invade Damien's chamber. Have you both lost your senses?" Damien heard her say.

"We thought we heard a cry of distress from inside. We were concerned that someone may be in need of assistance," Penelope said, in indignant defense.

"That is the most ridiculous excuse for what you were attempting that I have ever heard. You have no reason to even be on this hall much less simply strolling about in the middle of the night. I caught you red handed and you know it. I recommend that you cease this reckless scheme you have devised to marry off your spawn before I make it known to the entire gathering at Ravenswood what you have been up to. It won't help your cause at all if you were to be known to be the unconscionable pair of schemers that you are. Do I make myself clear?" he heard Matilda thunder.

If the entire gathering wasn't already informed by her tirade, it would be miraculous. He was sure everyone in the entire wing could hear her. They must have been sure too because it was apparent by the sound of retreating footsteps, that Matilda had won the battle again.

Damien removed the chair that was barring his door, unlocked, then opened the door. He peaked out and saw Matilda glaring at the retreating figures as they made their way to their own wing.

"What would I do without you, Aunt?" he asked smiling at the victor.

"Perhaps, you should double up with the baron. I have a feeling we haven't seen the last of those two," she said ignoring his gratitude.

Matilda was angry. He hadn't seen her in such a state in many years. She was an awesome force to be reckoned with and he was glad that she was on his side.

Along the hall, other doors creaked open as people were finally overcome with curiosity and decided to see what was afoot but he noted that neither, the baron or Celia came out to see what had transpired right outside their doors.

He decided that, sleeping soundly must be a Sheraton trait. He suddenly felt a twinge of envy as he was exhausted and would love to be oblivious right about now. He turned to his aunt and kissed her on the cheek.

"Go back to sleep Matilda, everything will be fine now. I doubt those two will risk your wrath a second time," he told her.

"Yes, well be sure you lock and bar the door again dear, you might think it's over but I have had dealings with their ilk before and I can tell you this was probably just the beginning. Make sure you are never alone anywhere while you are here. Make sure Celia, the baron or myself are with you at all times, as you will undoubtedly have need of a witness in your defense," she advised.

"You're serious, aren't you?" Damien asked in wide eyed astonishment.

"Yes, and you had better take heed, my boy or you will find yourself in quite an unfortunate dilemma," she told him, as she returned his kiss.

Her last words made him shiver. He took her advice. Locking and barring the door, he tried to go back to sleep.

*****

Chelsea didn't hear the commotion as she wasn't in her room when it came about. Instead she was tucked behind a tapestry that was placed over a niche along the wall not too far from Nigel's chamber that gave her a good view of his comings and goings. She had left her room earlier, taking up her position there, in hopes of gleaning some useful information to aid her cause.

After an hour or more she heard low murmurings by what sounded like two women and a man as they made their way up the hall. She couldn't quite make out what they were saying. It sounded like they were arguing about something, so she strained her ears to hear. Unfortunately, it was being hampered by the thickness of the tapestry, making their words sound muffled as they drew nearer.

She continued to listen and became aware that the women's voices she heard were those of the Duchess of Warwick and her disagreeable daughter.

She held her breath in an effort to hear better and distinctly heard the duchess say "Nigel really, we aren't incompetent as you say, it is not our fault that Matilda interfered, the woman is a termagant. I dare say she was waiting for us. It's as though she suspected our plan. No sooner had we arrived and Tess tried Damien's door, then there she was, threatening to expose us to the entire household. What were we to do?"

Chelsea gasped, loudly, then covered her mouth with her hand, hoping she hadn't given herself away. The nerve of them! She regretted now that she and Damien were not already married for if they were, then she could protect him from those two hags.

She suddenly realized that it was quiet out in the hall now and feared that she was about to be uncovered, but then she heard Nigel say, "Just go to bed and let me give this some thought. Obviously, you two are miserable failures and I will have to come up with an alternative plan and execute it myself. Get out of my sight, the both of you, you disgust me," he told them.

Chelsea heard the retreating footsteps and wondered if it was safe to come out. She dare not make a move now but she wanted to get away as soon as possible. She sat in silence for a few more minutes, willing her heart rate to slow down. She was beginning to feel like she was suffocating behind the enclosure.

She was about to take a peek to see if it was safe when she heard a soft sinister laugh. It was right on the other side of the tapestry from her. She knew then, that Nigel knew someone was behind the wall hanging and suddenly realized the foolishness of her actions.

The only thing that separated them now was some ancient work of art. She was about to be discovered spying on the devil himself and he would probably kill her.

She patted her thigh to assure herself that she had her knife and when she confirmed that she did, she quietly lifted her skirt to remove it from its sheath. She firmly grasped it in her hands, lifting it above her head so she could maximize the force of her strike, if he discovered her.

She was ready and her heart was about to leap out of her chest. She was shaking violently and felt the familiar icy tendrils of fear slithering up her spine. She tried to will herself into a calm that was impossible to achieve but she fought valiantly as she knew she couldn't afford to succumb now. Not now, when she was about to be able to fulfill her mission or be forced to defend her life.

She waited for what seemed an eternity but then was surprised to hear the sound of a cheerful tune being whistled, accompanied by the sound of retreating footsteps. He was leaving…just like that…he was gone.

Chelsea was stunned. She slid down the wall and landed on her rump, shaking and trembling. He was toying with her, she realized with a sick feeling in her gut.

Well, in all truth, he didn't know who was behind the tapestry but the way he had been staring at her all day and night, and she at him, he would have to be pretty dim not to be able to guess correctly, who was there, spying on him. Indeed, he wasn't stupid at all. He did recognize her, she was sure or it now. She felt exposed.

The hunter has become the hunted. She no longer felt confident in her ability to kill him. The way she had been shaking while she held the knife would have made any blow she could have struck totally ineffectual. Her arms felt limp and useless from the tremors.

It's time to get out of here, she decided and with that she peeked out and saw no one about so she quickly darted down the hall and took the hall that lead back to her quarters. She got to her room, dashed inside and quickly locked and barred the door. She jumped in her bed, pulling the covers over her head and allowed the fear to have its way with her.

*****

Indeed, Nigel wasn't stupid. He knew the Sheraton chit was hiding behind the tapestry to continue her voyeurism. She had been watching him all day and evening. This wasn't the first time he had caught her near his chambers. To what end, he wondered.

Is it possible that she knows, somehow? Her sister had been alone that day so he was fairly certain that couldn't be it. Unless the child had recognized him and reported it to her sister before she died.

He supposed that was possible but he didn't think it likely that the child knew who he was. She did have an agenda, of that he was certain. He didn't think that she had overheard anything too damaging before he became aware of her presence.

He wouldn't have noticed her there at all, if it hadn't been for the soft sound he had heard and the slight movement of the tapestry right after, to tip him off. Perhaps, Damien told her about what happened and the silly girl seeks vengeance. Aye, that's not only possible but probable.

Well, the bitch will have to go. He couldn't have menaces like that interfering with his plans. He would take care of her. But first he had to help his nitwit daughter catch a reluctant husband. 'Must I do everything myself,' he inwardly grumbled his complaint.

Nigel pondered ways to be rid of the nuisance. He would have to make it look like an accident of course, he decided. Ah, the secret passageways that lead to the sea…yes I remember hearing about them.

I could kidnap her and take her out through the passageways and drown her in the sea. No one would be the wiser. It would be assumed she was taken out too far by the currents and succumbed to exhaustion before she could make it back to shore. Tomorrow I shall go exploring in the castle and see if the rumors of the passageways are true.

He was suddenly very relaxed. He hadn't counted on killing anyone this weekend. Now that he knew he would, he was quite looking forward to tomorrow or the next day, there was no real rush after all.

It might even be wise to wait until he got his daughter compromised by Damien first. Then, people would assume she drowned herself from her despair. There was nothing like a good suicide, to liven up an otherwise dull party.

The nosey bitch was almost as bad as her sister, with her schemes to fool him. Well, he would take care of her and reunite the twin troublemakers. He was just disappointed he wouldn't get to play a few games with her first.

It wouldn't do to leave marks upon her body, indicating torture when one was trying to make it appear to be a death of her own doing. He could terrorize her a bit, he supposed. Get her excitement flowing just before he shoved her under the water. She would fight and thrash about making the whole thing worthwhile. Yes, it had promise, if he did it right. It wouldn't do, to waste a perfectly good opportunity to play games.

Though, he hadn't played games with a woman in many years, he thought it would still be enjoyable. The last time was when he was a green lad about the age of five and ten. The stupid whore said his manly parts were as useless as teats on a stallion, just because she repulsed him and he couldn't perform.

Well, he showed her and he would show the Sheraton chit, too. No one crossed Nigel Cullen and lived to tell about it.

*****

Chelsea wasn't the only one watching Nigel. The baron had witnessed the whole episode. He too, had been hiding in an alcove in an attempt to see what Chelsea found so interesting about this man. Now he knew....the woman called him Nigel.

It was all he could do to keep from killing him then and there but he refrained as he didn't have a weapon on him. Nigel was a big man and he didn't think he could over power him in hand to hand combat. He cursed himself for a fool, not to at least have his knife. He wouldn't make that mistake again.

He wished he could be sure this was the man who had harmed her so many years ago. He supposed he should be prudent and observe a little longer before he took fatal steps.

Aye he would keep a close eye on his baby lass, to gauge the matter accurately. Then he would strike. Whatever it was about this man, was distressing to her. This much he knew for sure.

But one thing that puzzled him about it, was that her behavior at being confronted by him was calm in comparison to other reactions in her past. Such as the recent event with that bad actor, Davenport. That was more along the lines that he would expect from her.

Perhaps, there was something else going on here that he wasn't aware of. His daughter seemed to have a secret. He needed to uncover it before he took a man's life. He didn't think he could come right out and confront her about it. She might become hysterical. He didn't want that kind of scene to be played out here, in front of so many witnesses.

He would just have to stick close to her, to make sure she came to no harm. If the man turned out to be her attacker, then he was a dead, man plain and simple. The baron had waited a decade to learn the identity of the monster that had harmed his precious daughter. He would move heaven and earth to send the bastard straight to hell.

Perhaps he could speak to Jenny or Matilda to see if they knew what her interests were in this Nigel Cullen. She was close to Jenny. She seemed quite fond of Matilda. It was possible she could have confided something to them. He would speak to them both to see what he could discover.

He would have to be careful not to expose Chelsea, of course, so he would have to handle the matter delicately. The baron made his way to his chambers, stopping to listen outside his daughter's door. All seemed quite in there now. He hoped that she wasn't lost in one of her episodes. Poor lass.

Chapter Twenty

Early the next morning, Damien was walking along the beach, contemplating the beautiful dawn. The rain had cleared away and it looked to be a promising day shaping up, weather-wise, at least. He still had this cursed house party to contend with. He was seriously considering convincing Celia that it was time to leave, today, the sooner the better.

Nothing good could come of their continued stay here and he didn't like the idea of having to fend off Tess and Penelope's machinations. Not to mention he didn't like the way that Celia and Nigel seemed to be constantly aware of one another. Nothing good could come of that either.

He didn't think there was an attraction there. No, it was something else. Celia found him disagreeable, he was sure of that and as he knew full well Nigel's predilections for boys, so he was sure there were no sexual attraction on his part. So, why all the interest? It was puzzling to say the least and it left him feeling quite unsettled especially in lieu of the situation last night.

As for Nigel and his absurd notions that Damien would have any interest in his daughter, Celia would simply be in the way and that would put her in a degree of danger. Damien had no knowledge of Nigel committing murder but he wouldn't put it past him to want to harm her if she got in his way and clearly she was in his way. To continue to stay within his reach was lunacy.

Besides, he wanted to be quit of this place and get on with his future as a married man. He didn't want to muck about with anymore of this foolishness. Damien was convinced. He would tell her when he returned to the castle after breakfast. It was time to put an end to this madness.

He turned to go back up the trail he had come from and stopped in his tracks. Nigel was coming out of a cave. He hadn't yet seen Damien. Damien hunkered down, behind a nearby boulder, so he could observe what Nigel was up to.

He walked about the entrance of the cave, looking around on the ground and feeling along the facade as if he were looking for something in particular. He didn't seem to find what he was after so he turned and went back inside the cave.

Damien sat there for over an hour waiting for Nigel to come back out but he never did. Curiosity finally won out. Damien went over to the cave entrance and listened for a minute before venturing inside.

It was so dark, he couldn't see anything beyond where the sunlight shone from the entrance. He looked around to see if he could tell which way the cave might lead but he could see nothing. He knew that it was pointless to try to go farther but Nigel had gone through somehow and that was very perplexing.

He wished he had a torch, but he didn't see anything lying around that could suffice to make one. He had noticed that Nigel didn't have a torch, so Damien knew that he had somehow managed to navigate the cave without one.

He moved into the darkened portion of the cave and started feeling around along the wall. About ten feet into the shadows he noticed that he seemed to be moving along a tunnel. He walked along the darkened tunnel very slowly in what felt like an ascending angle. He could feel the stress on his calves as he traversed along. That indicated to him that he was moving upwards, which seemed logical if it were to lead back to the castle, as he assumed it must.

He wasn't sure how far he had come but he knew it was very far. He could no longer hear the surf behind him, but he felt sure that he would have to go a least a quarter of a mile before he reached the castle. He decided to continue his exploration, as he had gone this far. To turn back now would be a waste of precious time.

He wanted to know what Nigel had been up to. This was the only way to know. He was fairly certain that Nigel was no longer in the cave and was probably already at the dining table breaking his fast with the other early risers, so continue on he must.

Finally after what seemed an eternity he bumped into what felt like a door. He felt around for a handle and located one. It seemed old and rudimentary but it worked. He opened the door and found himself inside the castle walls, quite literally.

The passageway was narrow and was lit sparsely with filtered light coming in through cutouts in the walls along the ceiling. Damien assumed it must have been some form of ventilation as it was a pleasant temperature within. It also allowed light in. However, it was still rather dark but not blindingly so, like it was before.

He found some narrow stairs and ascended them. He found himself on the second level in a passageway that lead to the sleeping chambers on what he thought was the wing he was staying in. He was intrigued now and wondered if the servants used these passage ways to navigate the castle unnoticed.

There seemed to be evidence of this. There were tables with buckets and cleaning supplies and there was a mop and broom leaning against the wall. These items weren't covered in dust, indicating that they were used recently. He found a door near where the mop and broom stood and put his ear to the door to see if he could get a feel for where he was. He realized that he was outside of Celia's room, as he could hear her and Jenny having some kind of disagreement.

He shouldn't be eavesdropping but his interest was piqued when he very clearly heard Celia say the oddest thing. "Jenny, I can't take it anymore, I'm going to confess everything to Damien when we get home and I'm ready to leave today. I can't stand living this lie any longer. I'm going to write Celia and tell her to prepare herself for our arrival."

Damien wasn't sure he heard her right at first, so he continued to listen for a moment more while his mind started grasping to understand what he was hearing. Suddenly, something his father said struck him like a bucket of ice water. 'One of the baron's daughter's' he said followed by the strange utterance of the word 'two.' Damien's mind started reeling as the memory of the twins tickled his brain.

Yes, the baron did have twins but one had died about ten years ago, or had she? He couldn't remember for sure and he couldn't even remember her name but he did remember now that the baron did have twin daughters.

Damien couldn't believe this. How could he have forgotten about the twin sister? In all this time it never occurred to him that she had been a twin and that he knew it all along. Not once did she ever mention her sister, even when he poured his heart out to her about Jacob. Was he really with the other daughter? Not Celia at all? What is this madness?

"My lady, you should have never concocted this idea in the first place. I told you nothing good could come of it but you wouldn't listen and you convinced your sister to go along with you and now look at you. You are worn to a frazzle and your nerves are nearly destroyed. You are losing weight and you aren't sleeping. If you keep on like this you are going to start having your episodes again," Jenny was chastising her.

The woman he had thought was Celia said nothing to this. Jenny continued after a moment, "You've been having them again haven't you?" she asked sternly.

Damien's muscles were tense. He had been duped. Fooled by a couple of chits and their maid, but why? He suddenly doubted everything that had gone on between him and this this…he didn't even know what to call her.

Frustrated beyond reason he started looking for a way out of this cursed passageway and went further up until he found another door. He put his ear to that door and didn't hear anything going on inside so he flipped the latch upwards and let himself in.

It was Matilda's room and she wasn't in it. He made his way out into the hallway and went to his so-called fiancé's door and knocked, loudly.

After a moment Jenny asked "Who's there?"

"Damien," was his curt reply.

The door opened and the woman he was supposed to be engaged to met him with a warm smile and evidence of shed tears.

"Damien, whatever is the matter?" she asked, after she took in his expression and reached the obvious conclusion that he was disturbed about something.

Damien looked at Jenny and said, "Leave us."

Jenny looked to her mistress to see if she agreed with such a command. She bobbed her head that she did. After giving Damien a look that told him that he had better mind his manners, she reluctantly quit the room.

"You have something to tell me?" he asked gruffly.

*****

Chelsea knew instantly what Damien was talking about. She could see the hurt and anger in his eyes and she just knew that he had overheard the conversation between she and Jenny, somehow. She would have preferred to wait until she was at Sheraton for this to come out but it couldn't be helped now.

She was tired from her continued lack of sleep and her nerves were on edge from the incident last night with Nigel. She had determined that she wouldn't have the courage or the strength to kill Nigel and the only thing left for her to do was expose him. She wanted to leave Ravenswood today as soon as she and Jenny could get packed, then once they had arrived home she planned to tell Damien her story and set about exposing Nigel. She supposed it didn't matter where it all took place so there was no sense in trying to fool him any longer.

"My name is Chelsea, Damien and before anything else is said, let me tell you that I love you with all my heart. I never inte…."

Damien cut her off by grabbing hold of her arms just below her shoulders and giving her a good shake, "You love me?" he barked at her. "I don't even know who you are, and you say that you love me," he added before releasing her abruptly and turning away from her in exasperation to pace back and forth.

Chelsea was afraid now, as Damien was seething mad and she was alone with him and he kept his pacing between her and the safety of the exit.

She decided now might not be the best time to tell him who she 'really' was after all, so she said, "I am the twin sister to the woman you met in London at the Simpson ball. We are identical twins as you can see and no one can tell us apart except for our nurse Hattie as she has been with us since our birth and is for all intents and purposes, our mother."

"Yes, yes, I can see that you are identical twins and you fooled me well, but what I don't yet see is the why of it? Is this some perverse game you and your sister play on unsuspecting gentlemen such as myself? What do you gain from it?" He demanded after rushing back up to her and towering over her in an angry stance.

Chelsea started shaking and shuddering and felt as though words were a foreign concept. She was suddenly unable to form a single coherent utterance.

When she remained mute, Damien grabbed her by the arms again and jerked her closer to him and their noses were nearly touching, "Don't stop talking now sweetheart, we are only just getting to know one another, please, do go on," he said sardonically.

"W-w-we, that is C-Celia and I, traded p-places because when I s-saw you in the g-garden, I w-wanted you for m-myself," she managed to articulate.

Damien released her as if she were an evil thing and spun around again into his pacing.

This wasn't going well at all, Chelsea realized. She drew in a few steadying breaths and forged ahead. "Damien please, I know that you are angry but please believe me when I tell you that I never meant to hurt you. Celia didn't want to marry you, so after she told me of it, I proposed that we switch places. If she didn't want you then I would have you," she said desperately clinging to the fabricated story.

"And I had nothing to say in the matter while you ladies decided my fate? Is that the way of it?" he roared.

Chelsea winced and stepped back a few paces to put some distance between her and the angry bear of a man towering before her. She felt the familiar feelings of fear. She knew that she would soon be unable to deal with him in the fast approaching condition she would be in and she didn't want to have the episode in his presence.

She shook her head and started running her hands along her arms in a fast motion to create warmth on her skin because she was ice cold and trembling violently. She couldn't hear him any longer but she was aware that he was still shouting at her and he looked as though he were fading away as the darkness started to surround her.

Damien rushed over to her again and roughly took her face by the chin. He was shouting something at her, but she couldn't make out the words.

Damien was surprised, when without warning and with an incredible amount of strength, she pushed away from him. She released herself from his hold and started grabbing at her skirts.

He stood there incredulous as it appeared that she was lifting them. Surely she didn't think to seduce him here and now, he thought with dark sarcasm.

He learned quickly that he was mistaken, as she withdrew a knife that was attached to her thigh and lunged at him. He barely had time to get out of the way from the wild woman, as she thrust the knife down at his face, in an over the head angle of attack.

She had a maniacal look in her eyes as she continued her attack and when she missed him, she began erratically thrusting at him every which way she could. Somehow, he managed to dodge and evade all of her attempts.

He saw an opening when one of her thrusts sent her into a spiral and she ended facing away from him. He launched his body forward and clutched her around the waist with one arm. He grabbed the wrist that held the knife and twisted her arm behind her to force her to release the weapon.

He spun her back around and she started thrashing, kicking at him and trying to bite him, too. He held on to the mad woman and tried to subdue her with all his strength.

After a moment, his efforts were rewarded when her body went limp in his arms. Damien allowed her to fall into his embrace and he turned her face toward him and saw the hollowed out eyes of a vacant stare. She was gone from this time and place and was no longer in a position to harm him or herself, he realized.

Damien slid down on the floor, cradling her in his arms. He first had to regulate his breathing before trying to bring her around. It was impossible to do the latter, he noted after several minutes so he made himself comfortable on the floor with her draped across his lap and just held her while he gently rocked her back and forth and spoke to her in a soft soothing manner.

He was ashamed of himself for behaving so recklessly with a so obviously disturbed woman. He should have taken into account her spells but he was so wrapped up in his anger that he hadn't given thought to her condition.

He realized while he was holding her now that he didn't care who she was and that he loved her no matter what. He would have her even if she was mad as she appeared to be now. He felt certain that her episodes were only brought about by stress and that they could be dealt with.

"I love you… Chelsea… and we will get through this, I promise," he vowed to her and squeezed her tighter against him. He was relieved, in a way, that he had finally discovered who the real woman was behind the many layers.

*****

Nigel was shocked. He too had overheard Chelsea's confession from his hiding place in the secret passageway. So this was the child from the wood and she hadn't died as he had always assumed. Instead she had been kept hidden away, like the dirty little slut she was.

Well, no one makes a fool of Nigel Cullen. He would take care of her, he decided as he made his way along the passage in retreat. She obviously hadn't told Damien a thing or vice versa as he had believed before. She wouldn't of course; it's too shameful for her to admit. Damien wouldn't have her, if he knew what a whore she was.

Well, no matter she would be dead soon, that much was still true. It didn't matter who she really was when he was drowning her, as long as she ended up dead in the end……

*****

The baron and Jenny burst into Chelsea's room and stopped dead in their tracks. They both took in the scene with a look of horror on their faces.

"I didn't hurt her, I swear," Damien said, defensively as his hold on her tightened. He wasn't about to let go of her now.

He didn't care what they had to say, propriety be damned, he loved this woman and would marry her right now if he could.

The baron was the first to speak, "I gather that you are aware now that you have been duped, my lord?" he asked in a frank manner, seeing no reason to continue the ruse.

"You knew?" Damien asked feeling himself grow angry all over again.

"Not in the beginning, my lord. I didn't even suspect that it was she until that night when that blackguard Davenport accosted her on the terrace. I decided then that whatever her reasons for doing this, that she loved you. I wanted to give her every chance at happiness, so I kept her secret even from her and allowed this drama to play itself out."

"I don't care who she is or why it was done. I only know that I love her and I will have her. So you have no fears where that is concerned. But perhaps you can enlighten me about a few things, as clearly she can no longer speak for herself. I need some answers," Damien said, as he continued to cradle her in his arms in a possessive manner.

The baron and Jenny both looked uncomfortable about the request, but after looking at each other for support.

"I shall do my best, my lord to answer your questions," the baron said, motioning for Damien to proceed with his questions.

"Perhaps you should have Jenny leave the room. I suspect that what we have to discuss should not be done so in front of the gentle sex," he said respectfully.

"I shall not leave my lord, it would be unseemly and I will not have my lady's reputation risked to scrutiny in such a way," she said, with squared shoulders and a look of complete defiance.

The baron placed a staying hand on her arm, "Please Jenny, go, he is her betrothed after all and no one will think badly of Chelsea with her father present," he implored her.

Jenny didn't like it one bit. She thought to defy them both by refusing to go but she knew she would be overstepping her bounds. She couldn't take the risk of being dismissed and being taken away from her Chelsea. So with great reluctance and a last look at Chelsea to assure herself that she was in no danger, she quietly took her leave.

Damien waited until the door was closed before asking with choked words, "Was Chelsea raped?"

The baron made a woeful sigh and went to sit in the chair beside the bed. He put his elbows on his knees and buried his face in his hands. He didn't want to betray his lass by telling her story to the marquess, so he said, "Please my lord, it is not my story to tell. When the time is right, allow her to do it. I could never betray her in such a way. I will tell you however, that as a child she was victimized, but she is still a virgin, if that is your concern."

Damien was relieved by that. It didn't matter that she was a virgin but he was grateful that the villain hadn't taken her innocence. Clearly whatever he had done to her was bad enough and it left traumatic scars on her psyche. But he felt that they could be managed with proper love and care.

"Did you ever catch the bastard?" he asked, with a hint of vengeance in his voice.

"No, I never knew who it was and she never told me. Until our trip back from Sheraton, I haven't spoken to my daughter in seven years. She has lived her life in her attic apartments as a recluse and refused to have anything to do with me. Only her maid Jenny, the nurse Hattie and Celia have been able to go near her. That's why I was so filled with hope when I realized who she was. It's why I didn't say or do anything to try and stop her. To see my daughter living again, was a treasure I jealously guarded with my silence. Please forgive me, my lord, but Chelsea is my special lass. I love her with all my heart and I only want her to have a chance at happiness. You have returned her to me and for that I will always be grateful to you. It is a miracle of monumental proportions as I would never have dreamed that she would ever be capable of the things that she has done. The last time I spoke to her was rather tragic. It ended in a violent tirade, after I told her that I couldn't stand to look at her. It was the drink, you see. I immediately realized my mistake and tried to reason with her but she cut me out of her life and never spoke to me again," the baron finished explaining with tears in his eyes.

Damien felt sorry for the man and couldn't imagine what it had been like for him, all those long years, being forced away from the daughter he so obviously adored.

So, seven years ago she had been attacked, he surmised. Not long enough to get over such a thing, if one ever could.

"I can't imagine how you must have felt and I'm happy that my presence has restored your daughter to you. I only wish that my presence could also cure her of her spells, but that's highly unlikely. I feel so helpless holding her like this while she is lost to me… how long do you think it will last?" he asked the baron.

"One never knows with these things. When she was first attacked, she was catatonic for many weeks. When she came around she would have these episodes whenever she felt threatened in some way. It seems to be some sort of retreat. It often restores her, I'm told. Sometimes, they last for hours and have been known to last more than a day. It's just hard to say when she might return to us, if ever she does," the baron said, then choked out a sob.

Damien took his words into consideration and the last part chilled his blood. The idea that she might not pull out of it was more than he could endure.

He began a slow stroking of her hair and kissed her temple before saying, "You should prepare yourself to leave this place. I want to go back to Sheraton as soon as she recovers. Once there, we shall be married. I think my cousin has a negative effect on her. There seems to be something odd between them and I don't like it. We must remove her from his presence. He is an unsavory man and I don't want to risk her safety. He has developed a plan to have me compromise his daughter. In point of fact there was an incident outside my door just last night. My Aunt Matilda caught Tess and her mother red handed, as they were trying to enter my chambers. She threatened to expose their treachery if they persisted but I don't trust that they will desist. By virtue of her betrothal to me, Chelsea stands in their way and could be targeted. So, the sooner we are gone from here the better," Damien explained.

The baron didn't mention to the marquess what he suspected about his cousin. He agreed that she was probably a target but for an entirely different reason. He decided he had to keep that to himself or else he would betray his daughter's secret.

He would just keep a close eye on the duke while they were forced to remain here. If he had to take up position outside of Chelsea's door to protect her from him, he would. He didn't think it would come to that however as he observed the possessive way in which Damien was holding Chelsea. She would be well guarded by him and that put his mind at ease, considerably.

"There is another matter I should explain to you, my lord'" he said when a new thought occurred to him.

Damien looked up at him and invited him to continue with a nod of his head.

"My other daughter Celia, I believe she may have eloped with Sir Jarrett. At least, that was the plan according to a letter she wrote to Chelsea while we were in London," he said cautiously.

Damien didn't know why but it struck him as funny. He laughed out loud and said "I'm not surprised at all… good for Jarrett," he mused aloud.

The baron was relieved by his response and said, "I suspect this whole thing was her idea. Celia told me early on that she preferred Sir Jarrett to you. She didn't want to leave Sheraton after she were married and she thought that Sir Jarrett being a poor knight would have been more suitable to her objective. I, of course, preferred you. You are a wealthy man and would have made her a fine husband. But where matters of the heart are concerned, it's best if a father stays well out of it, unless the daughter makes a bad choice that could put her future at risk, of course. I admit that I have a liking for Sir Jarrett so I am not concerned with her decision."

"Jarrett will make Celia a fine husband, on that you can count. He is a very noble man and I would trust him with my life," Damien said honestly.

The baron was pleased with this, saying, "My lord, if you would like to rest, I will stay with Chelsea until she comes around and you can see to our arrangements for departure."

"No, I will not be leaving her in this condition, I will stay right here. I want to be here when she recovers so I can tell I'm sorry and how much I love her. I hope you understand," he said, in a tone that brooked no further discussion on the matter.

The baron didn't see the harm in allowing it so he nodded his approval and left the room.

Damien was alone with Chelsea now. He quietly began telling her how much he loved her and what their future would be like while he gently caressed her face. They would get through this he vowed and together they would come out stronger on the other side with a bond no force on this earth could put asunder.

Chapter Twenty-one

Later that night, around eleven of the clock, Chelsea slowly came around. She was disoriented and confused and felt a slight bit of panic when she remembered what had happened. She tried to get up but found that she was being held in place by a set of very strong arms.

She looked over to her right and saw that Damien was stretched out beside her, looking at her with pure love in his eyes. She relaxed a bit, seeing that he was no longer mad but she still needed to get up, so she could relieve herself.

Her throat was dry. She swallowed trying to moisten it before rasping out, "You're still here?"

"Aye, 'tis where I belong. Where else would I be?" he asked smiling tenderly at her. "Are you thirsty? Allow me to get you some water," he added. He got up from the bed and went to the sideboard to get her a drink of water.

He handed her the glass and assisted her as she sat up enough so that she could drink it. "Better?" he asked.

"Yes, thank you but, I believe I need to a moment of privacy, if you don't mind," she answered shyly.

Damien immediately caught her meaning and excused himself from the room to allow her to take care of her needs. When she was through, she went back to the bed and sat down on the side of it, considering what would happen next.

It didn't take long for her to figure out that he was expecting to finish their earlier conversation. With a sigh, she called out, "You may enter."

Her heart skipped a beat as he re-entered the room. She knew that she had to explain her behavior. He deserved the truth but she was struck mute as she watched him turn and lock the door and then approach her.

He stood before her now and went to his knees so he could put his arms around her waist. He placed the side of his face against her bosom and held her tight. It was such a sweet and tender action that she was quite overcome.

Tears formed in her eyes and rolled down her cheeks. He must have felt them drip on him because he looked up at her and moved to wipe them away with his thumbs.

He kissed her then and said, "You are mine Chelsea, and I will never let you go. I love you, no matter the reasons for the ruse that you and your sister played. I was mad at first and I'm deeply ashamed of my behavior. I humbly ask that you forgive me," he said with contrition.

The sound of her name from his lips for the very first time was breathtaking. Her body reeled with a rippling current of pleasure. She savored the feeling as she looked at him. It was so like Damien to take all the guilt upon himself and ignore her own.

She wrapped her arms around his neck and kissed him with an open mouth, inviting his tongue to mingle with her own. He accepted the invitation and they continued their embrace as they slowly and tenderly devoured one another lips.

Damien pulled back from the kiss after a moment and looked into her eyes. It was as though he were trying to see into her soul and she felt exposed. She knew that she could no longer hide from him. He deserved to know everything and so she would tell him.

She placed her palms on his cheeks to cradle his face and returned his gaze for what seemed like an eternity, "When you look into my eyes like that, what do you see?" She asked.

"I see the woman I love. I feel a deep connection with you that I cannot explain. It's almost unearthly the way that I am naturally drawn to you through your eyes. They pull me in and then I'm inside you and I can see your soul, it's a beautiful soul and mine begs to merge with it," he said with another tender kiss.

Then, a thought occurred to him, "I'm fairly certain but I want to be sure that I never…kissed your sister," he said seriously, but with a light heart and a mischievous grin.

He was sure he never had because he didn't feel the same connection to Celia that he had with her and he was sure of the moment he met Chelsea for the first time was that morning at breakfast because it was a completely different feeling. It was pure and deep, whereas with Celia, it had been merely lustful, a simple physical response.

Chelsea couldn't help herself, she laughed and hugged him tight, "I would never have allowed you to kiss my sister, you were mine from the moment I saw you in the garden with her and Sir Jarrett," she assured him.

Damien kissed her then, deeply. It was soul-searing, and he never wanted it to end. He wanted to climb inside her and merge their hearts and souls together and coexist inside one blissful being of contentment.

But he knew they had much to discuss and he couldn't allow himself to be distracted. Reluctantly he pulled away from the embrace and moved to lay on the bed behind her. He gently tugged her around the waist so that she would join him.

He spooned his body behind hers, wrapping his arm around her and said, "Now, tell me what you must so we can put it behind us and go forward into the future with no secrets between us. I want nothing to stand in the way of our happiness, Chelsea."

The moment of truth had arrived. The moment she had waited for and knew she couldn't avoid another moment longer. She wasn't afraid that he would reject her but knew it would be hard to tell him everything. She searched her mind for the right words, so as to soften the impact of the awfulness that she must deliver.

With a heavy heart but one of confidence, she took a deep breath and said, "I have always loved you, you know…from the moment I first saw you…that day so long ago, in the forest," she said, pausing to see that he understood.

He was silent for a moment and she wasn't sure he understood what she meant. She worried that she would have to be more direct, but she was spared.

She knew the moment her words made their impact because he burrowed his face into her hair and his hold on her tightened. He groaned a sorrowful sound of agony and his whole body trembled as he began to weep. She was suddenly afraid that it had been too much for him and wished she could take it back but she couldn't.

Damien felt as though his heart had just been ripped from his chest as the meaning of her words finally made sense to him. At first the words made no sense at all and then all the clues he had gathered since he had known her, fell into place and he knew without a shadow of a doubt then, that he now held the child from that day in his arms.

His mind tried to reject it but couldn't. The truth of the words was evident in all that he had observed. He couldn't believe he hadn't seen it sooner. He was such a blind fool to have not put it together before now.

Even his subconscious mind had known the truth and had tried to speak to him in his dreams but his conscious mind had been unable to accept what had been staring him in the face. Her eyes alone should have told him who she was.

He had never forgotten those eyes and the connection he had made with them that day as he watched her suffer and he felt her pain. He had been so overwhelmed with her agony that he felt it in the very depths of his soul. He shivered at the memory and held her tighter, continuing to weep.

He couldn't help himself as the emotions just flowed out of his body. He felt so consumed with guilt and pain because he hadn't been able to spare her from what she had suffered.

If he had gotten there a little sooner, she wouldn't have been so abused. He silently cursed himself and God for failing to protect her.

Then, the full weight of her words rested in his mind and he remembered where they were. He remembered that he was here, too. Nigel was here now under the same roof as she and she was in danger. His protective instincts kicked in. Suddenly, his heart started thundering and he was in a state of panic.

He sat up quickly and turned to her, "We have to get you away from here," he said, as he started to get out of the bed.

She reached out for him to try to stay him but he had moved much too fast and he was just out of her reach, "No, Damien, let's wait and go with the dawn. We are safe here in my room, he won't come here," she said, understanding the source of his sudden upset.

"I will send you home with your father and Matilda. I will stay here and kill the bastard. Then, as soon as I safely can, I will join you and we shall marry right away, if you will still have me, that is" he vowed vehemently.

He felt a moment of insecurity that she might not wish to marry a man related to that sick animal.

She jumped up from the bed and grabbed him by the arm so that he would face her, "This is not how it should be, Damien. Let's wait until morning and leave this place and Nigel behind forever. We don't ever have to see or think of him again, if we don't want to. We can be married as soon as you say, only please don't kill him. I don't want you to bear that sin on your soul. He isn't worth it, I know because I came here to kill him myself but I couldn't do it. I don't want you to do it, either. We can expose him later, for what he did, if it would please you, but please don't kill him," she begged him.

"You would defend that villain?" Damien asked in total disbelief.

"No! I would defend you, and in so doing I would beg you not to kill him. What would I do without you if something were to go wrong and you were hurt or killed…or hanged?" she nearly choked on the words. "I can't lose you now. Damien, please stay with me here and now. We can leave this place with the dawn. I beg you." she continued to implore.

Damien gathered her in his arms, holding her tight. Every fiber in his being was begging to get her away and to kill Nigel once and for all. He couldn't stand the idea, that the monster lived and breathed another second. But he couldn't deny her this heartfelt request, so he relented.

"It shall be as you say," he said, guiding her back to the bed where they lack back down upon it. They were both silent for a long time laying in their comforting spooned position.

Damien's heart was aching and he could feel the tension in her body as he held her. He began a slow sensual caress along the length of her upper arm with his index finger in an attempt to soothe her. He was rewarded when she made a soft sound of contentment and burrowed her backside closer to him to encourage him to continue.

He leaned his head down and started speaking softly in her ear, "We are going to have a beautiful life together, you and I. When we get back to Sheraton, I will call for the parson and we will marry then. I cannot wait another day, without being able to make love to you Chelsea," he said.

Damien was ashamed that he could be aroused now at such a moment but he was. He knew that the last thing she would probably want was to be pawed at by some randy bugger but he couldn't help himself. She felt so warm and soft in his arms. He knew that his arousal was nudging at her bottom but he tried to ignore it as he continued with his sensual caress.

He noted that she didn't respond to his words about their making love, so he asked, "Do you think you will be able to make love to me when we are married, without feeling scared or uncomfortable?"

She silently nodded her head, then turned her body toward him to look at him. Her eyes were filled with sorrow and it hurt him to see it, "What is it," he asked.

Her bottom lip was quivering and tears were welling in her eyes before she managed to speak, "Are you sure you really want me…after…"

Her words were cut off. Damien plunged forward with a kiss to keep her from speaking such blasphemy. He wanted to assure her that no matter what, he adored and worshipped her. He allowed himself the pleasure of showing her how much he desired her. Then, he lost himself to the wonder of it.

She responded in kind. Together, they were swept away on the current of their passion. Their bodies were pressed against one another and the kiss had become devastatingly intense. He knew that he shouldn't allow such ardor loose upon her but his body was raging to take her now.

He didn't want to disrespect her by taking her out of wedlock and was torn between his body's demands and his conscience. He allowed himself a few more moments to revel in their embrace, then began to explore her curves with a knowing hand.

He ran his hand along the side of her breasts and torso before coming to rest on her hip where he gave it a tender squeeze of appreciation for her voluptuous form. She was all woman. Her breasts filled his large hands and spilled over, just as he liked. She was perfectly formed, full where she should be and tapering off at her slim waist before rounding out nicely at the hips and her well rounded backside.

He had no appreciation for a skinny frail woman as he was an aggressive lover, placing high demand on his partners but he wasn't selfish, no. He wanted just as much demand placed on himself by an equally aggressive woman to maximize the intensity of the experience.

His woman wasn't intimidated at all by him as she demonstrated with a pleading whimper trying to mesh herself even closer to him. He was nearly undone when she began an exploration of her own. Before he knew what she was about, she had unbuttoned his shirt and her soft little hands were caressing his bare chest without the slightest hesitation.

He briefly considered the wisdom of allowing this to continue but quickly put the foolish notion aside and began untying her night rail. Jenny had come in earlier to remove her clothing and put her into her night clothes after it had become apparent that she wouldn't be recovering from her spell for awhile. It was her thought to make Chelsea more comfortable. He was thanking her now for her thoughtfulness. It was driving him to a fevered need knowing that the only thing that separated his skin from hers was a thin piece of linen.

Once he had the ties and the buttons undone, he briskly pushed the material aside, in a rush. He was desperate to gaze upon her breasts. He was captivated by the sight before him as he looked upon her attributes with a feeling of appreciative awe, "You are the most beautiful woman I have ever seen," he murmured.

Then, without further ado he leaned forward, kissing each nipple before returning his lips to her mouth. He took their passion to a near frantic level with another kiss of hot blazing intensity. He could feel his heart thundering in his chest and his pulse was pounding in his ears as he was being consumed by desire.

He tried to fight his need into submission but soon understood that this was a need that couldn't be denied. He felt the pressure building in his shaft and it was painful to the point that he knew that if he couldn't control his passions soon, he might frighten her with the fierceness of his lovemaking.

He didn't want to be gentle now. He had waited for her so long but he knew he must be for her sake. He wanted to grab, plunder and ravish the magnificent bounty she offered him with a savage hunger.

His Chelsea wasn't frightened though. She was bold in her exploration, as well as demanding of him with her needs, too. Damien did nothing to discourage her as he knew that she needed to do this to prove to herself that she could meet him on his terms as well as her own.

She needed to be assured that he did really want her, and that she was capable of reciprocating. So, he resigned himself to obliging her and did not hold anything back. It wasn't a difficult thing to do. Sure, he would have preferred to wait until they were properly wed but he was beyond that now. It was clear to them both where this was leading.

As he deepened the kiss, he began to knead and caress her breasts, first one and then the other in a show of possession, showing equal ownership to them both. When he had her nipples peaked to perfection he bent his head to suckle and nip with his teeth, trying to pay as much attention to one as the other because he was a greedy man.

She moaned in appreciation of his attentions. He took that as permission to advance their loving and allowed his hand to explore the lower extremities of her soft and pliant body. He ran his hand along the curve of her hip and beyond to her thigh so he could gather the hem of her gown into his hand. Then, he slowly lifted it up and placed an arm behind her back to lift her off the bed so he could pull the offending material over her head.

Modesty drove her to cover herself, as she was completely nude now, but he moved her hands away and said, "Don't hide yourself from me, love, for my eyes ache to behold you."

She obeyed and didn't make another attempt to hide herself. She allowed his eyes to take their fill as he sent a heated hungry gazing roving over every inch of her body. He made it clear to her that she was his for the taking and he was feasting on the vision before him.

He realized then that he wanted to see her with her hair down, as he had that day at Sheraton. He wanted it draped all around her on the pillow, to frame her beautiful face. He removed the ribbon at the end of her plait and unloosened it, running his fingers through the silky raven strands. He marveled at the color. The candle light beside the bed made it glisten with shades of blue.

He brought a handful up to his nose and breathed in the scent. The essence filled his nostrils and sent a jolt of appreciation to his staff, as he placed it just so all around her.

She was perfection, he decided. He dove into her mouth again with a demand that was staggering even to him. She met him in intensity without a single sign of distress or hesitation.

She began to move her hands down his torso. When she got to his breeches, she fumbled at his waistband until she located the buttons and tried valiantly to undo them. She had a difficult time and made a cry of frustration when she was unable to get them undone. He took mercy on her then and took over the task.

As soon as he had them undone, she started aggressively pushing the fabric aside in a frustrated rush to uncover his manhood and his buttocks. Her hands reached around and she grabbed handfuls of the muscles in his backside. She kneaded them with such strength that he nearly found it painful, as her fingernails were long and digging into his flesh.

He didn't mind that at all because she was trying to communicate her need to him the only way she knew how. He moved out of her embrace, sitting on the side of the bed so he could remove his boots, hose and shirt. Then, he finished the removal of his breeches, not caring where they landed when he tossed them aside.

She gasped when she saw his endowments for the first time. For a moment he thought she would balk and call an end to it. "Are you afraid?" he asked her.

She shook her head that she wasn't, so he moved over her body again and reignited the fires between them with another heated kiss and urgent caresses. She slid her hand down between their bodies and wrapped her hand around his arousal and squeezed and stroked until he had to push her hand away in self defense.

She was becoming very demanding now. He feared he would be unmanned before he could have a chance to pleasure her first. He grabbed both her wrists into one of his large hands and lifted them above her head. He held them there, retaking control of the situation.

After a moment she began to resist the hold he had on her and tugged her hands to get them free. He understood her distress and allowed it so he could better explore her body. He needed both hands to fully engage.

He decided to change his plan of action and started a slow heated path with his lips and tongue. Starting at her neck, just under her ear, he very slowly and methodically began to work his way down to her breasts.

He rested there to lave the tips and pay homage to her bountiful offerings for several hot sultry moments before moving even lower down her body. He ran his tongue along her ribcage and gave one last worshipful kiss to the underside of her breast before continuing on to his intended destination.

Once he rested his lips on her thighs to signal his intent, she grabbed him by the ears and forced him to stop. He looked up at her and read the uncertainty in her eyes. He assured her with his own, that it was his desire and that it was perfectly normal between lovers. She received his assurances and released her hold and laid her head back to allow him to continue his ministrations.

With slow deliberation he began a sensual kiss at the entrance of her heated center. The pain in his arousal was acute. He breathed in her scent and soldiered on. He was determined to give her pleasure first.

He separated her soft delicate folds with his fingers, running his tongue over the sensitive nub of flesh. She bucked and whimpered at the sensation of it, so he held her hips in place with a firm hand on each side and aggressively continued to have his way.

Soon, she began to writhe and moan as he was relentless in his pursuit, giving her no quarter. He could feel her legs begin to tremble and he knew that she was close to her release. He pressed his thumb on her sensitive spot and rotated it, as he pushed his tongue inside her.

The response was immediate. Her whole body shook and shuddered. She cried out, wracked with the spasms of her climax. Damien continued his intimate kiss, keeping her prisoner in the throes of ecstasy.

He brought her back down gently by slowing to a stop as she went through the rest of her spasms. Once he was satisfied that she was safely delivered, he kissed his way up her stomach to her breasts and latched on to her left nipple. He took it gently between his teeth and bit down with just enough pressure to cause pleasure instead of pain. Her body shuddered hard one last time and he knew that she was completely satiated.

She took his face into her hands and brought his mouth to hers, thanking him with a searing kiss, as she sent her hand seeking his erection. She found it and started stroking it with her thumb and index finger. She wasn't a selfish lass. She was thinking of his needs now and this touched him profoundly.

"We don't have to do this now if you don't want to, I can wait," he assured her, searching her eyes for her answer.

She wanted to pleasure him, too but didn't know how to communicate it to him verbally, he realized. So when she encouraged him with a firm squeeze on his arousal and a tilt of her hips, he moved her thighs apart with his legs and positioned himself between them.

"Are you sure," he asked wanting to give her every opportunity to change her mind. Tears formed in her eyes. She smiled sweetly at him and nodded her head that she was.

He put his hand between them, guiding her hand with his own, to her entrance and began to slowly work himself inside her. Once he had the tip of his shaft inside her, he moved their hands away to begin the slow slide into her passage. She was slick and hot from her release but her body went rigid with the intrusion. But she didn't cry out.

He stopped himself at her thin barrier, knowing there was no help for what he was about to do, he said softly, "I'm sorry." Then, he plunged his way through without giving her a chance to react to his proclamation.

She gasped, clawing into his back with her fingernails. So, he held himself still, gently kissed her about the forehead and cheeks, and told her that he loved her. He kissed her mouth and she openly received him. After he was sure the shock of his intrusion had subsided, he allowed himself to start a slow steady movement in and out of her tight passage.

She quickly caught on to the rhythm and met him stroke for stroke. She lifted her hips and ground herself against him. That movement nearly drove him to completion. He slid his hands under her rear, roughly brought her hips upwards and deepened his thrusts.

She seemed to revel in the feeling as she began to kiss him about the face and neck. She grabbed on to her right breast, offering it to him, inviting him to suckle while he thrust harder into her. Not wanting her other breast to feel left out he moved over to it and latched on to the tip, just as he reached his own summit. He was rewarded by the distinct throbbing of the walls of her passage as he spilled his life giving essence inside her.

She had found her own climax with him deep inside her. The knowledge of it pleased him, immensely.

"God, Chelsea, I love you so much," he said, kissing her one last time. After a momen,t he became aware of his own weight and feared that he would suffocate her. So, he moved off of her and brought her with him, tucking her under his arm as they willed their hearts and breath into submission.

When he was calmed he became aware of something warm and wet on his chest. He realized that she was crying and was horrified that he might have hurt her. He lifted her face by her chin, so he could see her and softly asked, "What's this?"

She shook her head, continuing to quietly shed her tears and he was beside himself with agony.

"Please tell me Chelsea, you're killing me," he pleaded.

She sniffed and wiped at her eyes, "Nothing is wrong, everything is right. It was so wonderful, even in my wildest dreams, I never imagined that it would be this way," she said sincerely.

Damien's stomach clenched, as his heart jumped inside his chest. Her words were a shot of much needed absolution, after believing, even for a moment, that he had caused her pain beyond what was natural for her first time.

"I'm sorry that I had to hurt you. It won't be so the next time, I promise," he said, with a tender kiss to her temple.

Damien had never experienced such a sense of pure satisfaction with a woman before. It was as if they were one now in both body and spirit, a marriage of their beings. He would never, could never, let her go, or he would cease to exist.

He never knew lovemaking could be this way, either, and he was a very experienced lover. This was something altogether different for him. He was immersed in a feeling of peace and contentment, such as he had never known. This woman was his world, his beginning and his end. She was everything thing he could ever want or need.

She brought him out of his philosophical wanderings when she said, "You didn't hurt me at all and I look forward to the next time with great enthusiasm. I quite enjoyed myself."

Damien couldn't help himself, he roared out laughter, rich and full of genuine happiness. He pulled her on top of himself and kissed her again. Before he could stop himself, he was aroused once more. So, he showed her how to have the control in their lovemaking taking her by the hand and wrapping it around his arousal, guiding himself toward her entrance.

Once there, he released his hold and she lowered herself down and they made love again. She didn't lie when she said she was enthusiastic. She put all of her energy into the love-play. She was a quick study, and adventurous, too.

She drove them both to a thundering completion. At the end she collapsed on top of him and nearly fell asleep.

Afterwards, they were both spent and exhausted but Damien couldn't allow her to fall asleep, soiled as she was. He reluctantly moved her off of him. He got up from the bed and went to the water closet, bringing back a bowl of cool water and a wash cloth. He set about removing the evidence of their passion.

She was embarrassed but didn't resist as he tended to her in this way. He comforted her as he administered to her by never taking his eyes from hers. When he was satisfied that she was cleansed properly, he rinsed the wash cloth and offered it to her so she could do the same for him.

He thought that by doing so, he would take some of the embarrassment away and show her that they were lovers now and as such would know each other intimately in every way. She seemed to understand his offering and took the cloth, lovingly cleansing away all traces from him.

When she was done, he took the washcloth from her, set it and the bowl aside and climbed back into the bed, positioning himself behind her in his favorite spooned position. Together, they sank into a contented peaceful slumber.

Tomorrow, they would wed as soon as they reached Sheraton, Damien vowed as he drifted off to sleep with the love of his life nestled safely in his embrace.

Chapter Twenty-two

Chelsea woke up about an hour before dawn. She felt wonderful for the first time in her life. She was deliciously sore, all over her body from Damien's possession and she blushed at the memory.

She looked over to see if he was still sleeping but the bed was empty where he should have been. She sat up in a rush. Then, she heard him in the water closet so she relaxed knowing that he was still near at hand and hadn't abandoned her.

She hunted around for her night rail but couldn't find it. She couldn't believe she had fallen asleep in the altogether without a single thought to modesty. Chelsea pulled the sheet up to her chin as she heard Damien coming back into the room.

He stopped inside the doorway when he saw that she was awake and smiled the warmest smile she had ever seen upon his face. It made her stomach quiver and she tucked her nose inside the sheet to hide her embarrassment.

Damien noticed the action and walked over to her, pulling down the sheet and lifting her chin so he could place a tender kiss on her mouth. "I'm glad that you are awake, love. We need to get an early start and be done with this cursed hellhole," he said.

Clearly, he had been up for some time because he was already dressed and shaved.

He was so handsome, standing there that she wanted to pull him back into bed and ravish his perfect body.

"I want to make love to you again, Damien. Do we have to leave this moment?" she asked, pouting.

Damien tweaked her nose, saying, "We will have the rest of our lives for loving, sweet. We shall be married this afternoon upon our arrival to Sheraton. So, up with you now. Let us put this place and its…occupants behind us."

She threw her head back onto the pillow and growled, "Oh, alright!" she gritted out between clenched teeth.

Damien thought she was adorable, in her pout. He couldn't wait to fulfill her wish again but he had to be practical. Jenny was already awake and waiting for him to take his leave, so she could get her mistress ready.

He had already woken the baron and Matilda. They too, were getting ready so there was no time to waste. He wanted to be gone before the household woke up and made a big to-do of their departure. He was hoping to leave as quietly as possible, so as to avoid any more encounters with his cousin and his harpies.

He bent down and kissed her once more, saying "I shall come to collect you in a quarter of an hour. Do be quick," he warned.

With that, he took his leave. Moments later Jenny came into the room and started fussing over her.

"I knew that scoundrel couldn't keep his hands to himself," she grumbled, as she took in her mistress's condition. "Are you hurt?" she asked.

Chelsea blushed and said, "He was a perfect gentleman, and no, I am not hurt. I am better than I ever have been in my entire life. We are to be married this afternoon, so do try to be happy for me, Jenny."

Jenny threw her arms around Chelsea and hugged her, "That's wonderful my lady, I am happy for you. Tis a miracle, that's what it is," she cried.

The two women embraced for a moment more, then Jenny said, "Let's get the bride ready, shall we?"

Chelsea liked the sound of that. The bride! She was a bride. Would have ever imagined such a prospect? She certainly never had and to be marrying Damien, oh, the wonder of it.

She bounced up from the bed and said, "Oh, do hurry Jenny. I'm to be married today."

Jenny laughed out loud. Her mistress was running around the room, naked as the day she was born and she had never seen her so happy. She decided that she would be kind to the marquess, after all. If he could work such wonders on Chelsea, then he was a worthy man, indeed.

*****

Damien returned to his room to write two messages that he would send by special messenger from the posting inn in the nearby village. One to Sheraton, and one to Evansdale to prepare for their arrival and the subsequent nuptials and celebration.

He thought it would be fair to give Jarrett and Celia notice beforehand, so as not to catch them unawares. They were most likely newlyweds now, after all. Knowing how he would spend most of his time with Chelsea in the very near future, he thought it was the least he could do.

He chuckled at the thought of Jarrett keeping his marriage to Celia a secret. It didn't upset him, how could it? As far as Damien was concerned, he clearly got the real jewel among the twins.

He thought about last night and his body shivered. She had been so warm and pliant and adventurous. She approached lovemaking with great eagerness and he looked forward to teaching her all the many ways to indulge in one another.

He went over to the writing desk, found paper and ink and set about his task. He thought it would be prudent to allude to his knowledge that they were married and was happy to congratulate them. He snickered quietly, thinking how he would love to see Jarrett's face when he reads it.

He wondered briefly, if Jarrett knew that Chelsea was the child from the wood. He felt a twinge of anger over his keeping that a secret. He supposed that if he were in Jarrett's place, he might not tell him, either. How would you tell someone you love such an awful thing? Wouldn't you want to spare them the heartache if you could? He thought so, and decided not to harbor any ill will toward him.

He loved Chelsea and they were to be married today. That was all that mattered, really. When he was finished writing the letters, he walked over to the nightstand by his bed to make sure he had everything that belonged to him before going to collect Chelsea.

He saw a missive on the nightstand he hadn't noticed before when he was dressing. He picked it up. It was in Jarrett's hand, he observed before opening it. He read the message, in stunned disbelief.

The words inside chilled his blood and turned his stomach. He was glad he hadn't eaten yet or he would have cast up his accounts. Nigel had murdered the two cut throats they had hired and not only did he kill them, he apparently tortured them and set them ablaze too, burning the building to the ground in the process. Ghastly!

His hand shook, as he read it over again. He shouldn't be surprised that Nigel would be a murderer, as well as a pederast. When one is willing to do such horrific things to a child it's no great leap to murder.

The implication of their situation weighed heavy on Damien's mind. He realized how close to danger Chelsea truly had been. He couldn't believe the woman was going to try to kill such an evil man herself. 'And she wants me to spare him?' Damien grunted at the thought. 'She is too good for this world,' he decided. How could she not thirst for his blood, even now?

He was glad that they were leaving and wished they had done so last night. He shouldn't have allowed Chelsea to sway him in his course, but he had. He was using the wrong head and was glad it hadn't cost them their lives.

What if Nigel had gotten hold of Chelsea, somehow? The thought made him sick at heart to consider. Nigel is insane and none of them were safe. Once they were wed and back at Evansdale, he would do whatever he had to do to see that Nigel was punished. Even if they had to expose him, and in so doing, shed light on what he had done to Chelsea.

He didn't like the idea of putting her through that, he quickly realized. Public scrutiny would be ruthless and blame would be placed on her somehow, he was sure of it.

No! He would keep Chelsea's secret. With a heavy sigh, he decided Nigel simply had to die and he would have to find a way to make it happen. With that he left the room and went to collect Chelsea.

*****

"I thought we would stop and break our fast at the posting inn in the village. I need to send two messages ahead, to announce our arrival and our wedding plans," Damien told his group, as they waited in the courtyard while their carriage was being loaded.

"That's sounds wonderful dear, I'm simply starving," Matilda said.

"Yes, I think we could all use some victuals before we set out," the baron agreed.

Chelsea was standing there with a faraway look in her eyes and a silly grin. She wasn't thinking about food, Damien noted. He gathered her under his arm and kissed her temple and whispered, "Soon love."

She shivered, blinked her eyes, then smiled the most amazing smile at him. That gave him an idea.

"How would you like to ride with me on Lucas? The weather is fair, not too chilly and he is a fine horse, can handle the both of us and I do get lonely out there by myself," he said hopefully.

"Oh, that would be grand Damien, I haven't been atop a horse in ages," she beamed at him.

Damien was glad to see she was so lively and happy. It warmed his heavy heart and helped him to forget his troubles, even if for a while.

He told the baron about Jarrett's letter and instructed him not to mention anything to the ladies until they had reached Sheraton. He didn't want to upset them and cause undue stress while in route to home. He unpacked his pistol and made sure it was loaded and put it in his coat pocket to have at the ready in case there was in trouble on the road.

He didn't think Nigel would tear out after them, but you could never tell what a madman would do. He decided to be cautious in all things concerning Nigel. He would have to remain vigilant until his body was cold and dead in the ground.

He shook off his troubled thoughts and returned his attention back to Chelsea, "We shall have to correct that and get you a horse as a wedding gift, so we can enjoy riding together," he told her.

"I would love that Damien. Thank you," she said still smiling at him.

The footmen finished loading their carriage. Damien assisted Chelsea atop his horse then mounted up behind and secured her within his arms. The baron, Matilda and Jenny ensconced themselves in the carriage and they set off toward home.

*****

The baron watched his daughter and her husband-to-be with a happy heart. He was overwhelmed, by the sheer joy he saw in his daughters face. If he lived to be a thousand years old, he could never do enough to thank the marquess for saving his daughter, in so many ways.

He had been able to get some information out of Jenny and had learned that it was the marquess who tried to save her that day in the wood. Damien had nearly lost his life for his trouble, as he had been but a green lad of only eight and ten, and was no match for such a monster.

When he arrived at Sheraton and Chelsea saw him she had decided to use him to find and exact revenge on her assailant, who he now knew, without a doubt, to be Nigel. It was all he could do, to leave the evil blackguard unmolested as they removed themselves from his vicinity. But Damien convinced him of the wisdom of it and kept his own counsel on the matter.

Tomorrow after the celebrations, he would speak to the marquess about taking care of Nigel, once and for all. He felt sure between the two of them, with the assistance of Sir Jarrett, they could come up with some way to satisfy justice.

He hadn't yet told him that he was aware of his part, on that awful day because he didn't want anything else to upset their apparent happiness on their wedding day.

"She looks more alive than I have ever seen her," Jenny said breaking into his thoughts.

"Aye, that she does. I was just thinking the same thing myself," he said, with heartfelt emotion.

He could feel tears welling in his eyes. He feared he wouldn't be able to hold them back in front of the ladies. What a predicament for a man to find himself in, he inwardly groaned, trying to sniff them away.

Matilda squeezed the baron's hand, as if to say that she understood and that it was alright to cry those happy tears. He was nearly undone and squeezed her hand in return, to say thank you.

"I'm very happy Chelsea has rejoined the world and that she will be married to my Damien. I had a feeling about the gel and I was right. She has breathed new life into him, too. They needed each other so desperately," she said.

Matilda had started to suspect that all was not what it seemed with the girl known as Celia. She remembered that the baron's other daughter had become a recluse after suffering some kind of traumatic event, but she didn't know what it was. After observing the girl, coupled with Damien's insistence that she had been abused, then hearing about her spell after that ghastly Davenport attacked her, she couldn't help but wonder if something were afoot and Celia was, in fact, Chelsea.

She hadn't told Damien what she suspected for fear he might have broken off his courtship with the girl, thinking she was defective somehow. She was glad that she kept it to herself and that the two of them had fallen in love, despite all the obstacles.

She had always adored the twin's mother. Chelsea was the most like her of the tw,o from what she remembered. Of course both girls had a strong likeness to their mother but only Chelsea had her spark. A little hoyden, not unlike she herself had been, she thought with a smile of remembrance.

She was very happy for them both. She and Chelsea would become the best of friends. Ah, to be young and in love again...

*****

Jarrett and Celia received Damien's missive and learned they were due to arrive within two hours time. They were overjoyed that they were to be wed this afternoon and set about preparing for the festivities. He went over to Parson Holloway's and asked that he arrive at Sheraton at luncheon where they would have the wedding, then, they would feast.

Later they were to all join at Evansdale for evening supper and more celebration. Jarrett was relieved that his good friend held no ill will toward him, as his comment about 'newly-wed couples being caught unawares' was a direct admission of knowledge that he and Celia had eloped.

Jarrett was troubled to learn that Nigel had been at the Ravenswood affair but was glad that no harm came from it. Jarrett had decided that Nigel needed to be killed after seeing what he had done to the men he had hired.

He no longer held the position that he couldn't help Damien with the task and decided that after the celebration, he would have a sit down with him to discuss new strategies. If he, Damien and the baron all put their heads together, they could come up with some way to do it, undetected.

Jarrett had learned a thing or two over the years, as a Bow Street man, about getting away with murder. If you were discreet and handled things properly, it could be done. Why, between Sheraton and Evansdale, there was vast acreage of forest where a body could simply disappear.

*****

"What are you doing in my room?" Nigel asked, as his repulsive wife barged in to his chambers.

She was the last thing he wanted to see when he first opened his eyes in the morning. She was dressed in her usual ridiculous fashion with cosmetics that looked like they were applied by a fingerless blind man. God, what a horror!

"I came to inform you that our bird has flown the coop," she said, with her hands fisted on her fat hips.

"What in all that's holy are you yammering on about, madam," he scowled at her. The very sound of her voice was like claws inside his brain.

"I'm talking about your cousin. He's gone," she told him.

Nigel sat up quickly, "What do you mean, 'gone'?" he demanded.

"Are you daft? Just what I said, he and his entourage left before dawn. They packed up and left the party," she said, scowling at him too. When he didn't reply, she added, "I thought you said you had it all worked out and that you were going to force him to marry Tess. I guess you failed in this just like everything else you do."

Nigel's reaction was instantaneous. He jumped up from the bed, naked and tackled his wife. He knocked her to the floor, straddled her chest and wrapped his hands around her throat.

It felt so good to be choking the life out of her. He had waited so long to kill the bitch and now he could no longer restrain himself. He continued to squeeze as she thrashed and kicked. She clawed at his hands to pull them away from her neck. She went for his eyes but he was too quick and stretched back so that his face was out of her reach.

Her face was turning red and her eyes were bulging out of their sockets. The sight of it gave him an erection that could plow through solid granite. Just when she stopped fighting and her eyes rolled up in her head, he heard, "Father?"

He let go of her neck and turned his head to see his daughter standing in the doorway. "Go away, mummy and daddy are having a little chat," he told her.

He heard Penelope draw a deep wheezing breath and he turned back to look at her, "Get off of me, you beast," she croaked.

Nigel knew he couldn't kill her now. He had lost control of his senses. How would he get rid of the body and explain her absence? No, this would have to wait. He got off his wife and stood up.

He faced his daughter and said, "What in the bloody hell do you want? Didn't that cow ever teach you to knock?"

She looked at her mom and wanted to go to her but with her father standing right there she was afraid.

"Mother come, let us leave father alone," she ventured while averting her eyes from his obvious arousal.

Penelope rolled over onto her stomach and grunted. Heaving herself up on to her hands and knees, she lifted herself up off the ground. She started staggering toward the door, when Nigel put his foot in the middle of her arse and shoved her toward the door. "See you later darling," he promised, then blew her a kiss.

The two banes of his existence left his room and he walked back to the bed, He stretched out in the middle and began to fondle himself. He brought himself to completion reliving the memory of the moments that had just past. It had felt so good that he wanted to savor the memory. There now, that's better. A man can't think when his cods are all in a bind.

So Damien took his harlot and fled did he? We'll just see about that. He jumped up from the bed, feeling refreshed and relaxed and called a servant to help him shave and pack. He would go after them, of course. They could't escape their fate.

*****

As Sheraton came into view, Chelsea's heart began to take flight. She was so excited that she could hardly contain herself atop of Damien's horse.

All the way there they had talked of their future and their pasts. She explained to him all the things that she never got around to explaining yesterday.

Damien wasn't mad at her for using him to find Nigel. He said he didn't blame her but he wished that he had known what she were up to, so he could have prevented her from putting herself at risk. He promised her that some way, somehow he would take care of Nigel. She had faith that he would and didn't question him about it.

He was genuinely happy for Jarrett and Celia and couldn't wait to give them his felicitations and a wedding gift. She was glad that she hadn't come in between their friendship.

She told him what she had been like before that day in the wood and what her life has been like since. She didn't intend to, but she reduced him to tears again. He had such a gentle soul and she really felt that she didn't deserve such a man as he.

He told her of what he had seen Nigel do to his brother and that reduced her to tears. Together, they cried and laughed all the way to Sheraton. She wouldn't trade a minute of it for all the gold in the England.

He was hers now and she was his. Soon, they would put the past behind them and raise a family. They talked about what their children would be like and what they should name their first born. He said he preferred Beauregard and she asked him if he was serious. He laughed and said yes, while he shook his head no.

She laughed and said Beauregard was a fine name but that she would prefer something a little more biblical like, Jacob. He cried again and she hugged him and it was decided that they would name their heir after his brother.

She lightened the mood by telling him that he could be named Jacob Beauregard and it was settled. With any luck Jacob Beauregard Vane would come into this world before a year had passed.

Perhaps even now she carried him in her womb. The thought pleased them both, but they decided that whether he was or not they would go through the motions to ensure that he was, just in case.

He told her about all the different ways to make love and she was completely amazed. Then she wanted to know where he learned them all. He cleared his throat, saying, from a book, but she didn't believe him.

He swore that it was true and said he could prove it because he still had a copy of The Kama Sutra, whatever that was. She told him she would believe it when she saw it. She found it was hard to believe any decent publisher would print such a thing.

She wondered who the writer was and asked. He told her it was someone named Mallanaga Vatsyayana. She accused him of pulling her tail and said there was no such person with a name like that. He thought that was funniest thing he ever heard and laughed real hard.

She didn't like him making sport of her like that and told him so. He kissed her to shush her up. It worked, but she still wanted to see the book.

When they got to the drive at Sheraton, Damien pulled Lucas to the side of the road to let the carriage pass and they followed behind. She was going to be married within the hour and she couldn't be happier. She looked forward to this evening, when they would spend their first night as husband and wife.

When they finally arrived Celia came running out of the house like a wild banshee. She threw herself into her sisters arms and together they cried and looked each other over to be sure they were both unharmed. Jarrett and Damien embraced and shook hands before they slugged each other in the arms. Then they called each other a few vulgar names, purely in jest. It was easy to see that they loved one another in their behavior.

Papa and Matilda watched the goings-on with big smiles on their faces and told them to quit all the nonsense because they had a wedding to go to.

Chapter Twenty-three

The ceremony was small, with Celia and Jarrett as witnesses. The baron's lip quivered when he gave Chelsea away. Matilda smiled like the cat that ate the crème through the whole affair.

She was now Chelsea Dolores Vane, The Marchioness of Devonshire. It had a nice ring to it, Chelsea thought, sitting beside Damien at their wedding breakfast. It was really luncheon but why quibble, food is food and she was ravenous.

She hadn't been eating well over the last few weeks and suddenly she was starved. Damien was having a good time, stuffing food into her mouth. He seemed genuinely pleased to see her appetite returned.

He leaned over and whispered in her ear "You may be eating for two, Lady Vane," he said. It made her shiver and she opened her mouth to reply and he stuffed a piece of bread in. He chuckled and lifted her glass of wine to her lips, so she could wash it down.

When she swallowed, she said, "Perhaps we should go home and make sure."

"We shall leave in about an hour. Jenny and Hattie need time to pack up your belongings as well as theirs since they will be moving too," he reminded her. She couldn't do without Jenny and Hattie. She was pleased that Damien didn't mind making a place for them in his household.

They were thrilled for her and couldn't wait to get started packing. They called in reinforcements to get the job done. Hattie positioned herself in the hall barking orders as well as any general in the king's army could have done. Four footman and a half a dozen maids made up her little battalion. They were busily scurrying around even as the newlyweds sat here and enjoyed their meal. Papa estimated three carts would be needed for the job and happily provided them.

Chelsea didn't think that she would miss her attic apartments. Aside from her bath, before the ceremony, she didn't even want to go up there for one last visit. It was part of her past now. She was looking to the future. She wouldn't have even gone up there, if she hadn't smelled like Lucas. Odd though, horse smells pretty good on Damien, she thought with a blush.

Damien noticed her blush and said, "Patience, love."

They were distracted when Papa stood up. He clinked his wine glass with his spoon to draw everyone's attention. "I have a toast," he announced. "To Damien and Chelsea, may their union be fruitful and may they always know happiness that only a marriage founded in true love can offer." Everyone said, "Here, Here!" and thrust their glasses together then swallowed the contents.

But Papa wasn't finished, "Though, my oldest daughter and her husband didn't see fit to invite me to their wedding, I would like to wish them the same. To Jarrett and Celia and Damien and Chelsea, may your lives be full of all your hearts desires."

Everyone agreed, it was a wonderful toast. Jarrett and Celia looked properly chastised, but happy nonetheless. Papa was smiling and clearly held no malice toward Jarrett for eloping with his daughter. He just wanted to tease them a bit because he could. Chelsea smiled at her father and wished that the last seven years had been different for them. So much time was lost and could never be reclaimed but she would make sure that he would be a permanent fixture in her life from this day forward.

He would make a wonderful grandfather and she couldn't wait to see him with a babe on each knee. Tears welled in her eyes at the thought and Damien thought she was upset.

"What's this?" he asked with concern.

"Papa!" Chelsea cried out, jumping up from her chair and running to him. He jumped up to meet her and they threw their arms around each other, holding one another for a long moment.

"Now, now lass, what's this about? It's your wedding day and you're supposed to be happy, child," he cooed at her.

Chelsea didn't care that she was making a spectacle of herself. This was her Papa!

She reached up and touched his cheek, saying, "Oh, but I am happy Papa. It's just that I have missed you so much. I had to let you know that I love you before I left for Evansdale."

The baron was overcome and he finally did what he had been trying to avoid, he blubbered. "Lass, I missed you too. You know I never stopped loving you. Can you forgive an old man for his stupidity?" he asked with a sob.

"I forgave you long ago, Papa," she said sincerely.

He hugged her again, saying, "You did good my Chelsea lass, real good and I'm proud of you."

"Thank you Papa. I'm proud of you too," she sniffed and wiped her eyes.

He returned her to her husband and said, "You'll take care of my lass, won't you?"

"Absolutely!" was Damien's earnest reply.

Papa believed him. He lifted his shoulders and smiled, saying, "You may call me Malcolm and I shall call you son," then returned to his seat.

Everyone in the room was struck mute at the drama that had just played itself out. After Papa was seated and it was apparent that Chelsea had settled down, the conversations resumed.

Damien reached for her hand under the table and squeezed it reassuringly, whispering, "That was a good thing that you just did for your father. He has been hurting for many years and you just healed that hurt. That will allow him to finally forgive himself. You are an incredible woman, Lady Vane."

*****

When the carts were loaded, Damien and Chelsea took their leave of Sheraton with instructions for everyone to come to supper at eight and to plan to spend the night at Evansdale. It wasn't a long trip, just a little more than half an hour by horse.

When they arrived, the entire staff of Evansdale came out to greet their new mistress. Chelsea was somewhat overwhelmed at the thought of being responsible for so many lives. Damien assured her that she didn't have to worry because Jarrett's mother would stay on as chatelaine.

That was a huge relief to Chelsea. She knew absolutely nothing about running a household and was glad to allow Mrs. Wellstone to take the lead and keep it. 'You don't get much experience running a household by living in an attic,' Chelsea mused. Damien didn't seem disappointed by this, so Chelsea wouldn't dwell on it.

Maybe in a year or two, she could take the reins, but she doubted it. By then she hoped to have children to occupy her time and would still want Mrs. Wellstone's assistance.

Once all the formalities were observed, they went inside. She and Damien went to their wing. He ushered her there with purpose and she was eager to see what that purpose was. Once he had her inside his room, he quickly started removing her clothing.

He seemed in an awful hurry. She wanted to take a minute for a little romance but he seemed intent in his mission. He had her stripped down to her chemise in an amazing amount of speed. Then, he started removing his own clothes and she felt a little like a gazelle on the menu of a very hungry lion.

She started backing up. He slowly advanced toward her, keeping his eyes locked on hers as he disrobed himself. Chelsea flinched when he jerked off his boot, tossing it over his shoulder with no thought to where it landed. Then, he did the same with the other.

By the time he was disrobed, he had her corralled between himself and the bed. Then, he pounced. He reached out, pulled her to him and placed a searing kiss on her lips. Then, he gathered the hem of her chemise and quickly took it off of her, leaving her as bare as he.

He picked her up, wrapped her legs around his waist and started to plunder her breasts. After satisfying his immediate hunger for her bosom, he laid her down on the bed. He remained standing himself, positioning between her thighs.

He leaned over her, continuing to ravage her breasts, her belly and her thighs. He lifted up her legs, placing her ankles on his shoulders and without further ado, plunged himself inside her.

It was an aggressive action. He pounded himself into her but it didn't scare her. She soon gave herself up to his need. He kissed and nipped her calves while he thrust into her heated core.

Chelsea was amazed that he could make love to her while standing up like that and briefly wondered if he learned this from that book, too. She forgot that silly notion when he placed his finger on her sensitive nub and began to work her into a frenzied need of her own.

It wasn't long before her body jerked and shuddered in release. He quickly followed, throwing his head back, roaring with his own release. He truly did sound like the lion she thought he was before. The sound went over her body like a current of warm water and she felt limp and well handled.

When he recovered, he shifted her into the middle of the bed and lay down beside her, "I'm sorry, I couldn't wait," he said, with a huge grin. Then he added, "Besides, our room will be invaded by Hattie's army soon and I didn't want to wait until tonight to claim my bride."

She felt claimed alright. She looked down at her breasts and thighs and saw the marks of his claiming, shivering at the memory of how she received them.

He followed the path that her eyes had taken, and got a look of utter shock on his face, "I had no idea I had been so rough," he exclaimed.

He got really quiet and that worried Chelsea. She had a good idea what he must be thinking and she didn't ever want him to restrain himself during their joining.

Making love to Damien was empowering for her even though he had been the aggressor in this instance. She had the power to drive him to the action in the first place and she never wanted that to change, so she said, "I loved every minute of it." Then, she assured him by rubbing his chest in a circular motion with her index finger.

He took her in his arms then and kissed her soundly, saying, "So did I." They both giggled and quickly made love again, though this time, a little less rough, and it was good.

*****

After Damien visited his father to see about his health, he met Chelsea in the drawing room. "Come with me, I want to show you something," he said, with a grin born of pure mischief. He led her to the library, closing the door behind them.

He led her to a spot on the shelves and pulled out a red leather bound book. It was titled, "The Kama Sutra". Chelsea gasped and grabbed it out of his hand. She thought he had been teasing her but here it was in her hands.

She skipped over to the sofa and sat down. He sat down beside her, draping his arm around her shoulders, so they could view the book together. Chelsea opened it up and started flipping through the pages.

Colorful images illustrating all manner of unusual copulation was splashed upon each page. She gasped anew, with every turn of the page. Every now and then, Damien would stop her from turning to the next page and say, "I want to try that" or "I think you would enjoy that" or "I can't wait to do that to you."

She was beet red and very warm, with perspiration forming on her forehead from looking at all the pictures. Damien was aware of her discomfort but he gave her no quarter, as he asked "Which ones do you want to try," with a sultry voice.

Chelsea wasn't sure that she was limber enough to try most of them but she did find several of them rather intriguing. After a few minutes more perusal she pointed to an image that depicted the woman sitting on the man's lap and they were facing one another and she said, "I would like to try that one, I think."

"What else?" he asked her

She continued looking through the book and saw another image that showed the woman on her hands and knees with the man on his knees behind her. She cleared her throat and swallowed hard, making a gulping sound.

For a brief moment, she had an ugly image in her mind from long ago. An image that she wanted erased and replaced with a new one. One that she would find enjoyable with the man she loved, who was her husband now.

With a shaky voice, she pointed to it and said, "That one."

Damien was surprised by her choice this time. He had wondered if he would ever be able to take her in that position without causing fear or discomfort for her. It was one of his favorite positions and he knew that he could make her enjoy it, so he said, "We shall do that tonight."

Chelsea blushed and nodded her head that she would try it. He took the book from her then and put it away. He walked back over to the sofa, took her by the hand and said, "Let's go out to the stables and choose a horse for you."

*****

Chelsea was excited to be able to pick out her own horse. She chose a five year old Bay mare named Delilah. Delilah has a sweet temperament and would be loyal to anyone that provided her with plenty of apples and carrots.

She and Delilah were instant friends. When she saddled her up and mounted, she and Damien rode around the park. Chelsea was in heaven. She had missed riding most of all, while she was hid away in her attic. To be free again and feel the wind in her face and the power of the beast beneath her was a heady feeling.

Damien was impressed with how quickly she became comfortable in the saddle again. He thought she looked adorable with her skirts hiked up and her lovely calves exposed, so she could ride astride. She never learned to ride sidesaddle as is proper for a lady.

When she challenged him to a race and won, he wondered if this horse idea had been such a good one. She could be with child after all and she seemed to be taking undue risks considering it has been a decade since she last rode.

He decided that he would have to caution her and remind her of the need to take care with her person and avoid such reckless activity in the future. He didn't think she would appreciate it but he was her husband and she would have to obey him in this.

When they returned to the stables, he would have to tell her but not now. He didn't want to take away from her obvious elation, so it could wait. They slowed their horses to a sedate walk, in route back to the stables. Lucas was tired from this morning's journey and he didn't want to overtax him.

He was a good strong stallion. He had just gotten him trained the way he liked and didn't want to suffer any setbacks because of lameness. He didn't think that their quick little jaunt would cause any problems but he wanted to be safe.

When they returned to the stables, they walked their horses back to their stalls so Chelsea could reward Delilah and Lucas with some apples. Damien said, "I hate to have to do this, but I must caution you about your reckless behavior. You need to keep in mind that you could be with child, and ride at a more sedate pace. I'm very impressed with your skills, but the jarring motion at such speeds can't be good for a fetus, and I would die if you were to be thrown and break your lovely neck." There, that wasn't so bad, he thought.

Chelsea gasped and for a moment he thought they were about to have their first real quarrel, but she surprised him by saying, "I never thought of that. Of course, you are right and I shall heed what you say. We mustn't let anything happen to Jacob Beauregard." Then she smiled magnificently at him.

Damien was relieved. He took her in his arms and kissed her, "Thank you," he breathed in her ear. He straightened himself up and said, "Come, let us go prepare for our guests."

*****

Chelsea was glad that Damien was thoughtful enough to remind her to be careful. She felt guilty she hadn't considered it herself. Of course, she wouldn't do anything to jeopardize their child. The thought that she could have, made her feel ill. She could tell that Damien didn't like to have to assert his authority as her husband and she loved him for it.

When they returned to their rooms to bathe and prepare for their guests, he surprised her again, by returning her knife to her.

"I want you to wear this, at all times, unless we are in bed of course, until we have resolved the issue with Nigel. I would not have you unprotected and it would comfort me for you to wear it," he said, lifting up her skirts.

She held her breath when he dropped to one knee, placing the strap around her thigh and tenderly kissing the flesh just above it. He put her skirts back down and stood before her, she asked, "But I almost killed you with it, how can you trust me like this?"

He chuckled, "I shall never give you reason to try and kill me again, this I swear." He kissed her soundly and they went down stairs to greet their guests who had already arrived.

All their guests were at the foot of the stairs applauding as The Marquess and Marchioness of Devonshire descended. After the greetings, cheers and jeers were dispensed with; they all went into dining room. Supper was a lovely affair. Everyone was joyous as they ate and drank.

After dinner, Damien presented Jarrett and Celia with the deed to one of his properties, a villa in Italy, as a wedding gift. Celia jumped up and down at the prospect of honeymooning in Italy. She ran around the table and planted a big wet kiss on Damien's cheek.

She checked herself and darted a quick look at Jarrett to be sure she hadn't overstepped but he was smiling widely at her. He came around the table too, to embrace Damien. They shook hands, Jarrett thanking his friend profusely.

Later in the drawing room, Chelsea couldn't help but notice that Papa and Matilda seemed to be mooning over one another. She wondered if there might be something between them. She would have to keep an eye on that situation.

Not that Papa didn't deserve happiness or anything like that; she wanted to know if there was any prospect, so she could tell Celia and they could encourage the match. Now that both of Papa's daughters were married, he deserved to find happiness again, too.

She smiled at the thought. Damien, not one to miss anything, leaned over asking, "What has you smiling so beautifully?"

She whispered in his ear what she had observed. After a few moments of his own observations, he laughed out loud, shaking his head. "He better rest up a bit before he takes her on," he mused aloud.

That made Chelsea laugh, too, causing everyone to look over at them expectantly. She and Damien chose to keep their comments to themselves. After a moment her outburst was forgotten.

They finished out the evening's entertainment by playing charades. Damien thought it would be fun to invite Jenny, Hattie, Mrs. Wellstone and the butler to participate. The more, the merrier he said, and it was as everyone became loud and rowdy as they shouted out their guesses while each player acted out his or her topic.

Hattie was the most comical when she chose to act out a fox hunt. Her plump figure bounced, jounced and jiggled all around while she mimicked riding a horse. She really should never attempt firing a hunting musket because clearly she has no idea how to load one. It looked as though she were churning butter and everyone got really confused.

No one could figure out what making butter, crying hounds and riding horses had to do with one another. And the part about the hounds, well, that was just hilarious. Finally, Damien figured it out and everyone groaned because they had not guessed it themselves, agreeing it was plain as day what she was trying to say. Chelsea didn't see it but, oh well. It had been a rousing good time.

When the evening was over, the gentlemen all had a quiet discussion of some importance, agreeing to meet in the library on the morrow around half past nine. Chelsea thought it was odd that they would have such a meeting but didn't question it as she had other things on her mind.

Damien leaned over, whispering in her ear. He had another wedding gift for her. He would deliver it with his promise from the book and she suddenly felt very warm all over.

Damien led her to their chambers and shut the door. He positioned her in front of the cheval glass, telling her to stay where she was. He went over to his wardrobe, returned with a black velvet box and told her to close her eyes. She felt him place a necklace around her neck that rested at the base of her throat.

He told her to open her eyes. She gasped at the sight of the most beautiful sapphire and diamond necklace she had ever seen. It matched her betrothal ring perfectly.

"Part of the Vane wedding set," he told her. He began to take down her hair, placing it just so about her shoulders. He moved his lips to her ear. "Lovely," he breathed, then set about unbuttoning her bodice.

He very slowly disrobed her as she watched him through the mirror. Soon, she was looking at herself nude. All that remained were her stockings, slippers and her new wedding gift.

She made to remove her slippers but he stayed her hand. "Leave them on," he said in a husky voice.

He ran his hands along the length of her body, stopping at her breasts and backside to give them a firm massage. All the while, he kept his gaze locked on hers in the mirror. When he was satisfied with his results, he turned her around to face him.

He removed his boots then invited her to remove his clothing. She did, all the while maintaining the precious eye contact. When she had him disrobed, he took her by the hand and led her to the rug before the hearth, positioning her just so. Then, he set about demonstrating the illustration from the book.

Damien put his own ideas into the position as he began to nip at the back of her neck. He licked his way down the length of her back while massaging the globes of her buttocks. When it was clear he was becoming agitated and could no longer hold himself at bay, he surprised her by wrapping her thick hair around his hand until it rested at the base of her neck. He gently tugged her head back and took her by the chin so he could place an arousing kiss on her mouth.

He swallowed her gasp of surprise as he thrust himself deeply into her passage. He reached around her to press on her sensitive flesh and began to massage her in rhythm with his thrusts. It wasn't long before she was blinded by a rush of intense pleasure as he brought them both to completion, each shouting out at their release.

She decided then and there, that she quite liked that red book. She wanted to look through it again to make even more selections to try with her new husband. Damien was a demanding but caring lover. She felt quite safe in his charge.

She trusted him not to hurt her and he didn't. Nay, everything he did was designed to give her the greatest of pleasure. She enjoyed the mastery he showed over her body and gave herself into his keeping. He always took care to make sure she found her release before taking his own. He stoked her passions with erotic narratives as he took what he wanted.

She knew that he must have honed his skills on many women before her but she didn't want to dwell on that. It was hard not to be jealous but she consoled herself in the knowing that he belonged to her now and that he would never have another as he loved her and everything he did confirmed it.

They tried two of Damien's choices after refortifying with a few minutes rest and wine. She realized that she was limber enough, after all when Damien followed up with two of his choices, then capped it all off with her other choice.

She really enjoyed that one because it allowed such intimacy as they were able to maintain eye contact the entire time. That seemed to add a higher degree of intensity to the release. She loved looking into his emerald green eyes. To do so while making love to him, well that was simply devastating.

Damien put every ounce of himself into showing her the pleasures to be had between a man and a woman and she was overwhelmed by the sensations. Just when she thought she had no more to give, he wrung another release out of her, each more powerful than the last.

When neither of them could take any more, they collapsed in each other arms, falling asleep, completely exhausted. The last thought Chelsea remembered was wondering what he had in store for her tomorrow.

Chapter Twenty-four

Damien woke up a little after dawn and watched Chelsea sleep for awhile. He worried that he had used her too harshly. If his aches and pains were any indication, she would be in misery when she woke up.

He slid out of the bed and went to the water closet to run a hot bath for her, while he shaved and cleaned his teeth. When the tub was filled to his satisfaction, he scented the water with rose and heather oils. Then, he instructed a footman to order breakfast for his wife and went back into the bedroom.

He kissed her awake, laughing when she whimpered and rolled over to go back to sleep. "No, you don't. I have a hot bath prepared for you. Come on, let's get you up," he said, rolling her back over.

He pulled back the covers, lifting her into his arms. He carried her to the water closet and lovingly placed her into the copper tub.

Chelsea thought she was in heaven, the warm water felt so good. "Mmmm," she said, as she sank herself down into it. She opened her eyes and looked up to see Damien smiling at her. "What's this for?" she asked.

"My body aches and I know yours must, too. I thought to comfort you before you break your fast. I have asked that a tray be brought to you, so you can rest up since I have loved you so...vigorously," he explained, with no hint of contrition.

He enjoyed what they had done and planned more of the same in the near future, but he didn't want to maim his wife. So, he thought he had better pamper her in between their loving as much as possible.

"Are you going to join me?" she asked.

Damien laughed at his wife. Surely, she wasn't trying to seduce him, after their marathon last night. The woman must be made of iron, if she could even conceive of making love now, he thought incredulously. "Only if you promise not to ravish me?" he teased.

Chelsea pushed out her bottom lip in a pout and gave that some serious thought. She took an accounting of her aches and pains, agreeing she could probably do with a respite. "I suppose that I shall spare you," she said.

Damien laughed and joined her in the tub. He took up the position behind her and pulled her into his arms. They soaked for a good while and enjoyed just holding each other in quiet companionship. Finally, Damien became cognizant of the time and remembered his meeting. Time to move things along, he realized.

He picked up the soap and a wash cloth, then set about bathing his wife. He enjoyed the task, working her skin into a lather and massaging her shoulders and neck. Once he had her sufficiently bathed, he worked on himself.

With great reluctance, he removed himself from the tub. He leaned over, kissed her and told her to soak for a while longer. After getting dressed, he went back into the water closet to make sure she hadn't fallen back asleep and she had.

He woke her with a kiss, assisted her out, wrapped her in a towel and dried her off. He slipped her into a dressing gown and carried her back to the bed. She was just about to doze off again when Jenny appeared with her breakfast.

With his wife well pampered and in the care of her maid, he took his leave, going down stairs to break his fast. Malcolm, Jarrett, Celia and Matilda were all there along with Mrs. Wellstone, so discussion of Nigel would have to wait until their meeting in the library.

*****

"Your idea has merit, Damien, but I should remind you that Nigel won't be easy to kidnap. We need to come up with a fool-proof plan to accost him," Jarrett said, as the meeting was well underway.

"True, this time we shall have to take matters into our own hands and trust no one to the task. I suggest that we go to London and follow him covertly until we can isolate him. Then, we nab him, keeping pistols trained on him the entire time during transport. Once we bring him back to Sheraton, we will take him down to the scene of his crime against Chelsea, and shoot him there. We bury him there, too, and remove all trace of our having had contact with him. If no one knows of his going there, they would never think to look. Even if they did, they could never recover the body." Damien said

"Why can't we just kill him in London and leave his carcass in an alley, like the rat that he is?" the baron asked. "Seems silly to risk his escaping again," he added.

"That would work if we didn't use pistols to dispatch him. We can't discharge a pistol in London without drawing attention to our crime," Damien pointed out.

"I don't suppose we could lure him here, somehow," Jarrett suggested.

"I can't think how we could manage that, what would we use as bait?" the baron asked.

The three men sat and contemplated the logistics of dispatching Nigel, without having to suffer repercussions.

After a moment Jarrett asked, "How do we decide who makes the kill?"

"I will make the kill," Damien said emphatically. He had dreamed of killing Nigel for a decade and didn't want to be denied the pleasure.

"That hardly seems fair, it was my daughter that the animal abused. I should get to make the kill. I have the least to lose. You two have just recently wed. You have wives, my daughters I might add, who will depend on your continued health and safety," the baron put in.

That was true, Damien allowed silently to himself but still, he wanted to do it.

"We could have a lottery, or draw straws. Jarrett shouldn't have to do it, so it would be between you and I. You mustn't forget that not only did I witness what he did to my wife but I watched him destroy my brother's life as well. I will admit that you and I have an equal stake in the matter, as we have both dreamed of killing that monster for a decade. So, a lottery seems fair," Damien suggested.

"We could tie him to a post and all three take a shot at the same time. That way, we'd never really know which one of us killed him and could all have the pleasure. Damien, you can just forget about excluding me right now. You are my best friend and Jacob was like a brother to me. I, too, have a stake in it. It is my sister-in-law that he abused, lest you forget" Jarrett said defiantly.

"We are getting off the track here. Let us first decide how we shall accost him," the baron reminded them of the real issue at hand.

The discussion continued thusly…

*****

Chelsea was had just finished breaking her fast when Celia came to her room. They hadn't had time to visit with one another since Chelsea's return and they had a lot to catch up on.

"There you are you sleepy head," Celia said, as she entered the room. "I take it married life is tiresome for you," she added with knowing smile and a wink. She bent over her sister, kissed her on the forehead, then sat down beside her on the bed.

"Exhausting, but hardly tiresome," Chelsea corrected.

They giggled and nodded in agreement. Then they set about going over all the details of the last few weeks.

After they had sufficiently caught one another up, Celia asked, "What are we to do about Nigel?"

"We won't do anything. Damien has assured me that he will handle it. I have every confidence that he will. I suspect that our husbands and father are, even now, devising a plan in their meeting. You and I are out of it now. It was foolish of me to believe that I could have done anything about him on my own. I learned the error of my ways and have turned it over to Damien. I suggest you do the same," Chelsea told her.

"You must have been so scared when you were trapped behind that tapestry, knowing that he was there on the other side, aware of your presence," she said with a shiver.

"It was terrifying. That was when I knew I could never stand up to him and win. I very nearly had a spell right then and there. I only just managed to get back to my room before it overtook me. Can you imagine, if I were to confront him, then right in the middle of it, I were to…," Chelsea couldn't even finish the thought. Really there was no need because Celia understood.

"Well thankfully, you were spared such a situation. I should have never agreed to the plan in the first place. But then, neither of us would have our husbands," Celia said, with a smile.

True, if they hadn't concocted the whole idea, their lives would be very different now. So, for that alone, it had all been worth it, Chelsea decided. Not to mention that she and her Papa had reconciled. Yes, the plan saved her life really. She wouldn't change a thing now, even if she could.

Soon Nigel would be gone. She would never have to worry about him again, but she had the rest of her life before her, with the man she loved. That was worth any amount of suffering she had endured while in London and at Ravenswood. She felt fortunate, indeed.

Her sister drew her out of her musings. "Is…is…Damien a good lover?" she finally rushed out, tucking her head down and blushing.

"Why Celia Wellstone, how can you ask me such a thing? Of course, he is," she responded indignantly. Then, she did her own blushing as she remembered just how good he was. "What about Jarrett?" she asked.

"I fear I will have to put him on rations soon. All he wants to do is stay in bed. I can't manage to get a thing done, lying about all the time," Celia complained. "I suspect that I will be with child soon, if not already," she added with a smile.

"Oh, I don't think I would like rations at all," Chelsea giggled.

"Wouldn't it be grand if we were to be with child together? Our children would grow up together like brothers and sisters. Oh, what if we have twins?" Celia asked excitedly.

Chelsea hadn't thought about the possibility of twins. Her brow furrowed in distress as she remembered her mother dying giving birth to them.

Celia knew what she was thinking and took her hand in hers, "Do not despair dear sister, it won't happen to us. Our mother was much too small to have twins. We are much taller and more far more robust than she. We are fortunate that we favor our father in our size. We can do it, you'll see," she promised.

Chelsea was comforted by her words. So, they set about discussing baby names and the happiness that the future would bring.

"I can't tell you how happy I am to see you this way Chelsea. Did you ever imagine in your wildest dreams that you would be where you are now. You are a marchioness and someday you will be a duchess. You are very lofty, my dear sister," Celia said, making a face of mock snobbery.

Chelsea laughed, saying, "I haven't really given it much thought. I don't think I will be a social duchess. I much prefer rusticating in the country, to all the falderal that goes on in London among the ton. I don't think I shall ever fit in and have no desire to. I don't think Damien likes it much, either so we suit rather well on that score," Chelsea explained.

"I am so proud of the way you handled yourself. I wouldn't have thought you capable of being around so many people, especially men and dancing. Oh my, you danced with half the men in London, Chelsea," Celia said laughing. Well, not quite half, but close," she said, laughing too.

"Some of those poor men were absolute toads. Others were quite charming," she added. Then, she snapped her fingers, saying, "Oh, I nearly forgot to tell you, I think father and Matilda might have feelings for one another. I watched them mooning over one another last night. I'm sure something is there," she told her excitedly.

"Oh, that would be grand, wouldn't it? She and father would make a fine match. We must play matchmaker and ensure that they come together," Celia beamed.

"Yes, we must show our support. I hate seeing father so lonely. He loved our mother so much and never did consider marrying again. We need to let him know that it our wish to see him happy and that it would please us for him to wed again…to Matilda, of course. Perhaps we should take him aside and give him our thoughts on the matter," Chelsea said.

The two of them went on in this fashion for a few more moments until Chelsea announced that she had better get her lazy bones out of bed. She planned to go to the stables to feed Delilah some apples and carrots. The sisters hugged each other and Celia took her leave as Chelsea called for Jenny.

*****

"Don't trouble yourself, Mr. Blake. I'm not going to ride. I just want to go in for a visit. I brought some apples and carrots to feed Delilah. So, you just go back to what you were doing and I shall be fine," Chelsea told the stable master, as she entered.

Mr. Blake tipped his hat, saying, "Very good, my lady. Thank you." He sat back down and went back to polishing a saddle on a work table at the entrance of the stables.

Chelsea sought Delilah out and opened her stall. She started rubbing her face and gently butting heads with her. She and Delilah were like old shoes already, she mused.

"We shall take good care of one another, you and I," she cooed at her. She opened up her sack to fish out a piece of apple and fed it to her. She was scratching her chest while feeding her and didn't hear the grunt that Mr. Blake made, or the thud his body made when it hit the ground. She was oblivious to it all, as she continued to bond with her horse.

Suddenly, Delilah became agitated, snorting and stamping her hoof on the ground. Chelsea backed away, fearing she was about to rear up. She backed right into a wall of flesh and turned to find herself staring into familiar evil eyes.

She dropped her sack of treats and tried to make an escape but he grabbed her by her hair, yanking her back against him.

"Where do you think you're going?" he growled in her ear.

Chelsea struggled to free herself but it was futile. He had one hand in her hair and the other around her waist. 'This can't be real,' she told herself, squeezing her eyes closed tightly. She tried to will the nightmare away but it was all too real.

Her heart was pounding so hard, it felt like it was about to burst out of her chest. She could hear her pulse and feel it thumping in her neck. She tried to gather her wits, so she could find a way to escape him but she was having trouble thinking, with the roaring in her head.

She was afraid she would fall to her curse soon, if she didn't get away from him, so she screamed inwardly at herself to fight him. She didn't know how she would but she knew she must.

She must have screamed aloud, as well, because he laughed saying, "Mr. Blake is dead. Scream all you like. No one will hear you and it gives me great pleasure."

She stomped on his foot then, trying to twist out of his hold. She very nearly managed it but not quite. He did release her hair, though. That was his mistake as she lunged her head forward and bit into his hand that held her at her waist. He did release completely then, howling in pain.

She didn't waste the moment and started to run. But he quickly grabbed her again from behind, lifting her off the ground. He gripped her in a choke hold with his arm, her chin resting in the bend of his arm.

"Did you think I wouldn't know who you are?" he rasped into her ear from behind.

Chelsea refused to answer him. Her mind was busy trying to figure out how to get herself out of this situation alive. She knew he intended to kill her. Why else would he have come? She remembered her knife then, and started slowly hiking up her skirts so she could reach it.

He didn't notice her movements because he was too intent in his taunts. "Did you think you could fool me again? No, you can't fool me. I see you for what you are. You like to play games and try to trick people, like you did Damien. You got him to believe you were your sister because you were too ashamed to say who you really are. Did you think that you and Damien would marry and live happily ever after? No, you whore. You are going to die, you see. There will be no happily ever after for you. I haven't waited all these years for my daughter to be able to marry Damien to let a slut like you get in my way. Don't worry though, Damien will join you soon. Once he marries the bitch, his fortune will be willed to her and I will have no more use of him," he promised. "But before I kill you, I will make you pay for your sins, rest assured. We will play the game. You see, I too, like to play games," he continued his threats while he kept her pressed against him in his hold.

Chelsea managed to get her knife into her hand and was trying to decide the best way to use it when he released his hold and reached into her hair again. He started pulling her backwards so that she trailed behind him. She couldn't see where he was dragging her but she thought it was toward the back entrance of the stables.

She decided it was now or never because once he got her out of the stables, she had no idea where he would take her. She spun around, wincing at the pain when her hair pulled, but she could see his back now.

It was difficult to see above the middle of his back. Her head was tilted down from the angle at which he was dragging her. She quickly raised the blade as high as she could manage. With all her might, she brought it down into his back. Her aim had been off and the blade lodged into his shoulder. It wouldn't be a fatal wound.

He staggered from the impact, though. She thought he might go down but he turned around, dealing a savage blow to her jaw, and she saw no more.

*****

"The nerve of her," Nigel grumbled aloud, reaching behind his back to pull out the knife. He threw it to the ground, giving her a good kick in the arse, before bending down and grabbing her up.

He slung her over his good shoulder and made his way out of the stables. He threw her over his horse's back and mounted behind her. He didn't take the time to tie her hands and feet because he wasn't going far. She would keep, he told himself.

He was angry and bleeding like a slaughtered pig. Oh, she would pay for this, he promised. He kicked his horse in the sides and the horse leaped into a run. He knew where to take her for the game. The old game keeper's cottage would do just fine. It was provisioned for such things, he remembered in fond memory of the times he had been there with Jacob.

He wished he wasn't bleeding so much. It would take some of the pleasure out of his plans. He reached back, wiping at the wound and came back around with a saturated red hand.

"Stupid bitch!" he shouted at the unconscious woman.

"Just you wait!" he continued his rant.

He reached the cottage and kicked open the door. He went to the bedroom and threw her down on the bed. Then, he went back into the main room to gather his supplies. He decided he had better try and stop the bleeding on his shoulder before he got started, so he removed his bloodied coat and shirt. He found a wash cloth and pressed at the wound until he was satisfied that he had slowed the bleeding enough to play his game with the whore.

He went back into the bedroom and ripped off her frock. He left her shift on because he didn't want to be repulsed. He felt sure he could do without that. Once he had her tied up properly, he slapped her.

"Wake up!" he shouted at her.

She didn't stir. He jammed his hands on his hips and stared at her incredulously, wondering if she were already dead. He paced around for a moment, trying to think. He didn't want her dead just yet. He had plans!

He walked over to her and lifted up her eyelids. They stayed open when he removed his fingers but her eyes were unseeing. He placed a finger to her neck and was pleased to feel a pulse.

He thought perhaps she was trying to fool him again. So, he waved his hand in front of her eyes and she didn't even flinch. He clapped his hands an inch from her face and still there was nothing.

"WHAT THE BLOODY HELL!" he roared. She didn't react at all.

Frustrated he went outside to the well and filled up a bucket of water. He went back into the room and threw it in her face. The bitch didn't even react to the ice cold water. Something wasn't right here. How could she have a pulse and be dead at the same time? This made no sense at all.

Perhaps I imagined the pulse, he thought. He leaned over and placed his ear to her chest and could hear her heart beating. He wondered again, if she were trying to fool him somehow. He took out his pistol and put the barrel in her mouth.

"Speak now or so help me, I will shoot you here and now," he told her.

Nothing! No sign of fear. No sign of anything. Nigel scratched his head in puzzlement. Completely flummoxed, he went over to the chair in the corner of the room and plopped down in it. He sat broodingly, staring at her, while trying to decide what to do next. 'How can we play the game if she doesn't show any fear?' he wondered.

*****

"Have you seen Lady Vane?" Damien asked Jenny, in the kitchen. He had been up to his room after the meeting and was going to make sure she got up and dressed for luncheon but she wasn't there. Her father and the rest would be leaving soon. He thought they would like to visit with her once more before going home, so he set about finding her.

After checking the drawing room and not finding her there or anywhere else he had looked, he was becoming concerned. Neither Matilda nor Hattie had seen her and he was unable to speak with Celia, as she was having a bath.

"Yes, my lord, she has gone out to the stables to feed Delilah some apples and carrots," she told him, with a fond smile.

Damien sighed in relief then, went out the kitchen door toward the stables. He didn't really like the idea of her going out there alone but with Mr. Blake there to oversee things she should be fine.

Damien thought about their bath that morning and smiled. It had been very enjoyable. He looked forward to doing it again, only next time he would introduce her to the delights to be had in the water.

He marveled at her stamina. She had completely exhausted him. His body actually ached. He had never had such strenuous lovemaking that he actually felt sore the day after and she acted as though she could have gone another ten rounds.

He shook his head and laughed. His woman was going to keep him in shape…or kill him. He wasn't sure which. But oh, what a way to go!

He thought about the book and her reaction to it and smiled. He would have to take it out of the library and bring it to their room so they could make their selections every night. A bit like browsing through a catalogue, he mused. He wasn't sure how many different positions the book had but he would like to try them all and she was the woman that would take up the challenge with.

He remembered taking her there on the rug, before the hearth, and he shivered. It was the most incredible orgasm he had ever had. The stuff of legends!

Too bad he was a gentleman because he would be the envy of the world, if he were to ever tell his friends what a treasure he'd found. He shouldn't have, but he wondered if Jarrett could relate. The ladies were identical twins after all.

Perhaps one day he would probe him to find out. He smiled when he realized he and Jarrett were brothers now. It was a good feeling. He supposed there wouldn't be anything wrong with brothers discussing such things with each other. He imagined that sisters probably did, especially those two. Neither he nor Jarrett would betray the other. He just needed to brag to someone soon or he would burst from the knowledge.

Damien rounded the corner of the stables and stopped dead in his tracks. Fear gripped his chest and made it contract as he took in the view! Mr. Blake was lying on the ground, bleeding from a nasty head wound.

"CHELSEA!" he screamed. He ran toward Delilah's stall and skidded to a halt. There before him on the ground was her knife and it was covered in blood.

Chapter Twenty-five

Damien's mind was reeling as he took in the scene around him. There clearly had been a struggle here and someone had been severely injured, but who? He recognized Chelsea's knife, allowing himself to hope that it was a good sign.

With as much blood that had been spilled here, he was rather distraught from not knowing for sure whose blood it was. He felt like Chelsea would try to fight him initially, but how long could she last before her fears overtook her and she was lost, at the mercy of a madman.

That thought propelled him into action. He grabbed the knife and stuck it in his coat pocket, quickly saddled up his horse and mounted. He paused briefly and debated whether he should go and warn the others or if he should just go after them himself.

He didn't know how long it had been since the incident had occurred. The blood was still fresh, so, he if went now, he may still be able to save her. That thought made up his mind up for him and he set out following the blood trail alone.

He cursed himself for not having his pistol, especially after making a point to tell Chelsea to wear her knife at all times. At least she had listened to him and had been able to put up some kind of defense.

Though he was only armed with a knife, he thought that if he could sneak up on Nigel, he could probably overtake him. He didn't know what kind of weapons that Nigel would have on him but he knew that he was a cunning devil who would be armed somehow.

The blood trail started to slack up about ten yards from the stables and his heart fell into his stomach. He panicked for a moment. Then, he calmed himself and started looking closely at the grass to see if he could see hoof prints. After a couple of minutes, he spotted a clear print that allowed him to determine the direction Nigel had taken.

As he continued in that direction, he saw blood drops in the grass every twenty feet or so. He knew he was still on the right path. Nearing the wood, he despaired he would lose the trail but continued on. He was relieved to see broken branches and more spots of blood, as he continued to follow the signs.

Damien was grateful that Nigel hadn't taken more precautions to cover his tracks. He must be injured, or surely he would have taken more care to conceal his direction. Damien hoped that was the case and that he would find his wife alive.

After about one hundred and twenty five yards into the wood he realized Nigel must have taken her to the old game keeper's cottage. His spirits got a shot of much needed hope that he would find them. He picked up his pace, feeling more confident as he went in the direction of the cottage. At this pace he should reach it within minutes.

He needed to formulate a plan of attack before he got there, so as to maintain the element of surprise. He decided he would leave his horse in the wood before the clearing of the cottage. He would sneak up to the cottage and have a look through the windows before he made his presence known. That way he could try and assess what kind of weapons Nigel may have and what damage he had already done.

His blood went cold at the thought of Chelsea lying helpless and at his mercy. He silently prayed to God, that he wouldn't be too late.

*****

Everyone had gathered in the drawing room and was awaiting Damien and Chelsea, so they could have luncheon. No one wanted to disturb the newlyweds to inform them that luncheon was being served, so everyone awaited them patiently.

But as many minutes passed with no sign or word from them, Jarrett turned to his mother and said, "Perhaps we should send a footman to inquire with Jenny, to see what is keeping them. They know we are to leave directly after luncheon, so I can't imagine why they would keep us waiting."

The baron laughed, saying, "I can imagine why they would keep us waiting and if you think real hard son, you could too." He winked and added, "I'm sure they will be along shortly."

Jarrett blushed at the implication but he was still concerned. Earlier, when he spoke to Damien, he very specifically said that he was going to get Chelsea and have her get dressed and come down for luncheon. That had been well over an hour ago. He thought that even if they had taken the time for a quick romp, they should have been down at least a half an hour ago.

He looked over at his mother and said, "Mum, I would feel much better if you would send a footman to inquire. If Chelsea is ill or otherwise…indisposed, there is no reason for us to continue to await them. We could go ahead and dine and visit with them when they come down. Damien isn't so stuffy that he would make us wait and I really am starving."

Mrs. Wellstone agreed with his assessment. She spoke to the footman outside the drawing room door, relaying instructions to inquire with Jenny.

"Chelsea was fine when I saw her earlier. We talked for a good while. Then, she said she was going to get dressed and go and see Delilah. Perhaps we should send someone out to the stables. Damien might be trying to find her this very minute," Celia thought to put in.

Jarrett looked at his wife and smiled, "Let's see what Jenny tells us first, love," he said.

"That's probably the hold up. They're out in the stables and have simply lost track of time. I think I'll go out there to tell them luncheon is ready. I'll also ask Mr. Blake to prepare our horses for the trip back," the baron announced. He got up and made for the drawing room door.

"That's an excellent idea, Papa. I'm sure they are out there as we speak, dallying around with Delilah," Celia said smiling.

When Papa was out of earshot, Matilda leaned over to Celia and whispered, "If I know Damien, and I do, he probably has her skirts tossed up over her head on a hay stack right about now."

Celia gasped and blushed. She quickly darted a glance at Jarrett and his mother to see if they had overheard. But he was busy fussing with his pocket watch and she had her nose in a book. Neither had acknowledged the exchange.

"Chelsea was completely exhausted when I spoke to her earlier," she whispered in return. Then, the two ladies snickered.

"Damien is well known for his prowess and will keep her well amused, I'm quite sure," Matilda whispered again.

"That reminds me; I couldn't help but notice that you and Papa seem smitten with one another. Chelsea and I spoke of it and we decided you two would make a grand match. We wholeheartedly approve and wanted you to know," Celia told her quietly.

Matilda laughed and said, "Your father is a dear man. If I were ever to marry again, he would be just the sort I would prefer. A big, loveable, bear of a man. No London dandies for me," Matilda said, with a rare girlish blush.

Right then, the footman returned. He told the group that Jenny said her mistress went to the stables and that his lordship had gone to fetch her about twenty minutes ago. Jarrett was relieved and thought that they would all return momentarily. He put his earlier concerns to rest.

*****

The baron went out to the stables and got a bit of a shock when he arrived. He saw that Mr. Blake was injured but seemed to be just coming around.

"What happened here, Mr. Blake?" he asked, assisting him to his feet.

"I don't rightly know, my lord. One minute I was polishing a saddle, then the next thing I know, you're helping me to my feet," the man said, rubbing at his wounded head.

The baron was alarmed by that. He went into the stables to have a look around. He went to where Delilah was kept and saw that the stall was opened but the horse was still there. There was no sign of his daughter or Damien.

He looked in several other stalls and saw that Damien's horse was gone. He didn't see anyone else about and was just about to go back to Mr. Blake, when he looked down and saw blood on the ground.

His heart thudded in his chest and he hollered, "Mr. Blake, come quick!"

Mr. Blake staggered a bit but went to the baron. He saw the blood and both men were stricken with fear.

"What do you make of it, sir?" Mr. Blake asked.

"I don't know, but something terrible has happened. Where are the other stable hands, Mr. Blake?"

"Timbo had the day off and Chip went over to the village to see the smithy to have some new shoes made for the horses, and pick up some supplies. He will be gone until after dark," he explained.

"Are you well enough to saddle a couple of horses for me?" the baron asked the man. The man seemed alright to the baron but with a nasty gash like that, it was better not to assume anything.

"Aye sir, which ones do you want," he asked.

"Mine and Sir Jarrett's, if you please. We shall return momentarily. I suspect we have had an evil blackguard here and he must have taken my daughter. There's a fresh blood trail to follow, so time is of the essence," the baron explained, on his way out of the stables.

He rushed back, with fear in his heart, to tell Jarrett what he had seen. Nigel must have followed them here from Ravenswood and gotten Chelsea.

He hoped that Damien's missing horse indicated he was even now on the trail. He must have decided he didn't have time to waste. He was comforted by that, but not by much.

This Nigel person was a dangerous foe who would be difficult to manage alone. He needed to get Jarrett so they could join forces and kill the black hearted devil.

Moments later, the baron burst into the drawing room. Everyone froze when they saw him.

"Jarrett, we have a problem. Go get your pistol and meet me at the stables," he barked at him.

"What's happening, Papa?' Celia cried out.

"The blackguard is here. He has Chelsea. You ladies stay inside and stay together," he said. Jarrett was stunned and didn't react immediately. The baron prompted him, "Please, Jarrett we don't have time to waste. Meet me at the stables in five minutes," he said, running out of the room. He ran for the stairs to get his own pistols.

Jarrett was hot on his heels. The two men had no need to meet at the stables, as after they retrieved their pistols, they met on the stairway landing. They charged out to the stables, mounting their horses.

"Damien's horse is missing, so presumably he is already following them. There is a blood trail at the rear of the stables. Keep a close eye to the ground and try not to trample any tracks," the baron advised.

Now was not the time to remind the baron that he was a Bow Street runner and knew how to track a criminal, so he simply followed. Jarrett feared that with all the blood loss, they may be too late to save Chelsea, but he kept his own counsel.

He hoped that Damien would be able to save her but it looked very doubtful. The two men set out to follow the signs with a mixture of trepidation and vengeance in their hearts.

*****

Nigel was a very unhappy man. The whore wouldn't cooperate so he could play his game. He had never been denied the pleasure of the game before. He wasn't about to be deprived now.

He had been sitting, staring at her for a quarter of an hour and she hadn't moved a muscle. She hadn't even blinked. She just lay there, staring at nothing. It didn't even look like she was breathing. For all he could tell, by looking at her, she was dead.

He suspected that she wasn't pretending anymore but instead was in some kind of shock. He needed to wake her up somehow. He had a moment of inspiration, got up and walked over to the bed. He took the pillow out from underneath her head and covered her face with it. He pressed down to see if she would stir when she lost the ability to breathe.

His efforts were wasted. She didn't even twitch a muscle. He didn't know what to make of this madness. He threw the pillow to the ground. Leaning over, he pressed his nose to hers and roared in frustration.

"I WILL NOT BE DENIED," he screamed.

Nothing! He shoved away, sighing heavily. Then, he turned and left the room.

He started looking through the pantry for something to drink. This was thirsty work and he was feeling a little weak. He needed a restorative. After some plundering, he uncovered a bottle of whisky.

"Ah, here we are. Good ole Scottish whisky," he murmured. He popped the cork and took a fortifying drag from the bottle.

When he coughed and sputtered, it gave him an idea. He went back into the bedroom and pulled her chin down to open her mouth and poured some whisky down her throat.

Nothing! He grabbed her up by the shoulders and shook her violently. When she didn't stir from that, he thrust her back down and started pacing.

After a moment he whirled around, leaned over and grabbed her by her face.

"Stupid bitch! You think to deny me my pleasure?" he shouted at her. He shoved away from her, kicked the bed in frustration, and it nearly went over on its side.

"Damnation! What do I have to do to wake the chit up?" he asked the empty room.

He took a couple of more drags from the bottle and left the cottage. He was feeling damned weak from loss of blood but he was determined to have his way. No one trifles with Nigel Cullen and gets away with it. He would wait until she woke up, he decided. She couldn't stay like that forever.

If she didn't come around soon, he would have to move her, of course. He didn't think it would be too much longer before they came looking for her. He thought he probably still had a couple of hours to play with before he had to make any decisions, though. If anyone did come, he would just kill them. He wasn't too worried.

But in the meantime he needed to perk up a bit. He went back to the well, pulled up another bucket of water and dumped it on his head. He growled from the shock of the water, shaking his head to remove the excess.

"There, much better," he said, satisfied he would be sharp as a tack now. He scanned the area around the clearing to make sure no one was trying to sneak upon him. He saw nothing to alert him so he whirled around and stomped back inside, slamming the door.

*****

Damien watched Nigel go back into the cottage from his position, just inside the wood, on the edge of the clearing. He had just arrived when Nigel was nearly at the entrance of the cottage. There was no time to go after him and still be able to keep the element of surprise.

He saw that his back was bloodied and was proud of his wife. She must have put up a hell of a fight. His pride was quickly overshadowed by a shot of fear. It ripped through his veins when he thought of the repercussions she might have suffered for her valiance.

He drew in a steadying breath and walked through the wood that made up the perimeter of the clearing. When he got to the rear of the cottage, he ducked down low. He quickly moved to get to the wall, where there was a window to the bedroom. He hoped he would be able to see inside to make his assessments.

Once he made it to the cottage, he stood up straight with his back pressed against the wall. He waited a moment to be sure his movements had gone undetected. When he was sure they had been, he hunkered down, positioning himself just under the window.

His heart was thundering in his chest. His breathing was strained from a constricting feeling there. His blood was coursing through his body and he could hear it as it roared past his ears. He steadied his breathing, trying to will his heart rate into submission.

Once he felt under control, he pressed his ear to the wall, trying to hear anything going on inside. It was deadly silent. Damien wondered if Nigel might have her in the main room, rather than the bedroom. That didn't seem likely, as there was very little in the way of furnishings other than a small kitchen table, a couple of stools and a couple of stuffed chairs by the hearth. So, there weren't too many options for where she might be.

He took a deep breath and inched his way up so he could take a peek inside. The window was dirty but he could see that she was lying on the bed, and she was lost to her spells. He was grateful for that because it meant she wasn't suffering or scared anymore. It appeared that she was otherwise unharmed.

He could see that Nigel had removed all of her clothing, save her shift. He was relieved that she still remained partially clothed and wasn't exposed to his evil eyes. He didn't like to think that he had...he refused to think it. He consoled himself with the knowledge that Nigel didn't like women. He shook his head to clear away the thoughts.

He couldn't see any obvious injuries, though she was smeared with blood on her cheeks and arms. He could tell it wasn't her blood. Nigel must have transferred some of his blood onto her when he was handling her. The thought of Nigel handling her made his body rage to get his hands on him. He looked further into the room and didn't see him. He tried the window. It was locked.

He crawled away from there, deciding he had to look in through the front window. He went around the cottage and hunkered down, positioning himself under that window and pressed his ear to the wall. He couldn't hear anything in there either. He began to wonder if he might be weakened from his injuries and had passed out. He doubted it, but with all that blood loss, it was a distinct possibility.

He lifted up a few inches to look inside. He saw him, sitting in a chair before the hearth. He was stretched out. His head resting against the back of the chair and his eyes were closed. He took in the scene and noted that Nigel didn't appear to be armed, other than a whisky bottle clutched in his hand that appeared to be nearly empty.

He surveyed the room as best he could and saw that his pistol was on the kitchen table, along with a knife and some rope. There was a jug of lantern oil and some candles but nothing else. He looked over at Nigel again and studied him more closely. He was bare from the waist up except for a black leather band on his wrist. He wondered at that. It didn't appear to be jewelry, just a leather band. It was time to make his move, he decided.

*****

Nigel was resting. He supposed if the bitch could, then he should, too. It wouldn't do for him to be tired when she came around. He wanted to give her his full attention and all his energy. His thoughts were occupied with all the wonderful things he had planned for her when she came around.

He was going to have fun playing with her. He was going to make the game extra special for her. He was going to remind her of her deceitful behavior years ago and punish her good for it.

Imagine running through the woods dressed like a boy to entice him, the very nerve of her! Well, he would show her the error of her ways. She'd probably enjoyed it as much as he had been, until he realized his mistake.

Yes, it was a mistake. He could admit that now. He thought that the boy had been too effeminate, but he'd ignored it, just like she wanted him to do, the whore. She probably played games like that all the time. Well, she would get to play one more game, his game. Then, she would die. He smiled at the thought of Damien's face when he discovered her body.

He would carve pretty pictures all over her and mutilate her grotesque figure. 'Perhaps I should dump her in one of the fountains in the front courtyard when I'm done with her,' he mused. So many possibilities… He'd make sure that it was his finest work, so Damien could get the full appreciation of his talents.

*****

"He must have taken her to the old game keepers cottage," Jarrett surmised, as he took in the signs that they had followed them into the woods. He was sure that had to be where he was going, as that was the only thing in that direction for miles.

"How much farther would you say that is?" the baron asked, eager to find his daughter.

"Not too much further. It we stay on the trail, we should be there in a quarter of an hour, maybe a little less.

"We've no time to waste, let us pick up our pace. You know the way, do you not?"

"Aye, it's just through there," Jarrett said, pointing the way.

They picked up their pace. Their nerves were on edge. Neither had spoken of the possibilities of what they would find but they both knew it was likely to be devastating. Nigel was a force to be reckoned with. It was possible that Damien might not be able to handle him alone.

They continued on in stony silence, each man planning his own version of revenge, should Nigel have harmed Chelsea or Damien.

*****

Damien decided that now was the best time to attack. With Nigel napping in the chair, he could take him unawares. He decided he would kicked down the door, charge in as fast as he could, and hope that he could subdue him before he ever lifted himself from the chair.

It was a good plan, the only one he had. His wife was in there and she needed him. He had to do what he must to rescue her. He only hoped she wouldn't be too traumatized when this was over.

She didn't deserve to go through this again. He simply couldn't fail her now. He told her that he would take care of Nigel and he would. He wouldn't allow the filthy bastard to touch her ever again.

He thought about his beautiful wife and how sweet she had been this morning when they were in the bath, soaking together. She was an amazing woman. He knew this to the core of his being. She had overcome such obstacles in her life and somehow managed to survive. Yes, she had spells when she was under extreme stress but that was a minor thing considering what all she had endured.

He knew personally, what she had gone through. The fact that she could function at all, was a complete miracle. She was so alive and loving, when anyone else who had suffered such an ordeal, would have become cold and hard. Or, they would have become lifeless shells of humanity, simply existing. But not his Chelsea. She was strong and vibrant, with so much love inside her. The fact that she could even stand his touch was another miracle in itself.

He would never give her a reason to shy from him, as to do so would be a sin against his very soul. She was his soul now. She lived deep within him and he could never be separated from her, for it would simply destroy him. The thought of never holding her in his arms again was too much to fathom. She was his whole life now. He would do whatever it took to save her.

He raised his face heavenward and asked for God's assistance. That done, he positioned himself in front of the door, "I'm coming for you, love," he quietly vowed. Then he raised his leg high and kicked the door as hard as he could, making it fly off the hinges.

Chapter Twenty-six

Damien burst into the room, launching himself at Nigel. As he had planned it, he was able to tackle him before he had a chance to react to his entrance. The collision of his body into Nigel's, knocked the chair and the both of them over onto the floor.

Damien didn't waste a second or give an inch, as he went straight for his throat. Before Nigel could respond, he had him in a fierce strangle hold and was choking the life out of him.

Nigel wasn't one to go down easy. He started clawing at Damien's face. Damien moved his head to the side to obstruct him from being able to gouge his eyes. This forced Nigel to change his tactic. He grabbed onto Damien's throat. Both men locked on to one another's throats and became engaged in a test of strength and will.

After a moment Damien started to feel weak from lack of oxygen. He wasn't going to last much longer, so he thrust his head forward, causing a clash of their foreheads. Nigel was briefly stunned. He released his hold on Damien's throat. Damien was a little dizzy, himself from the impact, but he quickly took advantage of the situation, straddled himself across Nigel's chest and jerked his head up by the hair. He proceeded to deliver several savage blows to his face.

Nigel lay motionless for a moment and Damien relaxed. That was a mistake. Nigel suddenly produced a dagger that seemed to be attached to the leather armband he wore. He swiped at Damien, cutting him across his chest and shoved him away. Both men jumped up. Damien reached in his pocket and drew out Chelsea's knife.

They circled one another, taking occasional swipes at the air, to keep the other from advancing. They held each other at bay thusly for a moment before Nigel decided it was time to move the situation along. He lunged his body at Damien.

They were thrust up against one another, with their arms tangled, as each man tried to stab the other with one arm, but restrain their opponent with their free arm. Another test of strength and wills that went on for what seemed an eternity before Damien realized the futility of it. He stomped on Nigel's foot to distract him.

This worked. It gave Damien a brief window of opportunity to lunge at Nigel. He thrust his knife into Nigel's gut, twisted it and pulled upwards, causing him to collapse to his knees. When he did so, Damien withdrew the knife and stabbed him once more just above the heart. Nigel fell over onto his stomach and became still.

Damien took a few moments to catch his breath before lifting Nigel's head to see if he were dead. His eyes were closed and blood was coming from his mouth. Damien threw his head back down roughly and ran into the bedroom to go see Chelsea.

He got to the bed, untied his wife and pulled her across his lap. He cradled her in his arms and started kissing her face. Tears began to flow.

"Chelsea love, I'm so sorry. I'm here, you're safe now," he crooned. He started rocking her back and forth. Tears flowed from his eyes for several moments. He didn't hear any movement or he would have realized he was no longer alone with his wife.

"You thought you could defeat me, you insolent pup?" a raspy voiced Nigel said from the doorway.

Damien froze with his wife in his arms. He looked up to see Nigel standing in the doorway with a pistol and it was trained on him. Nigel was weak and fatally wounded as there was no way to survive such a stab wound to the gut. He had already lost tremendous amounts of blood.

It stunned Damien that he could even be speaking, much less standing there with a pistol aimed at him. His complexion was ashen and he had to use the door frame to hold himself up. But he kept the pistol fairly steady as he aimed it at Damien.

Damien didn't think he could survive a shot at such close range. He would surely die, but maybe Chelsea would live and that was all that mattered to him. He moved to lay her back down, blocking her with his body as best he could. He faced Nigel squarely and prepared to die.

Nigel cocked the pistol, levering it at Damien's head, "Tess will be so disappointed," he rasped out.

"You weren't supposed to die until you married the stupid gel, but there has been a change in plans. You simply must die now," he added.

"You're going to die as well, Nigel. You may kill me but you will soon follow. You have lost too much blood to live, and I will go to my maker proud that I have killed you," Damien vowed defiantly.

Nigel laughed, then, started coughing up blood, "No matter. I will follow you and drag you to hell with me, long before you reach the pearly gates. You won't be able to escape me, even in death. I will torment you for all eternity," he gritted out, clearly struggling to hang on to his last few minutes of life.

Damien drew in a breath as he knew that the moment of his death had arrived. Never again would he hold his beautiful wife. He would never see her smile and he would never make sweet love to her again. He cast one last longing look at her, when he heard the shots and felt the wind from a bullet whizzing past his head.

He jerked his head back around just in time to see Nigel hit the floor. This time he was dead; he knew as he was missing a big piece of the top of his head. It now decorated a large part of the wall opposite where Nigel had been standing.

He wondered what miracle this was and soon had his answer. Jarrett and Malcolm appeared in the doorway, each holding a smoking pistol.

"What took you so long," he said with a huge grin. "I thought I was a dead man and was saying my last goodbyes to my wife," he added still grinning.

Jarrett and Malcolm said nothing to this. Each grabbed one of Nigel's legs, dragged him out of the doorway and left him in a bloody heap on the floor.

They went back into the room and Malcolm said, "We got here as soon as we could. How's my lass?"

Damien stood up and allowed the baron to see about his daughter. Jarrett quickly embraced his friend and brother. The two men held each other as though they hadn't seen one another in twenty years.

"Thank God, you're both alive. I saw all that blood and I thought…." he choked on the words and could say no more.

The baron was satisfied that his daughter would be alright, after he assessed that she had no obvious wounds.

"Looks like she was spared the worst of it. Her spells must have protected her from further harm, somehow," he said a little mystified.

"Nigel wanted to torture her. He wouldn't have enjoyed himself unless she was terrified. When I got here Nigel was asleep in the chair, probably waiting for her to wake up. Chelsea had managed to stab him in the back. He was fairly weak from loss of blood, otherwise he wouldn't have fallen asleep. I took him unawares. We tangled and I managed to stab him two more times. I thought he was dead. I can't imagine how he lived through all that," Damien explained.

"Nigel was insane, and insane people often have an incredible amount of strength. It's strange really. It's almost like they become invincible," Jarrett explained. He had seen his fair share of insanity as a Bow Street man and never ceased to be amazed by the things a lunatic was capable of.

"I suppose that explains it." Damien said.

"Well, the question of who gets to kill him seems to have been answered. Seems we all got a piece of the nasty blackguard. Even my lass managed to get a good swipe at him," the baron said smiling.

They all had a good laugh at that and the baron always one to plan ahead said, "Looks like we have a mess to clean up, boys. Should we just burn the place down, it would be the easiest," he suggested.

Damien nodded his head and said, "Let the bastard get a taste of the hell that awaits him."

Damien gathered his wife in his arms while Jarrett and Malcolm set about preparing the cottage to burn. Moments later the three men stood in the clearing and watched the cottage go up in flames. Damien hugged his wife closer to him, whispering, "It's over, love." He turned to leave the raging inferno behind.

Jarrett and Malcolm followed. Jarrett said, "When the ashes cool, I'll come back and remove what's left of the bones and bag them up for burial by the stream like we discussed."

Damien and Malcolm grunted their approval of his plan. Malcolm took Chelsea from Damien so he could mount his horse. Then, he lovingly handed her up to him. Damien cradled her close to him while the others mounted their horses to take leave of the clearing. They all rode back quietly, thanking God for their good fortune.

*****

"Please come back to me, Chelsea. I need you so much. Please come back," Damien pleaded with his wife, as he lay behind her on their bed. He had her tucked against him, in his favorite position, as he had for most of the last three days. For three long days, since Nigel's death, she lay in a catatonic state.

The doctor said she may never come out of it but he refused to believe it. So, he kept vigil round the clock, refusing to leave her side except to take care of personal needs.

Everyone had come up to try to cajole her out of her spell, but she hadn't moved a muscle. He had been able to manage to dribble broth and water in to her mouth, and coax her throat to accept it by massaging it. He worried that if she didn't come around soon she would wither away and die.

The baron assured him that she had endured for many weeks in this condition once before. She had come out of it a little thinner but otherwise healthy. He hoped it wouldn't last that long and did his best to encourage her to wake.

The days and nights were agonizingly long, heart wrenching and he was exhausted. He hadn't yet fully recovered from his bruised throat and wounded chest. The doctor told him if he didn't rest, he might succumb to the fever he had been fighting off for the last two days.

He felt sure the only thing keeping him going were Hattie's tonics. Every few hours, she came into the room and forced him to drink the ghastly stuff. She spooned some to Chelsea, too, saying it would keep her strong. He hoped she was right and clung tightly to every piece of hope she and the baron gave him.

They had seen it before. They had faith in her will to survive. He did too, but he was troubled that she hadn't come around by now.

He needed his Chelsea back and nothing else mattered. She had to be in there, somewhere. She had to. Damien drew her closer and kissed her on the temple. He wouldn't let her go. How could he?

*****

Four days later, there was still no change in Chelsea. Damien was inconsolable and had become difficult to manage. He refused to leave Chelsea's side. He was raging with a fever and his wound on his chest was festering.

Matilda called the doctor to come and try to sedate him, so he could rest to help the healing. It took Jarrett, Malcolm and two footmen to do it. He fought like a crazed animal when they tried to remove him from his beloved.

He had fire in his eyes and threatened to kill anyone who touched her. When he was subdued, he was given a good dose of laudanum. After trying to fight the effects for nearly an hour, he finally succumbed and fell asleep. Even in his drug induced sleep, he clutched his wife to his bosom.

Matilda despaired that he would die if Chelsea didn't pull through this soon. She was sitting beside their bed.

"Poor bugger," Malcolm said, looking at Damien. He pulled a chair beside Matilda and saw that she had been crying. He took her hand in his, saying, "Fear not, my love, they will come through it."

Matilda threw herself into her lover's arms and wept. He wrapped his strong arms around her, holding her tight. Together, they sat through the night, watching their loved ones for any signs of change.

*****

On the twelfth day since Nigel's death, Damien finally recovered. His fever had broken and his wound was healing nicely now that the festering was gone. He went right back to keeping his vigil.

There had been no change in Chelsea and he had become very solemn. He continued to talk to his wife and encourage her to wake. He had closed her eyes that first night. He couldn't bear to look at them and see the lifelessness.

It was easier to deal with if he simply thought of her as sleeping. The doctor had advised it anyway, so they wouldn't dry out and cause blindness, so it was for the best. He missed her eyes and wished he could see them again while they looked back at him. He thought of all the times they had looked into each other's eyes and saw into each other's soul.

His soul was lonely for hers. He felt like a part of him had been ripped away. He had decided that if she didn't survive this he would follow her. He wouldn't tell anyone that, of course or they would sedate him again. He didn't want that. But he knew what he would do as he couldn't live without her.

*****

"You have to go back Chelsea, my brother needs you," the boy told her.

"I can't, I'm too scared," she said. She hugged her legs and pulled them closer and buried her face in her knees.

She and Jacob were sitting by the stream. She was peaceful here. The sky was a cloudless blue The grass was greener than she had ever seen it. The stream was rushing by, like it did after a good heavy rain, and the sound of it soothed her.

"Chelsea, Damien will die without you. I saw him and I know what he is thinking. Please you must go back," he pleaded.

Chelsea lifted her head and thought about that. She did miss Damien terribly and it hurt her to ignore his cries. But she was afraid that the bad man would come again. She was safe here. Everyone was safe while she was here.

She knew that the man had no interest in her while she was here therefore everyone else was safe too. She remembered him trying to bring her back. Finally he left her alone, once he realized she was gone.

"I can't go back. He will come again if I go back," she said after a moment.

"He can't come back. He is dead now. Please you must believe me. I would never lie about a thing like that. I saw him go. I swear," Jacob pleaded.

Chelsea shook her head and started rocking back and forth, trying to tune him out. She didn't think he would lie to her about it, but she didn't trust the bad man. He could trick them all and come back.

Jacob got up and took one of her hands and pulled her to her feet, so that she was facing him. He reached out and touched her belly over her womb, smiling. "You are with child" he told her.

Chelsea gasped in surprise, "With child?" she asked in disbelief.

"Yes, even now, my namesake grows within you. So, don't you see? You must go back, my brother needs his family. You carry his family within you, so you must go back," he said smiling at her. "Come, I'll take you home," he said. He gently tugged her hand and started leading her away from the stream.

Chelsea didn't resist this time. She was going to have a child, Damien's child. She was full of love and wonder, while together, they walked back to Evansdale, hand in hand.

*****

"Damien," her soft voice said.

Damien jumped at the sound. He looked at his wife and found himself looking into her eyes. Those eyes…those beautiful blue eyes. They had returned to him, at last, and they were looking at his.

"I thought you would never come back," he said, tears clouding his vision. He sat up, pulled her across his lap and hugged her with all his might.

"Don't ever leave me again," he said on a sob, as he buried his face in her neck and wept.

She wrapped her weakened arms around him, holding on as best she could. She didn't mind that he was squeezing her uncomfortably, because she loved him so much.

"I won't ever leave you again, I promise," she told him, with gasping breath. "Damien, we stink," she added, after the horrible odor became overwhelming.

Damien threw back his head and laughed the happiest laugh she ever heard. He said, "What do you expect when neither of us has properly bathed in a fortnight"

"Oh, my God! You mean to tell me that I was gone for an entire fortnight?" she asked incredulously.

"Yes and I felt every agonizing moment of it. Don't ever do that to me again," he chastised.

Then added, "Stay where you are, I will run us a nice hot bath. We can bathe each other until your nose is content." He hopped out of the bed and hurried to the water closet.

Chelsea smiled at her silly husband and wondered when she should tell him about the child.

Epilogue

Eight and a half months later

No one ever came looking for Nigel. They had learned that Penelope and her daughter Tess were living in grand fashion, touring the continent with some of the highest ranking libertines of the ton. They were living a life of celebration and debauchery.

Tess still hadn't found a husband. It didn't appear she was really too serious about the hunt, as she and her mother seemed quite content in their new found freedom. The Times made a big to-do over Nigel's disappearance. They still occasionally mentioned the need for information on the whereabouts of his body, dead or alive.

The baron and Matilda wed soon after Chelsea's recovery. They honeymooned at Sheraton. Jarrett and Celia had gone to their new villa in Italy to celebrate theirs. Damien was happy for them both but he was confused about the family connections now. He wasn't sure if his new father-in-law was now his uncle, too, and his wife was now a cousin. He tried not to dwell on it much, as it really didn't matter.

Several months after Chelsea's return, the old duke passed quietly from this world. Damien assumed the title with pride and acceptance. He would miss his father. He hoped that he and his brother could find peace now.

Chelsea had told him about her strange visits with Jacob while she was away. Damien remembered his strange dream of Jacob and Chelsea holding hands as children and wondered if his brother had a guiding hand in all of this somehow.

The thought pleased him. He hoped, now that all was resolved and their lives were filled with joy rather than tragedy, that Jacob had moved on to his reward.

Nearly nine months to the day of their wedding, The Duke and Duchess of Evansdale became parents. It was a hectic day when her water broke. Damien sent the whole house into an uproar to make preparations.

His wife had grown uncommonly large during her pregnancy. He began to suspect that if she didn't have the child soon, she would burst. She had been miserable and could hardly walk, stand, sit or even sleep without agonizing discomfort.

He called for the doctor. However, he was out on another call and wouldn't be there for hours, so Hattie and Jenny rushed in to take charge. Damien stood out in the hall, barking orders out to the footmen and the maids to bring this, that or the other.

He sent a messenger to go and inform the baron of the impending arrival of his grandchild. Within two and half hours, the baron, Matilda, Jarrett and Celia arrived to await the birth. Celia shouldn't have made the trip as she was fast approaching her own confinement, but she wouldn't miss being here for the world and refused to be left behind.

Damien stood outside the doorway, with a sense of extreme agitation; listening to his wife's shouts and curses, all of which were directed at him. He didn't like the idea of his wife in so much pain. It worried him that she could have one of her spells.

The thought was terribly unsettling. He was unable to relax, but he took a kind of uneasy comfort in her continued curses. He would gladly suffer all the things she promised to do to him and then some, as long as she was safely delivered of the child.

At first, it all seemed like a normal delivery. Then, Hattie announced that the child was breeched. Damien despaired that she could die, but Hattie worked a miracle and was able to turn the child.

Moments later, Chelsea delivered his daughter, whom they had later decided to name Marianna Danette after Chelsea's mother. But apparently she wasn't finished yet, as the shouts and curses resumed and continued for another half an hour.

Then, he heard the cries of a second child and couldn't take it a second longer. He burst into the room just in time to see Hattie holding up Jacob Beauregard, high to the heavens in joyous communion with the lord. And Damien…Well, he looked the situation over and promptly fell to the floor in a swoon.

The End

PostScript:

Oh, and in case you're wondering whether Celia had twins, too…the answer is no. They had a bouncing baby boy, little Robert Jarrett Wellstone, heir to the Sheraton fortune.

About the Author

Gina Rose is the pseudonym for a very prolific author who spins tales in the Regency Romance genre.

"Keeping Chelsea's Secret" is the first to be published for public consumption.

Look for many more or her books to be available soon at all online bookstores.

Check her website, ginarose-author.com, often for more information and reviews.